The Seduction

The Seduction

Julia Ross

BERKLEY BOOKS, NEW YORK

A Berkley Book
Published by The Berkley Publishing Group
A division of Penguin Putnam Inc.
375 Hudson Street
New York, New York 10014

This book is an original publication of The Berkley Publishing Group.

Copyright © 2002 by Jean Ross Ewing.
Jacket art by Greisbach and Martucci.
Text design by Tiffany Kukec.

ISBN 0-7394-2623-0

PRINTED IN THE UNITED STATES OF AMERICA

This book is respectfully dedicated
to the memory of
Dorothy Dunnett.

Lymond will remain forever unequalled.

PROLOGUE

*H*E HAD LOST. INCONCEIVABLY HE HAD LOST!

Shock reverberated, choking.

Everything he owned—investments, jewels, weapons, even his home, Gracechurch Abbey—would not be enough to cover what he had just wagered and lost.

Lace cascaded as Alden pressed his handkerchief to his lips.

He had piled risk on risk with reckless abandon. Yet he had been almost abstemious tonight—or had he? He couldn't quite remember. His pulse careened with an unnatural excitement, as if he might dissolve at any moment.

Shadows raced over the candlelit study, sliding over bottles and glasses, across the cards and the mad deluge of promissory notes on the table, to lose themselves at last in the mullioned windows. Beyond that wavering glass, King George's London schemed and reeked, indifferent to the fate of Alden Granville-Strachan, Viscount Gracechurch, who had just gamed away everything.

Dread desiccated his mouth and hammered in his veins.

I am obliterated!

Lord Edward Vane, long jaw sleek, as polished as ivory, pinched out a guttering candle. "I' faith, Gracechurch! Still so unmoved by your losses, sir? What the deuce would excite you? Double the stakes?"

Alden met the man's cold, oddly vacant stare—a petty nastiness not uncommon among the younger sons of peers—last faced that morning across the point of a rapier. An exhilarating fencing partner, the lean and hungry Lord Edward Vane: Alden had never been quite sure that the duke's son would not, on a whim, thrust home to the heart.

Yet that interesting exercise had brought Alden here, to game away the night in Lord Edward's townhouse. A chance encounter. A narrow victory against a more skilled swordsman than himself. An invitation to cards—to give the duke's son his chance at revenge. Alden had no one to blame but himself.

Perfume from the handkerchief uncoiled like a snake in his nostrils.

He was not among friends.

The third player's powdered wig grew like an excrescence above his red face. In his garish coat and dirty lace, Sir Reginald Denby seemed a deuced odd companion for the duke's exquisite son. Yet Denby's heavy fingers splayed over his winning cards, where Alden's queen and knave lay stiff with unconcern as they faced their little court of fellows, all trumps.

To have lost such inconceivable sums to Lord Edward Vane was to have plunged directly into the jaws of the beast. To have lost even more to a bluff country squire like Sir Reginald Denby seemed almost ludicrous.

Yet the repercussions echoed, tolling deeper and deeper. Devastation. Ruin to innumerable blameless souls.

Alden did not expect mercy, not even for the innocent.

So he must find a way out. There was always, always a way out. Failure was unthinkable.

His heart raced. The room seemed fuzzy at the edges. He was aware of nausea, as if he were at sea once again, returning home . . .

With a flamboyant gesture Alden dropped the handkerchief and scrawled his signature across another unholy slip of paper.

"I believe I am ruined, Lord Edward." He pitched his voice to be careless, bored, as if such losses meant nothing. "Allow me to give you another vowel, though if I continue to play, you'll be dunning me without hope of remittance. I shall have to leave the country and become a hopeless old roué in Paris."

"*Hopeless*, Gracechurch?" Lord Edward laughed. "Not from what I hear! Yet it is my little conceit to ruin at least one fellow libertine a year. A small amusement of mine. So what hazard would tempt you to stay in the game?"

Denby triumphantly gathered cards. "Triple the risk, what?"

"When Dame Fortune is robbing my purse without recompense?" Alden yawned. "I never allow a lady to be so coy, sir."

A heart-shaped patch creased at the corner of Lord Edward's mouth. It seemed almost obscene. "The infamous *Gracechurch* doubts the favors of a harlot like Dame Fortune? They say no woman has ever refused you, sir."

"Rumor exaggerates," Alden said.

Though it did not, of course.

Lace burgeoned at his wrists. It graced the backs of his hands and foamed at his throat: a witty froth of cherubs and tiny bells, like snowflake babies cavorting in sea spray. He was decadent with lace. It spoke of wealth, of taste, of refinement, with—in the circumstances under which he was known to have obtained it— amusing overtones of wickedness.

It was among the more famous witticisms ever offered in St. James's: Surely Viscount Gracechurch could only obtain such very feminine lace from a certain unmentionable place?

Amid much masculine hilarity, several such places had immediately been mentioned.

Alden had, naturally, won the indelicate wager that had followed.

How could Lord Edward not have heard the tale? This was how the world worked. To survive at the tables, in the fashionable drawing rooms, the clubs and coffeehouses, appearances were everything.

Alden leaned back in his chair and winked. "Alas, my pockets are as empty as my wit, Lord Edward. I have not the head for cards tonight. If you insist on more play, pray offer me a hazard I can win."

The duke's son grinned. Lead powder creased, showing the dark flesh beneath. "Then let us have a wager over a woman! What say you, Sir Reginald? Name any wench in the country and Gracechurch will have her favors by Friday."

Denby's color deepened. "He will not, sir—if I name the wench!"

"Then we have a new challenge." Lord Edward opened his betting book. "Well, Gracechurch? Do you agree? A little rutting should present you with no difficulty. Let Denby name the lady. Succeed with her and I will pay off these vowels, Denby's as well as my own. Fail and pay us in full next Saturday morning—with some amusing further forfeit of my own choosing, perhaps? You approve, Sir Reginald?"

"I'm game, sir!" Glass clinked as Denby poured himself more wine. "And a further five thousand against his success, for I warrant he'll fail with the Jezebel I have in mind."

Alden folded the absurd little square of linen with its impudent edging. Flames sparked in his rings, family heirlooms. He noticed them with poignant regret.

"Failure is not in my vocabulary, Sir Reginald, yet I am aquiver with curiosity. What creature would you like me to ravish to redeem my debts?"

"One I can guarantee will resist."

"Then she is virtuous? Don't say you're about to name me a virgin? I am charmed."

Denby scratched under his wig with an ivory wand he kept for the purpose. "It wasn't a virgin I had in mind."

Alden stood up to hide his relief.

Nausea clouded his brain. Absurd, in the face of the enormity of this—the deadly slips of paper that represented everything he owned and a great deal more that he didn't. Yet now there was a chance. It wasn't over. What matter if Denby named a hag or a harlot? As long as he wasn't expected to ruin some innocent girl!

"Perhaps you should name me a wife?" Alden said.

"Who could resist such glorious temptation?" Lord Edward showed discolored teeth. "Is there a wife left in the shires that you haven't already sampled at one time or another?"

Alden bowed. "What a magnificent reputation to have, to be sure! You put very little trust in the fidelity of wives, Lord Edward."

"Lud! I put no faith in the institution of marriage, sir. Neither, obviously, do you, since neither of us has been fool enough to get leg-shackled."

"Indeed," Alden said. "Why marry a wife of your own when you may enjoy someone else's? Obviously you agree, Sir Reginald?"

"She's not a wife either," Sir Reginald Denby said doggedly. "She's a widow. Lives in the village by Marion Hall—my country seat, don't you know."

Shadows leaped as Lord Edward's laugh broke up into hiccups of merriment. "Plague take me! You're the very devil, Denby! The very devil! A glorious wager! So, Gracechurch? What do you say? You may take back your vowels and another five thousand, if you can tup this relict—willing or no'—by midnight on Friday."

"Alas, I only take my women willing, Lord Edward." Alden bowed from the waist, with an ostentatious flourish of his handkerchief. "Just a personal quirk—like preferring my hair without powder—an odd whim, but mine own."

Denby's face shone scarlet. "If you want her willing, I guarantee you'll lose."

"Oh, no. He'll win." Lord Edward winked over his wineglass. "No one can resist him."

"She's not had a man in her bed in five years—"

"But not for want of them all trying!" The duke's son was still chortling. "You had your attempt at her, didn't you, Denby? Even proposed marriage, you told me, and just for the sake of her eyes, damn it all!"

His heels rapped on the floor as Alden walked to the window. "You also know the lady, Lord Edward?"

"Only by hearsay, sir. Hearsay. Yet they say she's a peach, a veritable peach, and not more than five-and-twenty. I begin to envy you the wager."

"Damme, sir!" exclaimed Denby. "She's hard as stone at the core."

"But sweet-fleshed." The heart-shaped patch creased. "No doubt, like a peach, very sweet-fleshed."

Denby looked stubborn. "How is Gracechurch's success or failure to be proved?"

"You don't think my word sufficient?" Alden asked. "Would you rather have the lady's?"

"No doubt she will find the experience delectable," Lord Edward replied. "And would tell the tale with a great many sighs and blushes. But then again, perhaps she is shy. Didn't you tell me the widow wears a locket, Sir Reginald?"

"Never without it."

The duke's son set down his glass. "Then also secure us the locket, Gracechurch."

"And wager your rings for that," Denby added.

Relief flooded through Alden's blood. Denby didn't realize his father's rings were already lost? They must think him wealthy beyond measure. Yet his pulse thundered, promising the devil of a head in the morning.

"For the locket, or as a pledge that I don't run off to Paris? My dears, for so amusing a wager, you could recall me from paradise."

"I imagine paradise awaits in the lady's bed." Lord Edward began to write in his betting book. "Here is the wager, Gracechurch: bed this widow at Marion Hall by midnight on Friday— Sir Reginald must allow you to enter the house with her, of course—and bring us the locket the next day. Then we'll forgive this small matter." He indicated the table with its scattering of cards and pledges of payment. "Agreed?"

Alden's reflection shimmered in the windowpanes: high-instep shoes of silver silk with gilt heels; white silk stockings; gold-and-ivory striped breeches that fastened below the knee with silver buttons; the long waistcoat embroidered in gold thread on ivory satin; his wide-skirted, gold-and-ivory coat and the amusing little dress sword.

All of it accented by lace. Avalanches of magnificent lace.

His manservant had set curls above each ear with a hot iron, tying the rest of his hair back with a black ribbon. His small affectation. No wig. No powder. Just his own pale yellow hair, absolutely clean. It shone like the precious metals on his fingers and sword hilt.

A fortune he didn't possess displayed on his body.

The effect was deliberate. More subtle than the chain mail of his ancestors, but just as important.

Would this widow be impressed?

The steady ticking of a clock dropped into the silence. The tables had always been his friend, his only promise for the future, before tonight. Before tonight and the mysterious tumble over the edge, the loss of balance, the inexorable slide into ever more desperate play and losses so absolute that he might as well have wagered his life.

Like a fox trapped in its den, he had been left without options.

It seemed suddenly absurd and unreal, as if a child pulled off a pretty mask to reveal a gargoyle. His wealth, such as it was, his house and his rings for a woman's locket—and her virtue, if she had any.

"I am enchanted by the notion," he said. "Of course, I agree."

Sir Reginald leaned forward. "Your rings, sir."

He had worn them since his father's death. Alden stripped the rings from his fingers and tossed them onto the table. If he lost this wager, Sir Reginald Denby would need to get them enlarged to fit over his fat knuckles—and Lord Edward Vane would see him to perdition.

She's a peach, a veritable peach. Not more than five-and-twenty.

Turning away, Alden flung up the sash and leaned out into the black night.

Cool air washed over his face, but it was not enough to calm the rapid thump of his heart or clear the dizziness in his brain.

"May I ask the lady's name, Sir Reginald?"

"Mistress Juliet Seton."

Juliet.

Alden had never known a Juliet, but he didn't like the name. It seemed sentimental. And, of course, doomed to tragedy.

"I' faith, a devil of a wind blows up," he observed casually. "I do believe it comes on to rain."

CHAPTER ONE

❧

$\mathcal{I}$T WAS A MODEST ENOUGH HOUSE, ALMOST A COTTAGE, RED brick under a thatched roof, tucked back from the main street of the village behind a stand of elms.

Alden leaned on the garden gate and surveyed it.

A three-cornered hat was tucked under his arm and a plain brown riding coat replaced the gold-and-ivory brocade. He had left his tired hack at the village inn. The Three Tuns was a rustic enough place, sanctuary for a handful of locals guzzling ale. Alden had taken the one guest room upstairs. At least the bed, being generally unused, seemed empty of fleas, though the landlord had been oddly unresponsive to the discreet inquiries of a stranger.

In some lost hour of the night he had returned to his townhouse and been sick. Shaking like a reed, he'd washed his head and hands in a basin that belonged now to another man and missed his rings. Whatever he touched—even his razor and hairbrushes—if he lost this wager, none of it was his any longer.

Was he left with anything? Did any skill remain he could trust?

It hadn't even come on to rain. The dry roads had rung hollow for the thirty miles from London to the village of Manston Mingate, the home of Mistress Juliet Seton. The air was oppressive, the sun a hot haze in unforgiving summer skies.

Less than five miles farther, Sir Reginald Denby's seat at Marion Hall, with its grandiose pillars and white facade, dominated the countryside. It was another ten miles to Alden's own home, Grace-church Abbey, now at risk of being lost forever.

Bed this widow by Friday or be ruined.

Ruin. It was a word one heard bandied almost casually about the clubs of St. James's, as if it had no stark reality to it, the way a man might joke about a skeleton in the family closet, never expecting that one day he would open a forbidden door and be engulfed in the fall of rattling bones. Now it yawned like the open grave, a pit of humiliation and degradation.

Ruin meant exile—eking out one's dishonorable days in a for-eign garret—or death. Death by one's own hand, preferably with a pistol, abandoning one's obligations and dependents, leaving one's friends the unpleasant task of finding the results. Why the hell was that considered an honorable option?

So the skeleton must be packed up and buried. Any alternative was unthinkable. Lord Edward Vane had offered him the way out, though God knew why. For Alden had never yet failed in the pursuit of a woman. It was his avocation, his pleasure, almost his calling.

He liked women.

The gate creaked under his hand.

His boots carried a coating of dust from his walk up the street. In his elegant coach with the family escutcheon on the door, his luggage and his valet had traveled on to Gracechurch Abbey with-out him. Alden had wanted the fresh air and the brutal exercise of riding, but to arrive here without fanfare had also seemed the wisest course of action, though he wasn't sure why. Just an in-tuition and the knowledge that Lord Edward Vane would least expect it.

So what could he discover about the widow from her home?

A rambling rose ran wild over the front porch. Thorned tendrils wrapped lovingly around the windows. Flowers of all descriptions clustered in random masses in the garden, divided only by worn brick paths. Behind a group of bee skeps, orderly rows of vege-tables and berry bushes marched along each side of the house. So she cultivated food and perhaps from necessity. There was a shabby look to the thatch and shutters that spoke of a restricted purse.

Three cats—one white, one ginger and one tabby—were sunning themselves on the brick, images of contentment.

He looked again at the rose. Was her nature revealed by that wanton growth, or by the sober, practical carrot tops and staked green beans? He had learned just enough at the inn to know that any excuse to make her acquaintance would send him away with a flea in his ear. Denby and Lord Edward obviously thought her an impossible target for seduction.

Why?

Would the gaze of this Juliet—like the snake-haired Gorgons—turn a man into stone?

Alden had learned only that she was not devoted to religion, nor known to be in love with another man. What other reason could she have not to take a lover?

He smiled as two rather indelicate memories fought for his attention.

The widow who'd wanted to be a nun had tried to reform him. In the end she had changed her mind instead of his and proved rapacious in bed. Then, when she'd discovered that Alden refused to declare undying love, she had taken all that unholy enthusiasm straight into the arms of a new husband.

After a very gentle campaign of flattery and flirtation, the second lady had been suddenly, desperately, willing, and he had wanted her with equal ferocity. Alas, half naked in his arms she had sobbed her confession: she did love the other man—her husband. It had taken a strong dose of nobility, but Alden had sent her back to her marriage untouched. Fortunate now, he supposed, for it had left him temporarily without a mistress.

There was no reason at all why this Juliet Seton shouldn't succumb, but perhaps she was deformed or insane. Lord Edward and Sir Reginald had no motive he could fathom for suggesting this wager, unless they were certain it would fail. Then he faced ruin and some further, unspecified price—*some amusing further forfeit of my own choosing*—the most dangerous hazard he had ever accepted.

The tabby rose and stretched.

It was time for another gamble.

Alden pushed open the gate and stepped onto the path, just as a woman came out of the front door. She was carrying a basket. He stopped, half hidden by a great clump of hollyhocks, and watched her.

She was wearing something voluminous—like a shepherd's smock in blue—over a white muslin dress. Keys and scissors clanked at her waist. Like his, her hair was unpowdered. Sunlight gloried in sumptuously rich chestnut waves, loosely gathered in a knot at the back of her neck: a round neck like a flower stem, leading to a tender, feminine jaw. She walked down one of the paths and began to clip blooms. Self-contained, absorbed, with an oddly withdrawn dignity, she moved in her own aura of concentration. The flowers fell one after another, bowing their heads to her scissors and falling into the basket.

His speculation collapsed into confusion.

In spite of the housekeeper's chatelaine with its keys and small tools, her movements betrayed her: the unconscious grace, the elegant carriage, a way of turning her head. Not simply a gentlewoman, but a lady who had been trained from earliest childhood to grace any drawing room.

A lady?

Every one of his planned openings seemed suddenly fatuous. He felt at a loss for a strategy. As the innkeeper had said with almost proprietary dismissal, she was fiercely protective of her privacy, never known to tolerate overtures from strangers. Alden could hardly force her even to talk to him, could he?

A lady would indeed know how to cut a man dead—like Medusa—with a glance.

He had five days.

A honeybee buzzed in and out of the hollyhocks. The insect carried little bags of pollen on its hind legs and an additional dusting of powder about the head and body. Its wings were ragged. This bee was already worked close to death for the sake of its colony.

A bee sting had once almost killed him as a child.

Deliberately, Alden reached out one hand and bit back a curse as the stinger sank into his palm.

The tabby ran off into the pea patch.

Mistress Seton looked up.

Her eyes were a deep cornflower blue under strong brows, drawn together in a frown. She was not a classic beauty. Her features were neither regular nor delicate. Instead she was lush. The succulent mouth promised a profound sensuality. Like the body beneath that absurd smock, soft and full in all the right places. A woman made for the bedroom. A peach.

Heady laughter fought for release. She really was a peach!

"Your pardon, ma'am, I pray," he said with a small bow. "It would seem that your garden has vigilant wardens to defend against intruders. I have been stung."

The blue eyes glared at him. "There's an apothecary in the village, sir. Scrape out the stinger with your thumbnail."

Her voice was golden, throaty, sensuous. A rich voice for a woman, with round, deep vowels.

His vision blurred. The breath struggled in his lungs. "I'm not sure—" He sat down suddenly on the bricks. "I'm not sure I can go so far, ma'am. If you will allow me a few moments?"

He dropped his head back against the gate and closed his eyes. A damned ignominious death—if this gamble failed—to die of a bee sting!

*J*ULIET HAD LOOKED UP AT A SMALL SOUND TO SEE HIM STANDING among her hollyhocks. Golden. Bright. Glimmering in the sunshine. Vividly male.

A sudden panic clamored for her attention. Mad images—of fallen angels, of the Heavenly Host singing of glory, of the golden band she had once worn on her finger—jostled and demanded for a moment. Her breath came fast, shivering up from her lungs in hot, angry gasps.

But he is so beautiful!

Damnation! Another man determined to disturb my peace!

Worse: a man of fashion—eyes exhilarated, intelligent, wary.

His hair was tied neatly at the back of his neck, but it rippled at the temples where a more elaborate style had been brushed out. The blond waves framed skin with the fashionable pallor of London, enhanced by a small patch high on one cheekbone. Arrogance was reflected in every line of his body, enhanced, not hidden, by the full-skirted riding coat, the tall boots, the fall of white linen at his throat.

A town gentleman, dressed for the country.

His moment of surprised admiration had been masked quickly enough, but it had been there. She had suffered from it all her life. It was the way men always looked at her, as if she were fruit, and ripe, and ready for plucking. Even after she suppressed her moment of panic, it still filled her with fury.

In a movement of pure aristocratic grace, he held out one hand, reddened in the palm, but his face had turned pale as death. His eyes dark with the body's reflexive, panicked shock, he slid to the path.

Juliet dropped the basket and ran up to him.

A damp sheen glistened on his cheekbones. He tipped his head back, breathing hard, seemingly incapable of movement. She knelt and took his hand. It was supple and long-fingered, with square knuckles and beautiful nails. A hand that further betrayed him: a hand inherited from a long line of nobility who disdained honest labor and valued their sensitive fingertips. Yet several rings had been recently removed. Rings he had worn a long time by the look of the indented traces.

A gentleman down on his luck?

An adventurer?

The stinger was steadily working itself into his palm, automatically pumping poison. With a quick scrape, she removed it, but his hand was swelling and the breath whistled in his throat. Alarm reverberated. She had seen this before a few times—people for whom a bee sting could prove fatal.

"Lie quite still where you are," she said. "Remain as quiet as possible. I shall be back in a moment."

In her kitchen she grasped a kettle of hot water. Hefting her load in both hands, she hurried back down the path, carrying a cushion, a blanket, some white cloth and the kettle. Fierce, exasperated anger flamed beneath her fear—that a golden prince risked death in her garden after first looking at her with that wicked flash of self-derision, of lust tinged with humor, that had made her knees weaken for a moment.

Her fury was not because the admiration of men did not affect her, but because it did. She could not afford it. She had never understood it. Now it was an intolerable burden, when her only future lay in concealment and denial. Yet sometimes loneliness caught her unawares, like a little beggar child suddenly grasping at her skirt, demanding her attention with heartbreaking need. She knew no defense against that, except anger. The world believed her a widow. Why couldn't men leave her alone?

He lay where she'd left him, among the lazy scents of summer.

The sunlight was broken, marking him with dapples where it sifted through the trees, creating one moderately cool spot in her hot garden.

He burned there like a fire.

As she approached he opened eyes blackened into midnight pools and grinned at her. It sent creases into his cheeks, disarming, making her anger seem absurd. The lines of his face were almost severe—clean, hard, shaped like a sculpture, easy to barricade against—but the smile made him human again, even frivolous.

Swallowing her uneasiness, Juliet slipped the pillow under his neck. His hair was the color of the cowslips she used to make wine. Silky under her fingers.

"Give me your hand." She poured hot water from the kettle

onto her cloth and wrapped the compress over the swelling. "Now lie still until you feel stronger. The pain and the weakness will probably pass."

"I can . . . stand them, ma'am." His voice was almost strangled by his erratic breathing. "But if they do not?"

"Then no doubt your heart will stop beating, sir." With relief she noticed there was no feminine tenderness at all in her voice. "However, it would be a considerable inconvenience to me if you were to die in my garden, so I pray you will concentrate on maintaining life."

She reached for the folds of his cravat and pulled out the knots. She did not want to touch him, but his tight clothes were a danger to a man in shock.

Her fingers felt clumsy and heavy as she unbuttoned the front of his waistcoat, then opened his shirt at the neck. The strong skin of his throat gleamed smooth and white in the mottled light. She noticed the perfect shape of his jaw at the strangely vulnerable junction where it curved up into his ear and felt a small surge of discomfort, as if she were a young farm girl winked at by a gentleman.

How humiliating to mark such things! So the man was handsome and golden in the sunshine. He was also spoiled by discontent and idleness. There was a petulant scorn to the set of his lips and a permanent disdain bred into the shape of his nostrils. A man of leisure, no doubt, and very probably a wastrel.

His clothes were simple, but sumptuously made, the fabric of his coat rich and thick. Without compunction, she wrenched it off, tugging at the arms. He was firm, superbly fit. So he fenced and rode. Of course. Most gentlemen did, however much they disguised that strength with the gloss of fashion.

His shirtsleeve stretched over his swollen wrist, so she slit the fabric to the elbow with the little knife from her chatelaine. His forearm was strong, carved with muscle beneath a masculine dusting of golden hairs. Juliet tried to ignore the unwelcome intimacy, the unwelcome feelings, but she held a man's naked arm in her bare hand.

The swelling blurred the fine shape, the powerful mesh of wrist to arm.

He was ill.

Steadily, she applied more compresses. Even his shirt was finer than anything in her wardrobe, soft and enticing to touch. So he was—or had recently been—a wealthy man. A little tendril of curiosity unfurled. What was he doing in Manston Mingate?

She bit her lip and suppressed the question.

It made no difference. She would be forced into his company for only a few hours of simple nursing—and even that was a compromise.

Juliet wanted to be left alone, but she did not want a corpse on her garden path.

*A*LDEN LAY FLAT ON HIS BACK AND STARED AT THE MOTTLED pattern of leaves overhead as he concentrated on each breath. *In. Out. Focus. Once again.* Had he finally gone too far? His heart rattled erratically in his chest. A cold sweat had broken out on his face. It had never been this bad before. His hand throbbed like the very devil, and the swelling had traveled up his arm.

What an insane risk to take! To die of a bee sting. In which case, the notorious Lord Gracechurch would go to his grave without having tasted the sweetness of Mistress Juliet Seton.

For without regard to the wager, Alden wanted her. *Just for the sake of her eyes, damn it all!* Why did she wear that ridiculous smock? From her face and hands, he could imagine the body that lay under it. She would be soft and female, with generous high breasts and a beneficent, slipping curve to her waist. Her skin was a pale cream, like a Caerphilly cheese, but with that hair and those eyebrows she would have dark nipples, as sweet as raspberries. If only he had a whole summer to woo her and tempt her, and win her little by little in a game as delightful as the final surrender!

Yet he had undertaken to bed her by Friday.

Why the devil had he lost all that blunt to Denby and Lord Edward? But if he had not, he would never have met her. Obscure little Manston Mingate with its impoverished, succulent widow was not on the usual way to Gracechurch Abbey. It wasn't on the way to anywhere.

Alden closed his eyes. His head was cushioned on something soft. Alas, that it wasn't her lap! Hot compresses were laid over his throbbing arm. Her clothes rustled. There was a clean, flowery scent—of roses and gillyflowers at dusk. Somewhere a cat purred. At last he felt his breathing become deeper, almost back to normal.

So perhaps he would live after all.

Then he would win her for one night of ecstasy, which would save him from ruin.

He glanced up.

The sun had dropped in the west. Long shadows raced over the flowers, gilding the red brick to flame, though the air still pressed, heavy and hot.

Her three cats sat beside his head, contemplating him, vibrating with feline intensity.

Mistress Seton was perched on a stool she must have fetched from the house, calmly shelling peas. The hem of her skirt lifted a little at the front. Cheap stockings wrinkled around her ankles. Delectable ankles, curving up into rounded calves and descending to soft insteps that would fit neatly into the palms of his hands. Desire stirred, then asserted itself with considerable intensity.

Yes, he would live!

He let his gaze slide up over her blue smock to the neck of her dress. If she wore a locket, it was hidden by her clothes. His attention lingered on her cheek and on each flutter of long lashes as they swept down over her eyes. What made her so provocative? Was it that very air of watchfulness, the guarded, severe turn at the corner of her luscious mouth? The suspicion and resentment clear in her eyes?

So she disliked, even feared, strangers. The thought thrust its way into consciousness: *she fears men?* No, not fear, exactly, but a definite rejection—a fierce commitment to privacy.

It wasn't going to be easy.

She looked down at him. Alden dropped his gaze so that she wouldn't see the desire in his. Surely he had successfully proved himself helpless, no threat at all?

"You have recovered, sir?" She glanced away. "You must be anxious to leave. May I fetch help? Or can you manage?"

He smiled up at her. His hand still throbbed, but his heart seemed to be beating its usual strong rhythm. "You have been very kind, ma'am. I would like to thank you by name, at least."

"Mistress Juliet Seton, sir. Now you have the advantage of me." She looked directly at him and stood, her cornflower eyes suspicious.

Alden managed to get to his feet without disgracing himself, but prudence acquired by a man living by his wits told him now not to tell her his title, nor offer her too elaborate a bow. "Alden Granville, your most humble and obedient servant, Mistress Seton."

"Where is your carriage? You did not walk to Manston Mingate, surely?"

"I left a horse, ma'am, at the Three Tuns."

The bow was his undoing. As he straightened, he staggered, dizzy.

Immediately she let the words tumble. "Mr. Granville, you aren't yet strong enough to ride!" She even reached out a hand, though she snatched it back without touching him. Sitting down, she plunged back into the shelling of peas.

Ah, so she was bountiful by nature! He was ferociously glad of it.

"I cannot think to impose on you any further, ma'am. The Three Tuns is only a short walk. I have taken a room there for the week."

A handful of peas fell through her fingers, bounced off her skirts and scattered on the path. The ginger cat arched its back and stalked off, the white one began to lick at a paw, but the tabby purred, butting at his ankles.

He crouched and rubbed behind its ears. "Does your tabby have a name?"

"Meshach." She sat as if helpless, watching his hands.

"Then the others are Shadrach and Abednego? I always loved that story as a boy. The three men of faith, cast into the fiery furnace by Nebuchadnezzar and rescued by an angel, survivors against overwhelming odds. Which is which?"

A spatter of water fell among the scattered peas. Then another.

The blue of her eyes reproached like a bruise. "Shadrach is the ginger—"

"And Abednego the white?"

More water splashed onto the path. The cats raced away. A cold breeze rustled the hollyhocks as a rumble of thunder boomed overhead. He stood and clutched at the gate with one hand, dizzy again.

"It's going to rain." She rose, fumbling with her bowl. "You had better . . ." The scattering of drops began to run together, wetting the bricks. "You aren't well—You had better come inside!"

She bent to pick up her stool, just as Alden reached for it. Their fingers touched. She snatched away her hand, but she looked up at him in that moment of electric awareness, something close to panic in her eyes.

Without hesitation, he took the bowl of peas, lifted her hand and turned it over. He ran his thumb over the roughened skin and the calluses on her palm.

"*Quel dommage,*" he said softly. *What a pity!*

She jerked away. He thought for a moment she was ready to weep. "Pray, sir, do not insist upon gallantry. It has no meaning for me, I assure you. I have been widowed five years. I do a great deal of my own work. I can carry a stool."

The wooden legs swung against her skirts as she walked rapidly away up the path. Thunder rolled again. Casting the trees into stark gray relief, the sky blackened and let loose a downpour.

She had left the front door open.

ULIET KNEW HE WOULD HAVE TO DUCK HIS HEAD TO STEP INTO her hallway. Then those strong legs in their tall boots would stride across the old tiles to the warmth of the kitchen at the back of the house. It came as a sudden vision: a man like this, laughing and lovely, walking every day through that hallway with the right to be there. Or better, better—taking her away from all this into his own bright world!

An impossibility.

She looked at her hand for a moment, furious with herself. Had it ever really been the hand of a lady? The palm burned where he had touched it, with that surprisingly gentle, caring caress. This was folly, wasn't it? Her vision was bankrupt, now and forever. She should have left him there in the garden to drown.

Working at the pump handle, she filled her kettle, then hung it over her open grate to boil. A scrubbed pine table with a long bench and two chairs filled the center of the room. Copper pots shone on the walls. She looked up as Mr. Granville came in, his head framed by her hanging bunches of herbs, his shoulders brushing her lavender. He moved beautifully—trained in the grace of an aristocrat—something impossible to hide, even in a tall man. A reminder of balls and suitors, of exquisite ladies and lords in silks and lace, dancing until dawn. A very long time ago.

She waved him to a chair, then folded her arms protectively in front of her.

"May I ask, sir, why you were in my garden at all?"

Alden set down the bowl and gratefully took the seat. He felt as weak as a puppy. But he met her gaze with his own as a dozen provocative, flirtatious comments came to mind. He dismissed them. The first move must still be played with caution.

"Your white sweet peas, ma'am. Flowers native to Italy."

"Are they?" She looked surprised. "I don't know."

"I recall a maroon and violet variety there, named for the monk who discovered them in Sicily, but white is an unusual color. They couldn't help but catch my eye in an English village."

Juliet turned to the fire, hiding her face from view. In a few deft movements she made tea and poured it. She had a lovely turn to her elbow and wrist, graceful and delicate.

"You like flowers?" she asked. "That seems odd, when bees may be lurking behind every petal to deal unexpected death."

"It's a fancy that creates certain difficulties, I admit."

Rain beat hard on the roof, racing in sheets off the eaves, pounding and gushing in sudden fits and starts past the windows. Thunder rumbled ever louder.

She set a dish of tea in front of him. He sipped at it gratefully.

"It has always been dangerous for you to be stung?"

"The first time it happened I was three years old and screamed for five solid minutes, then terrified my nurse by turning blue and limp in her arms. The doctors predicted the permanent loss of my senses. They say I stayed swollen for a week and barely survived." He glanced up at her between narrowed lashes. "Still there is something about a delicate petal that draws me, even though I know I court danger."

She looked away, as if annoyed. "Flowers must guard themselves. It's why roses have thorns."

Ah, even against her better judgment, she was playing already! "Yet the thought that an insect can reduce me to such infirmity is the most appalling insult imaginable to my pride."

"Then I am fortunate you recovered so quickly this time."

"Indeed you are, ma'am. For I have been led to understand that swollen and blue I am a hideous sight. Can you imagine the humiliation the second time I was stung, when I was ten? It happened at school in front of twenty other lads. It took me three years to live it down."

Almost reluctantly, she smiled. "But it happened again?"

"Unfortunately, it did. On the third occasion my father beat me with a switch on the theory that if I tried hard enough I could prevent the reaction. To no avail, alas. My life was feared for each time."

"That was barbaric. To beat a child for an illness!" Her emotions seemed almost transparent, a vulnerable sincerity she simply couldn't hide.

"Oh, no, ma'am. It was wise. I was more afraid of my father's wrath than I was of the bees."

"Yet the fear of his punishment was not enough to stop you brushing past my hollyhocks?"

"He is dead, ma'am. But, alas, I am often enough a fool and I am paying the price. Think of the dreadful disadvantage of being forced to lie helpless on a stranger's garden path for an entire afternoon. Imagine my chagrin!"

She laughed—a genuine, rich laugh that made Alden think of honey and red wine. It filled him with delight. Mistress Seton did not know it, but Lord Gracechurch had already begun to seduce her.

"No, I don't think you feel much chagrin, sir. You don't seem humbled and you are not a fool by any means. What are you doing in Manston Mingate?"

His reply was deliberately casual. "I am looking for a retreat hereabouts. Something modest, with flowers."

A single clap of thunder boomed almost directly overhead.

Her dark brows flew together. "But such a risk would be a daily challenge to your wits."

"I like challenge, ma'am, as I would guess that you do." Alden had already scanned the room. Among the herbs and the rows of jars and bottles, he had found treasure. "How many ladies keep a chess set in the kitchen? While we wait out this storm, will you test my wits and give me a game?"

He had guessed correctly. Genuine longing flashed in her eyes. She instantly turned away and busied herself with the tea things.

"There will not be time—" Her voice was drowned out by a

rumbling drumroll as a crack of lightning lit up the kitchen. She jumped, then nervously shook her head.

"My nurse used to say that thunder was the sound of giants playing ninepins. I think their game has only just begun. I thought we might while away the time, but if my presence makes you uncomfortable—"

Abednego jumped suddenly onto his lap.

Juliet glanced around at her cat in surprise. Aloof Abednego, who never welcomed strangers!

He tickled under the white chin until purrs rumbled as loudly as the booming rumbles outside. "You already have someone to partner you, a companion?"

"No," she said. "Miss Parrett died last year." Dear Miss Parrett! Spry, valiant, the one person who had stuck by her throughout her disaster. Juliet forced herself to sound matter-of-fact. "She shared the house. I have not played chess since her death."

"I am very sorry. I intrude on your privacy. I should leave." He looked down at the cat and gave it a wry smile. "Yet, alas, it would seem that I am pinned. . . ."

This was a dreadful foolishness. A man so appealing to her senses—she should thrust him back out into the storm, whether he was fully recovered or not. Surely she had learned her lesson? Learned what physical desire could destroy? Yet she craved intelligent, educated company, and it seemed that she must permit his until the storm was over. In which case, there might be less harm in an hour's play than in an hour's conversation, for she was being charmed and he was doing it deliberately.

Any gentleman would do the same if unexpectedly closeted with a lady—offer a little coquetry, a few compliments. It was the way of the world. She knew that as she knew it was a madness to respond to it or want it. Yet there was an oddly appealing courage revealed by his dismissal of his illness. His sorrow when she'd mentioned Miss Parrett seemed genuine, more than just courtesy. And, after all, this was only a chance encounter, random, harmless. He wanted to leave.

Abednego had closed his eyes in feline bliss.

The ninepins rollicked across her roof and echoed down the chimney. Rain drummed.

What harm could there be in a chess match—by its nature impersonal, safe from emotion? Or even in his carefully restrained flirtation? As long as she was careful—

"You cannot go out in this downpour," she said. "Your heart has had a shock. It would be dangerous to stress it."

Juliet reached to the shelf and brought down her chess set.

Rapidly she set up the board and offered him the white men, which play first. Fortunately, he had been stung on his left hand and he was right-handed. She watched his fingers as he began with his king's pawn, a classic opening, telling her nothing of his skill. She responded with the same move. His king's knight followed. In the next few moves there were no surprises. He did not offend her with concessions, or distracting small talk, or more veiled flirtation. He seemed intent on the game.

She relaxed.

"Would you recommend this area for a single man?" he asked after a moment.

"It's very quiet here."

"Perhaps you're right. I'd forgotten how dull it can be in the English countryside."

Before she could stop herself, she looked up. "Because you have traveled—"

"Indeed, ma'am. I lived several years abroad."

What a wealth of treasure lay in that one word! *Abroad!* A reminder of the world beyond Manston Mingate—of sparkling, sophisticated conversation about travel and culture and art—her birthright. He had known Italy and seen sweet peas in Sicily. She longed to ask him about it. Yet she mustn't allow anything but a casual exchange with this stranger. She concentrated on the board.

"I believe a single gentleman would find more to amuse him closer to London."

He looked up, a lazy, smiling glance, while his fingers stroked the white fur. "Perhaps. But this single gentleman is very easy. . . ." His last move had left her a perfect opening. With a small surge of exhilaration, she stepped her queen forward. He picked up his knight as if about to fall into her trap, then caught her eye and laughed. ". . . to amuse, that is."

His knight leaped in another direction entirely. For a wild moment, she felt an answering laugh struggling for release. She suppressed the mad bubble of merriment.

"Then I wish you were harder to fool."

"We are too well matched," he said. "I offer you a wager, Mistress Seton, to spur us both to better play. If I win this game, will you allow me one game of chess each day this week?"

"Sir, I can hardly—"

"Otherwise I fear my stay at the Three Tuns will require me to exchange pleasantries with rustics in the taproom, until I forget that I ever knew anything besides turnips and mangel-wurzels. You cannot be cruel enough to condemn me to such a fate. A simple wager, an incentive to try harder?"

Ah, that last play! She had almost forgotten the delight of facing a competent opponent across the board. Yet her gambit was still stronger. With unalloyed pleasure, she planned her path to checkmate.

"And if I should win?" she asked.

"Then you may claim anything from me that you like."

She was genuinely surprised. "Rather a hazard for you, sir!"

"What venture is worthwhile without risk, even a chess game?" His lashes swept down over his eyes in a gesture that was at the same time gently submissive and shamelessly seductive. "I can be sure you wouldn't demand more than honor could bear. I will trust you, Mistress Seton."

Her heart pounded, echoing the rain. He had just made an error by moving a critical pawn into the path of her bishop. It was enough to give her a definite advantage. She knew she was playing well and she wanted his best possible game—

"Very well," she said with every expectation of victory. "Let us play for a wager, but I would demand one more condition."

"Name it." The corners of his mouth pulled down in regret as she took his pawn.

"I don't have much spare time. Most days I have only one maid-of-all-work to help me. She comes in from the village, but she's been taken ill this week. If you should win, you must make up for my loss of time—do some chores for me, whatever I need."

"What kind of chores?" A little wrinkle marked his brow. "I'm rather useless when it comes to practical affairs, especially rural ones." The wrinkle disappeared as sudden laughter flashed over his face—as if at a thought so impossible as to be absurd. "Will you expect me to feed pigs?"

So the merest hint of labor would indeed drive him away! A poignant disappointment pierced her, in spite of the apparent success of her ploy—to make sure he wouldn't come back, whether he lost or won, yet still secure his best play. But how foolish to feel sad when she had just achieved what she wanted! She had everything to lose and nothing to gain from any man's daily visits.

"I won't ask anything I would not think within your talents, sir. I don't keep pigs."

He raised elegant brows and smiled. "Then I am your servant, ma'am—whether I win or lose. However, if I do your chores, then whenever I win a game, you must also grant me a wish."

It was dangerous, but he'd just made a move that put his queen's knight at risk. Very soon she could open her path to checkmate and it would all be irrelevant. Juliet captured his knight, ready to set up her trap and secure victory.

"I accept," she said. "On the same terms."

Abednego thumped to the ground and stalked away, tail in the air. Juliet watched him leave, a bundle of indignant white fluff, then glanced back at Mr. Granville. A cold trickle of alarm ran down her spine.

An intense concentration had fallen over him, as if he were

hardly aware of her. That hint of disdain had disappeared from
the corner of his mouth. He looked as grave and austere as a carved
saint in the local church. His shirt still lay open at the neck. Her
gaze wandered over the waves of gold pulled back over his ears,
and the pulse that beat normally now at the base of his throat: a
man's beautiful, strong throat, which promised a honed body below it and invited kisses.

Damnation! The man was a stranger, merely passing through.
It was only a chess match.

He made his move, momentarily blocking her rook, but achieving nothing she could understand. She answered it, driving her
plan forward—five more moves, maybe six, and she would win.

He didn't look up. Abednego curled into a ball by the fire.
Shadrach sat in the window, eyes closed.

Rain drummed.

Meshach wove a pattern about his legs, purring and bumping
his boots.

Occasionally he dropped a hand and touched the tabby with
long fingers, caressing the soft fur, sensuously rubbing the most
sensitive spots with his thumb. Purrs rumbled. Shadrach thumped
down and crossed the room to commandeer his lap. While Meshach spun a web about his feet, around and around, he massaged
his other hand through the marmalade fur as Shadrach settled on
his thighs.

Powerful, tender fingers, stroking hypnotically.

Purring echoed louder and louder. Purring and warmth. Drum-
ming rain, purring cats, and the warm crackle of the fire. Her
blood swam lazily, in hot, silent eddies. Little tickling sensations
shivered in her thighs. Nervously smoothing her skirts, Juliet
made her move and looked back at her unwelcome visitor.

Such beautiful bones. Such sensual hands. His thumb brushed
the head of his white queen, as if seeking among bunched drapes
of white linen, white lace, exploring the shape of a woman's naked
thigh.

Hot blood rushed to her cheeks.

Yet she'd known it since the minute she'd seen him sliding down to sit on her brick path. The heavy lids, the charming smile, the potency that breathed from his skin. The fine shirt, the satin waistcoat and the ripples in his blond hair chanted a wicked, witty refrain: *We can afford to be pretty,* they said, *because a rake's appearance is only a whimsy to counterbalance the hard steel underneath—were you fooled?*

Juliet wrenched her mind back to the chessboard. His queen had moved five squares. It was another play she hadn't foreseen.

Steadily, inexorably, the game ran her closer and closer to the edge of her skill. She was forced onto the defensive. Her plan for checkmate evaporated. He captured both a bishop and her queen's rook, while he had lost only a knight and fewer pawns than he had taken. Meanwhile, the patterns were shifting on the board— pieces regrouping, webs of threat materializing as if from nowhere, surrounding her men, breaking their cohesion—a network of alternatives all leading to one outcome.

A strangling panic seized her by the throat as she realized the enormity of her mistake. Unless he made another error, he was going to win. She had misjudged and allowed this stranger into her life.

Because he had lain so helplessly on her path—

Because he was gentle with her cats—

Because he had come inside only at her insistence and had even seemed anxious to leave—

She had broken all of her rules. She had thought the threat insubstantial.

Now it was too late.

He leaned back and stretched both arms above his head in an exuberant gesture of triumph, filled with masculine power.

"Checkmate in two moves, Mistress Seton!"

Chagrin and humiliation tasted suddenly very bitter. Juliet studied the board, confounded by his strategy.

"I see I must concede victory to you, sir. You're a deep player, aren't you?"

He laughed. "As you are, ma'am. It was too deuced close! I was told that you are beautiful, but not that you have so many skills."

Her chair clattered as she leaped up. The cats scattered. Damn him! She had been outwitted, outclassed by a bolder player than herself. Now he didn't scruple to flaunt it.

"Told by whom?" she asked bitterly. "What else have you heard? So it was not chance that brought you to my garden gate. Nor was it my white sweet peas, was it, sir?"

CHAPTER TWO

ELATION ALMOST BLINDED HIM FOR A MOMENT, BEFORE HE RE- alized in the next breath that he had very nearly thrown it all away. In a rapid attempt to recover, Alden decided quite deliberately to take the next chance. He even had a vague memory of some Seton from whom—in one of those exhilarating runs of luck—he had won six hundred guineas in a single hand.

He leaned back and smiled up at her. "The innkeeper described you to me, Mistress Seton. I thought perhaps I had met your late husband once in St. James's. That coincidence led to a small conversation about you at the Three Tuns. If that was an impertinence, I pray you will forgive me."

A deep flush spread slowly down her neck and across her cheeks. Her eyes darkened to violet in contrast.

"You knave!" she exclaimed. "You mountebank! It is a damned impertinence, sir! I beg you will leave this instant."

He stood and gave her a flourishing bow. What had he said to bring about such a violent reaction?

"Mistress Seton, you have been good-hearted beyond measure. If I have offended you, I must beg the kindness of your forgiveness. These last few hours in your company have been nothing but a delight to me."

"Stop it!" she said wildly. "Do you think you're the first rake to wander in here and try to pay empty compliments to the poor, lonely widow? I am not frustrated, sir, nor foolish. Neither am I looking for a lover, nor another husband. Good day to you, sir. It has stopped raining. You know the way out!"

*A*LDEN STOOD IN THE MUDDY STREET AND STARED AT THE HAT in his hands. He had made a splendid mess of that! But he had learned something. Mistress Seton was far from foolish, but she was frustrated and lonely, even if she denied it. His mention of her dead husband had triggered not sadness, not fond memories, but desperation—even fear.

Had her marriage been that terrible or that good?

He hoped it was the strength of her own passion that terrified her, for he intended to help her unleash it and he had four more days. He thrust the tricorn onto his head and strode away toward the Three Tuns.

Within half an hour he was riding north through the long summer twilight. Ten miles passed in a sparkling blur of wet trees and hedgerows, until Alden stopped his horse and gazed up the valley to the cluster of buildings on the rise at the other end. There was nothing left of the medieval abbey, except a few foundation stones and the ruined remains of a cloister. Instead a great house sat nestled in the trees where monks had once droned away the hours.

Alden sat for a moment, staring at the house and the scattering of cattle in the grounds.

His cows—unless he lost this wager.

His fields, his crops, his woods, his fish in the ponds.

His inheritance, with all of its encumbrance of tenants and retainers, as well as the responsibilities he'd voluntarily taken on, believing at the time he could afford it. Gracechurch Abbey, his ancestral home and the seat of what little power and wealth he had ever possessed—until the madness of one night's gaming.

A fierce possessiveness took him by the throat.

Nowhere else and nothing else had ever belonged to him. Nowhere else in the world bore his name. He was on the edge of losing it forever.

He *must* bed Juliet Seton by the end of the week. He could imagine nothing more enticing. Her round ankles and graceful wrists; the smooth, creamy skin. He wanted his hands on her, his lips. He wanted to bury himself in her soft, female flesh.

Yet as he remembered her face, severe, lovely, bent over the shelled peas, the desire almost dissolved in a sea of questions. She seemed to be a lady, yet she lived by herself and did her own work? No one had no family at all—no cousins, uncles, aunts. Even if she had no living relatives, a respectable widow always had friends, social connections, to find her a home. How could this Juliet be completely alone in the world?

It spoke uncomfortably of disaster, like her name. Or of a forbidding secret. This Miss Parrett she'd mentioned—who the devil was she? And why Manston Mingate?

Damnation! He didn't *want* to know. There was a fortune at stake. A fortune and more lives than just theirs—one in particular whose existence meant more than all the rest combined.

For a moment he thought of riding up to the house and routing Sherry out of bed. Sleepy blue eyes would open and stare up into his. Plump arms would wrap joyously about his neck. Then the child's tutor would subtly admonish Lord Gracechurch for costing the boy his sleep and exciting him over nothing.

Mr. Primrose would be right. Alden couldn't stay.

He had a widow to seduce.

It was his one undisputed talent. It would not be difficult to find excuse enough in himself to do it. What was her virtue to Juliet Seton? She wasn't an innocent. She had been married. He would steal his prize and take her locket as proof, but he would pay for that theft with a wealth of pleasure—worshipful, delectable, slow. Whether her marriage had been happy or sad, she would not be the loser.

Perhaps she wasn't even a lady, but an actress practiced in aping her betters. There was, after all, only one other thing—besides

tragedy—that could account for her living alone. That one thing
was sin.

His qualms dissolved in a cornucopia of voluptuous images.

Alden turned his horse's head and rode back to Manston Mingate and the tiny room at the Three Tuns.

*J*ULIET FACED THE NEXT MORNING WITH A HEADACHE. IT WAS
overbearingly hot, threatening unreleased thunder. She had
slept badly, disturbed by dreams. George glowered at her, his
black brows beetled together, as she ran endlessly down the corridors of a great country mansion, throwing open door after door.
Every room was empty, but when she reached the window at the
end of the hall and looked down into the courtyard, Mr. Alden
Granville was there. Golden, graceful in the sunshine and far too
beautiful, he flung himself back into a border of massed white
flowers. A wave of scent rushed up to envelop her.

"The bees!" she shouted through the window. "The bees!"

He looked up from the multitude of petals, his shirt collar open
to reveal his strong white throat, and laughed—while the flowers
began to buzz angrily, so that she awoke with a start.

Juliet climbed from her bed and walked to the front window.
Her garden lay beneath her in its orderly rows. So he claimed to
have met a Mr. Seton in St. James's. Perhaps he had, but he had
not met George, her disastrous husband. Plus, if Mr. Granville
had been in London then, he would have heard of the scandal.
Though, of course, there was no reason why he should connect it
with her. Seton had not been her name at the time.

She forced herself to be calm, not to panic, but the dark fear
beat at her heart. He had revealed a further deception in that last
formal speech and court bow—the gesture of a man who knew
his own power and had the conceit to show it or hide it as he
desired. He was not merely a gentleman down on his luck, he was
an aristocrat.

Why had he chosen not to reveal that?

And why was he here, in Manston Mingate?

Barely conscious that she had laid one palm over her locket, Juliet turned from the window. Very probably she had seen the last of him anyway. Alden Granville would hardly return to be faced with some menial task in exchange for another chess game. And with poor Tilly sick, there was a great deal of work to do and no time for a headache or thoughts of this man.

After her regular chores, Juliet draped herself in her blue smock and went through the house to her stillroom. It was time to bottle her cowslip wine. Two and a half pounds of sugar, two lemons and four quarts of wild cowslips, gathered in May, had been added to each two gallons of pure water. The wine had been fermenting in the barrel for a month. Several bottles had been ordered by the parsonage, more by Mistress Caxton in Upper Mingate, the next village. It was one of Juliet's small sources of extra income.

She opened the tiny north-facing window and left the outside door ajar so that air from the shadowed courtyard could flow through the room. The floor beneath her feet was flagged with stone, making the place invitingly cool. A cast-iron handle worked a pump which brought water up from the well when she needed it, splashing the excess into a shallow stone sink. She took her crates of clean empty bottles and began to transfer the bright liquid into each one, content, concentrating on the task.

A man's voice dropped into the silence, like honey from a comb.

" 'Neither must you let it work too long in the butt, as it will be apt to take off the sweetness and flavor of the fruit or flowers from which it is made. Let your vessels be clean and dry, and before you put in the wine, give them a rinse with a little brandy,' " the voice read—then with a flash of humor: "Alternatively it seems to me you may drink the brandy and save yourself a great deal of work."

Juliet looked up. Mr. Granville stood, as golden as the wine, in the doorway. He held her little leather-bound housekeeping book and was reading aloud from it.

She set down the wine bottle before she should drop it, flushed with her awareness of him.

Today he wore a blue velveteen coat over a long waistcoat embroidered with silver thread on peach satin. No longer in riding boots, he had walked from the Three Tuns in black buckled shoes, a little dusty from the road. Except for the lack of powder in his hair, it was the grooming any gentleman might use to make a formal call on a lady: a lady he was courting. But, of course, he was not courting. He was here in the village for a week and bored, that was all. His comment about her late husband had been random. It meant nothing. They had met only because Mr. Granville had been ill, momentarily helpless.

Yet he was not helpless now. His presence filled the room, a bold masculine power, tempered only by his grace and the laughter barely hidden in his voice. In spite of everything, Juliet knew that she wanted it, the humor and the intelligence. In spite of everything, she wanted *him,* to fill the dreadful void of her days.

But it was too late. Too late. Thanks to George, her days must remain forever empty.

Oh, God, don't let this happen! Please, please, please!

" 'When the wine has done fermenting, bung it up close, and after being properly settled, it will draw to your wishes.' Will it, Mistress Seton?"

"What are you doing here, sir?" She hated the panic she could hear in her voice.

"I'm sorry. It was unforgivable for me to startle you. Let me assist you."

She pulled back, almost wildly. "No! Let it be! Why have you come back?"

He closed the book and set it on the slate shelf. "Only to play chess, ma'am. One game a day was our wager, was it not? You gave me your word."

"I have a great deal to do."

"Then allow me to help. That was also part of our bargain."

"No! Later! I can do this by myself."

"Then I'll wait until you're finished. I shall be in the garden."

With a slight nod of his golden head, he was gone. Juliet leaned against the stone sink and laid her forehead against the cold pump handle. The iron was beaded with tiny drops of condensation. After a moment she rubbed the moisture over her face with both hands.

She had taken a wager! She had promised! A chess game each day for a week. And foolishly, foolishly, she wanted it, because the wine and the bees and the flower garden couldn't play chess, and the villagers couldn't challenge her wits, and underneath all of her care and her efficiency, she was hideously lonely.

As she turned, her elbow caught the half-filled wine bottle and sent it toppling toward the floor. Somehow, in a desperate swoop, she caught the green glass before it shattered on the stone, but liquid spilled across the front of her skirt, soaking her with the wild scent of cowslips. She sat down on a three-legged stool for a moment, while her damp petticoats clung to her legs.

Damn him! Damn him and his golden charm and the lovely, enticing curl to his lip. Damn him and his deliberate ruse to pursue her!

For she saw it clearly now. The offer of a chess game. He had known it would disarm her and he had known he would win. But his illness had been genuine enough, so could his presence otherwise be a coincidence? Had he once met some Mr. Seton? The innkeeper had very likely spoken of her and told Mr. Granville she was widowed. There could not be any real threat there, could there?

He was bored. No more. It was just chance that he was here.

She had taken a wager. She had promised.

Why not meet it with audacity?

With a wry smile, Juliet took up the clean towel lying by the sink and mopped her skirts. She looked about the small room at the neat rows of bottles, the whitewash peeling slightly from the spot on the north wall where the damp crept in, the scrubbed shelves and the worn stone floor: all the evidence of her years of struggle and discipline.

Whether she ignored it or tried to laugh at herself, loneliness contaminated her days, immune to her attempts to chase it away. She had been lonely even when Miss Parrett shared the house. Now loneliness waited in the empty corners and echoed about the garden. Yet she had won something close to equanimity—a kind of calm, practical acceptance—through hard work and a saving sense of humor.

Now this man, with his insolence and his certainty of conquest, threatened her life like a summer thunderstorm, with its towering clouds swept by high winds and carrying hail, to batter down her flowers and her runner beans, flood her hen coop and her beehives, and ruin all hope of security for the coming winter.

A vision of the golden Mr. Granville incongruously found among her staked runner beans caught her out. She felt a gurgle of laughter. It welled up to swamp all of her prudence and reticent pride, and tinge her thoughts with a bright edge of hysteria.

Juliet swallowed her mirth and methodically continued her bottling. If Mr. Alden Granville wished to wait among the sweet peas, he would have to wait for two more hours at least. Maybe another bee would come along and sting him in the meantime.

LORD EDWARD VANE REINED IN HIS MOUNT. SUPREMELY ELE-gant, he sat his horse with careless grace and stared across the valley toward Manston Mingate. The church spire towered above a thick grouping of trees, but no houses were visible. A black tricorn sat firmly on top of his wig. His face was as heavily powdered as always, though he had replaced the heart-shaped patches that he wore for evening with plain round ones. They did little to disguise his smallpox scars.

Sir Reginald Denby scowled at his back. He did not like being forced to straddle a horse.

"So Gracechurch has begun the courtship, has he? Already gained access to her house? Damn his eyes! How the devil did he do it?"

The duke's son tapped gently at his lip with the butt of his riding crop. "Courtship? You think he intends to wed her? My dear sir, nothing is less likely, I assure you."

"I think he will ravish her—"

"But this lady is hardly a virgin plucked fresh from the schoolroom, who would simply squeal and faint into the arms of a lover. I fear Mistress Juliet would very likely unman one with a glance— though not Gracechurch, of course, if rumor is correct. He has such a lovely reputation. I would so like to discover that it's true."

Indignation flared. "But then I would lose my damned money."

Lord Edward sat in silence for a moment, before he glanced back and smiled.

"Pray, don't distress yourself, Sir Reginald! You will bring on some unpleasant physical ailment. If Gracechurch insists on taking Mistress Juliet willing, he will indeed lose, for she will never succumb. What I do with him then is my own affair. But he can't pay you either way."

Denby felt the shock like a blow. "What, sir?"

"Surely you knew he was bluffing? If he fails in this wager, he is ruined. He could not redeem even a fraction of his debt to us, sir. The man hasn't a feather to fly with."

"But Gracechurch Abbey—?"

"—is already mortgaged to the hilt. Gracechurch had no idea of it until he came back from Italy. His father was a rakehell and spendthrift. Spent every last penny and left his son a hollow inheritance and a worthless title." Lord Edward slipped the brass cap between his lips and suckled it before he went on. "Alas, the value of your anticipated win is a great deal less than you hope."

"Then why the devil did you set this up? What do you want with him?"

"Nothing to signify, dear sir. Perhaps he might yet throw up her skirts and rape her, but if he fails in this wager, I fear he will whistle about it and try to repair his purse in Paris. In which case, we will lose both the man and what little money he possesses, and neither shall we have a delightful spectacle to entertain us."

The indignation was turning into rage. "What the hell do you suggest?"

Lord Edward bared his discolored teeth in a grin, the brass cap still lying on his tongue, and gave Denby a wink.

"I suggest," he replied with an unpleasant lift to one corner of his mouth, "that you allow me to buy all his debts from you now."

*J*ULIET STARED AT THE NEAT ROWS OF BOTTLES. THE STILLROOM was swept and washed, everything put away. She could not put it off any longer. Mr. Alden Granville was waiting for her in the garden and she had given her word.

She saw the gleam of his hair first, golden under the leaves of her grapevine. He was sitting at the little table that the Manston Mingate blacksmith had made for her under the arbor. He stood as soon as she appeared.

Their eyes met.

Juliet felt the burn and knew the answering heat in him, before he dropped his lashes and gave her a small bow.

"Shall we play here?" He indicated the chess set already laid out on the table. In contrast to his strong, masculine hands, the lace at his cuffs was very fine, with a pattern of small bells and angels, expensive. "It's your turn to play white, so the advantage is yours today."

Juliet sat down. The slow flame where his lightning had struck her was her problem alone. Yet she felt nervous and awkward in her stained gown. Her hair was untidy. Wisps fell annoyingly against her cheek, but she had been determined to make no concessions to this man and had refused the luxury of tidying herself—not in spite of the fact that she had felt the urge to try to look pretty for him, but because of it.

Every morning her mirror reflected her round chin and full mouth, blue eyes and fair skin. Though she liked her reddish hair and was glad it was healthy and abundant, she wasn't fine-boned or refined. When she changed her dress and caught sight of her reflection in nothing but petticoats and chemise, she didn't see a fashionable figure. She never had, even in the days when a maid had laced her into her corset. Juliet had never been slender enough, nor swan-necked enough. She was too rounded to fit comfortably into the long, slim bodice that made dresses look elegant.

Yet the sight of her always brought that particular look to men's eyes.

When she was only fourteen she had overheard her mother talking to her father. "Men won't be able to keep their hands off her, Felton. We must arrange a marriage right away."

Alas, her face had not been her fortune, but her downfall!

Now she wished she had at least gone into the house to wash her hands and comb her hair. The afternoon was unbearably hot, as if the entire atmosphere pressed down, close and suffocating. She longed to hear the distant rumble of thunder, anything to clear the oppression from the air.

Instead this golden man waited quietly, facing her across the board. The tails of his coat draped elegantly as he crossed long legs at the knee. The buckles on his heeled shoes shone under their thin coating of dirt. Faintly dusty white stockings outlined his firm calves. A man's calves. Muscled and hard.

"Very well," she said. "It's my opening. Pawn to King's Bishop Three."

Juliet snapped the pawn into place. She would throw him the game and get rid of him. Alden raised a brow, but he responded with a standard play: Pawn to King Four. Juliet moved her pawn to King's Knight Four. She had just opened a path directly to her king with no possibility of escape. His queen to Rook Five would give him checkmate in the next move.

He sat back and gazed at her. His eyes were a deep, dark blue. Why had she thought them brown? Because the blue held a depth of color that seemed close to black, unless the light was very brilliant as it was now in her summer garden—or because his pupils seemed to dilate whenever he looked at her?

"This is the opening for Fool's Mate, Mistress Seton. That's not what we wagered. You agreed to give me a game, not an insult. I believed you a lady of more honor and more courage." He left his queen untouched and moved a knight instead. "Come, give me a run for my money, ma'am! I wager you can win if you wish."

Chagrin left her feeling hot and flushed. She replied angrily to hide her embarrassment. "What do you wager this time, sir? You have already won a game for each day this week—and a wish granted the winner."

He looked up at her, the skin creased a little at the corners of his eyes. "Are you concerned that I might demand more than some small forfeit? Let me assure you that—if I win—I will ask for something harmless."

"What if your definition of harm is not the same as mine?"

He gazed straight into her eyes, adding fuel to that slow, agonizing fire in her heart. "If it is not, then you may refuse to pay, of course. Small and harmless, and you shall define it. If I lose, you may ask anything of me that you like, as before—in addition to whatever chores you need done, as we agreed."

"Do you reserve the right of refusal, also?"

"No, ma'am. I like to risk everything. Anything that you ask, I swear to fulfill it. Now, I will give you five moves to recover from your disastrous opening and then it is war."

Juliet studied the board. If she won, she could demand he leave Manston Mingate and never come back. But how could she recover? She tried to concentrate.

He watched her move and made his own. Meshach had come out of the house. The tabby stretched out in the shade under the table. Mr. Granville leaned down and gently flicked the cat under the chin. Meshach began to purr.

Even her cats were traitors!

"It is very hot, ma'am. Would you give me permission to remove my jacket?"

She glanced up. "It would be a discourtesy, sir. I would prefer you to wear it."

He took a handkerchief out of his pocket and touched it gently

to his face. The lace edging was exquisite, feminine. The contrast
with his lean fingers and hard bones was deeply tantalizing. "Even
if I melt?"

Juliet dropped her gaze. Let him swelter! "That's not my concern, sir."

"You are heartless, ma'am. Cruel." His voice held irrepressible
humor. "You will have a puddle on your hands."

"You are thoughtless to wear velveteen on such a hot day."

"I' faith," he said indignantly, smoothing his hand over the
plush sleeve. "It was chosen with a great deal of thought. I wanted
to look pretty for you."

Before she could stop herself, she laughed. *"Pretty?"*

"Pretty." He moved his rook.

"Like all that lace—so very effeminate?"

"Indeed, ma'am. My lace is both feminine and royal, a prize
won from a visiting European princess."

"The result of another game?"

"If you like." He smiled. "What do you suppose is the purpose
of chess, Mistress Seton?"

His position was still stronger—except for one little opening.
She took it. "To capture the opponent's king, of course. Check!"

He blocked the threat in a way she hadn't expected and destroyed her strategy. "But the king is never captured. He is only
pinned down and forced to surrender. Meanwhile the queen can
sweep any other piece to destruction. It's odd, don't you think,
for the lady to have so much power?"

The blue eyes were gazing at her through narrowed lashes. Blue
eyes. Blue velvet. Beneath a great arch of blue sky. The color
echoed and re-echoed, gaining depth and timbre. Her pulse res-
onated as if it responded to that silent orchestra of color. Heat
flooded her face. She had made a dreadful mistake, letting him
lull her into a false sense of security by his illness on her garden
path.

She looked down and moved her queen's bishop two squares.
"Why odd?"

"It suggests that chess is a metaphor for seduction."

Disquiet throbbed. It was getting difficult to concentrate on the direction of her new attack. She could see where his moves were leading him, but it made little sense. It was too obvious a play.

"I thought we had agreed that chess is a war game."

"It is, of course. Yet all's fair in love and war, they say." His knight blocked her, but gave her another opening. "Both must win surrender of the opponent. Although any tactics may secure victory, there are certain rules, aren't there, that must be followed if the winning is to be honorable? Even when the game involves royalty. No, without question, chess is a model for seduction. Look at what is happening on the board: a pursuit, a pinning, followed by a forking check."

The words hung between them for a moment, rich in suggestion. The sun burned onto her hair and sent a flush of heat through her limbs. She wanted to peel off her hot, sticky dress and plunge into something cool and dark, like the village pond. Instead she was trapped here at her own garden table with a man who blazed like the sun. A faint trace of perspiration lay along his cheekbone. It sparkled, distracting her. Juliet dragged her mind back to the board.

He had slipped away from her thrust and she was in check. She moved her bishop as she had planned and challenged him again, quite deliberately, because she couldn't bear the uncertainty, the sense of impending disaster.

"It's a totally false analogy, sir! Am I to assume that you wantonly reveal your true purpose, after all?"

She'd put as much indignation as she could muster into her voice, but he laughed.

"My *purpose* is only to win this game. But my desire? I would very much like to seduce you, Mistress Seton."

She looked up, her face burning, hating herself for bringing it out into the open where the delicate game must be shattered. Had she ever been so young that she had thought flirtation harmless?

"This sudden lurch into candor will achieve you nothing, sir. I'm not interested."

He was smiling, just a little, the sun flaming gold in his hair. Not a muscle moved except a slight narrowing of his eyes, but the depths of those black pupils offered a searing invitation to eroticism. The coward in her wanted to leap up from the table and flee. Instead she funneled her anger into a determination to beat him, to leave him humbled, his king pinned on the last rank, helpless before her massed attack.

"Oh, no, ma'am. Do not prevaricate." His voice was very soft. "You are interested. Don't let it disturb you. We are civilized creatures. But should I pretend that I don't find you lovely, that my blood doesn't burn for you? Why? It would be an absurd falsehood. Yet you hold the power. If the lady allows no room for maneuver, the game is over before it begins."

That my blood doesn't burn for you? Her blood raged in her veins.

"And if she is tricked into allowing that room, sir?"

Two more moves and she would have him trapped—if he did not see her strategy, if he continued to pursue the path to checkmate she could see—-the game would be hers. A trickle ran down her spine, stinging and hot. Her skirts were a suffocating burden.

He mopped a fine bead of moisture from his upper lip with his handkerchief. The lip curved, pouting sweetly in the center. The gesture was delicate, elegant, designed to provoke. It infuriated her.

"She was not tricked," he said. "She played to win and lost. But only because she played to lose at the beginning and couldn't catch up." He closed one blue eye in a slow wink, then he moved his rook all the way up an empty file to penetrate her side of the board. "Checkmate."

Juliet stared at the chessmen. She had not seen it coming and even now she was not sure she was defeated. Yet a moment's examination of the board proved he was right. She looked up at him with a humiliating blur of tears in her eyes.

"You play a very subtle game, sir. I am outclassed."

He leaned back and watched her. The dimples had disappeared, leaving that lean, stern look to his cheek and jaw. "No, you are not. You began with a disadvantage that couldn't be recovered because you misjudged my reaction to your strategy. You offered me Fool's Mate, thinking that conquest was more important to me than the game. Now you've discovered that it's not. Tomorrow, you will begin knowing that and we'll be better matched. If the play is worthwhile, what does it matter who wins?"

"Because the winner," Juliet said with a mixture of anger and foreboding, "may claim a forfeit."

She knew what it would be. He would kiss her. It felt as inevitable as the hot, oppressive twilight that would follow this blazing day. He would demand a kiss, mouth to mouth.

Juliet closed her eyes. *You may refuse to pay, of course.* Panic rose clear in her throat. *Small and harmless, and you shall define it.* So he could not force her, but when he asked, how could she reply? *That a kiss is never harmless, that I wish you had never come into my life.* Because it would be a lie. A lie to add to the one she had already told him.

She tried to stop herself looking at his mouth. His lips were mobile and expressive, firm and full. In a furious mix of emotions she leaped to her feet. "What do you claim, sir?"

His eyes narrowed against the bright sun. "It's your turn first." He seemed merely casual and courteous, though his voice betrayed him. "Before I claim anything from you, I owe you a small chore, some task, as we agreed. By all means, name it."

Juliet turned her back. Summer shimmered over her garden—her world, her realm, the one place where everything was under her control.

"The bottom meadow," she said over her shoulder. "It needs mowing. There's a scythe in the shed."

"A *scythe*?" He sounded genuinely horrified. "How many acres?"

"Two. Of course, you cannot do it today. Haymaking must be started at dawn. You may begin tomorrow morning."

"Who usually does it?"

"Farmer Hames, from the farm to the west—next door across the lane. He brings his men every year to make the hay for me. But he can't come for three more days—"

"How long would it take Farmer Hames and his men to cut this terrifying meadow?"

Juliet turned back to face him. She already regretted it—impulsive, too much! It made it clear that she cared. She should have picked something trivial. "Last year it took four men three hours."

The lines of merriment deepened around his eyes. "A very dangerous chore, Mistress Seton."

"Dangerous? Why?"

He stood up, took her fingers in his own and kissed them briefly. Then he brushed his folded knuckles over her cheekbone. "You have given me twelve hours' labor during which to think up what forfeit I shall demand in return."

A little leap of panic forced her to swallow before she replied. "Something small. Harmless, you said."

"So I did. But we are playing a perilous game, Mistress Seton. You know it. I know it. Anyway, it's tomorrow's forfeit of which I may dream while swinging that scythe."

He walked away a few paces.

She stared at the powerful lines of his back. "You might lose."

"So I might. We'll find out tomorrow. Meanwhile, I may still claim today's little prize."

Abednego appeared from behind the arbor. Juliet picked him up, her heart thumping. "What do you want?"

Silence stretched. Her mouth flamed with almost forgotten memories. What would it be like to kiss a man like this, golden and hot and glorious in the sun? What should she do, if that's what he demanded? She licked her lips and swallowed nervously.

He spun around and bowed. "My forfeit today, ma'am, is that you give me permission to remove this damnable blue velvet."

She hugged her cat to her chin, feeling foolish, then almost laughed aloud as she recognized her own absurdity. Of course he would not claim a kiss—a complete stranger! He was bored, so he thought to indulge in a little flirtation with an available widow. It meant nothing to him. It was indeed just a game, for his·idle amusement.

You offered me Fool's Mate, thinking that conquest was more important to me than the game. Now you've discovered that it's not.

He lifted both brows. "Before I do indeed melt?"

Abednego's purrs rumbled against her cheek as she rubbed her face in the white fur. "As you wish."

"Thank you, ma'am."

He stood silhouetted against the dark texture of her grapevine. Very slowly he peeled off his jacket. Blue velveteen bunched and flowed, carried by the weight of the heavy cuffs as it draped down off his shoulders. Powerful shoulders. He shook the fabric free and dropped the coat. Gathered shirtsleeves of white lawn, slightly damp, clung lovingly to the muscles of his arms.

Trickles of desire ran over her body.

His close-fitting waistcoat was embroidered with peacocks. His shirt cuffs frothed like white foam as he stretched languidly, beautifully—a display of potency—like a cat. Muscles flexed. Peach satin hugged his flexible spine, the forceful lines of his back. Peacocks rattled golden feathers, glorious in their embroidered garden, icons of male boldness entrapped in satin over a man's firm flesh.

She thought she might weep with yearning and rage.

Meshach leaped onto his discarded coat and began to knead, purring like a beehive on a hot day. Idly he unfastened a few waistcoat buttons and bent to lift the tabby away. It was the movement of a dancer, precise and graceful. The cat disappeared indignantly into the marigolds.

Juliet collapsed onto the seat.

Only a whimsy to counterbalance the hard steel underneath—were you fooled?

No, I'm not fooled. She thought she might even have said it aloud.

He smiled down at her, his coat folded over his arm. "Not so dangerous a request after all, ma'am?"

She stood up, Abednego rumbling in her arms. "A petty one. *If* you win again, will tomorrow's be more interesting?"

"Oh, yes," he said. "After I cut all that hay? Only consider, ma'am, when you ask such a Herculean task of me, what size forfeit—*when* I win—does that justify my demanding in return?"

CHAPTER THREE

ALDEN DEMANDED BUCKETS FROM THE INNKEEPER, STRIPPED off his waistcoat and shirt, and sluiced himself with cold water from the tap in the yard. The rustics gaped. He grinned at them and strode up to his room with his hair plastered to his head, leaving a trail of moisture along the hallway.

She was glorious. Devil take it, Mistress Juliet was resplendent, brilliant! She would not win, but she was an extraordinary adversary.

He whistled as he toweled his hair and shoulders dry. Victory lay within his grasp. He was going to win her favors, the wager and that extra five thousand from Denby, enough to solidly enhance his network of investments. He liked risk, but this was the game he loved better: the ruin of a woman with her ardent consent, but only after a chase—a seduction—worth the effort.

Juliet Seton was well worth the effort.

He shrugged into a clean shirt and buttoned a plain linen ruffle to the cuffs, discarding his lace. Stepping out of his shoes, he tugged on riding breeches and boots, then donned a simple gray jacket. He paused for a moment as he reached for his gloves. The tracks of his rings were starting to fade. He turned one hand over and looked at the palm.

Of course, he knew nothing of manual labor. He had no idea how to swing a scythe. As his clothes advertised to the world, he was a gentleman. He had never worked with his hands in his life.

He had taught his fingers other skills, ones that left no trace, except at the end of a rapier—or in a woman's soul.

Had she imagined his expert fingertips on her naked body? Was that why she had picked this impossible task? Desire burned in her. She couldn't hide it. So she wanted to see him make a fool of himself. She planned to gloat, to glory over his punishment in a hay meadow, so that she could deny her own feelings and keep herself safe.

"Alas, sweet Juliet," he said aloud to the empty air. "You don't know it, but you are already in the palm of my hand."

With a laugh, he donned gloves and tricorn, caught up his riding crop, and ran down the stairs to the stables.

THE SOUND WOKE HER. SOMETHING DIFFERENT, RHYTHMIC, clanking beneath the twitter of songbirds. It was morning. A new day. Juliet struggled up from her dreams and listened.

Creak, whir. Creak, whir.

She climbed from her bed and peered from the window at the back of the house. Dawn streaked the sky. Chill shadows submerged the cluster of work buildings around her small courtyard. Her chicken coop slept in the shade of Mill Spinney. Still clinging to traces of night, massed trees slumbered on in the fold of the hill on the far side of Manston Brook—the woods that bordered the edge of the Marion Hall estates.

Juliet unbuttoned the neck of her nightdress and laid one palm over her locket. The gold felt warm: warm, but not comforting. She felt for it automatically every morning—her tangible remembrance of the purest, brightest love of her life. Yet she wore it almost as a monk wears a hair shirt: in penance as well as in memory. With a small sigh, she opened the hasp to look inside.

Creak, whir. Creak, whir.

She closed the locket with a snap just as the sun broke over the top of the rise. Color flooded the landscape. Bordered by the stream and the little lane to the west—the one that ran down to the ford, before cavorting away to Upper Mingate—her hayfield suddenly sparked green, fired with sunlight. A rooster crowed, then another. The songbirds' melody reached a crescendo. Two cornrails flew up, trailing pale legs. They nested in the fields every year, filling the countryside with their rasping cries.

But this was a sound made by man—*creak, whir, creak, whir.*

It was the turning of the whetstone in the shed.

Juliet raced downstairs and filled her jug with water, still warm from last night's coals. She washed rapidly before scrambling into a fresh chemise. With fumbling fingers she hooked her corset and grabbed clean stockings from the dresser. She tied her garters, then wrenched her dress over her head. She caught a glimpse of herself in the mirror. Her plait had come undone in the night. She looked wild, her hair rioting about her face.

She sat down on the bed and began to laugh—letting the laughter have free rein, bubbles of madness welling up, making her sides ache. It was a struggle to regain control, but at last she picked up her comb and began to unweave the night's tangles, before brushing out the long chestnut waves and plaiting them into a knot.

The sound echoed. *Creak, whir. Creak, whir.*

Mr. Alden Granville was sharpening metal!

*S*HE SAW HIM AS SOON AS SHE STEPPED INTO THE YARD. HE WAS leaning casually against the door of the shed, a bottle-green tricorn tucked under one elbow. His gaze was speculative, as if contemplating the results of his labor at the whetstone. The scythe lay propped against the open field gate, fifty feet away. The newly honed blade sparkled in the sunlight.

Juliet stopped, torn between astonishment and the dying shreds of her laughter.

His gilt hair was curled, immaculate, tied back neatly in a dark green ribbon. A fall of lace snowflakes foamed at his throat. A full-skirted, dusky-pink brocade coat lay unbuttoned to reveal a leaf-green waistcoat, exquisitely embroidered in gold thread, over pink brocade breeches. More layers of white lace fell from his extravagant cuffs to caress the backs of his hands. The rich lining of the flared coat framed the lean length of legs and hips. Outlining the hard shape of his calves, silver-and-white striped stockings disappeared into red-heeled, white leather shoes, fit for a ballroom.

His face pale, composed, with one tiny, discreet patch placed high on one cheekbone, Alden Granville shone in her yard like a rose.

"What a flower!" she said dryly. "You sharpened the scythe?"

He turned his head and met her gaze with an amused lift of the brows. "Until lethal."

"You cannot really mean to cut my hay."

"Why not?" His smile struck her with undiluted force, like a sea wave knocking the breath from a child.

"You're a gentleman."

He bowed his head. "Worse, ma'am."

"*Worse?* Worse than what?"

"You might say I am a popinjay." Humor danced in his voice. "I am disappointed you did not." He flicked one finger over his cuff. Sunlight caught his profile for a moment. "This is Mechlin lace."

"A gift from a princess."

"Nevertheless, I still mean to cut your hay."

She smoothed her palms down her blue smock, then tucked a stray wisp of hair under her flat straw hat. Absurdly, her heart still hammered too hard and fast. "What if I no longer wish it?"

"I'd be desolate."

"You *want* to do it? Dressed like that!"

"Dressed like what?" He set the tricorn on his head and strolled to the field gate. "This is my usual morning attire."

She marched after him and leaned both elbows on the gate. "This I must see," she said, genuinely amused. "By all means begin mowing, Mr. Granville."

He stared for a moment at the tall grass, sprinkled with buttercups and clover, then glanced back at the scythe. The blade curved dangerously. "Which end do I hold?"

"Why not the sharp end?"

"Flowers may have thorns, ma'am, but you do not distinguish between risk and foolishness?"

"Do you?"

His smile caressed. "Only when it involves death—or love, of course."

He bent and correctly grasped the two grips on the scythe handle before striding to the top corner of the field. Powerful shoulders flexed. The blade swung in a long, low arc.

Swish.

A swath of grass fell neatly to one side. He stepped forward. The rose-pink jacket stretched and relaxed across his back.

Step, swish.

Another patch of grass fell. Lace fluttered over his hands as he swung the scythe in long, steady strokes.

"You wretch!" she shouted. "You took lessons! Who taught you?"

"We agreed to trade forfeits," he said without breaking rhythm. "Do you now wish to trade secrets?"

"You admit to having secrets?"

"Only ones worth having." *Step, swish. Step, swish.* "There's nothing arcane about slaying all this innocent grass."

"You are expert at the slaughter of innocence?"

"Innocence doesn't need to be slaughtered. It just lies down and surrenders." There was only a slight catch in his breathing. "I find experience far more interesting."

Juliet didn't reply. He would need all of his breath. Anyway, what reply could she make? She had been innocent once, until she had done more than lain down and surrendered.

Meshach rubbed at her skirts. Shadrach and Abednego followed. The cats leaped, one after the other, onto an oak branch that formed part of the hedge. Folding their paws, they sat and watched the stranger in the rose-pink coat. Six feline eyes stared at him as if he were the god of cats.

Like her pets, Juliet couldn't tear herself away.

It was incongruous, bizarre, beautiful. He shone like a jewel against the backdrop of the woods: a study in contrasts—this man in his exquisite clothes wielding a workman's tool with such precision and grace.

Step, swish. Step, swish.

The cats rumbled contentedly, purring.

A small trickle of guilt disturbed her amusement. He was strong. He was clever. But, even though he had somehow learned the knack of swinging a scythe, he was obviously unused to such work. Twelve hours of it would destroy his hands, scorch a tearing pain into his muscles. It was a very cruel price to demand for a chess game!

She closed her eyes for a moment, unsure of her emotions.

"Look like you could use a hand there, sir," a stranger's voice said. "Are you hiring?"

Juliet looked up to see a man in a laborer's smock standing in the lane. A giant of a man, he carried a scythe over his shoulder.

Mr. Granville had worked down that side of the field and was close to the gate. "A very kind offer, i' faith," he said without stopping. "I'll trade you, but only for something I have on me."

The man eyed him speculatively. "Your hat, sir?"

Alden Granville took the green tricorn from his head and tossed it to the giant. The man jammed the hat onto his head, flung open the gate and began working. The tricorn sat jauntily on his brown hair. It was obvious he knew all about the scything of hay. Yet Mr. Granville kept pace with him.

Juliet closed the gate and climbed up to sit on the top rail, fascinated, like a prisoner who sees the bright world ring by beyond a barred window.

The two incongruously dressed men worked on down the field.

Within ten minutes a second stranger had stopped. This time a swarthy fellow with black hair accepted the rose-pink coat. He replaced his smock with the gorgeous brocade and preened for a moment, checking the fit across his narrower shoulders. Then he also began to expertly swing his scythe.

Mr. Granville's white shirtsleeves glittered in the sun. Royal lace frothed over his hands. Embroidered gold-thread flowers and birds fluttered on his green waistcoat, leaping to life with each swing. Yet he kept step with the two laborers.

Step, swish. Step, swish.

Juliet pressed one hand to her throat. Her runnel of remorse had evaporated like a thin sheen of water spilled under a hot sun. She only wanted to laugh. How on earth had he arranged this?

The sun was rising higher above Mill Spinney. The chickens needed feeding. Climbing down from the gate, she hurried away and rushed through the most urgent of her chores. As she threw out the grain in the chicken coop and refilled the water pan, sudden cheers rose from the direction of the hayfield. She heard them again as she set her bread out to rise. *Cheers?*

She raced back to the gate. Five men now worked steadily through the hay, shoulders swinging in rhythm. Each of the new arrivals wore some article of gentleman's apparel, absurdly added to his work clothes.

The brown-haired man had pulled the tricorn down solidly over his forehead. The dark fellow sweltered in the pink coat. He wiped his face on the gorgeous cuffs and grinned as if at some tremendous joke. A wiry newcomer—not much more than a boy—was almost swamped by the glorious green waistcoat. The embroidered birds flapped about his skinny thighs. Another stranger sported lace—*Mechlin* lace—on his coarse homespun shirt, but he had pinned the cuffs above his elbows so the expensive lace fluttered about his brawny forearms without damage as he worked.

Mr. Granville stepped and swung in time with them, stripped now to shirt and breeches. In contrast to the others, he looked calm, elegant, even comfortable.

A crowd of locals had gathered in the lane—men, women, mothers with young children in their arms. The babble of their

excited voices and the yap of village dogs drifted across the flattened hay. The cats had abandoned their post on the oak branch
and were now leaping in pursuit of the mice disturbed by the
mowing. It was just the same when Farmer Hames cut her hay,
or when any group of men gathered for the communal tasks of
the countryside—an excuse for a party.

And she was the hostess.

Juliet managed to catch young Jemmy Brambey's eye.

The boy ran over, his round face flushed beneath his freckles.
"Morning, Mistress Seton! It's a rare sight this, then, eh?"

She smiled. "It is, Master Brambey. Would you do a favor for
me?"

Jemmy nodded and followed her into the house, where she
raided the little hoard of coins she had been saving. He listened
and nodded as she gave him his instructions, then he ran away
into the village. Juliet went back outside. Another stranger, a
redhead carrying a scythe, had shouldered through the giggling
crowd in the lane to lean on the gate.

Mr. Granville didn't break step. The other men winked to each
other as they also kept working. Only the brown-haired man
stopped for a moment, lifting the green tricorn to mop his brow.
He met the newcomer's gaze and grinned.

The redhead grinned back, then nodded to the blond gentleman in the field and shouted out to him. "Look like you could
use another hand there, sir."

"I'll trade you." His breathing was definitely broken now—
with labor or with laughter? "But only . . . for something . . . I
have on me."

A cheer went up from the lane.

"Your shirt, my lor—sir?"

The cheer redoubled.

Alden Granville set down his scythe and peeled off his white
shirt. Muscles rippled in his back. His skin glowed. Juliet imagined living marble, mysteriously lit from within, as if a Greek
statue had come miraculously to life. The tail of gilt hair curled

down over his strong, sunlit shoulders, the ends of the dark ribbon startling in contrast—a supreme elegance of form knit to deadly male strength.

It was a terrible weakness to want that, to find it so beautiful, to feel it devouring her peace and making her breathless. Decent ladies did not admire men in that way. Her mother had never looked at her father and had such thoughts. Only she! Only she— a natural wanton among women! This man symbolized everything she had tried to renounce and she was trapped here. She couldn't flee. It was her hay meadow.

The grass was almost all cut. The sun blazed. The men labored on.

The strangers in their fantastic clothing had begun a kind of chant to keep the rhythm. It swelled up into the summer air. Their faces shone with sweat as their arms swung. No doubt now that they were truly farm workers. Yet she had never seen any of them before, certainly not on the road to Upper Mingate—no more than two farms and three cottages—a lane rarely traveled by anyone except locals.

Only Mr. Granville didn't know the song. He shone among the others like Apollo. His bright blade bit through the grass and buttercups. His hard muscles, his certainty of movement, his fine white skin, mocked her. The wretch wasn't even tired yet! Was he entirely ruthless to have created this dance of wit and defiance in her hayfield?

Working side by side, the six men again reached the top of the field. The last swatch of grass fell. It was done.

The crowd in the lane cheered again as a cart rumbled toward them from the village. Mr. Sandham, the innkeeper, sat on the box driving a brown horse.

Jemmy Brambey raced up to Juliet, his freckled face beaming. "Here he is, ma'am! With the ale for the men, as you wanted! But Mr. Sandham said to keep this." The boy thrust out the coins she had given him. "The fancy gentleman had already ordered it all this morning at the inn and paid for it—the usual ale and food, he said, for haymaking, with some extra for onlookers."

Juliet thanked Jemmy and gave the boy a farthing for his trouble. She walked into the house to put the rest of her coins back into their hiding place. For a moment she looked about at the low-ceilinged room, then suddenly envisioned the high blaze of white plaster that had soared overhead during her childhood. Strident images swarmed, making the breath catch in her throat. Not something she usually allowed. She never let herself indulge in vain regrets. Now they came rushing back. The aching void, slashed through the lives of everyone she loved. The terrible price they had all paid in pain and sorrow. Her fists clenched as her eyes burned with tears.

Damn this man! Alden Granville had cut a swath through her contentment with his keen, sharp presence, as if to lay open all of her defenses. It was intolerable. She turned around to march out into her hayfield and confront him.

The five laborers, joined by the gaggle of spectators from the village, were now quaffing ale and tearing into large chunks of bread and cheese by the lane gate. The brown-haired giant had set the tricorn reverently on the gate post. Pink brocade hung from the hedge, while the swarthy man mopped his face with a handkerchief and accepted slaps on the back from his fellows. Waistcoat, lace cuffs and linen shirt were all being folded and laid carefully out of harm's way, while their new owners laughed and nodded at the merry throng of faces. There was no half-naked gentleman with yellow hair among them.

"It would spoil their party if I joined in," he said.

Juliet looked around. He had flung himself full length on a patch of mown grass near the hedge by the yard, one hand over his eyes to shield them from the sun. Her attention focused on his mouth, on that lovely curl of lip, the little smile lingering at the corners. A tiny sparkle of gold glittered on his jaw. More gold shone on his forearms. Firm muscles ridged below his rib cage. A line of hair ran down his chest, then disappeared beneath his breeches.

She lifted her chin, feeling the mad awareness creep over her skin.

Her cats had curled up beside him, a tumble of multicolored fur, purring. The god fallen, but still worshipped.

"You cheated," she said.

He moved his fingers and opened one blue eye. "Did I?"

The indignant cats uncurled and arched their backs. Abednego stalked off through the grass.

"You found laborers to help you." She bit her lip and glanced away. It wasn't what she wanted to say.

"The hay is cut. I was the instrument of that." His tone was entirely innocent, good-humored. "I think you have your prize, ma'am."

She bent to pick up a beheaded buttercup. The petals glowed like yellow fire. "And do you think you are any closer to yours?"

"No, alas." He sounded almost merry. "This forfeit is all for you."

Shadrach stretched and walked away. Tail high, Meshach ran off toward the yard. Juliet watched them go, her disloyal pets.

"I did not gain much by it," she said.

"Yes, you did. You wanted me to feel humiliation. I did not. But you also wanted me to feel at least some modicum of pain."

It was true, wasn't it? "And do you?"

He started to laugh. Still laughing, he rolled over to bury his face in his hands. Blond hair, tawny with moisture, clung to his spine. Even the brocade breeches were damp, though his washed skin was no longer sticky with sweat and pollen. He must have cleansed himself at the yard pump, dumped water over his head and muscular shoulders, then let himself dry in the sun.

If she moved closer she would catch his scent—be able to breathe it deeply into her starved lungs—the honest tang of freshly mown grass with a deeper note echoing the damp heat of clean male flesh. Her pulse beat darkly in forbidden, secret rhythms as her rage grew.

"I ache from head to toe," he said at last. "Every blessed muscle. I' faith, but I had no idea mowing hay would be such deuced hard work."

She dropped the buttercup. Caught by a slight breeze, the petals drifted onto his naked back. Gold shone against the strong indentation of his spine.

"Because you have never before done a day's work in your life," she said. "Which is why you cannot join the men for their ale. They'd be far too uncomfortable if you socialized with them. They know their place. As you know yours—*my lord.*"

His spine stiffened. "Yes," he said. "Does it matter?"

Juliet stared across the field to the group lolling and drinking by the gate. Of course it mattered! Nothing else mattered as much in this England. One class of men born into privilege and wealth, another into unceasing labor. Yet the burden of the aristocracy was the greatest—theirs the responsibility to hold the whole system together. Alas that there were members of that class, like herself, who had not understood the price that would be exacted from any who broke the rules.

"One of your men almost called you by your title," she said. "You are a lord. Who?"

His back flexed. His muscles slipped smoothly. The buttercup petals slid away to be lost in the cut grass. He turned over and set one hand behind his damp head, while the fingers of the other shaded his gaze once again.

"If I tell you my parentage, will you tell me yours?"

She stared down at him, lying abandoned at her feet. "It is none of your business."

His eyes narrowed. "Then let us remain strangers, Mistress Juliet. It adds spice."

"*Spice?* You are a peer of the realm—or your father was—yet you come here on some kind of whim. You entrap me, a perfect stranger, into your madness. You steal my time and my contentment. You glory over my discomfiture. You make a fool of me in front of the people among whom I must spend the rest of my days, long after you have returned to your life of idleness and dissipation. It is all an amusement to you." Her hands had balled into fists. She shook them. "*You*—all of you!"

"All of whom?"

Juliet took a deep breath. Rage surged in her blood. "Three years ago Sir Reginald Denby, my neighbor at Marion Hall"— she stabbed a forefinger to the north—"blew up the mill dam on Manston Brook to amuse some cronies. They were racing toy boats. When the miller complained, they laughed. Last year Sir Reginald drove his carriage at a gallop down that lane—" She waved her hand to the west, indicating the road to Upper Mingate. "At the ford he killed six geese belonging to Mistress Caxton. No recompense was offered. *You*—in your silk and lace and finery—you are all parasites on the land!"

"Lud!" he said calmly. "How fortunate we are that you're not also a member of that execrated class!"

Her anger died. Why had she railed at him about this? Of course not all landowners were like Sir Reginald Denby. Her father had always worked harder than any of his tenants, fulfilling the responsibilities of his position before ever indulging his own pleasure. So had many of his friends. She knew that.

She turned to leave.

"You're an actress?"

Surprise stopped her in mid-turn. "Of a kind."

His hand seized her ankle.

Juliet almost tripped. She stopped dead, the strength of his fingers pressed into her bones. Outrage left her momentarily speechless.

"Alas, another predicament, ma'am?" he asked softly. "If you move, you will fall. If you struggle, you will create a scene. The villagers will notice."

"And may well exact a swift enough vengeance on you for my

discomfort." The firm grip held steadily, just enough to prevent her wrenching away. "What humiliation do you plan now?"

"None." His palm burned warmly on her stocking. She was searingly aware of it. "I just want to let you know that you are right."

"Right about what?"

"That this is all an amusement to me. Why shouldn't life be amusing, full of joy? Why the devil are you so full of regrets, Mistress Seton? When you sat on the gate and watched us cut hay, you seemed filled with longing for the wicked, immodest world. Why have you allowed it to leave you behind?"

"I regret nothing except that I let you cozen me into this mad agreement."

"I have barely begun to cozen you, but I won't do you any harm." His hand slipped open-fingered over her ankle, sending keen shivers up her calf. "Whereas you have already caused me grave injury."

"You are in that much pain?" she asked derisively, looking at the obvious strength of his arms and shoulders.

"Not of the body, ma'am—though I shall know a merry enough ache in my limbs for a day or two. The real injury you have caused me is to the heart."

The absurdity of it, his sheer nonsense, made her want to laugh. "You have no heart, sir. Meanwhile, you have me pinned by the foot! What am I supposed to say? 'Unhand me, sirrah'?"

He grinned. "I would never obey so melodramatic a request."

Juliet lifted the edge of her skirt and stared at his hand on her ankle. "Why not? Do you think 'undress me' is more likely?"

His fingers flew open as he was startled into laughter. He rolled over again, covering himself in cut grass and shredded buttercups, his shoulders shaking with mirth.

Juliet spun about and walked rapidly to the house. She slammed the kitchen door behind her and raced up the stairs to her bedroom. Ribbons flailed on her straw bonnet as she wrenched it off and threw it to the floor. The clumsy action caught hairpins, so her hair tumbled down around her shoulders. He had almost made her join him in hilarity—which felt dangerously close to surrender!

She seized the chestnut mass in both hands and pushed it away from her face. Her flushed reflection stared back from the mirror. High color flooded her cheeks. Her eyes burned like blue sapphires. She was still young. She was comely enough. Her blood pulsed with vigorous desire. Did he think her reasons for rejecting him were trivial?

Juliet dropped her hands and let her hair fall.

She had closed all those doors five years ago and none of them could be opened again. Unless— Horrified at her own thoughts, Juliet paced to the window and looked out, one hand over the locket hidden beneath her dress.

The villagers had piled onto the inn wagon and were riding away. Mr. Granville was talking to Farmer Hames. A gang of men from the farm, joined by the five strangers, were already raking the downed grass. One of the lads was bringing the hay cart in through the gate. It would take them the rest of the afternoon, raking and turning, letting the sun dry the hay. So he must have arranged that, too, as he had arranged for the ale from the Three Tuns. He might be a wastrel, but he knew about rural customs. Obviously he had estates of his own somewhere.

She turned away. It was better not to know.

Meanwhile, she had work to do. She secured her hair neatly at her nape, picked up her bonnet and hung it carefully from its hook. For a moment she leaned one shoulder against the wall, fingering the worn ribbons. Perhaps with what Mr. Granville had just saved her in getting her hay scythed for free, she could buy herself a new bonnet. Juliet laughed aloud and went downstairs.

*A*LDEN LEFT THE MEN MAKING HAY AND WALKED BACK TO the inn. Four cows grazing on the green lifted their heads and watched him pass, their long-lashed brown eyes gazing stupidly after him.

He was only a little regretful about the pink brocade and the waistcoat. They had been a necessity for a particular court appearance and had cost a deuced fortune. But the lads from Gracechurch Abbey could carry off their winnings, along with a grand tale to tell, to sell or keep as they wished. If he won the wager, he could afford it. If he lost, it didn't matter. He was giving away clothes that had already been lost in a card game, but he was damned if he wanted Sir Reginald Denby—a man who had destroyed a village mill pond for sport—to decorate his callous exploits with royal lace and gold-thread embroidery.

At the Three Tuns Alden ordered his daily hot bath, much to the consternation of Mr. Sandham. The innkeeper was mystified by the peculiar cleanliness standards of his guest.

"You'll be aching, then, sir?" the man asked, scratching his head.

"I' faith, Mr. Sandham," Alden replied. "Since my last tub I have ridden thirty miles, taken lessons with a scythe until dawn, broken my back over a whetstone, then swung that sharpened blade at a killing pace for two hours. I am going to bathe and sleep. I do not wish to be disturbed."

The innkeeper grinned. "Then you'll visit Mistress Seton again?"

Alden paused at the foot of the stairs. "You truly don't know who she is?"

"On my life, sir! Miss Parrett, as used to have the cottage, was fetched one morning in a carriage. No one in the village had ever seen it before. She come back the next day with Mistress Seton. It were five year ago."

"The lady was widowed before she came here? Was it a recent loss, do you think?"

"She were dead with grief, I'd say, when she arrived—pale as a ghost and sick with a fever. Miss Parrett nursed her. But the ladies always kept themselves to themselves, sir. That's all I know.

'Tis all anyone knows. Though she's well respected around here, Mistress Seton's never had friends or visitors—till you."

"And Miss Parrett. Who was she?"

"Why, I don't rightly know, sir. She weren't born around here. She were quite an old lady when she bought the house. She had genteel enough ways. I thought to myself perhaps she'd been a lady's maid, but she said not. That's all anyone knows."

"For your trouble." Alden pressed a coin into the man's palm. "I await the hot water."

*J*EMMY BRAMBEY HAD TO WAIT UNTIL AFTER HIS SUPPER TO ES- cape his mother. He left his brothers and sisters playing on the green. It took him over an hour, running much of the way, before he knocked at the back entrance to Marion Hall. Sir Reginald Denby never allowed him into the fancy part of the house, so Jemmy sat in a hallway near the kitchen. Nothing to complain about, since the cook had given him a large slice of mutton pie to keep him occupied.

When the plump form of Sir Reginald finally approached, Jemmy had already finished his pie and wiped his mouth on his sleeve.

"You have more news of Mistress Seton, lad?" Sir Reginald asked.

Jemmy stood and gave the hair over his forehead a quick tug. Another gentleman, tall, thin, richly dressed, his wig powdered, had also entered the hallway. He leaned against the wall and stared at Jemmy through a quizzing glass.

"How amusing!" the stranger said. "You have many such spies, Denby? Very effective, I'm sure!"

"I'm not a spy, sir!" Jemmy said indignantly. "I bring only the common news."

"Lud, the creature has a tongue!" The stranger smiled. A patch creased at the corner of his mouth. He was handsome enough— a lord, most like! "Of course, as seigneur, Sir Reginald must know what is happening in the parish attached to his manor. Don't let me intimidate you, lad. Here's an extra penny for you."

Metal spun. Jemmy snatched the coin out of the air and thrust it away in a pocket. Mother needed all the extra he could earn. Anyhow, the stranger was right. He had no idea what a *say-nure* might be and no one liked Sir Reginald, but there was nothing wrong in telling him what he was bound to find out anyway. Besides, the Marion Hall cook made a splendid mutton pie.

ULIET BURIED IT, ALL OF IT—ALL THE MEMORIES, ALL THE EMOtions—as deeply as she could. She vigorously cleaned her copper pots, turned out a cupboard and scrubbed her pine table. After a quick meal she carried clean sheets upstairs to her bedroom and made the bed. For just a moment she lay down on the lavender-scented cover and closed her eyes.

Her gold chain twisted against her neck. She tugged at the locket to free it, then kissed the warm metal. Images swarmed: a golden-haired boy ran laughing through a summer garden; spread toy soldiers before a wintertime hearth; held her hand in trust or pulled away in momentary rebellion. In spite of her resolutions, searing tears welled up, ugly and self-indulgent. She would not allow it! She would not. . . . She tucked the locket away and tried to breathe deeply, stifling the sobs. . . .

Something was shaking her, a tentative hand at her shoulder. Juliet opened her eyes to see her maid-of-all-work smiling down at her. Tilly Brambey was about five years older than her little brother Jemmy, and already courting. *Walking out with the wood-cutter's son,* as she put it.

"La, ma'am!" Tilly exclaimed. "You're all worn out, not having any help. I planned to come back to work in the morning, but I felt ever so much better, so—"

Juliet glanced at the window. She must have been asleep for several hours. It was early evening, the warm summer day winding down into dust motes and haze. It was an effort to sit up, to act as if nothing were wrong. She felt drained, even desperate.

"Thank you, Tilly. You are quite well now?"

The maid pushed a wisp of hair back from her freckled face. In the other hand she held a feather duster. She looked excited, like a child with a secret. "La, Mistress Seton! It was just a touch of the influenza that's going about, though it made my nose look red as a beet. I wouldn't have had my young man see me like that!"

"Does the thought of your young man always bring such a blush to your cheeks?" Juliet asked.

"It's not that, ma'am." The maid's color deepened until her eyes sparkled. "There's a gentleman come to call."

So he had charmed even Tilly, brought that bright, becoming look to her face!

"Did this gentleman give his name and business?"

Tilly turned to whisk her bundle of feathers over the mirror, smiling at herself in the glass, thrilled by her own prettiness and the dominion it gave her over the woodcutter's son—thrilled that even the gentleman who'd come to see her mistress had complimented her hazel eyes.

"It's the gentleman 'as cut the hay, ma'am. Mr. Granville, as is staying at the Three Tuns. All the village is talking of it." Innocent mischief was as plain as the freckles on Tilly's round cheeks. "La! He's a very comely gentleman. Oh, ma'am! Mr. Sandham says he takes a bath every day!"

In spite of herself, Juliet laughed. "So you thought you'd come back this evening to see this notorious fellow for yourself?"

The feathers danced as Tilly dusted the frame. "He says he's come to play chess. Where's the harm in that?"

Had he flirted with Tilly, trying his luck? Was he a rake who didn't hesitate to take advantage of that keen female vulnerability—even in a maidservant—the terrible power of any handsome, unprincipled man, when a foolish girl thought she had charmed him?

Juliet slid from the bed. "I fail to see why the thought of my playing chess brings you so much happiness, Matilda Brambey."

The maid spun about. "Oh, ma'am! It's so exciting! He said all this work was too much for a pretty girl like me all by myself. He's sent three maids to help for the remainder of the week. They're downstairs."

Three maids! With unimaginable arrogance, without even consulting her, he had hired three maids? If she upbraided him, she would only seem petty and stubborn. Yet if she accepted it, she allowed him an outrageous liberty—for a chess game! Indignation left her speechless.

Juliet stalked to her washstand and splashed cold water on her face. With vigorous strokes, she brushed out and pinned up her hair, then selected a fresh fichu for her dress. Apart from her high color, a respectable widow stared back from the mirror, as if defying the world to declare the image a falsehood.

Tilly's artless face waited in the background. With one hand on the door latch, she gazed expectantly at her mistress. "What shall I tell the new maids, ma'am?"

An unwanted gift with far too high a price attached! Juliet was free to play chess, free of her daily chores—as if she were still a lady of leisure—for a week. Then she must return to her regular life and think herself lucky for this memory? The irony of it was almost cruel. It was past time for her to turn the tables.

Juliet smoothed her bodice, fitting the fabric properly over her corset. Three maids! She had grown up in a household with forty. When she turned back to Tilly, her tone was dispassionate.

"This invasion force must be given beds, of course. You know where the linens are. Tell these new maids to wait for me in the kitchen."

"Yes, ma'am." Tilly gave a clumsy little curtsy, her eyes bright. "And the gentleman?"

"Please inform Mr. Granville that he may set up the chessmen in the arbor."

"Yes, ma'am."

Juliet smiled and reined in her annoyance. "You may also tell him that this time I intend to win."

CHAPTER FOUR

⟡

$\mathcal{H}$E WAS NOT IN THE ARBOR, THOUGH THE CHESSBOARD WAS laid out on the little iron table. Perhaps he had tired of waiting and returned to the Three Tuns? Juliet ran her finger over the black king's wooden crown, surprised by a keen rush of disappointment. Was she mad? She resented his presence, she regretted the wager, yet she was *disappointed*? Disappointed because, in spite of everything, she wanted to play chess—she wanted to match wits with this man? Laughter ran far too close to tears!

Juliet looked up at the wash of green leaves overhead. Summer life spiraled and surged all around her. Until now she had been content enough with her unchanging days. She had even been proud of her tenacity and courage. With Miss Parrett's help, she had learned to find a new dignity and fulfillment in work—something she had never imagined in her girlhood. It had taken immense determination. What an absurdity to find all that hard-won accomplishment lying empty in her heart because a handsome knave wanted to play games!

Trying to negate her odd mood, Juliet went back to the kitchen to fetch a basket of scraps to feed her chickens. She had interviewed the maids: three solid, respectable women. Betty and Sarah were competent in every task from the kitchen to the dairy, but Kate had curtsied with a quite different air.

"I'm a lady's maid, ma'am, for your personal needs, your clothing, your own room, whatever you wish."

Juliet suppressed her astonishment. "You have been hired recently, or you come here from Mr. Granville's own home?"

Kate curtsied again. "I can't rightly say, ma'am, but you will find me as well trained as any."

A lady's maid! Stolen from his wife, sister, mistress?

With a few brief instructions, Juliet had sent the women upstairs to settle in. He might have guessed she wouldn't embarrass them by a close interrogation, but did he think she would send such help away? Even a lady's maid! It felt almost reckless, to be forced back into a role she had never thought to fulfill again.

She could spend the rest of the week without lifting a finger. Yet she liked feeding her poultry herself. There was something fearless about hens—they didn't have the brains to be apprehensive. Contentment could turn into squawking panic in an instant, but chickens didn't worry about the future or have regrets for the past. Juliet smiled as she pulled on her old blue smock. Everything in life had its compensations.

Carrying the basket, she walked out through the yard, only to see Alden Granville leaning against the woven fence of her chicken coop.

The breath caught in her throat.

In the dappled half-shadow of the trees he stood absolutely still, the lines of his body graceful and lithe. With one buckled shoe propped on the bottom support rail, he stared down at the hens as they dusted in the shade.

Gold-and-red embroidery swirled over his tan satin waistcoat, echoing the trail of ribbon tying back his hair. Hooked on one forefinger, his jacket was flung over his shoulder. The other hand at his hip pushed aside the skirt of his waistcoat to reveal elegant breeches and white stockings. The impression of soft elegance was belied only by the smallsword hanging at his side and the virile tension in his stance that said he knew how to use it.

My lord, the laborer had almost said. The still center of a wave of disturbance that had raced through her zealously guarded sanctuary.

Juliet moved forward, clutching the basket to her hip. So the sight of him agitated her pulse! He was beautiful. He was undoubtedly a rake, who sought some casual amusement at her expense. His identity was entirely irrelevant. He—and his maids—would be gone in a week.

Like the sweet kernel hidden in the walnut, perhaps she could find some amusement of her own in his presumption and let the costs all be his.

He looked up. For a moment his eyes seemed bleak, then a smile broke over his face, the entranced smile of a man who greets his lover's return from a long journey. It seemed as if he might open his arms to welcome her straight into his embrace.

Her heart faltered.

"You have a broody hen," he said. "She's very fierce. As soon as I appeared, she called to her babies with the most imperious cries I have ever heard outside of the Countess of Roxham's withdrawing room."

Juliet stopped dead, disconcerted he could still catch her so off-guard, almost as if she were waking after a long sleep to find herself surrounded by playmates who had grown old and become strangers, a fearful discontinuity that left her floundering for a moment. *But I remember Lady Roxham—she was indeed feathered with shrillness and ribbons!*

It reminded her only too clearly of what she had lost, that she was indeed a lady, yet it was far too intimate a greeting, as if they had been close friends for years.

He glanced back at the broody hen, releasing Juliet from the ephemeral madness caused by his smile. "Now she has all those helpless little chicks hidden under her wings while she glares and bridles at me. Will she suffocate them?"

"If hens were so inept, poultry wouldn't survive." Her tone was deliberately acerbic. His hand still rested comfortably on his hip, his fingers whiter than hers, perfectly manicured, yet with a deadly strength. "As society would fall apart, no doubt, were gentlemen *always* to forgo the formal courtesies."

"Ah," he said. "I didn't bow."

"And thus omitted the true purpose of a gentleman's scraping his greeting: to negate his inherent male threat." Expectant chickens came running as she walked up to him. "The obeisance shows his weaponless hands. The dropped head reveals his intention to be peaceful—"

"—in spite of the blade at his side? Or perhaps the presence of sheer loveliness—the simple sunlit ivory and blue of it—leaves a man bereft."

Her blue smock flamed against her legs, her wrists ivory in the sun. "Yet even my hen recognizes danger when she sees it. You think her attitude unreasonable?"

"It's producing a great many ruffled feathers without due cause," he replied. "I don't intend her any harm."

"Thus says the fox."

His eyes filled with innocent merriment as he met her gaze, as if he recognized her own hidden impulse to mirth. "You think I am Reynard, come to prey on innocent chicks? I would never aspire to be a fox in a hen coop. I like the hunt to be more evenly matched than that."

"I'm not sure Tilly thought so."

"*Tilly?*" His astonishment seemed genuine. "Your maid? Lud! She's not more than what—fourteen?"

"She is fifteen."

"It's a valiant concern, but an absurd one. She is quite safe from me. I never create havoc among baby chicks."

"The proximity of the fox creates havoc, whether he means it or not. When is any servant girl safe from the attentions of a rake?"

Sunlight glimmered over his hair. "Rarely, I admit. It's commonly understood that a parlor maid will sacrifice her virtue for two ribbons, whereas the lady's maid will demand three. Yet I have always lived by a code that leaves the maids to their sweethearts." He slung his jacket over a nearby oak branch. "Does that surprise you?"

"It only surprises me that you expect me to believe you never flirt with the maids."

"Flirt?" Folding his arms, he propped his shoulders against the dappled trunk. "I have been known to flirt with grandmothers— an innocent pastime, amusing to both parties. I thought we were talking about a lady's more intimate favors, which I *never* purchase, especially with something as tawdry as ribbons."

Juliet threw the contents of her basket over the fence. The chickens scrambled to snatch the choicest pieces. "You expect such favors to be granted freely?"

"Of course, since I grant mine freely in return."

"But there is no equality, is there, between men and women in such matters? Women give of themselves, men only take."

"That's not true."

"Isn't it?"

He bowed his head. "I speak, I am sure, ma'am, from far more experience than you."

"Yet you have never seduced a servant?"

"Never." His voice held pure wickedness, rich with masculine conceit. "Why would I, when the lady of the house is always willing?"

"Always?" She laughed. She wanted to snap her fingers in his face. "Then you admit without a qualm that you are indeed a rake?"

His smile warmed, like the sun, as he gazed directly into her eyes. "Do you *wish* me to admit it?"

"It's nothing to me."

"Yet let any gentleman enter a ballroom and the flutter begins behind the fans: *Is this a man I might marry or is this one of those dangerous, predatory creatures my mother warned me against?* A pet dog or a fox: a delicious quandary for any lady of spirit. She knows the dog is too tame. Must she believe the fox to be too perilous?"

"You are saying she is wrong to be wary?"

"No, but only the fox thrills the blood as he races by after dark."

"Then how much more exciting to run with the foxes!" Tension made her voice high, too bright. Did he notice? His expression didn't change, yet layers of intelligent awareness lay in that casual gaze. "No doubt the hens would agree?"

"Reynard doesn't waste time on tame chickens, safe in their wattle enclosure," he said. "He has far more sophisticated tastes."

She felt giddy, as if she were being whirled around and around in too fast a dance.

"Either way he deals death!" She regretted her vehemence immediately and paced away.

His voice pursued her, gentle but relentless. "The lady might think she is dying, but if she is one of the wise—like you—who knows what she wants, I assure you she survives to *die* again the next night. It's why intelligent ladies prefer rakes: either a man knows how to bring his lady a pleasure worth dying for, or he doesn't."

Agitation inundated her veins, a rush of feeling, heady and foolish. Grass crushed under her shoes as she strode back toward him, her simple hoops swaying, her heart beating too fast.

"How can you claim to know what I want?"

"Your breathing tells me, as the disorder in mine should tell you." His eyes spoke of mischief, a jester in a fox mask reveling in a forest.

"Because you vibrate as if you were the center of an invisible whirlwind? Because your lace trembles with such a fine tumult? I thought perhaps you were afraid."

"Is that what your rapid tumble of breathing should tell me? Or your eyes when you look at me, or your supple spine when you turn away? What about the glorious wisp of chestnut that dances, escaped from its pins, over your nape? The quick color flooding your skin?"

The laces of her corset constricted like a vise. "What should they tell you? That I am discomposed, embarrassed, irritated—"

"Nonsense." Laughter lit his voice, warm and seductive. "The fox knows desire when he sees it. You can't blame him if he stands and quakes, captivated by the loveliness of it."

Hot color burned her cheeks. Strands of hair caressed the back of her neck. Her legs wished to fold, to carry her down, quivering, onto the crushed grass.

"I don't claim to be immune," she said. "But I am no baby chick. I have my own ways to ward off spells."

"Spells?"

"Charm," she said. "In the old, original meaning of the word: *casting a spell*. There is nothing personal about the charm of a rake, it's as natural to him as his heartbeat. Thus, there's no honesty in such compliments."

"Yes, there is, Juliet. True compliments are driven by an exact and passionate observation. The dishonesty is the lady's for denying the truth."

"The truth is that the intelligent lady does not prefer a fox, because she resents being used only for his pleasure."

"Unless she wishes to use him for hers."

"She does not."

He shrugged—the elegant, commanding shrug of the fencer loosening muscles for a duel. "Then how can she be harmed?" His gaze held hers, blue on blue. "No lady gives herself to a lover, if there's nothing in it for her. Why do you so mistrust men, ma'am?"

"I do not mistrust men, sir," she snapped. "I mistrust you."

"About *Tilly*?" His voice mocked openly, yet the undertones were still melodious, seductive, like the voice of the incubus, whispering in a dream. "Her infantile thoughts revolve around her plans for matrimony—eagerly, even lustily anticipated. She's in love with the woodcutter's son and means to marry him. She told me so. It's not for such a downy chick that Reynard gambols and frolics to try to lure her out into the mysterious night. I'm not interested in Tilly, ma'am. I *am* interested in you."

She retrieved the basket, clutching it against her blue skirts. "So the compliment becomes a declaration? How very bold, sir, when all we're committed to is a chess match! You expect me to be flattered?"

"I expect you to be amused. You are not likely to succumb. Though a lovely enough rose, you are well surrounded by thorns."

Stray feathers clung to the fence. A small clutch of eggs—brown, white, speckled—filled a nest of dead leaves under a bramble that had crept into a corner of the pen. Juliet stared at them. She hated the image of herself as a prickly, hostile plant—like a thistle or a stinging nettle.

She bent to reach through the fence to gather the eggs. "Oh, I am amused, but don't try to tell me you aren't dangerous, sir. The fox isn't all fun and games. You well know how to use that smallsword, don't you?"

"Would you rather I told you I wear it only for show?"

She glanced up. He had moved silently across the grass to stand beside her, heightening her awareness of him, of his nearness, of the very scent of him, male and hot, tempered only by traces of fine soap. He held out one hand to help her up. The beautiful, open hand of a lover.

Without hesitation, she set a brown egg on his palm. "No doubt you have reveled determinedly enough on a dueling ground?"

"Men duel because it's the ultimate wager. Certainly, it's the only one where winning is guaranteed."

"Now you speak in riddles." She straightened up, keeping her back against the fence. "Victory is never certain."

"Just to survive is to win." His fingers closed gently around the egg. "The dead, poor fellows, no longer have any opinion to express, but every man that survives a duel has experienced the most intense gamble of his life." He took the remaining eggs from her hands and set them in the basket. Sunlight gleamed on his hair and warmed his satin waistcoat to bronze. "The nearer he came to death, the greater the victory when he emerges unscathed. That's seductive enough to make men crave it, over and over again. It's like an addiction to wine, an ecstasy."

"Because there's exhilaration in risk?" She almost laughed, triumphant. "I think it an appalling philosophy!"

His innocent gaze met hers. "Yet you cannot deny the pleasure in this, can you, ma'am? The purity of debate, the fun of leaping after an idea, the game of it. Men aren't the only creatures who enjoy a challenge." The waistcoat flexed over his spine as he gestured toward her broody hen. "This female is as ferocious as any male."

Juliet opened the wicker gate and went into the coop. The broody hen ruffled its feathers and fixed its eyes on her face, but did not move. She knelt and slipped a hand underneath one wing. Her fingers closed over a soft ball of down, then another.

"This is what the hen defends," she said, stepping back out of the pen with the tiny chicks cradled in her hands. "It's the purpose of her whole existence, not just an exercise in vainglory and arrogance, however amusing that may be."

"Amazing!"

She glanced up at his face, puzzled. His tone was suddenly serious, even reverent.

A little breeze stirred through the spinney. Leaves rustled. A soft strand of gold danced against the carved line of male cheek. He was staring down at the chicks as if fascinated.

Without moving his gaze, he held out one hand, palm cupped. "May I?"

She stared at the corner of his mouth—the texture of smooth lip against the subtle roughness of a man's jaw. He had beautiful teeth and such a mobile, expressive mouth! Above the lean line of his cheekbone, his eyelashes were as long as her own, the lowered lids hiding that disturbing blue gaze.

"I should give the chicks directly to the fox?" She reached for sarcasm, but it came out as a whisper, too husky. The babies huddled in her hands, as if they could hear the strong beat of her heart.

He glanced up and smiled again—that thoughtful smile this time, like a carved saint.

"You trusted me with the eggs."

Juliet felt the impact in her bones, far deeper, more perilous than the simple flush of arousal. It was as if she had been racing like a girl in short skirts and was abruptly arrested by a flood of mysterious adult awareness.

"You know I am in truth harmless to chicks, ma'am," he added gently. "And I would like it, very much."

As if bewitched, she placed the baby birds into his hands. He cradled them both in one careful palm and stroked their heads with a fingertip. The chicks huddled down, secure under his caress.

"Lud!" he said. "They're incredibly soft—except for some remarkably scratchy little feet." He laughed. "Too bad they're doomed to turn into chickens!"

Her back was pinned against the fence. Unable to move away, Juliet stared at the babies, so she would not have to look at the devastating tenderness in his eyes. One chick peeped suddenly, its beak a cavity of red in the tiny mottled-brown head. The broody hen launched herself at the fence, scattering the rest of her brood.

"Now we have maternal panic." Juliet held out both palms as the hen flapped her wings and squawked, distracting her. "Let me have them."

He placed one chick in her hands. The other began cheeping piteously.

Soft fluff touched her face. Startled, Juliet lifted her chin. He was holding the remaining bird cushioned against her earlobe. His knuckles slid, carrying the baby. Its soft down tickled a path across her cheek. His thumb followed, over the small hollow by her nostril, the tormentingly sensitive corner of her mouth, past her jaw.

Her senses caught fire. Her mouth ached. Her skin bloomed.

She bit her lip, so the sensations couldn't take form in a resonant breath.

He let the chick nestle in the hollow of her neck.

Instantly the baby became quiet. Silky soft. Soft against the tender skin of her throat and her too rapid pulse. The little scratch of feet tickled as the chick settled into the curve between her neck and her collar. She could imagine it there, eyes closed, securely hunched down against her living heat.

He stepped back. If she moved, the chick would fall.

"But what about you, Mistress Seton?" he asked gently. "While you nurture all this fecundity, has your own life crystallized into a static wasteland? Do you truly wish to live here forever like a fly in amber, while the world buzzes and clicks by without you?"

The trees of Mill Spinney were lit like lamps by the sinking sun. Maddeningly, tears blurred her vision, scattering the bright leaves into multiple images, as if they all shook in an invisible, silent breeze.

She gave a broken half-laugh. "I am a chicken or maybe a vixen; a rose or maybe a thorn; and now I'm a fossilized insect?" Emotion roughened her voice. "Such a splendid mix of images! What are you, Mr. Granville, but an importunate, profligate stranger, imposing on my time for your idle amusement?"

A quick brush of his fingertips. The soft warmth left her neck. He took the other chick from her hands and crouched down to let them both run back into the pen. Clucking, the mother hen gathered her brood and led them all away, balls of down tumbling and running on pink spiked feet over the rough dirt.

"Then you have the right of it," he said. "I am no threat to you. Unless you ask me, I won't touch you again."

"I will never ask!"

"Faith! Then you have no cause for concern."

Her hands closed involuntarily on the rough wattles at her back, as if she must hold herself upright. "Ha! You are all appearance, without substance—no more than a butterfly flitting through a garden, lighting up each flower for a moment before moving on. Why should that glittering track leave any permanent impression on the petals?"

Alden glanced up at her, at the bright chestnut hair, at the curve of her neck, at the long lashes, damp and spiky, spilling shadows over her cheeks. She'd seemed so very alone and valiant, in her blue smock with the fluffy chicks in her rough hands. He'd felt a dangerous surge of tenderness.

He felt it now.

He wanted to feel the rich silk of her hair. He wanted to kiss her pale nape where a thin gold chain showed above the neckline of her smock. He wanted to offer comfort and protection: to hold her, soft and yielding, cradled like a chick in his hands.

Far too costly! The gold chain no doubt held the locket for which he had wagered his future. A few days only remained until Friday. How fortunate that desire also stirred! Sex fit far more comfortably than this odd stirring of emotion into his scheme of things.

Would she allow him to kiss away the tears?

Soon.

Ask him to carry her away to the short grass under the oak tree and lay her down with her blue smock billowing beneath her long, naked legs?

Soon. Soon.

Her mouth invited his, her skin invited his hands, as the sweet peas invited the bees.

Hot desire became insistent, urging simple male need. *A few more days,* he told himself. *A few more days!* Now it was time to reassure her, win her confidence, so that he could press his advantage when she finally surrendered her guard.

Yet something else still disturbed him. Nothing he could give name to, but it felt vaguely uncomfortable. Ignoring the odd feeling, he stood and walked back to the tree to retrieve his coat.

"All the tender life that you protect here is quite safe," he said. "We are only chance acquaintances, whiling away a little time—a holiday, if you like, which I am able by chance to provide. I certainly hope to amuse you. It has never been my intention to distress you."

"You don't have the power to distress me, sir." She had turned her head. He couldn't see her face. "You are as out of place here as a silk fan in the hands of a cowhand. Far too hideously exquisite for such humble surroundings as these!"

In spite of the still-warm air, he shrugged into the coat, carefully arranging the cuffs, and deliberately made his voice light, teasing. "Then I may provide you the merriment of contrasting my evil town decadence unfavorably with your honest country values. The silk fan is unquestionably designed only to amuse, for I fear it's an absurdity otherwise."

"Oh, I'll never believe *that*!" Her feet moved like a dancer's beneath her worn blue smock. Her face was set in a bright smile— the smile of a courtier, a lady, determined on triumph. "I' faith, I am tired of chickens, sir. Let us play chess. There you may indeed entertain me, for this time I intend to win."

HE PLAYED A TEASING GAME, LETTING HER CAST HER NETS WIDE and breaking them gently. She was concentrating intently, but he was still winning—she just didn't know it yet. In spite of her suspicions and her reticence, she was generous: a fine, magnanimous nature, for some reason buried here in this backwater. Her pleasure every time she almost pinned down his king was obvious. She seemed able to escape into the moment with the purity of a child. Had she forgiven him for confronting her with what already lay between them? Forgotten that he had deliberately brought tears to her eyes?

Obviously she knew she was being played, yet she was falling directly into his trap. The fox danced and gamboled in the moonlight. The prey was rapt, until finally thrilled to yield into Reynard's smiling jaws. Did it matter that the fox just followed his animal nature? On Friday he would use her for his own ends, then abandon her. He must at least make it a rapturous, willing surrender.

Alden glanced at her beneath his lashes. It was hot in the arbor, the air heavy and still. Dying sunlight played harmonies in her hair, rich reds and browns, like the gleaming pebbles of a stream-bed. She had taken off her smock to reveal a plain workaday dress underneath.

Meshach and Shadrach had settled at his feet. He dropped a hand occasionally to caress a tabby or orange head. Abednego lay a little behind him, out of reach, curled up where a twist of grape leaves bent down from a broken place in the arbor to make a comfortable nest.

With an unconsciously elegant gesture, Juliet ran one hand around the fichu filling the neckline of her dress, loosening the fabric from her moist skin. His attention concentrated on the soft whiteness of her throat, the swell of her breasts. Desire surged, overwhelming, almost as if he were still a callow youth, at the mercy of his own racing pulse. He forced himself back to the cool, logical analysis of the chess match and the game of seduction he had equally coolly begun.

"If you win," he asked as he sacrificed a bishop, "what would you ask of me?"

"*When* I win!"

He replied automatically, disturbed by the intrusion of such sensual images when they hadn't been invited. "Very well. When you win."

"I believe I shan't ask for anything, sir. After all, you are empty, nothing! You've never known anything but pleasure. Will you tell me that isn't true?"

"I am serious when rare occasion warrants, but I am a professional at pleasure."

She laid one hand flat on the table. His attention riveted there, unable to stop the image of her fingers on his naked skin.

"And you think I should take advantage of that expertise?"

"Of course, ma'am. It's entirely at your disposal."

"Then I admit it's a pleasure to play chess with you, sir, even though you're going to win this game, too."

Alden leaned back, surprised by the humor in her voice. "I am?"

She laughed. "Of course! I already cannot recover, can I?"

He moved his queen's rook. "Check. No, you can't."

She touched her king with a fingertip and let the piece topple. "Then I concede the match. However, you might do well to remember that though you may win each battle, you will never win the war."

He gave her a deliberate smile. "I'm not fighting a war, ma'am. I'm pursuing a seduction. Whether I succeed or fail, whatever the outcome, you will be the winner of that."

In a flash of white fur, Abednego hurtled onto the board, scattering the pieces. Juliet jumped up. The other cats leaped to chase the pawns, rooks and bishops rolling about on the flagstones under the table. For a moment it was pure feline chaos.

Juliet burst out laughing, letting him kneel to retrieve the lost men among the havoc of hunting cats. He glanced at her ankles— no reason not to enjoy the resulting surge of male hunger. Yet his desire seemed to have mutated into something mysterious, multilayered. An odd feeling caught his heart suddenly, an unnameable feeling: mirth, lust and that strange surge of tenderness, unexpected and subtler than he could immediately fathom.

Alden sat back on his heels and gazed up at her. "We may have been wrong to indulge in such wanton talk of foxes, ma'am. Your cats have a far better gift for disorder."

"No," she said, stifling her merriment. "Our talk of foxes was very valuable to me. Meanwhile, you have won the chess match. You may claim your forfeit."

He stood and placed the chessmen on the table. The cats disappeared.

She raised her brows. "I am waiting. I expect something extravagant."

He dropped the pieces one by one into their box. "Extravagant, ma'am?"

"In trade for your Herculean task with my hay—"

"Extravagant," he repeated, gathering his scattered wits. "Yes, if you like. Though what I have in mind is quite simple. We'll play chess tomorrow as if we're in Italy."

She looked puzzled. What had she expected? That he would ask for something she could simply and in honor refuse? Or that he would ask for her favors directly and let himself be so easily spurned?

"Now I *am* surprised," she said.

He gave her a small bow. "What I really wish for, I shall never ask. I am content to wait until you offer it."

"Which will never happen."

Alden looked away toward the carefully tended garden. It was all practicality, yet the indulgence of flowers spoke of a longing for beauty, even for frivolity—or did they all have some use, like the cowslip wine?

He had no idea.

The whole place spoke of unceasing toil. Why did she do it? Most widows, especially ones with her looks, would hasten to remarry. Instead she buried herself here and labored alone. It spoke of a great reserve of courage, but Alden couldn't understand it and he wanted to, very much. Yet how could he, if he was to carry this through? Lud, he was behaving like a moon-calf! She was only a woman. What harm would it do to bring her a few hours of pleasure?

He turned back to her and bowed again, the exact, gracious obeisance of the court. "In which case, let us amuse ourselves with more innocent pastimes. Your face lit like a lamp when I mentioned Italy. I cannot take you there, so let me bring a little of her flavor here. Just follow the instructions I send you and meet me here tomorrow as the sun is going down."

She looked suspicious, but something else flamed in her eyes— a longing, an intense curiosity. It moved him.

"Very well," she said. It was almost breathless.

"And my chore? What task do you have for me?"

"What chores can I possibly have left, now I have three maids?

Was that your idea when you sent them?" Her voice mocked. "You think you avoid your debt so easily?"

"Not at all. You may ask for anything."

"Then my task is this: I need a pineapple."

At the splendid incongruity of it, he laughed. "I am overwhelmed," he said. "Why?"

"To eat. It is my fancy."

"Where would I find such a thing?"

"In London? When I have it, you may claim your forfeit. Then we shall share our evening in Italy."

"The hunt for this fruit will certainly take me away from Manston Mingate."

"That's the idea," she said.

He turned and gave her his most elaborate bow, with flourishes and an expertly used handkerchief. It had once caused a lady to faint away on the spot.

"I fear, ma'am, you will cost me another night's sleep."

"What would you do with sleep, sir?" She spun away, as if she wore wide skirts and panniers instead of her plain working dress, and would dismiss him with a wave of an imaginary fan. "Dream in vain about me?"

CHAPTER FIVE

❧

I̅T WAS DARK WHEN HE ARRIVED AT GRACECHURCH ABBEY.
Sherry would be long abed. Alden nevertheless went straight
up to the nursery. He spoke quietly to the nursemaid, assuring
himself of the boy's perfect health, then softly opened the bedroom
door and walked in. The child slept, his blond head cushioned in
shadows, one hand flung out on the moonlit pillow. A chick,
helpless in sleep.

Alden stared down at him for several minutes. What would
happen to the child if Sir Reginald Denby seized Gracechurch? If
Alden fled to Paris and tried to recoup his losses at those alien
tables, he could hardly take Sherry with him. Yet how could a
nameless orphan survive in the world without a protector?

He resisted the urge to smooth back the lock of butter-yellow
hair that had fallen over the boy's forehead. If it came to a choice
between sacrificing the child or Juliet Seton, the answer was obvious. Alden even thought she might understand, if she knew.

Silently he walked out of the room and went down to his study.

He sent first for his head gardener. Their interview was brief.
The man came in and touched his forehead with one bent forefinger. "My lord?"

"I need a pineapple, Mr. Appleby."

The gardener scratched his grizzled head. "I've not put any
pineapples under glass this year, my lord, what with Your Lordship not usually in residence—"

"Does my mother have any at the Dower House?"

Mr. Appleby's face brightened. "Why, Her Ladyship well might, my lord. Shall I send to inquire?"

"I'll go myself. Meanwhile, please have a footman send for Mr. Primrose."

The head gardener touched his forelock once again and left.

Peter Primrose smiled as he came in. He gave Alden a short bow. "Lord Gracechurch. I hope I see you well, my lord?"

"And you, sir. Come and sit down."

Alden indicated one of two chairs placed comfortably on each side of the fireplace. The tutor's brown eyes were already wreathed in the fine wrinkles of years spent squinting at books, enlivened by frequent laughter. Peter dressed soberly, but put him in silk and lace and he'd easily pass for a lord. Alden liked him.

"Sherry is doing well with his studies?" he asked.

"He's very bright, my lord. He's reading better than many a boy twice his age. He especially likes Greek—"

"Since you intersperse Homer with reenactments of Trojan struggles in the shrubbery. He told me, last time I was here. Sherry can recount every clash between Achilles and Hector, and supply the dialogue in Greek." It was almost too easy to slip into the role of lord of the manor, in charge, as if nothing were wrong, as if he hadn't already risked the child's future.

Peter smiled. "No lad is improved by being whipped to his books—"

Alden walked across the room. "Lud, sir! You don't need to convince me. It's why I hired you. My own school days involved enough encounters with the cane. I did not learn any better for it." A small shiver ran down his spine. Without thinking, he voiced a fear he'd never had to contemplate before. "Yet I fear our kindness won't prepare Sherry very well for the outside world."

Candlelight shone silver on the tutor's powdered hair as he turned his head. "I beg to disagree, my lord. The child is developing a self-confidence and certainty of his own worth that will enable him to face down any bully. By letting him spend half his days outside, he's growing fit and strong. The world won't faze him—even if you send him to school when he's older."

Alden buried the unease and deliberately turned his concern into something general. "I can't fix his parentage, sir. He'll always be a bastard with an unknown father."

"As I was." Peter steepled his hands together, fingertips meeting under his chin, and grinned. "I was fortunate to be raised as a gentleman, even if I was not raised by a viscount with expectations of that patronage."

Expectations! Of course, he must fulfill them. It was unthinkable that he not! "I could hardly have done otherwise, Mr. Primrose."

The young man colored, as if to acknowledge that it might seem unmannerly to talk to his employer so freely, though Alden always encouraged him to speak his mind. "My lord, are you entirely unaware of how extraordinarily generous it is, in the circumstances, to give the boy a home here?"

Alden suppressed his slight annoyance at this question—the answer was so completely obvious to him.

"Sherry was born here," he said simply. "Where else should he live?"

IT WAS TWO MILES TO THE DOWER HOUSE. ALDEN RODE ALONG the dark track through the woods, listening to the occasional hoot of an owl and the answering rustle of nighttime creatures in the undergrowth. Did a fox also slink by on the prowl? Were the mice and the voles stunned into silence as Reynard trotted past?

Yet Juliet was like a wildcat, sensuous and fierce, hunting by herself on the lonely moor. Strong, ferocious, her passing in the night would leave its own wake of disturbance. Alas that the wildcat was no match for the fox in cunning—especially when the fox had a cub to protect. Would she mourn him after he abandoned her? Or would she go back without a second thought to her solitary ways?

He wasn't sure which question disturbed him the most.

The Dower House was lit from top to bottom. Dismissing his troubling thoughts, Alden looked up at the facade. His mother kept town hours, even in the country. She would be up until three in the morning, then sleep until noon. The one part of the wreckage left by his father's death for which Alden didn't have to be financially responsible, Mama had her own independent income. Her son had the burden of worrying about her affairs, but not the necessity to supply her with funds.

A footman let him in. Alden strode through the house and knocked on the door of his mother's boudoir. She called out a vague answer. He opened the door and went in.

The widow reclined in a cloud of white silk and lace on a chaise longue. High-heeled slippers, supported on an embroidered cushion, peeked beneath the hem of her robe. Still pretty and girlish, she wore her powdered hair tied up with bows and knots of silk flowers. It ought to have been absurd, but somehow the style was only charming on Lady Gracechurch.

"Alden," she said without any other greeting. "Light another candle. Oh, and give me my wrap." Her voice embodied plaintive resentment. "You haven't been to see your mama this age. I am quite, quite neglected. No one cares what becomes of me."

Alden lit an entire stand of candles and set the wrap about her shoulders. "Mama, I visit you every week and I had the pleasure of your company only last night, when I asked you to lend me a competent lady's maid. You are still quite well, I trust?"

She pouted. "Not at all! I have been most unwell. I don't recall any lady's maid."

"Kate Winsley. You hired her to assist with your wardrobe, but your woman Polly objected that she needed no help. Kate was in danger of dismissal."

"Oh, that! It's such a problem finding good help these days. Have you brought me a present from London?"

Alden held out his empty palms. "Alas, Mama, I didn't come from town. I'll make you a present of wit, if you like."

He could smell her scent, a little cloying, as she wrinkled her brow. "What kind of present is that? Is it a new kind of sweet-meat?"

Not for the first time, Alden wondered how, with such an empty-headed mother, he could have any brains in his. "Never mind, Mama. I'll bring you a gift next time."

She leaned back. "It is the least you could do for your poor mama. It was the worst day of my life when I found I was increasing with you."

Alden was damned if he wanted to discuss that one again. "I regret that my conception caused you distress, Mama. It was none of my doing——"

Fortunately the change of subject was hers, as his mother sat up and pointed her finger at his chest. "You have come here straight from that boy, haven't you? I swear you will break my heart!"

He strode restlessly about the room. "Mama, we have talked of this before. You won't change my mind. I am sensible that Sherry's presence at the Abbey is hurtful to you, but he is an innocent child."

Lady Gracechurch laid the back of one elegant hand on her mouth and closed her eyes. "Hurtful! The knowledge of his existence is like being torn apart in a thornbush. Now he comes between us—mother and son!"

"Your choice, Mama. Perhaps if you would let him visit, you'd see that——"

She swooned melodramatically on the couch. "Next you will tell me that he's a charming child, the image of—Oh, I cannot bring myself to speak her name! Mrs. Sherwood! It was all enough to have sent me quite, quite mad, and then your papa could have locked me up as a lunatic. It's what he always planned. The Duke of Gessham did it to his wife and she was a duchess. That I should be sent away to be caged like a wild animal with a broken heart!"

Alden handed her a lace-edged handkerchief as she began to sob. "I'm sure it was very difficult, Mama, but Father would never have locked you away."

"You don't care what I went through. What happened—and all because of that woman! For all those years, you stayed in Italy, while I had to sit across from my husband's mistress every morning at breakfast."

Not something he could argue, though he had every sympathy for his father. He remembered Mrs. Sherwood, a quiet, attractive widow, who had moved in as his mother's companion just before Alden left England. She had without question almost immediately become his father's mistress and remained so for five years. Then for some mysterious reason she had taken a second, unknown lover on a visit to London and conceived a child by him—a fact she had concealed from Lord Gracechurch until it was too late.

"Yet can you feel no compassion for her orphaned baby, Mama? He'll never even know his father's name."

This only released a flood of tears. "Men are all alike! Even my own sons! Nobody cares about me. The burden forced upon me by that wicked, wicked woman. Oh, I am quite, quite unwell!"

Alden rang the bell that sat on the table. It was impossible to get his mother to talk sensibly about it. She seemed to enjoy the mystery, like a child with a secret.

A maid opened the door and curtsied.

"Tea for Her Ladyship," Alden said. "With some of Cook's orange biscuits."

Mama was suddenly all smiles, dabbing at her eyes. "You darling boy! How did you know orange biscuits are my favorite?"

He leaned forward, picked up her hand and kissed her knuckles. "They've been your favorite for as long as I've been alive, Mama."

"Oh." She giggled, then pouted again. "Well. And you know all this boy's favorite foods, too, no doubt?"

Fresh cherries and ices and raisin cake. "Not really," Alden replied diplomatically. "His nursemaid and tutor tend to his needs."

"He ought never to have been born. You should have sent him away."

Alden took a deep breath. "I came back from Italy to find Father dead. You were unwell and wouldn't speak to me. I had to learn about Mrs. Sherwood's death from the butler. Two weeks later, after you had removed here to the Dower House—as you said you preferred—I discovered a baby in the nursery. The maids had been afraid to tell me, in case I left him to the mercy of the parish. A *baby,* Mama!"

"The world is full of babies, thousands of them!"

"But this one fell to me. He is my responsibility."

"Mrs. Sherwood was unfaithful to your father. I thought she was my friend. How's that for ingratitude?"

He didn't quite see the logic of this, but then logic had never been his mother's strength. "You'd rather they *had* remained faithful to each other, Mama? Why?"

A knock at the door heralded the arrival of tea, accompanied by thin wafers of pressed orange and sugar—exactly the kind of over-sweet confection Alden hated. He made himself eat two, while his mother devoured the rest.

"Oh, I wish I'd never been born! No wonder you won't marry, with such an example before you!"

"Very likely, Mama. Now may I kiss you good night?"

"You are leaving already? Oh, take something with you! Whatever you like!"

He stood and bent over her hand: the generous mother who, perhaps, loved him. "Thank you, Mama. You are very kind. It is my intention, with your permission, to raid your glasshouses."

She waved one hand and closed her eyes. "Take anything you like. Really, I have never liked babies—"

Alden slipped from the room.

*J*ULIET WAS WOKEN THE NEXT MORNING BY A SMALL NOISE. SHE had been dreaming again. A golden man had been holding out both hands, cradling something mysterious and precious, something for which she had always yearned. She looked longingly into his palms, anticipating treasure . . .

Kate stood beside the bed with a jug in her hands.

"I trust you slept well, ma'am."

What had he been holding—? The elusive images faded away.

Juliet glanced at the window. Kate had already opened the casement. It was full daylight. She had slept late, something she never did! But now, just today—thanks to him—it didn't matter. She had three extra maids.

"I have brought up hot water, ma'am." Kate dropped a small curtsy. "And breakfast." The maid nodded toward the small table by the door. "It's a lovely morning. Promises to be fair hot again today."

Juliet sat up and wrapped her arms about her knees. A warm breeze stirred outside, carrying the scent of the garden and the far woods. For a moment she imagined herself back in her father's house. Bemused, as if still enfolded in the warm atmosphere of her dream, she let Kate pour water to wash her hands and face. The maid then set the covered tray across her lap on a little table with short legs. She remembered ones like it from her girlhood.

The tray was draped with a fine linen cloth. An embroidered monogram had been worked in white thread on the corners. Juliet lifted one edge to look at it. An unfamiliar crest and a single letter: *G.*

Kate lifted the cloth away.

On one corner of the tray, a card sat pinned between two chess pieces: white king and red queen. The queen toppled as Juliet plucked out the card.

The handwriting was firm and confident, a man's hand, but one tempered by social grace into fluidity: *Madam, your wish is my command—G.*

Juliet laughed as she set down the card. *Even in bed?* She felt pinned by a piercing diversity of emotions: a sudden heady delight mixed oddly with a bittersweet sense of loss. Her thoughts spun. *Your wish is my command.* The words of the genie in *The Arabian Nights' Entertainments?* The book sat somewhere on a shelf downstairs: *Mille et une Nuits.* One thousand and one nights, when a new bride named Scheherazade had woven a spell of tales so her husband would not execute her in the morning.

The tray was silver, heavy and expensive. The spoons and knives were also silver, the handles inlaid with gold. She picked up a spoon. The gold picked out a sinuous engraving: *G*. Alden Granville.

It all spoke so clearly of him: the exuberant joy in beauty, the love of sensual indulgence—and the seductive small joke, like a little wink, of the two chess pieces. An intimate awareness stirred her blood, almost giddy, almost as if he were here in the room, waking her from a long sleep and giving her that tiny, knowing gesture, the quick drop of an eyelid over one startlingly blue eye.

Your wish is my command.

His crest was echoed again on the corner of a napkin. To one side, a fully open red rose nestled among a host of white sweet peas in a flat crystal vase. Juliet plucked out the rose and inhaled its rich scent. Where had he found such a bloom so early in the summer? It spoke of an extra care, that he had troubled to find such a flower for her.

She was being served breakfast in bed. She had three extra maids. Contemptible, luxurious excess! Why not appreciate it?

A bubble of mad laughter fought for release. With determination, she swallowed it, but the humor danced in her throat, making her feel wanton—like a girl.

Juliet set the rose behind one ear.

On the other side of the tray, the spouts of a silver tea service steamed gently next to a blue-and-white china tea-dish, edged in gold. More fine china held strawberry jam and butter. Flaky pastries threatened to crumble at a touch. Other dishes lay covered with individual silver lids. She lifted one: newly baked currant buns. Another: eggs. As she leaned forward to inhale the mixed aromas, the rose fell from her hair. It landed, shedding petals, in the butter.

She pressed both hands over her face as the laughter soared to the surface. Mad, like the release of months—years—of tension.

The maid stepped forward as if to remove the offending flower. Choking back her hilarity, Juliet waved one hand to stop her.

"You didn't know roses were edible, Kate? Indeed, they are very good buttered." With a grin, Juliet popped a petal in her mouth.

The maid stared at her in open astonishment. "No, ma'am." She curtsied. "Yes, ma'am."

"As eggs," Juliet said earnestly, "are very good with jam. Thank you, Kate. You may go."

Her round face stiff, Kate curtsied again and backed out of the room.

Mirth burst out in a great shout of glee. Juliet laughed until the bed shook, threatening to spill her luxurious breakfast. She held on to the little table with both hands while hilarity rocked her.

Oh, Mr. Granville, might I wish for the moon? And would you deliver it, wrapped in roses and polished silver? Would you deliver me a whole new past? What about a new future to go with it?

In the center of the tray sat another dish, its contents also hidden under a cover. As soon as the mad laughter died to an ache in her side, Juliet lifted the lid, knowing quite well what she would find.

She sat and gazed at it for a moment, while she picked up a pastry. With a silver knife, she spread strawberry jam over the crumbly, hot surface and bit into it. Ambrosia! Flakes of floury, buttery flavor burst on her tongue, mixed with the sweet-tangy strawberries. Still studying the contents of the center dish, she set down the pastry and poured tea. As she sipped at it, she tipped her head on one side to better appreciate the chef's work.

The spiky green top had been sliced off, then arranged as a decorative surround. Intertwined with hothouse flowers, it made an exotic setting: exuberant, foreign, speaking clearly of paradise. But true paradise lay inside the natural cup formed by the rind. Each slice of fruit had been carefully removed, then cut into an individual flower shape before being set back inside. They glistened there like liquid sunshine.

Juliet set down her tea and picked up a fork. She speared a single piece of golden fruit and closed her eyes, before she bit down into this wondrous heaven. Juice ran down her chin to be licked off with a blithe tongue.

Not the moon, exactly. Fresh pineapple.

*K*ATE HAD BEEN RIGHT. IT WAS ANOTHER HOT DAY. STULTIfyingly hot. After a quick tour of her garden, Juliet retreated into the cool parlor. The occasional burst of talk or the rattle of some implement did little to disturb the close air. Tilly and the new maids were doing all the work that usually kept Juliet occupied. She had a whole day to indulge herself, to take a holiday. She could read, lounge at the window, luxuriate in having absolutely nothing to do. Surely she could enjoy it?

She ran her finger along the spines of the books and pulled out *The Arabian Nights*. Here was fantasy, magic, sweeping adventure in exotic worlds. Here was a woman who had wed—unwisely? Juliet smiled a little grimly to herself. Obviously Arabian ladies had very little choice and learned to make the best of it. But Scheherazade risked death each morning if she did not keep the sultan entertained with another wondrous tale the night before. That was not, of course, the usual danger of an unwise marriage! Life was a little less dramatic than fiction, even if sometimes just as painful.

Meshach, Shadrach and Abednego rubbed about her ankles, complaining until she sat down. It was too hot to have a cat curl up on her lap, but they each picked a spot on her spread skirts, pinning her to the sofa. She gazed at them, her only companions. Yet even the cats had come with the house, another legacy from Miss Parrett. Of course, no cat ever truly belonged to its owner. Not the way Scheherazade had belonged to the sultan. Not the way a wife was the property of her husband.

There. It was out. She almost repeated it aloud. *A wife belongs to her husband.*

The cats purred, a dry rumble. A snatch of the maids' chatter blew by the open window. The hum of bees drifted. Dimly in the distance, black rooks cawed and swirled, argumentative and noisy, in their rookery in Mill Spinney.

Mr. Alden Granville thought her a widow. The village thought her a widow. Her secure future here depended on that. But Juliet wasn't a widow. She was a wife.

Five years ago, after the tragedy, George had abandoned her and left her destitute. It didn't matter that she had no idea of his whereabouts. They were still married—until death. If he discovered her here, he could march into her life and demand all his rights: her property, her attention, her person. Not even her body was her own.

She was a wife.

A wife belongs to her husband.

She mustn't forget. Mustn't think for one moment that this little episode with a charming stranger changed anything about her circumstances. It was playing with fire even to entertain him, and a madness if she thought she could warm herself at those flames and not be burned. If she took a lover, she could never stay hidden. Sooner or later it would become known and she would be discovered. She had also taken vows and paid heavily for them. Not something she took lightly, whatever the results of that hasty wedding. And yet— And yet—

Someone knocked on the door. Juliet leaped up, dislodging cats. They gave her three variations of the same disgusted look and resettled themselves where she'd been sitting. But it was only Betty with a question about some chores. Thrusting away her thoughts, Juliet walked through to the kitchen and plunged into work.

*   *   *

*A*LTHOUGH IT WAS ALREADY EARLY EVENING, IT WAS STILL HOT when the boxes arrived, delivered by private carriage. Pushing her hair back from her damp forehead, Juliet oversaw the few minutes of clunking confusion as a footman brought three of the boxes inside and handed her a sealed missive. Her name surged across the front in the handwriting she'd first seen that morning. Perhaps he had sent his excuses and would not come for their chess game that night! It was a moment of piercing disappointment. Dear Lord, how foolish!

The maids stared at her with open curiosity. Juliet straightened her spine and walked into the parlor. The wax seal held the same crest as the spoons. She broke it open and started to read:

Madam: Imagine an Italian evening. It is the very hot end to a very hot day. The stars will soon blaze in a velvet sky. White stone houses glow like lamps. The very earth breathes heat. Yet presently, perhaps, a cool breeze might stir to carry the burning air away across the parched hills. Perhaps the zephyr will pull a moisture-laden current from the wine-dark ocean. Perhaps it will bring us a serene breath from the icy moon. Will it waft the spiced scents of history and foreign blooms onto our deeply shaded patio? Shall we drink wine and eat a light supper? Shall we play chess together? I have sent you a dress in the Italian style. I think it might please you—G.

She sat for a moment and gazed blindly at the paper. Then she walked back into the hallway, where the maids were still fussing over the boxes.

"Oh, ma'am!" Tilly's freckled face beamed like a sunrise. "This one's labeled for the kitchen, Betty's to see to that. This one says it's for the bath and is for Kate. The other's all in foreign."

Juliet read the label on the largest of the boxes. *Vestimenti di confidenza.* She did not know Italian, but she could guess the meaning.

"It's for me," she said. "Leave it here."

"You aren't going to open it, ma'am?" Tilly was openly dismayed.

Juliet shook her head. *A dress in the Italian style.*

"There is another note attached here, ma'am."

Kate gave her a folded paper. Juliet broke the seal and walked away to read it.

It would please me very much if you would wear it. I shall wear mine—G.

*J*ULIET WENT THROUGH THE REST OF THE EVENING LIKE A NERvous filly. It continued hot, the air heavy with unshed moisture. Jumping and starting at each small sound, she felt taut with anticipation, waiting for him to arrive. She imagined herself winning the chess match. She imagined herself repudiating him, berating him, sending him away. She imagined herself madly asking him to kiss her. She did not dare to imagine an Italian supper.

Why wouldn't it rain?

Why didn't he come?

She couldn't eat for nerves. In the heavy, sticky dress she'd been wearing all day, she burned as if he had already set the flames.

I am not a widow. I am a wife.

She paced the limits of the parlor, went up and downstairs several times, strode about the hallways and the close confines of her bedroom, where—through the uselessly open windows—the hot air under the roof mingled with the hot air outside. She must win the game, that was all!

Do you truly wish to live here forever like a fly in amber, while the world buzzes and clicks by without you?

A bat flitted past the window. Juliet sped over to the open casement and leaned out. The sun had almost disappeared behind Farmer Hames's woods to the west. He must come soon.

As the sun is going down.

"Ma'am," Kate said behind her. "I have filled a bath."

Juliet spun about.

"In the porch off the kitchen," Kate added. "The tub was delivered not an hour ago."

"A tub?"

"Yes, ma'am. And another note." The maid held it out.

The wax seal fell away as Juliet tore it open.

In Italy to change into our most casual clothes and sit quietly on the patio with friends is just a gentle, civilized way to spend a summer evening. But rest assured, our Italian supper does not begin until you arrive in the arbor—G.

So he would not burst in on her as she bathed? At the eroticism of the thought, Juliet blushed scarlet. What was the matter with her? She threw up her chin, her father's daughter. Of course, no gentleman would do anything so scandalous!

Her petticoats stuck to her hot skin.

"Yes," she said. "I should like to bathe."

She had not soaked in a bath in years. It would have been far too much work to heat that much water, let alone to fill and then empty a tub. Juliet had contented herself with basins and a daily wash with a cloth.

The air scorched in the kitchen, but the porch door had been built in two sections, as if for a stable. The top stood open. Beyond, the courtyard lay shadowed and silent. Cooler air flowed through now to where Kate had set the tub and filled it with the help of the other maids. The scent of mown hay mingled with drifting smoke from the chimney. It felt safe and quiet, the tub standing in this little vestibule with the vast countryside stretching away outside.

He had sent soaps, thick white towels and a linen bathing robe—wildly improper gifts no lady should accept. Juliet laughed and changed into the long gown. It was bliss to sink into the tepid water and let a lady's maid wash away the residue of the day. The tub was also hung with cloth, so as Kate washed each part of Juliet's body, just that one limb or area of skin emerged whitely from the damp drapes. It was an oddly coy dance, poised between modesty and abandonment.

Kate turned aside, busy with some detail. A small noise made Juliet glance up. There was nothing there. No golden-haired man leaned grinning on the sill of the open stable door. Nothing but the quiet summer evening. Nothing to disturb her.

If he did burst in on her, what would he see?

Juliet glanced down at herself. The gown draped thinly, sticking to her wanton skin. Her breasts glowed pink under the wet fabric, her nipples dark in contrast. Heat burned through her blood. *If he burst in on her*—

Yet she knew he would not. Even without his reassurance, she knew he would not. Alden Granville was far more clever and more subtle than that.

Kate washed Juliet's hair in a preparation of suds and herbs and rinsed it in clean water. She helped her out of the water and dried her. Immediately, in spite of the cool bath and her damp hair, Juliet was too warm. Must she dress again in petticoats and hooped skirts, with the bodice laced tightly over her corset and her fichu tucked into the neckline?

"I'll fetch the Italian dress, ma'am," Kate said. "I took the liberty of unpacking it for you. There's another note."

Standing wrapped in towels, Juliet read his swirling handwriting:

The company has shed all the day's formal clothes. We find the ladies in slippers instead of shoes. No heavy overdress or stiff, pointed bodices. No hats or hoops. Just muslin sleeves tied with ribbons, and a simple lute-string petticoat.

  Improper? Only a little.
  Sensible? Eminently.
  And very liberating—G.

She could almost see his smile.

"What do the gentlemen wear?" she asked.

Kate stopped in the doorway. "In Italy? I really can't say, ma'am. No doubt they have very foreign ways and fashions."

A white garment hung over the maid's arm, light and inviting. Dark blue muslin bunched and draped. Ribbons fluttered. *Vestimenti di confidenza.*

Did he think Juliet had too little nerve?

Obviously not. He expected her to wear it.

She put on her stays first, with one of her own chemises under it. Even Italian ladies surely did not receive company without them? But then she let Kate comb out her hair and tie it back in a ribbon. Almost as if it were a dream, she slid into the gauzy petticoat with the ribbon-tied sleeves. The fine muslin robe that went over it was dyed a deep indigo—*the wine-dark sea.* It all felt so insubstantial, falling over her skin with a feather-light touch.

Kate held out a pair of slippers. Simple, without heels. Juliet slipped her bare feet into the blissfully cool leather. Filmy cotton caressed her bare legs and arms as she moved.

She walked into the kitchen to stand in front of the window, glazed with reflections now it was growing dark outside. A stranger gazed back: a woman in loose-fitting robes with her damp hair spilling down her back and her skin rosy from the bath. The low neckline exposed her throat. Ribbons trembled.

Her gold chain disappeared beneath the neckline of the petticoat, less revealing than a ball gown, to where her locket nestled hidden between her breasts.

The dress was not immodest.

It only felt that way.

CHAPTER SIX

*M*R. GEORGE HARDCASTLE SPREAD HIS COATTAILS BEFORE THE fireplace, though the grate lay cold. He was dark, certainly handsome enough—the dramatic coloring and strong bones that often appealed to the ladies.

"So what the devil can you tell me about my wife, sir?" he asked.

"Was Russia never warm enough?" Robert Dovenby put as much sympathy as he could into the question.

"Just a habit, sir." George dropped his skirts. "I don't generally stay in the stink of London in midsummer. I am here now only because—" He stopped as if uncomfortable. Poor fool! "Well, I've had a small reversal in fortune, truth be told." Real distress slipped into his voice. "Rivals ruining my business. Faith, sir! Don't even know who they are!"

Dovenby raised a brow. "Deuced bad luck, sir. But to answer your question: Your wife disappeared years ago. No one's seen hide nor hair of her since."

"Disappeared? Plague take it, how can she have disappeared? Her father—"

"Disowned her." Dovenby picked up his glass and sipped at his wine. "After the unfortunate scandal and the tragedy. She has very probably changed her name."

"Then how does she survive? Whoring, most like! Who keeps her?"

Dovenby lost any last shred of sympathy for the man—a dangerous development for Hardcastle. "If she were being kept as a mistress, sir, we'd all have heard of it."

"Then the rumor is true that she came into an inheritance?" Hardcastle stepped forward. "Devil take it! How much?"

"I have no idea. I have heard nothing of her since you left for Muscovy."

"Because you bloody well tried to get into her skirts, most like!"

Dovenby smiled, though he did not think it amusing. "I would probably have done so, had the chance arisen. It did not."

George stared at him. "They still call you the Dove?"

The ruby liquid swirled with dark shadows. It was so simple to lead a man like Hardcastle exactly where one wanted to go. He would do so now without compunction.

"Only my most intimate friends—or sometimes my enemies— take such liberties, sir. You will be pleased, I am sure, to use my correct name?"

The man flushed. "Do you still claim to be the most notorious rake in London, sir?"

Dovenby glanced up at the man who had just chosen, if unwittingly, to become a pawn in a very wicked game. "Alas, Viscount Gracechurch stole that distinction as soon as he came back from Italy."

George Hardcastle broke into peals of laughter. "Heard it already in the hallway—Sir Reginald Denby's been putting the story about! Involves a hayfield? The lady said she'd tup Gracechurch if he scythed twenty acres for her. Imagine! Stripped himself naked—displaying to a gaggle of rustics everything God gave him—cut the whole damned field in an hour, then tupped her in the haystack! Is it true?"

"I wasn't there, my dear fellow."

"Yet he did tup her?"

"*Gracechurch?*" The word expressed a world of incredulity. "No woman ever refused him!"

"Who was the wench?"

"No idea, sir. Yet the libidinous viscount has not been seen at his London lodgings for a week. Neither is he at Gracechurch Abbey."

"And the place falls apart while he games away his fortune: that's the story I heard—just hadn't put it all together till now." George struck one fist into the palm of the other hand. "Women are a man's ruin, sir! Meanwhile my wife enjoys her inheritance!"

"How very distressing." Dovenby set down his wine. "With your own affairs so ill-starred, what will you do?"

"I'll have her property from her, of course," George Hardcastle said. "As soon as I can find her."

The door opened behind them. Heels clicked as another man walked into the room.

"A pretty tale," the newcomer said. "May I join you, Dovenby? Hardcastle? I couldn't help but overhear."

George scrambled to his feet and bowed. "My lord!"

Lord Edward Vane sat and stretched out long legs. "Can't stay, alas. Leave town within the hour—off to Marion Hall, Sir Reginald Denby's place in Hertfordshire. Yet I must speak with Dovenby. Hardcastle, if you wouldn't mind—?"

George blushed and bowed. "Of course not, my lord." He bowed again. "Dovenby."

Lord Edward watched him leave. "Money-grubbing fellow. Is he completely to let, Dovenby?"

Dovenby stood up and stretched. He must do whatever necessary to complete his vital plans regarding Lord Edward, but he did not have to particularly enjoy it.

"Shall we say his business fails to prosper."

The duke's son closed his eyes and leaned back. "So unfortunate. The unavoidable consequence of your private venture into his trade and my own investment therein. He has taken the hint that his wife has her own income and property?"

"Hardly hers. Anything she possesses is Hardcastle's by right."

The Dove turned and studied the powdered face, the slight sneer about the nostrils. "This lurid tale about Gracechurch. *Is* it true?"

"Who knows? Perhaps not in the details. Does it matter? What matters is that we know the whereabouts of Mrs. George Hardcastle. When the time comes, I suppose we must let it slip to her husband, if only from a sense of duty—"

His distaste deepened. "You have no concerns about Gracechurch? That the viscount might be a dangerous choice for your game?"

"Lud, sir! Thus speaks the notorious Dove. Are you jealous I didn't choose you for the role?"

Dovenby bowed. "Touché. She's rumored to be a damned beauty, of course. Yet she must be very alone in the world."

Lord Edward opened his eyes to stare at his business partner. "Hardly alone, sir, when she has a living husband."

THE PATH TO THE ARBOR WAS LIT WITH SMALL LANTERNS. JULIET followed them like a moth. It was almost fully dark now. The trees hung silent in the placid air. Hot brick radiated. The petticoat and the lightweight indigo robe billowed about her legs as if she floated.

A cloth had been spread on the table. Silk cushions covered the rustic seats. Drapes of white muslin stirred gently in the now-cooling air along one side of the arbor. Glass sparkled in the soft glow of more lanterns, hanging from the arbor roof. Two wine-glasses, bottles, several covered dishes waited on the table.

The pieces were already set up on the chessboard.

Juliet touched the white king with one finger.

"A light supper," he said softly behind her. "And our game, of course."

She froze, standing completely still with her back to him, looking down at the chessmen, while her blood sang with awareness and her hands trembled at her sides. She seemed to feel his gaze run over her body like the brush of a feather.

A hot blush flared on her cheeks.

Juliet lifted her head. Her shoulders longed for his touch. Her waist anticipated the span of his hands. Her hair waited for him to stroke it aside, to put his fingers, his mouth, on her sensitive nape. The deadly, knowing treachery of the body. The desire that had led her into a disastrous marriage. Her great weakness.

She waited, tortured by that beckoning of the flesh. She knew he would see it, yet not act unless she invited him.

She would never invite him.

"I am wearing the Italian dress," she said. Her voice was too sharp. She took a deep breath. "You do not compliment me on it?"

"Would you like compliments?" The husky tones caressed. "They would be superfluous."

Light fabric brushed over her burning thighs as she turned to confront him.

His long white robe fell smoothly from shoulder to ankle. A black dressing gown draped over it, embroidered in silver thread. The open collar revealed his naked throat and chest, the muscle that meshed from masculine shoulders into strong neck. His skin shone like ivory. Only loosely gathered by a ribbon, his hair— pure as beaten gold—flowed down his back.

Simple flat slippers, similar to hers, had allowed him to approach silently, like a nighttime creature.

The garments were more shocking on a man, too close to night attire, a frightening abandonment of formal coat and cravat. Yet she had seen him half-naked, cutting hay. Why was this worse? Juliet glanced down, trying to gather anger or indignation, hoping he would not see the confusion in her eyes.

"The question the English visitor usually asks in Italy," he said dryly, "is whether the gentleman wears any breeches beneath his gown. It is, of course, too immodest a question to answer."

Her cheeks burned, but she looked up and laughed at the sheer impudence of it.

He smiled as he held out a hand. "Wine?"

She put her fingers on his and allowed him to help her to her seat—a defiance, if he expected she would be petty over such minor details. Such a foolish convention, that a gentleman must assist a lady as if she were completely helpless! Yet as he touched her hand, a sense of fragile femininity unfolded at the core, as if she truly might shatter without his support.

"I would like wine." It took nerve to speak at all. "Thank you."

In a smooth flow of robes he sat down opposite her. The lantern light burnished the table, but cast the man into shadows. Only his hands were lit as he filled the glasses. Hungrily she watched his loose sleeves fall back—that beauty of masculine strength, knit smoothly from forearm through wrist into long, square-tipped fingers. A perfection of form. Stunning.

Red liquid poured from the bottle like melted rubies.

Leaning back into her own cocoon of darkness, Juliet sipped at the full-bodied wine. Better than she had tasted in years. Delicious. Heady. She wasn't surprised.

"Supper?" He lifted the lids from the serving dishes. The scent of bread enveloped her: warm, fresh, fragrant with rosemary and onion. "May I serve you?"

A lady, delicate, helpless, unable to serve herself—? She had almost believed it once.

"Thank you," she said.

He sliced white cheese and a red fruit, which oozed juice and small seeds from a starred center. He sprinkled it liberally with salt and black pepper.

"The Italians call these the apples of love," he said. "Otherwise known as the tomato. We don't usually eat them in England."

She lounged back against the luxurious cushions—as if she were perfectly comfortable to be in her garden with a man in his nightclothes. "They are commonly thought to be poisonous."

He set slices on two plates. "That's a risk we must take."

"And you like risk."

He gazed quizzically down at the tomatoes. "So do you."

Her pulse was pounding, a madcap rhythm, galloping. She felt exhilarated, alight with exuberance. "Only in safe doses."

Juliet watched as he tore apart bread to layer cheese, tomato and basil leaves on the warm surface. Apples of love and rosemary bread.

There's rosemary, that's for remembrance; pray, love, remember.

"By definition, risk cannot be safe," he said. "It is all or nothing."

"I refuse to believe that," she said. "I make my own rules, tonight at least. So why *apples of love?*"

His gaze locked with hers. His hair shimmered, shadows and golden gleams in the night. He smiled. "Because they're an aphrodisiac, of course."

The whisper-soft petticoat tingled over her thighs. "Thus a favorite food for a rake?"

His eyes were dark, echoing the mysteries of night. He set her plate down in front of her, then speared a piece of tomato on his fork.

"You think a rake's pleasure is to be found only in the bedroom?" He bit into the red fruit.

"Where else is it found?" With a mad bravado, she deliberately let her fingers fondle the stem of her wineglass.

He swallowed the tomato, then lifted his wineglass and matched her gesture, the smile haunting his cheeks. "My pleasure isn't simply in bedding a woman. It's in seducing her."

"Because her heart is a trophy?"

"No, because the better the seduction, the better what happens later in bed."

"Ah," she said. "Then if she gives you her heart, that's just an unfortunate accident?"

His glass tipped. He took a long swallow. "Why unfortunate?"

"You've never been in love?"

He bit into the bread, savoring it before swallowing. His gaze scorched over her like a hot wind. "Of course. Madly, passionately."

Juliet tried to control her breathing, the rush and flood of emotion. "Where?" she asked. "In Italy?"

He speared a piece of tomato and held it up. "Italian food. Toxic or an aphrodisiac. What do you think?"

She leaned forward and boldly took the fork from his hand. "Either way, perhaps it is only deadly to women—"

He leaned back, cradling his wineglass as he watched her taste the red fruit.

Sweet, tangy, salty, peppery, the taste burst on her tongue. Saliva filled her mouth. "It's very good," she said, surprised.

He laughed. "I' faith, ma'am, would I bring you something that was not?"

Another slice released a torrent of flavor in her mouth. "How can I know, sir? They say the Italians are equally proficient at poisons and love. Do you claim to have found only love while you were there?"

He speared another slice. "Her name was Maria. She was like honey, a distillation of flowers. I found only love."

Like honey! A bat flitted past, a silent shadow. "Did you marry her?"

"She was already married. In Italy unmarried ladies don't go out in society."

Juliet set down her fork. "Yet you and she became lovers."

"Her husband was sixty-seven. She was nineteen. I was a lot closer to her age than his. I carried her shawls, accompanied her to the opera, helped entertain their friends. Of course, I also shared her bed. Would you have had us do otherwise?"

"Her husband knew?"

He sipped wine, still watching her. "He and I shared an interest in antiquities. When I came home, I brought back a collection of Roman sculpture, dug from fields and the foundations of new houses. We became good friends. Of course he knew. We liked each other. He was proud that his wife had taken an English lover."

The cheese was smooth, tangy. She tried to concentrate on the taste of it, close out the enormity of what he was saying. "You make it sound so civilized."

"It was. As long as certain rules are followed, it's a common enough arrangement in Italy, especially when the husband is so much older."

She could imagine them, Romeo and Juliet, nineteen-year-old lovers, and the husband, wise enough to accept it. Insanely, her heart felt like breaking, shattering into tiny pieces.

"Is passion ever civilized?" she asked. "Only the poor wed for love. Society marriages are for property and status—"

"So passion must find its own path." His smile remained soft, almost sweet. *Like honey*— "Yet there's no reason it cannot be civilized."

"Of course! It's the way of the world, where rakes seduce married women. So much safer and easier, especially when the husband is compliant." He didn't seem to react to the sharpness in her tone. "Yet it's not so simple for females. Did Maria also love you?"

"Yes." Light flickered over his face, highlighting his severe bones as he leaned forward to refill her wineglass. "Passionately. Madly. Or she was clever enough to let me believe so. Italian women are very good at managing men. They have to be."

"How else should a female protect herself? Even English girls learn how to flirt and tease—"

"Which can be used to control a man, turn his desire against him."

She wanted to press the point. "It's her only power—"

"But is essentially dishonest."

"Certainly, it comes with a cost—"

"Maria had no regrets. We indulged our passion flagrantly. It went on for six years."

Wine flowed, heady and strong, into her blood. "Yet you came home and became a rake?"

"I was already a rake." It was almost a whisper, soft with smiles.

"What else should I do with all those Italian skills? With everything Maria had taught me?"

The darkness breathed intimacy, safety, the hush of night-shrouded secrets. Juliet caught a breath and let her next question escape her lips unhindered. "So what did she teach you?"

He leaned back. His features disappeared in the duplicitous shadows, though his eyes glittered. Lantern light glimmered richly on his wineglass and highlighted his fingers.

"How to make a woman tremble with a look, moan with a touch, melt with a kiss. How to take my pleasure from pleasuring her. How to yield to her as she does the same to me. Maria's husband had fifty years of experience. He taught her. She taught me. Now I teach others."

Shivers ran up and down her spine, as if her skin wished to melt, to moan, as if her heart trembled. "Love isn't enough?"

"Every plowboy falls in love, but pity the poor maid who's doomed to know only his inexpert fumbling." Light flared across his supple hands. "Physical love is an art—it deserves comprehensive practice."

"With many partners . . ."

He refilled her glass. "Neither Maria nor I was faithful, which is how we perfected our skill."

A white shape flitted through the shadowed flowers. Abednego hunting.

"There's no room in your philosophy for romantic love?"

"A boy fell romantically in love with an Italian girl who had nothing to offer but honey. A man prefers a keener passion, which he feels for every woman who enthralls, engages, delights him—body, mind and spirit. Yet true intensity cannot last, so a passionate man loves many women. From fairness, he does not expect constancy."

She tried to match his lightness, the sophisticated cynicism, though she didn't feel it. "So you learned irresistible techniques for flirtation—"

As he leaned forward his smile interrupted her, a smile carrying intelligent, worldly-wise humor. "I' faith, it rapidly grows more visceral than that. Flirting and teasing are for children. Adults go to bed together."

It hung between them for a moment. That it had been so lightly said was oddly reassuring. She wondered if this was how men talked with their friends, with this open, unemotional honesty. *This is how it is. We all accept it.* She felt completely safe.

"With someone else's spouse, of course," she said.

He smiled over his wineglass. "Unless you both agree not to act on what lies between you—usually the lady's decision."

"And you would argue that it's better to have such an affair, where the rules are clearly understood—" She was distracted by a sharp rustle in the flower border.

He picked up the wine bottle. Light played over the ruby liquid. "Less damaging than false protestations of undying love, certainly."

Dark marigolds quavered. Abednego appeared for a moment with something in his mouth, then raced away up the path.

"That wasn't what I believed when I married," she said. "I thought I was in love. I meant every word of my vows. But it was only a child's attraction to something that glittered."

"Like gold?"

Juliet glanced back at him. "More like ice: gleaming in fascinating drapes over a winter pond, but destined to melt into vapor when the sun returns. Gold implies value and permanence. Yet both are cold at the core." She reached up one hand to tip a lantern to dazzle for a moment on his face and hair. "However superficially alluring when gilt gleams in the dark."

Released, the light swung back to illuminate her in her turn. Her hair lay over her shoulder, soft against her cheek, the color intensified to mahogany.

"Ah," he said. "Which is why gold longs for a rare wood, smooth and warm under the palm. Yet you wear gold for love, Juliet."

She glanced down. Her locket hung outside the neckline of her petticoat. The metal gleamed softly. She clutched one fist over it and closed her eyes. "This locket was something I shared with the only person, other than my parents, whom I truly did love." The words came out in a rush, as if she couldn't stop them. "My baby brother."

The wine bottle hit the table with a small thud. "Your *brother?*"

Distress twisted wildly as she thrust the locket away. "Don't ask me about him. He is dead."

Immediately she was horrified. She had confided in this man, this stranger, as if she really could trust him. She had broken her own resolution to play lightly, to enjoy the evening as an amusing episode. *A comfortable evening with friends.* Now she had shattered everything.

Because of the shifting shadows? Because of the dark night? Juliet dropped her face in her hands.

He rose in a rustle of muslin. His slippers struck softly on the path.

Was he angry that she had introduced such a bane into his beautiful seduction of rosemary and love apples? Or could he turn aside what she'd said, find a way to recover the carefully orchestrated mood? If he did that, she would hate him. Yet for a moment she felt bereft, devastated at the thought that he would simply walk out of her life.

Silence stretched, broken only by the thump of her heart.

"I also lost a brother," he said starkly. "Five years older than I. He died while I was in Italy. There are no words sufficient to comfort such a loss. Nothing ever really heals it. I won't ask you, Juliet."

Breathlessness entrapped her, made her frantic. Stunned, Juliet fought for equilibrium, thinking she might need to gulp for air, but the breath still moved in and out of her lungs. The night remained quiet, though her eyes burned with tears.

"Nor I you—I am sorry."

"It's all right." His voice gentled. "News of his death finally broke my ties to Italy."

She looked up through a glaze of tears. Scattered with the remains of their supper, the table still glowed. Beyond the halo of lamplight, night wrapped its mystery about the garden. Dark on dark—only his hair gleaming in gilt mockery of the moon—Alden Granville stood with his back to her, gazing at the sky. A small breeze stirred his silver-and-black robe, fluttered the inky muslin draped from his broad shoulders like a necromancer's gown.

Perhaps it will bring us a serene breath from the icy moon. Will it waft the spiced scents of history and foreign blooms onto our deeply shaded patio?

She had felt the shimmer of his presence in her body and in her blood, the vital charge sparking between male and female. Now she felt it in her heart—a bond of sympathy, of shared tragedy, of a loss understood. Far more terrifying. *All or nothing?*

"So you came home? And Maria—?" She bit off the question, hating herself.

"Maria had died of a fever a few months earlier."

The breath congealed into a hard lump in her throat. It hurt as if she'd been struck by a hammer. "I'm sorry. I thought—" She forced herself to start again. "I don't know what to say. I assumed you had abandoned her."

"If you like." His robe moved as if caught in a dark flood tide. "The passion died first—by only six months, but it had died—for both of us. Alas, I found I wanted more than a flower, however sweet, and she had found a new interest. She and her husband had a child by then. I mourned my friend's loss and their child's loss, but she did not break my heart, nor I hers. In the end, I wasn't so important."

"After six years?"

He nodded. "What else would you like to know?"

"Nothing, nothing," she said desperately. "I did not ask for this relationship, these strange games that seem to spiral into something else. I don't wish to feel too safe with you. I don't think we should exchange such personal confidences. I am sorry."

"The apology is mine, ma'am," he said formally. "I will ask no more questions and tell no more secrets. I am not a man of much principle. I am indeed a rake. It was never my intention to do more than amuse you."

"Tomorrow is Friday," she said. "The sun will burn away all of this false intimacy and the next day you'll be gone—"

He turned. "Yet I like you, Juliet, very much."

She suppressed a sob. "You don't even know me! Perhaps I am a shrew."

He walked silently back to her. He took her fingers, then bent to kiss them. It was done with a light, gallant humor, though something else, something deadly serious, lurked beneath.

"And what's wrong with a shrew?" his voice teased. "A private, beneficial creature, otherwise known in various localities as the nursrow, shrove mouse, nostral, rannie mouse, skrew mouse, thraw mouse, rone mouse, or herdishrew. You have read your *Historie of Four-footed Beastes* far too carefully, ma'am. Alas, it's full of lies."

She tried to smile. "What?"

He folded her fingers into her palm and returned her hand to her. "Topsell's *Four-footed Beastes* is every schoolboy's favorite text. Far more amusing than all that Latin and Greek. Allow me to quote: 'The shrew is a ravening beast, feigning itself gentle and tame, but, being touched, it biteth deep and poysoneth deadly. It beareth a cruel minde, desiring to hurt anything, neither is there any creature that it loveth, or it loveth him, because it is feared by all.' "

"But none of that's true!"

"Just foolish country tales. We are bedeviled by them. The shrew is no more poisonous than the apple of love—and neither are you."

Juliet gazed up into the mysterious, intelligent smile. "Then what am I?"

His smile widened. "A sad lady in need of diversion." He sat down. "Let us play chess, ma'am. It's your turn to win."

Yet she knew she would lose before they began. In spite of his charm, he was deeply disturbed and he couldn't quite hide it. She had shredded the magic atmosphere and let it spiral away into smoke. She knew he only wanted to leave and would do so as quickly as possible.

She was right. Ruthlessly taking her pieces and destroying her strategies, he ravished the board like a miniature battlefield, scattering her defenses. As if it mattered! There was only one more day.

"What do you claim for your forfeit this time, sir?" she asked at last.

He looked up at her with something close to desperation in his eyes, but he laughed.

"That we play chess somewhere else tomorrow. We have played once in the kitchen and thrice in the grape arbor. Why not a fresh location?"

"Very well," she said.

"And my chore for the day?"

She pushed away from the table and stood up. "I think you have already fulfilled it, sir. You brought supper."

Juliet spun out of the arbor and hurried away up the path.

$\mathcal{A}$LDEN WATCHED HER GO. THE ITALIAN ROBE FLOWED OUT behind her like wings.

Tomorrow. He must bed her tomorrow at Marion Hall. Failure was out of the question. Ruin was simply too great a punishment for one night's mad gaming: for himself, his servants, his mother—and above all little Sherry, who wouldn't even understand enough to condemn him for it.

Yet he didn't seem able to play the game as he generally played it. Because so bloody much depended on the outcome? Or because Juliet had touched so much deeper than usual? *She had lost a little brother. She had married for love.*

He had followed the first three stages of any seduction: shown her his flattering interest; created a physical awareness in her; begun to dispose of her objections so she would feel secure in his company. Juliet was almost ready, surely, for the fourth stage: his clever hands and more clever mouth.

Why had he told her about Maria? Of course, it was a simple enough truth. While little more than a boy, he had loved. He had stayed away from England because of it. His Italian mistress and her fatherly husband had helped form his life and his expectations. Yet the thought of Maria no longer moved him. When it was over, it had not broken his heart. Perhaps he had no such vital organ?

Only Gregory's death had ever really mattered, and there was no one—not even his mother—to whom he could talk about his beloved older brother. Lady Gracechurch simply behaved as if she'd never had another son, as if Alden had always been expected to inherit.

Had he thought he must warn her? Tell Juliet in so many words that he was faithless, superficial? Why had he allowed the evening to slip from his careful design, let the mood change, slide away from his sensual onslaught? Created the moment when she had told him about the locket and he had felt forced to mention Gregory? He had wanted to win her confidence, make her feel safe with him, but he hadn't wanted to delve so deeply into the personal.

He struck one fist into the palm of the other hand. Was he doomed to bring pain to a woman he liked? For he truly did like her.

Abednego appeared at his feet, purring. The white cat dropped a small creature from its mouth. Alden bent to look at it. Not a shrew. Only a mouse. Quite dead. He moved it with his slipper. Abednego pounced on the carcass and raced away with it.

This locket was something I shared with the only person, other than my parents, whom I truly did love. My little brother. . . . Don't ask me about him. He is dead.

Her words felt like a curse. Yet by tomorrow he must deliver her locket to Lord Edward Vane, or see his world go up in flames. Alden had no doubt that he would find it in himself to do it.

*J*ULIET AWOKE THE NEXT MORNING TO THE SOUND OF HAM-mering at the front door. Sunlight flooded her bedroom. She had asked Kate not to wake her. Throwing on a wrap, she leaned from her window. The sky already blazed blue above her head, the air thick. Another hot, oppressive day filled with dust.

Jemmy Brambey stood on the brick path in front of the house and was squinting up at her.

"Message from the Three Tuns, Mistress Seton!" The boy waved a scrap of paper in one dirty hand.

Cats scattered as Juliet hurried down the stairs. Tilly had already thrown open the door. Jemmy exchanged a few words with his sister before he ran off with a farthing in his pocket.

Carrying the note, Juliet walked into her parlor. The paper was sealed with red wax, impressed with his crest. She stared at her name on the front, while her heart thumped uncomfortably in her breast. For several minutes she sat perfectly still, holding the note as if it had come from beyond the grave. She could not afford a repetition of what had happened last night, that dangerous slide toward real intimacy. Yet she wanted *something* out of this odd encounter, something to remember—

She opened the sheet and rapidly scanned the few lines, then read them again. Suddenly she laughed.

It had been five years since she had done such a thing! A whole day away from her house. A whole day to rub in the knowledge that she would never have another chance at a man's love, the past squandered, the future destroyed.

Yet, of course, she could not go. It was too dangerous. She would have to find some excuse. For the note read:

My dear Mistress Seton: If I might beg your kind indulgence, our chess match today will take place in a folly a few hours' drive from

Manston Mingate. The distance will necessitate a picnic lunch, kindly provided by mine host of the Three Tuns. I trust these arrangements will cause you no great inconvenience. It is impossible to describe the pleasure with which I anticipate such an outing in your company.

I shall arrive with a carriage and pair at ten o'clock.

We may, of course, expect another checkmate.

Whether yours or mine remains to be discovered.

I remain, dear madam, your most obedient, humble servant—G.

Humble servant, indeed! He obeyed only his own whim. Yet when had she last traveled in a private carriage? Taken a day's outing? A drive, a picnic, a visit to an interesting and beautiful place, and a chess game.

Their last day.

She had given her word to fulfill his forfeits whenever she lost a chess match.

Yet she could not go.

What if she were seen by someone who remembered her? Someone who could convey the information to George? Her husband lived. She knew it in her bones and that soul-deep knowledge was backed, every once in a while, by a scrap of news. George Hardcastle was making a name for himself, running his timber trade. He was gone often to Russia, but he also spent time in London— only thirty miles away.

Juliet stood and walked to the door. She opened it and called to Kate.

The lady's maid appeared and curtsied. "Yes, ma'am?"

"Do you think me mad, Kate?"

The maid curtsied again to hide her obvious discomfort. "No, ma'am."

Cradling the note, Juliet laughed. "Then you are wrong. I am about to do something quite lunatic. I shall need your help— yours and Tilly's."

* * *

*A*LDEN STEPPED DOWN AND LEANED BACK FOR A MOMENT against the wheel. He had brought a light open carriage and pair: the matched grays from Gracechurch Abbey, sent down the previous afternoon. It was going to be another blazing day, yet he had dressed in the full formal clothing of an English peer: dove gray coat; lace; crisp, clean linen. He crossed one heeled shoe over the other and let his gaze drift over the trailing roses. As when he had first seen them, Shadrach, Meshach and Abednego sat serenely on the brick path, watching him.

Mistress Juliet Seton.

He had bedded lovelier ladies and ones of more consequence: ladies of the royal court, dukes' wives, and once, a visiting German princess, who had gifted him with her lace. He had been inveigled into bed by females with the skills of Delilah, beguiled noblewomen and harlots. Sometimes they were one and the same.

It wasn't a life he had ever questioned. It had always brought him a profound pleasure, an intensity of sensation—at the tables, in the exquisite food and wine, in the voluptuous knowledge of each woman's body—a life filled with potency.

Now he was here to complete his seduction of this widow. It should be no different from a hundred other seductions, just more important. Alden cursed under his breath. He wasn't used to feeling so vulnerable, and—lud!—such a great deal hung in the balance.

This was the last day.

So he had decided on another gamble: to enlist the aid of those enchanting false ruins, the folly at Gracechurch Abbey, and Juliet's surprise when she discovered his identity. After weakening her with the amusement of the grounds, he would take her into those cool, gracious rooms and let his house destroy her defenses by its very loveliness. The awe-inspiring ceilings. The art. The collection of Italian and Roman sculpture in the long gallery. The home of each Viscount Gracechurch for several hundred years.

The only weapon he refused to use was Sherry. Peter Primrose had been instructed to take the boy out for the day. Foolish, perhaps. The child was bound to soften any female heart. Yet he couldn't quite bring himself to do it, even though Sherry's future depended as much as Alden's on his success today.

His servants would see that everything was in readiness. The kitchens would produce a feast of sumptuous food and heady wine. A tour of the house would include alcoves and private sofas. Every bed would be aired and made up with clean linen.

If he took her to Gracechurch, he would know every secret of her body by the end of the day.

He would do her no harm. He would bring her nothing but pleasure.

He concentrated on that one thought as he opened the gate. The cats stalked away and disappeared into the flower beds. Alden stopped and watched them leave, surprised.

The door opened. He looked up.

The breath was snatched from his body.

The impoverished widow of the blue smock and wine-stained skirts was gone. The soft, vulnerable lady of the Italian gown and petticoat had suffused into smoke. A new Juliet Seton stood facing him, her eyes as brilliant as the sky. Her chin was up as if she challenged him to a duel.

A straw hat, decorated with sweet peas and ribbons, nestled over elegant powdered ringlets. They were real sweet peas, wafting their fresh perfume among the fluttering satin streamers. A thin dusting of powder and rouge enhanced her perfect skin. She even wore a patch that danced coyly at the corner of her mouth as she smiled.

She stepped onto the path. Her rose satin gown shimmered in the sunlight. White satin bows decorated the bodice and sleeves. Deep ruches of lace frothed at each elbow. The belling skirts were supported by extravagant hoops, tipping and swaying as she walked. Petticoats rustled. Dainty high-heeled slippers with matching satin bows rapped on the brick, beating the rhythm of his heartbeat.

White-hot desire flooded through his veins.

Lud, lud! Mistress Juliet Seton! Would you try to match me at my own game?

It took him a moment to realize that the dress was five years out of style and a little faded. His body derided such an irrelevant observation.

The narrow, corseted bodice forced up her breasts in deliberate invitation. Lush, rich, female—just as he had imagined. Their swelling curves were framed by a pleated ruffle around the deep, square neckline, a display for male delectation. Her gold locket glittered against tender white skin. The deep cleavage begged for a touch: of aching fingers; of a clever, lascivious tongue.

With the brazen rush of lust came the knowledge that she recognized his purpose and did not shrink from it. It would be the sweetest, most glorious conquest he had ever made. With a shock that left him floundering, Alden knew that his desire was not only for her body—displayed with all the deliberate provocation of a society gown—but for the high courage it must have taken her to wear it.

Yet from somewhere he felt the smallest blossom of rage, though he had no idea why.

She flipped open a fan that hung from her wrist and held it to hide her décolletage from his eyes. The movement was one of pure coquetry, learned in a ballroom.

He took off his tricorn and swept her a complete court bow.

"Madam," he said. "I am ravished."

And knew to the bottom of his heart that he meant it.

T HE DRESS HAD BEEN WRAPPED IN LAVENDER AND PAPER IN THE chest in her bedroom for five years. What call was there in Manston Mingate for such finery? Juliet had carefully folded back the layers of paper and taken out the gown, as images of a life lost forever had come rushing back. Evenings at the theater exchanging glances over her fan. Afternoons at embroidery or the harpsichord. Five years ago she had sold every last dress but this one.

While Tilly worked frantically at pressing the creases out of the rose satin, Kate had dressed Juliet's hair. She had even produced powder and rouge.

"I would never attend a lady without it, ma'am," she had said through pursed lips.

Kate had also worked expertly at the tight lacing the dress required. Then Tilly had come in from the garden, red-faced and giggling, carrying a posy of sweet peas.

"For your hat, ma'am!" she cried. "Oh, ma'am. You do look splendid! Wait till I tell Jemmy and the rest!"

"I am to travel in an open carriage," Juliet replied. "The entire village will no doubt see me depart."

She felt breathless, gasping at the unaccustomed constriction of the tight stays. The high-heeled slippers made her feel unsteady, as if she might totter, but she hadn't forgotten how to walk so that her skirts dipped and swayed, provocatively displaying glimpses of ankle. Had she ever dallied away an afternoon in such clothes?

She wasn't sure why she had put them on now and decided against every better judgment to defy the fates. Because she was worn down with her life and with the requirements of secrecy? Because she longed to take a wild, uncalculated risk, just for once? Because she wanted to see that admiration in Mr. Granville's gaze turn into a recognition that he tormented a lady—his equal?

She stepped onto the path and saw his admiration turn into something quite different.

He took off his tricorn and swept her a complete court bow, elegant, graceful, deadly. The fleeting vulnerability left his face. She thought he might even be angry.

For a moment it was as if the entire world stood still, crystallizing her in place, like Lot's wife turned into a pillar of salt. Then a small anger of her own blossomed in return. How dare he! How dare he sweep into her life with his overweening confidence, then leave unscathed in the morning? Did he think she couldn't match him in this?

"Madam," he said. "I am ravished."

Chapter Seven

❧❧

ᵀT WAS A DANCE, THEIR MOVEMENTS PERFECT, AS HE HELPED HER
into the carriage. Each action precise, practiced. In a rustle
of petticoats, with the dainty rap of high-heeled shoes, she settled
herself on the seat. Her billowing skirts and stiffened panniers
filled most of the space.

Alden stepped up to sit beside her. Rose satin surged against
his thighs. If he had retained any last doubts, they were gone now:
that grace had taken a lifetime of training. Backboards and com-
portment lessons. Dancing masters. Straight-backed chairs and
rigid corsets. Trained for a ballroom from earliest childhood.

The value she placed on her word and her privacy said the same
thing. She had been raised as a lady. In which case, there was no
explanation that justified her life of solitude and hard work, except
some mad self-immolation or romantic denial of reality—either
one essentially selfish at the core.

He was glad. He must ravish her, leave her, and not look back.
That she had become this stranger in rose satin only made it easier.
Yet he didn't like her like this! Something in him wanted the
Juliet of the garden and the chicken coop, not just another society
lady, flirting over a fan—

What was the matter with him? Deliberately he thrust away
the memory of her as she had been last night in the Italian gown,
a mad trick of muslin and moonlight. He shuddered to remember

that flawed moment when he had almost told her about his brother's death. I' faith, he didn't want any such intimacy!

Alden signaled the driver. The grays started forward.

"John, our driver, is stone deaf—" he began.

"What a considerate employer you are, not to turn him off, when he suffers such a convenient affliction!"

He laughed, though in truth John's deafness was inconvenient more often than not. But the man had driven for the viscounts of Gracechurch his entire life. It was out of the question not to provide employment for him. Another innocent soul whose future depended on Alden's success today.

He leaned back and smiled. "I thought, perhaps, you wouldn't come. I see I was right."

"What do you mean, sir? I am here." She fluttered her fan, forcing the hot summer air past her face. "You think I have so little courage that an outing in a carriage would make me quail?"

"I' faith, ma'am, I imagined Mistress Juliet Seton was reluctant to leave the security of Manston Mingate. I am right—Juliet stayed home. She did not have the temerity to come. Instead we do indeed have the actress."

Her eyes smiled over her fan, but he had definitely raised her ire. A little anger often helped in a seduction. Let the day move into the well-practiced, meaningless provocation he was used to, without the trickery of moonlight and the slide into some unwelcome, truly personal exchange. Let their physical attraction be out in the open under a blazing sun on the hottest day of summer!

"I am still she, sir. Perhaps, in the formality of this gown, I feel armored and can thus play chess with more confidence."

"You believe that satin and lace move our game to a level that can be more clearly understood by both sides?"

"You are in satin and lace of your own," she replied. "It merely levels the field for me to be similarly attired."

So she would, indeed, play! "It makes both of us warm, ma'am, where the trapped sunshine turns into a furnace in the blood."

"Does it, indeed?" With a flick of the wrist, she folded and flipped open the fan. A tiny sheen of perspiration glimmered on the soft curves blatantly displayed beneath her locket. "I thought our game was to be chess?"

She was, deliberately, flirting with him. He had wanted it, so why did it now make him angry? "Oh no, ma'am, you are not such an innocent."

The fan fluttered. "You contradict me with so much certainty! How do you know what I am?"

Without dissembling he could never play cards. Calling on those long years of practice, he hid his confused emotions—simply another skill—and smoothed a fold of her skirt over his thigh.

"I know you to be a lady of superior understanding. I know you have decided to play to win this time and use every weapon in your arsenal. But if the divertissement changes—if we move from the vegetable garden to the more highly cultured blooms of high society—you must remember that I am a more practiced player in that game, too."

Color mounted in her cheeks. "But do you always win, sir?"

He glanced at her with something close to derision. "Always."

The sweet peas nodded on her bonnet as she turned her head. "Even though you said the game was worth more to you than the conquest?"

He spread her skirt further, covering his legs with the soft pink satin. "Madam, in the game of seduction the play and the conquest are all one."

She glanced down at her skirt, then up into his eyes. The fathomless blue filled with a desperate anger, but she did not move the fabric away.

"You are wrong," she said.

"I am right. Look at your fan, one of the tools of the pastime. Close it and hold it to your heart as if in withdrawal, what does it mean?"

She left the fan still. "Tell me, sir. You are such an expert."

He lounged deliberately, smoothing her skirt over his lap. "Even a closed, withdrawn fan still means: *You have won my love.*"

"So it does, should I be foolish enough to signal that."

"Alternatively, leave the fan open. Drawn across the cheek, it yet says: *I love you.*"

"You are selecting only those gestures most suitable to your purpose—"

"Then keep it half-open, pressed against your lips. The message then is: *You may kiss me.*"

She glanced away, as if studying the passing countryside. The tip of her tongue was just visible between her moist lips, like that of a child lost in concentration. The immediate effect it had on him had nothing to do with children.

He wanted to trace the deep curve of her upper lip with his own and feel the touch of that delectable tongue in the secret places of his mouth.

"However you move it, you invite my attentions," he said. "Thus any lady with a fan has already begun to surrender."

She glanced back at him from half-closed eyes. This was blatant encouragement!

"But like this," she said, bringing the fan up to her face, "placed against my ear, it means: *I wish to be rid of you.*"

Her lace cuffs, falling from the open elbows of her dress, brushed against his hand. He caught a trail of lace between thumb and forefinger. He was absurdly desperate to kiss her. "During which time, ma'am, we are still in conversation."

With a snap of the wrist, she moved the fan again. He released the lace.

"And like this, drawn through my hand: *I hate you!*"

He laughed. "In this game even 'no' means 'yes' eventually, and hatred, they say, is close enough to love."

She drew the fan through her hand again. "An interesting philosophy. Is the price worth it?"

"To whom? It has always been worth it to me."

She placed the fan against her ear. "But rarely, if I guess correctly, to your opponent."

"Opponent?"

"No other word will do, will it? I would venture that your lovers are always your adversaries."

The sway of her body next to his had already brought him to the knife-edge of desire. With a perilous raising of the stakes, he decided to tell her more of what it really meant to be a rake. Hardly from a sense of fair play! Then why? Because the least hint of his reputation had always proved to be an aphrodisiac in the past? Or simply because, for no reason he could fathom, he was still angry—with a wild, undirected rage at his own unprincipled desire?

The risk was indeed all or nothing now, was it not? Let Juliet Seton leap from the carriage and damn him to hell if she wished!

"Lovemaking is always improved by strife," he said. "Like a lover's bite—"

Color flooded her neck. "Yet you always part amicably?"

"There have been a few regrettable scenes."

"Have there, sir? Pray, enlighten me."

It seemed the most outrageous gamble he had ever taken in his life. To freely admit to her that he had indeed left a trail of broken hearts. When this time he must win!

"Since I came back from Italy, ladies have berated me, cursed me, even tried to have me killed—or their husbands have."

"You're not dead."

"I have a certain gift with a sword. When you accused me of being a rake, you were right. This is what that means: I never ruin servants, that is true, but when it's an even game, I play to win, whatever the consequences."

"So the lady risks her happiness and you take your pleasure—"

"It's a fair exchange. She finds her pleasure, too, I promise you." He touched the naked back of her wrist. Her skin held a tiny bloom of moisture. The touch was electric. "Yet I have always won, because I have always become bored first."

Her gaze riveted on his fingers. Her lashes were dark beneath the shadow of her bonnet. "So it's a contest to see who has the least heart?"

"Or to see who has the most passion—it is never my intention to involve hearts."

Her knuckles tightened on her fan as she looked away again. "Have you recently become bored with a particular lady?"

He thought for a moment of that young wife and her sudden desperate admission of true love for her husband. He could still have bedded her. Why had he instead let her go? Was it as simple as boredom? His own question annoyed him. What else?

"Oh, yes," he said with a small laugh. "Very much so."

"And before her?"

"That lady wanted to be a nun. I disabused her of the concept."

"After which you abandoned her."

"Of course."

He had. Quite coldly. He hadn't even liked her. Yet it did not feel like such a splendid admission, which annoyed him even more.

"So the lady went away utterly defeated," Juliet said.

This time it was undoubtedly true. When the would-be nun had come to him weeping and begging, he'd only wanted to spurn her the more. She had been such a hypocrite—pretending all that purity, while doing everything to entice him into bed!

"Yes," he said.

"And thus you were defeated, also."

He was surprised enough to take her chin and turn her head so she faced him. "Do you think so?"

She looked him straight in the eyes. "I would venture that both parties lost, sir, but that you have more pride, that is all. You are quicker to see the end coming and so you salvage yourself first. No doubt that's what really happened with Maria. You have never had the nerve to risk anything else."

Alden laughed at her—a low, lazy laugh—to hide his flare of anger. He released her chin. Why should he be irritated? He was winning. He had made clear what it meant to dally with a rake and she had not panicked. The line of her neck and upswept hair beneath the back of her bonnet held an intense allure. He wanted to touch that soft white skin, trace his fingers over the curve of her collarbone and down the swell of her lush breasts. His body reacted instantly. The trace of anger dissolved into ardent need.

"What is there to risk, ma'am?"

She glanced back, her color still high. Her eyes were stunningly blue. "Oh, affection. Constancy. True intimacy. Love."

"Emotions you have known?"

"No." She seemed starkly virtuous. "But I have believed in them."

"You have also known desire, which is more genuine." The throbbing pleasure in his groin made his voice a little husky. "You feel it now."

"Yes," she said on a breath, looking away. "Why deny it?"

Pleasure tightened, growing in intensity. "And you know it is worth it, even without love or constancy. What is more, you know it is safest to explore that ardor with a rake, because he expects nothing else and promises nothing else."

The horses' hooves clopped along the hard road, a heavy counterpoint to the jingle of the harness and the rustling of leaves overhead. It was a strangely innocent accompaniment to the outrageous surging of his blood.

"You think so?" she asked.

"Why else are you here?"

"Perhaps because I agree with you." Her breathing was rapid, nervous. "It doesn't have to go any further than this: If a rake asks for more and the lady refuses it, he will forget her and go his own way. If she would prefer to be forgotten, that is better for her. She would be left to her work and her garden, with the memory of a harmless moment of foolishness."

He felt like crowing, shouting to the far blue sky, a male shout of triumph, though he kept his voice calm, even found a dash of humor. "What kind of foolishness?"

"That remains to be seen."

"What if he asks for more and she agrees?"

"She will not. She would then truly prove herself to be a fool."

He closed his eyes for a second to regain control. A madness. He wasn't a boy to be swept up by sexual excitement, and yet he felt a blaze of urgency—

"So though she believes a rake to be unprincipled and dangerous, those very things make it safer that for this one day she can flirt—even kiss him—with the chance to scorn him afterward?"

"Yes," she said bluntly. "That would bring its own satisfaction, don't you think? If she is left unmoved and he is the one still trembling for more?"

"Fair enough, if she has judged her own reaction correctly." He slid one hand along the back of the seat until his fingers touched lightly on her nape. Heat burned from her skin. He stroked gently up to her hairline and back. "Let's find out."

Her face flamed. "You do believe attack is the best strategy, don't you?"

He untied her bonnet and tossed it aside, then traced the line of her jaw with his thumb. Her breasts rose and fell rapidly beneath the gold locket, as if her very skin sang in harmony with his touch. His pulse hammered.

"To be always on the defensive guarantees losing," he said.

She dropped her fan to her lap, but she did not pull away. Her breath fanned his lips, tantalizing, a fast harmony in rhythm with his own. "Yes, attack is always good strategy—in chess."

"Though in life it may lead you further than you want to go?"

"How far is that?"

"At least this far, Juliet."

He touched one thumb to the sensuous corner of her mouth as he lowered his head to hers. Her lips met his softly, lightly, with a small sigh. In spite of the urgent surge in his blood, he answered with delicacy. He kissed her upper lip and the corners of her mouth, then took her full lower lip between both of his and suckled gently, playing with sensation.

Sweetness flooded his mouth.

He pressed for more, let her feel the slight bite of his teeth as he changed the kiss to include her upper lip, then followed it with the soft touch of the tip of his tongue.

She responded with artless bravery. Surprisingly innocent.

Desire began to burn white-hot. Yet he teased, exploring with subtlety, waiting until she began to demand the intensity he was still holding back. At last she clutched at his coat and moaned, then slipped one hand behind his head and opened her mouth to his invasion. Sensations exploded. His blood roared its male exultation, thundering in his ears, as he put his heart and soul into kissing her.

Before he entirely lost control, he broke the kiss, with small nips and caresses—to her neck, her eyelids and earlobes. She sighed, her head pillowed on his arm, her mouth swollen and hot.

"Ah, Mistress Juliet," he whispered, rubbing his thumb over her cheek. "I am the one conquered."

"No." Her pupils were dilated, huge, as she glanced up at him. "Don't be dishonest now. I know this means nothing."

"It means that I am on fire for you, Juliet. No truth ever burned brighter or more starkly honest than that."

Her fingers touched lightly on his cheek, as if she would trace the lines of his face and commit them to memory. "You think to add more fuel to the flames?"

"I'm damned if I care. Let's create a conflagration!"

He kissed her again, deeper this time, while his fingers trailed down her throat and over the exposed swell of her breasts. The soft ball of his thumb lingered in the crevice, pushing aside her locket, as he kissed deeper yet.

Deeper. Deeper. With every ounce of his skill and experience. With a surprising and unlooked-for passion. Devouring her mouth. Exploring the soft shape of her breasts.

Intensity erupted in a flood tide.

His very bones responded with stark need. To touch her, anywhere, everywhere! Consume her with hungry hands and starving mouth. Invade her lush beauty and meld his flesh into hers. Now! Now! Make her body sing as his lips were singing—keen, sharp, burning with desire. Bury himself in her hot female heart. Find a soul-shattering pleasure. Sweep her with him to their mutual release.

Now! Lust soared in crescendo. More! Further! Deeper! *Now!* His control began to slip—

His legs were entangled in pink satin. His palms met only whalebone and lacing. He dropped his head to tongue her breasts, wanting to slide her dress from both shoulders—wanting to see her naked—feel her naked—and tasted a mouthful of lace from her cuffs as she pushed him away.

He glanced up into her eyes as he opened his hands and released her. "Juliet, please!"

"You have failed," she said, turning away. "You leave me cold."

For one split second he believed that she truly repudiated him. The pain of it paralyzed him.

"For pity's sake," he said at last. "We have hardly begun—"

"To play this game?" She laughed. "But we shall see, sir, who forces checkmate."

Alden spun away from her and leaned back into his corner of the seat. His breath rushed uncontrolled from his lungs. His mouth felt bruised, burning.

"There won't be checkmate," he said. "I concede and withdraw my forces. If you wished to wound me, you have succeeded beyond your wildest expectations."

She covered her mouth with her fan. The fan trembled, quivered as if shaken by an earthquake. She clasped one hand over the other as if to keep it still.

In the language of the fan: *Forgive me.*

He caught her by both shoulders and turned her to face him.

Her breathing, her color, her dilated eyes gave her away. She was brimming with courage and a determination to beat him at his own game, but if he asked now, she couldn't refuse him. What the devil did Juliet Seton think she was doing, trying to match wits with a rake? Although she didn't know it, her body had already betrayed her.

His blood surged and sang, while his mind filled with victory. "I am burning for you. You are truly different, Juliet."

"For today," she said. "For now. Pretty lies."

"Why would I dissemble now? Do you want me to pretend I'm not frantic with desire? I've never felt this desperate before." It was true—all of it.

She glanced down and bit her lip, absentmindedly opening and closing the fan. *You are cruel.* "If you are wounded, sir, it is only in your pride."

"Perhaps, but it feels like a much deeper laceration than that and not one that I fathom at all. In truth, I feel a little dazed and uncomfortably vulnerable, neither of which are my normal reactions to kissing a lady."

She clenched her hands in her lap, staring down at the closed fan. "It was only an experiment—"

"An experiment! And what did you feel?"

The fan snapped open. "Nothing—"

He laughed then, a great shout of laughter, filled with joy. "Oh, Juliet! What a blatant untruth! It's all right to admit it. Faith! It can still stop here, if you wish. I may never touch you again, but the truth is this: I've never known such a kiss—"

"Flattery," she said desperately.

"Lud, no! Why the devil flatter? It's more true than the blue sky. If you insist otherwise, then I might insist we do it again, just to prove you wrong."

"I think—" She grabbed her bonnet, thrust it on her head and frantically tied the ribbons under her chin. "I think we should not."

"Hush, hush," he said. "Valiant Juliet. You have stabbed me to the heart. It's not something I'm used to, but I won't die. Meanwhile, the control is all yours. If you say it stops here, it stops here."

She turned her head so he couldn't see her face and said nothing.

"Alas, ma'am. Your sweet peas are wilting."

He signaled John to stop the horses and leaped down. Red campion grew along the roadside. Alden picked a handful of the wild blooms, then swung himself back into the carriage. The grays started forward again.

Her hands were locked on the edge of the side panel, her back turned toward him. She was looking away through an opening in the trees.

"What place is that?"

He tore his gaze away from the gathered drapes on the back of her dress and the vulnerable white nape framed by the rose satin neckline. In the blue distance a house nestled in its grounds, hazy in the afternoon heat. They were already approaching the southern borders of his lands.

"Gracechurch Abbey."

"Who lives there?"

He pulled the dying flowers from her hat. One by one, he dropped them into her lap.

"The viscount, though he's seldom in residence."

She sat as if frozen, clinging to the carriage door, staring at his house. "Viscount Gracechurch?"

Alden wove the fresh wildflowers in place of the sweet peas. "The fellow's a gambler and wastrel, but the very devil, they say, with women."

He leaned down to kiss the tender curve where her shoulder met the column of her neck. Once. To show her his control. To remind her of his skill.

Apart from one quick, intaken breath, she didn't move.

He could imagine the next scene as clearly as if it were a play he had written. There was no need to go all the way to the house. She was already his. In another mile he could signal John to stop the horses, leap down from the carriage and take her by the waist to swing her into his arms. In a cloud of rose satin and lace she would land against his chest.

He would kiss her until she was on fire and helpless, then he would lead her through the little spinney and kiss her again. Where the trees thinned there was a private, sunny dell filled with wildflowers, sheltered by the curve of a ruined wall, an ancient, abandoned outpost of the Abbey that his father had rebuilt into a charming folly.

There he would remove the glittering dress. Peel away petticoats and corset. Slide off the beribboned high-heeled shoes, untie her garters, kiss away her stockings. His coat would cushion her powdered head, his shirt make a soft bed for her naked back. She would press her lips to his bare chest as he kicked away his shoes, moan into his mouth as she helped slide down his breeches. He would take her, there in that dell, as she begged him not to, then begged him not to stop.

His blood burned.

His knowing, practiced body was hers to use however she desired.

In exchange, he promised her ecstasy.

It was no overconfident fantasy. It was the simple truth. She wanted him as much as he wanted her. There among the crushed thyme and forget-me-nots, he would devour her. When she was enthralled, helpless, he would bury himself to the hilt in her sweetness and her courage and her fortitude, and win her.

No woman had ever denied him. He could take her to Marion Hall before midnight, certain that she could refuse him nothing. Whether she realized it or not, Mistress Juliet Seton was already his lover. The wager was as good as won.

With gentle fingertips he stroked the back of her neck, marveling at her silky white skin.

The matched grays trotted confidently toward the spinney.

Alden had already put out his hand to tap the signal to halt, when she turned to face him. Her eyes were brilliant, dilated, her color high. There was everything there he had worked for: her body's craving and its female vulnerability. The answering pressure of his own desire raced hot through his blood, importunate, demanding. He cradled her cheek in one palm as if to kiss her again.

She clutched at his hand, pulling it down.

"I cannot," she whispered. "I cannot win. I was lying. You have defeated me. If you have any mercy at all, you will not touch me again."

Checkmate!

He was stunned into silence.

Alden dropped his hand.

There was a distant growl of thunder. A raindrop splashed on his knuckles.

He glanced up. Black clouds had gathered and built, rapidly boiling up into thunderheads. A cold breeze blew her skirts and fluttered the ribbons on her bonnet. Raindrops began to patter audibly on the road.

"Thank God," she said, tipping back her head and closing her eyes as the water ran down over her ravaged face. "At last."

He fought for escape, desperate to find a way past his unwelcome surge of scruples. Gracechurch Abbey was close. They could arrive wet from the rain. Comfort and warmth would be a simple prelude to a civilized seduction in a drawing room, or a bundling in towels and warm sheets in a bedroom. Easy to tease a woman out of her damp clothes and into his arms. He had done it a hundred times.

Then afterward he would take her, soft and glowing from his lovemaking, to Marion Hall, where he would ravish her again to satisfy the wager with Lord Edward and Sir Reginald Denby. Where he would give them her locket as proof—or be ruined.

He had been so certain he could do it. Why the devil not?

It would be something he would regret to his dying day, if he did not make love to Juliet Seton. If he failed to bed her tonight at Marion Hall, it would cost him his home and his future, and very possibly his freedom. It would cost him Sherry and Peter Primrose and the future of all of his dependents—

Alden didn't know what else he thought it would cost him, except that it would be a travesty to take her in a field or under a hedge like a farm girl—and the act of a blackguard to take her to Gracechurch Abbey only to feast off of her vulnerability.

With rage at his own incomprehensible feelings tearing at his heart, Alden signaled John to turn the carriage.

"Then I had better take you home," he said savagely. "Unless we wish to play chess in a downpour."

He let his mind run through every blasphemous curse that he knew. From somewhere, unlooked for and unwelcome, some tiny shred of honor or pity or restraint seemed to have become seeded and sprouted into this unlikely plant.

The notorious Lord Gracechurch was going to refrain once again from making love to a willing woman that he passionately desired. Even though this time it would cost him his home and his future, and very possibly his freedom.

He had gone mad.

*T*HE HORSES TROTTED ON. FOLDED KNUCKLES PRESSED TO HER burning mouth, Juliet huddled inside his coat. He had insisted on taking it off and draping it around her shoulders. The thunder shower had faded to a sprinkle, then stopped altogether, but she didn't return his jacket. She sat enfolded in its dry warmth, with the carriage blanket tucked over her knees.

Eyes closed, arms folded, Alden Granville lay back on the seat next to her. Rain had soaked his hair, his shoulders and waistcoat, plastering the fabric to his body, washing over the severe, beautiful lines of his face. His expressive lips lay still, robbed of words, robbed of kisses, dampened only by rain.

If he had asked, he could have made love to her right there in the carriage. Tossed up her skirts and thrust himself boldly into her moist, willing body. He had not, though he had, of course, wanted to. She believed him in that.

She did not believe it was because she was special, or because she had moved him in any unique way. He wanted to, because he was a rake and she was female.

He was a libertine, a man who broke hearts for a pastime. She was a married woman, who—in spite of everything—felt bound by the vows that had cost her so much and was even more bound by her fear of discovery. She was not free. And even if she were, she would never be just another mistress to a man who had casually enjoyed so many. Though she wanted him with a longing that shook her to her soul: wanted the wit and the attention, and the lean masculine body.

Juliet pulled his coat closer about her shoulders. The fabric carried his essence, that clean, male-and-soap smell that she wanted to breathe forever deep into her lungs—to hold in some part of him, even if only his scent.

How foolish, when it was so thoroughly over! The pretty game and the play at seduction. Destroyed forever. He would go on his way and leave her to hers.

Yet her skin craved the touch of his hands. Her mouth silently called out for the press of his lips, for the demon knowledge of his mouth and tongue. Her palms longed to feast on the muscles displayed, clean and hard, beneath his damp shirt. If he asked now, even with a look, she would not be able to deny him.

He did not ask.

So, in spite of his avowed vocation, he was merciful!

Juliet turned her head away, just as two horses came crashing along a track through the woods. In the lead cantered a stout black cob, carrying a small blond-haired boy. The second rider was a slender young man on a bay.

The boy took off his hat and waved it. "Lord Gracechurch!"

"Look out!" Juliet shouted. "There's a ditch!"

She had a confused impression of blue eyes and a stubborn young mouth, then the blond head dipped as the child grabbed for mane with both hands. The black plunged awkwardly. The boy tumbled forward. His hat went flying as he fell over his mount's shoulder and disappeared.

Alden had already vaulted from the carriage. He ran six paces and slid down into the ditch.

His face white, the man on the bay dismounted.

John pulled up the grays and Juliet clambered down, stripping Alden's jacket from her shoulders. In that one glimpse of the child's face, she had seen a ghost. Some trick of the light, no doubt. Some mad jolting of memory, of an image of another blond boy running away from his nursemaid, laughing at the world. Why must the sight of any carefree child bring back such excruciating echoes?

"It's all right, Peter," Alden said. "He's unharmed."

Juliet ran to the edge of the ditch.

Ignoring satin breeches and high-heeled shoes, Alden Granville knelt in several inches of muddy water, holding the little boy in his arms. The lace at his wrists was solid with muck. The hem of his embroidered waistcoat dragged in the mire. The child's mouth was clamped shut under a layer of wet grime, his stubby fingers clamped onto his rescuer's clothes as Alden wiped the boy's face with a lace-edged handkerchief. The child was trying very hard not to cry.

Alden glanced up at Juliet and smiled.

She dropped the jacket into his outstretched hand. Alden wrapped the child in its folds and held him tightly as the little boy shivered against a broad shoulder.

"My lord," the man named Peter said. He had tied the horses: his own bay and the child's black cob. "I am—You are sure he's all right?"

"No broken bones. A few bruises, a bit of a shaking—and a dunking, of course. We must get him inside and warm." Alden looked down at the boy with infinite tenderness. "Very precipitate, Sherry. You must prepare your mount properly before a leap, or he'll take it awkwardly and dump you in the ditch. It takes concentration. Besides, a gentleman never leaps his horse while waving his hat to a lady."

The child coughed up a little ditch water onto Alden's shoulder and wrapped both arms about his neck. "But you did. Mr. Primrose told me."

Peter Primrose colored. "Alas, my lord, I did. I told him how you leaped your horse right over the thorn hedge while waving your tricorn at Lady Gracechurch."

"Thereby making my mother scream. Very bad manners. I have never done it again."

The child tried to grin, but his lip wobbled and tears pooled in his eyes.

Alden smoothed the yellow hair back from the round forehead. "Never mind, sir. I'll take you home and have Cook make you some currant buns."

He handed the child, wrapped in the jacket, up to John, before he climbed out of the ditch. Peter Primrose hurried ahead of them to make a bed from the blanket and his own coat as the coachman carried the boy to the carriage.

"*The very devil, they say, with women,* Lord Gracechurch," Juliet said dryly.

He glanced down at her. She couldn't read his expression.

"He's your son?" she asked.

"Lud, no."

"Obviously the child cannot ride home and you must take him back in the carriage."

His expression was remote, almost cold, as he stared away toward his house. "And also carry a lady into my den of iniquity, when she is so deuced unwilling to go?"

"I will not come back with you. It would achieve neither your purpose, nor mine."

He ran both hands through his damp hair, pushing it back from his forehead. The ribbon had slipped away. Blond strands straggled across his shoulders and back. He looked rugged, very male.

"My purpose being to ravish you shamelessly and add you to my list of conquests. Yes, it's true."

"So it failed," she said. "See to the child. My purpose now is only self-preservation. I don't need you for that."

Before she could react, he leaned down and kissed her once on the mouth. His lips were icy. "Yes, my seduction failed. We shan't see each other again. But the joke is on me, ma'am. I'm in love."

Her heart stopped, then leaped back to life, pounding heavily. "But we part here. Good-bye, Lord Gracechurch."

"Madly. Passionately." He gave her a lighthearted grin. "So, you see, you have won, after all. However, we still have a problem: I cannot leave a lady abandoned beside the road."

"I will borrow one of the horses."

"You can hardly ride home in hooped skirts and without a lady's saddle."

"Watch me," Juliet said.

Still meeting his gaze, she backed up to a tree and reached up under her skirts at the back to untie laces. He lifted one eyebrow—incredulous.

Juliet raised her chin. Her hooped petticoat fell to the ground. She stepped out of the folded whalebone and gathered her limp rose satin skirts in both hands to walk swiftly to the tied horses. The black cob was little more than a pony. With the help of a nearby stump, Juliet climbed astride onto the child's saddle. She adjusted the stirrups, arranged her dress, and turned the animal's head toward Manston Mingate.

She didn't expect Lord Gracechurch to stop her or say good-bye. He did not.

Without a backward glance, in all his ruined finery, he spun about, strode to the carriage and stepped inside. The child cuddled against him, rubbing one fist over a tear-streaked face.

"You will escort Mistress Seton to the Dower House, Mr. Primrose, where you will secure a carriage to take her home," Lord Gracechurch said over his shoulder. "John will take Sherry back to the Abbey with me. Meanwhile, I pray you will not be careless enough to allow this lady to end up in a ditch."

CHAPTER EIGHT

❧

$\mathcal{T}$HE CARRIAGE BOWLED AWAY. JULIET GLANCED BACK. SHE would never see him again. Restless emotions surged—whether anger or heartache she wasn't sure. Had he, in one week, forever destroyed her peace?

The young man rode up beside her on his bay. "My name is Peter Primrose, ma'am. I pray you will allow me to escort you?"

"Of course, sir." She tore her gaze away from the departing carriage. "Nevertheless, we shall ride straight to my home."

He colored a little and pushed his tall bay to block the road. "Lord Gracechurch is an indulgent employer, ma'am. However, it would be wiser to secure another carriage. The Dower House is quite close." He glanced at the sky. "It's going to rain again."

A chill breeze stirred through the damp leaves. It was at least ten miles back to Manston Mingate. The Dower House was probably unused except for storage. The rational choice. It would be senseless to insist otherwise.

"Very well, Mr. Primrose," Juliet said. "I put myself in your hands."

They left the road to follow a track across the fields. Peter Primrose stopped his horse to open a gate for her.

"The little boy," she asked. "Who is he?"

"James Sherwood, ma'am. We call him Sherry. I'm his tutor. He's a brilliant child, remarkable for his age." Mr. Primrose maneuvered his mount so that she could ride past him into the next field. "He's an orphan. No relation to the family."

"Yet Lord Gracechurch gives him a home?"

He glanced at her with thinly veiled scorn. "I'm sure it seems odd to a lady such as yourself for Lord Gracechurch to care so much for his dependents, yet I would say that he and the child love each other like father and son. Without the viscount's protection, the boy would starve."

A lady such as yourself! What did that mean to this severe young man with the look of a cleric? Among other, more obvious and insulting, implications, that she was incidental, irrelevant, to the viscount's life, to this tutor's life, making a home for an abandoned child.

Yet she replied gently. "You are very loyal to your employer, sir."

He seemed to soften a little. "As is everyone at the Abbey. When the viscount came back from Italy, he found nothing but debts. Creditors were out for his blood. Anyone else would have sold up or at least trimmed the staff, forced ruthless frugality. Lord Gracechurch promised to pay, then assumed the burden of a ruined estate and all of its dependents without a second thought." He closed the gate and rode up beside her. "His servants are more than loyal. They're devoted."

Juliet looked away across the open farmland. Every cow, every blade of wheat, every worker—his responsibility. Was it a romantic madness to make no economies, keep on all the old servants?

"Yet if the viscount fails, all of his dependents will suffer, instead of just a few. When his debts are so severe, how can he possibly recover?"

Mr. Primrose rode ahead of her and tossed the answer over his shoulder. "Through the only path open to any gentleman, ma'am: he gambles."

Juliet followed, not wanting to think about what she'd just learned and could clearly imagine. An old estate encumbered with dependents. Servants too ancient or infirm to find employment elsewhere, retired workers, widows, children . . . and an orphan boy. Lord Gracechurch tried to support all of them and still stave off his creditors by relying on wins at the tables?

"There are other options," she insisted. "He's a viscount. He could marry for money."

The tutor stopped his horse and turned to face her. "That is hardly my business, is it, ma'am?" he asked. "Nor yours."

He spun the bay about and rode away down the track.

Alden, Viscount Gracechurch. A man who, when he married, must marry an heiress. Why had he not done so years ago?

Her family must have known his, of course, though she didn't recall ever meeting any of them. She had never known anything about Alden, the younger son, not even his name. The heir, Gregory, had been killed, she thought, in a duel—?

Five years older than I. He died while I was in Italy. There are no words sufficient to comfort such a loss. Nothing that ever really heals it. I won't ask you, Juliet.

Another part of the tenuous bond, deeper than mere physical attraction, that had somehow sprung up between them. But he had not been the cause of his brother's death, whereas she had been the cause of hers.

She concentrated on mundane details, the passing scenery, the flexible spine of the young man who rode ahead of her, until they arrived in the stable yard of a large mansion. The rain started again.

Mr. Primrose helped her dismount. A closed coach already waited for them. Alden—*Lord Gracechurch*—had obviously sent word as soon as he'd arrived home with the little boy. Holding her trailing skirts off the wet cobbles, Juliet walked to the carriage.

"Lady Elizabeth Juliet Amberleigh?" a woman's voice asked.

In stark shock, Juliet spun about.

Peter Primrose bowed deeply to the lady who had just joined them. "Lady Gracechurch, your servant, ma'am."

Though a paler, more abstracted copy of her son, it could be no one else. Alden's mother stood in the archway that led to the house. She glanced away, as if not quite paying attention, or as if paying equal attention to the clouds or the cobbles or the horses harnessed to the carriage. Then she looked directly at Juliet once again and frowned.

"I remember you as a girl, Lady Elizabeth," she said. "You were an ungrateful child. Children are a great trial to their parents. If I'd had daughters, I would have wished them to have been more obedient and grateful. Yet sons are so very, very difficult. Your father has no children, does he? Not now?"

Juliet felt ill, as if struck by a knife. She did not remember ever having met Alden's mother, but Lady Gracechurch must have seen her at home when she was still in short skirts. One of that procession of nameless fashionable guests to whom she had made her curtsy before being ushered back to the schoolroom.

Lady Gracechurch would remember the scandal. She would know what had happened.

Your father has no children, does he? Not now?

Alden's mother turned away and disappeared. Juliet lifted her head and climbed into the carriage. Peter Primrose swung himself onto the step, ready to come with her.

Juliet forced herself to speak calmly. "Pray, sir, go straight home to the little boy. I am quite safe. Sherry needs you far more than I do."

The tutor glanced at her face, bowed his head, and stepped down again.

Two minutes later Juliet sat alone in the coach as it started out for Manston Mingate. Was rage the only antidote to despair?

ALDEN HELD SHERRY ON HIS LAP, WRAPPED WARMLY IN A towel, and told stories—stories Gregory had told him when they were children, of the foolish brother who fished for the moon, of Jack who found the magic beans beside the road.

Children died every day from fevers and chills. A serious influenza had been going about. Yet by the time they arrived back at the Abbey and a gang of nursemaids had fussed over Sherry, putting him in a hot bath and feeding him currant buns, the child was glowing with health. Half an hour later, replete with tales and warm drinks, he fell happily asleep with his guardian by his bedside and no trace of fever.

Alden strode to his room then and ordered a bath of his own. Lud, he looked as if he'd been dragged backward through a hedge! His hair was still damp. The mud-covered shoes, stockings and breeches would have to be thrown away—even the coat and lace cuffs were ruined.

Nothing could be more irrelevant. His clothing had only ever mattered when it served a direct purpose, although when he put his mind to anything, he liked to do it well. Alden turned away from the mirror.

For a split second something seemed to reflect pinkly behind him. He almost spun about, as if he would see Juliet in her rose satin gown standing in the room, but no one was there.

Watch me!

Devil take it! She'd have done it, too. Ridden all the way back to Manston Mingate on the child's pony, shedding campion and heartbreak.

I'm in love. Madly. Passionately.

He shivered. Just words, of course. He'd used them before to countless women. He'd never meant them. Faith, he definitely did not mean them now!

Yet whatever he'd meant, for whatever insane reason, he had failed to win her. He had lost the wager and forfeited his entire estate.

He was ruined.

Nausea twisted in his gut. He shivered again. Somehow, from somewhere, he must still provide for Sherry. Was there time, before midnight tonight, to salvage something, set up some kind of trust that Lord Edward couldn't claim?

Why the *hell* had he been so confident of victory?

Alden glanced around as a string of menservants entered the room. Bathtub. Hot water. Towels. Fresh linen. The silver coat with the matching shoes and rose-and-silver waistcoat. The clothes he'd planned to wear for his triumph at Marion Hall, symbols of a life that now seemed only brutally empty. He laughed. He would still sport all that gilt finery. But only to admit his failure and take his punishment.

If it weren't for Sherry, he wasn't sure he would care.

JULIET WALKED STRAIGHT INTO HER KITCHEN. TILLY HAD ALready gone home. Betty and Sarah were scrubbing the floor. Kate was busy with the flatiron.

"Leave it," Juliet said, swallowing hard. "Leave everything. Lady Gracechurch's coach is outside."

With a thud, Kate set the iron back on the hob. "Ma'am?"

"Your services here are done. Collect your things. Do not keep the coachman waiting."

They obeyed instantly. She had known they would. Whatever arrangements Viscount Gracechurch had made, these maids were used to Gracechurch Abbey or the Dower House. Quite a comedown to be employed in a cottage in Manston Mingate!

Juliet sat alone in her parlor until she heard the coach leave. The mud from her shoes had tracked across the rug. She had stepped into the wet road, hadn't she, when the child fell into the ditch? Would all small boys, always, remind her of her dead brother?

The pain came in sharp waves. She wrapped her arms over her breasts and concentrated on breathing steadily. It was foolish, self-indulgent, to let the memory do this to her after all these years.

There are no words sufficient to comfort such a loss. Nothing that ever really heals it.

Yet what loss should she weep for? It was even more foolish to regret the loss of a libertine's empty flirtation.

A rake had promised a few hours of ecstasy. No more. No less. Pleasure without consequences. Without ties. Why hadn't she grasped the opportunity? Why not have kissed him again and kept kissing? What loyalty could she possibly owe to her husband? George had abandoned her. Was she to live here in lonely celibacy until she died of old age?

She stood up and began to pace. And she had thought she was brave! Now it seemed only a wretched cowardice to have made a life hiding here in Manston Mingate. Why hadn't she gone to London and faced down the world? Become a courtesan or actress? Because she couldn't face the reaction of her father, or because she had been forced to be realistic about the power he and her husband held over her?

Francis Amberleigh, Earl of Felton, might have abandoned his daughter to her fate, but he would never have idly stood by and seen her disgrace the family name in public. In truth, there had been no other option but this retreat into a private sanctuary. Anything else was just a romantic fantasy.

As was loyalty to an abusive husband? Or fatuous ideas about honor and chastity? Or the hubris of false pride?

The day was fading outside. Deep shadows fell across the parlor window.

"You fool!" she said to the empty air. "What did you have to lose?"

"Lud, ma'am," a man's voice said behind her. "What is this? Regrets? He's a wastrel and gambler, like his father, but very charming. Did you enjoy his attentions? Did you long to allow him into your bed? No one, they say, is more skilled there."

Breath stopped.

Like Lot's wife, she thought wildly, *a pillar of salt!*

She had fallen into a nightmare where even if she ran and ran until her lungs shattered in her chest, she would go nowhere. But it was not yet night. She wasn't asleep. This was real.

It took intense self-control, but Juliet waited until she was able to breathe normally. Meanwhile, without looking around, she reached for the tinderbox and lit a candle on the mantelpiece. The light would throw her into shadow while illuminating the face of the intruder. Not that she needed to see his face. She would recognize his voice anywhere.

At last, with the single flame dancing and flickering behind her, she turned to face him.

"Lord Edward Vane," she said. "To what do I owe this unexpected pleasure?"

*M*ARION HALL WAS LIT FROM TOP TO BOTTOM. ALDEN'S SHOES rapped up the steps. Lace rustled. The smallsword at his hip clinked once. Silver satin whispered its own song of luxury. The elaborate clothes of the court. The dress that spoke of wealth and fashion, with those witty little touches that hinted at hidden power.

Such a pretty irony, when he felt ferocious, wild, as if he were about to fight a duel to the death.

His harsh steps echoed as he strode along hallways and through doorways, until at last a footman flung open a door and he stepped into a small parlor.

A blaze of candlelight assaulted him. Every face turned in his direction.

Alden stopped and pressed his whimsical handkerchief to his lips for a moment, before giving the company his most exquisite bow.

"Dear me," he drawled. "A party."

Lord Edward Vane, Sir Reginald Denby and some other gentlemen lounged about the room, drinking. Three of them were men he had fairly recently encountered during long evenings at the tables: Lord Bracefort, the Earl of Fenborough and young Kenneth Trenton-Smith.

The last guest, Robert Dovenby, was a man Alden hardly knew, except that he had a rather odd reputation and was sometimes referred to, rather mockingly, by a nickname: the Dove. As if to flaunt the bird he was named for, he was dressed entirely in shades of soft gray and silver. His expression was bland, but a keen intelligence lurked in his deep hazel eyes. Alden met that shrewd gaze for a moment, before he glanced back at the others.

Why Dovenby?

Alden didn't imagine for a moment that the guest list was arbitrary.

Lord Bracefort he thoroughly disliked. In one evening's play the man had lost badly, then offered his wife's favors in payment. Alden had refused. A duel had, unfortunately, resulted. Bracefort had fainted before the fighting began and been forced to withdraw—a humiliation not easily forgiven.

Fenborough, alas, had possessed a wife who was more than willing, then tried in vain to defend her dubious honor at sword point. His left arm was probably still in bandages.

Trenton-Smith had not only lost a great deal of money to Alden—though not more than he could afford—he also had a sister: who had wanted to become a nun.

Dovenby, obviously, must have some connection to Lord Edward. What, exactly? Alden rapidly considered everything he had ever heard about the man. It wasn't much, but it was certainly food for thought. Why was such a man here, tonight?

The men stared at him in silence as Alden closed the door behind him.

He glanced at their faces with indifference. Nothing mattered here tonight but Juliet's good name—his to save, if he could.

"Were the conversation more lively, I should think I had stumbled into an Oriental bazaar," Alden said. "Such an overwhelming display of bad taste! Bracefort, you really shouldn't wear puce, unless you truly *wish* to indulge in some bloodletting—"

Bracefort choked on his wine.

"—and my dear Fenborough, that brilliant green does not become you, though I am relieved to see you so well recovered from your recent sad accident."

Fenborough's hand flew to his sword hilt as he leaped to his feet. "My injury was no accident!"

"Then you plunged deliberately onto my blade? Faith! How original! Trenton-Smith! How is your sister? Enjoying unholy revels with her husband or has she already taken a new lover?"

Like an uncoordinated marionette, Trenton-Smith began to lunge across the room.

Alden ignored him. "And Mr. Dovenby? You and I have no quarrel that I remember. Is that because there is none, or because you are too insignificant for me to remember? Don't tell me that you are here—like myself—just from idle viciousness?"

Dovenby smiled as if only he had escaped insult, as perhaps he had. "My viciousness is never idle, Gracechurch. Like you—if I hear correctly—I take great pains to perfect it."

Alden laughed. He felt truly amused.

"Do sit down, Fenborough, Bracefort." Lord Edward Vane thrust out one hand to grip Trenton-Smith by the arm. "Gracechurch will apologize."

"By no means, sir. I meant every word of it." Alden helped himself to port from a side table. "Young Kenneth defends his sister in vain and knows it. Although Bracefort might be indistinguishable in appearance from dowagers past a certain age, that particular shade of puce really should be reserved for those ladies. And alas, that green casts bilious shades of envy across Fenborough's leafy countenance."

"My coat, sir!" Fenborough sputtered, his fist still closed on his sword hilt. "You scorn my damned coat!"

Setting down his wine for a moment, Alden stripped off his silver brocade to toss it to the earl. "Never mind, sir, you may have my own jacket, although it won't fit your regrettably pugilistic purposes—too snugly cut for a brawl."

Sir Reginald Denby lurched up. "Do you mean to insult us all, Gracechurch?"

"Of course." Alden raised his glass in salute. "I would never insult anyone by mistake."

"Let it go, Denby! Fenborough!" Lord Edward said. The patch at the corner of his mouth winked as he grinned up at Alden. "So tell us, Gracechurch: How goes our wager? Did you already tup the lady in the shrubbery or under the back stairs? Do you bring us the proof we agreed on?"

Alden waited a moment, gathering absolute attention. Then he dropped his words like ice crystals into the expectant silence. "The lady's virtue remains irreproachable and unblemished. I discovered a personal distaste for the terms. Thus I have lost our wager."

There was silence for a moment, before Denby leaped up in triumph. "He has failed. What did I tell you, sirs? Gracechurch has failed."

Lord Edward smiled like a snake. "Thus everything he has is mine, including his lovely person. As it happens, I am in need of a personal servant to empty my chamber pot."

Alden raised a brow. "But Sir Reginald is also my creditor. Doesn't *he* have a chamber pot?"

"I have already purchased from Sir Reginald your entire obligation to him," Lord Edward said. "Thus your debt and your forfeit are mine alone."

A small shock, though not one that mattered—everything was lost either way.

"My pleasure, of course," Alden said. "One chamber pot is less work than two—or do you both share the same one?"

The duke's son stood and crossed to a desk at the side of the room. "No amount of bravado can change the facts, proved here before these witnesses. You have lost. You are mine." He looked up. "Do come here, Gracechurch, and accept your punishment like a man."

"Like a man, sir? Or like a woman?"

Lord Edward's face reddened beneath the powder. He picked up a quill. "You waste your breath. I have already designed a pretty enough recompense for your loss of our wager. You may begin by signing these papers."

"Not yet." Alden raised his glass and downed the contents. "It is still two hours to midnight."

The quill bent. "At midnight, sir, you will sign. Title to Gracechurch Abbey, your funds and investments, your personal effects—"

"And my carcass, of course. The pound of flesh."

"To put your person at my disposal—for a year, shall we say?—is the added forfeit I have chosen for your losing our last wager and not redeeming it now. An unofficial form of indentured servitude—"

"I forgot to ask at the time. Careless of me." Alden strode to the window and stared out. "Though I imagined something of the kind."

"Do you wish to wager for further terms?" Lord Edward asked. "Another day to win the lady? What is her virtue worth to you, sir? One more year in my service? I might even agree. I' faith, I'm sure every gentleman here would think me most generous if I did."

The steel blade at his hip felt cold, whispering its own frost-bitten need. Alden kept his back to the room, not quite trusting himself to control his expression. "Your servant, sir—after midnight. Yet while my person is still my own, I have the rest of the company to insult—"

The door opened. Chairs scraped as men scrambled to their feet.

Alden froze where he was.

A haze of rose satin danced at the edge of his vision like a half-remembered dream to reflect its scattered petals in the window glass.

He did not have to look around. His entire body—blood, sinews, bones, skin—would know her scent anywhere.

Catastrophe coalesced into an intense, bright pain.

Juliet.

A silken curtsy rustled in his ears, then her high-heeled shoes walked farther into the room. Her scent intensified until he knew she stood directly behind him. Questions formed and broke in his mind as he waited for her public denunciation—the deserved blow to the heart. He felt stripped, without defenses, offering her only his rigid back and the broken rhythm of his breathing. It seemed to roar into the quiet night as if a lion were surrounded by jackals.

"I am given to understand by Lord Edward, sir, that you sought my acquaintance only in order to win an infamous wager," she said. "Is that true?"

He forced himself to turn.

Her hair was powdered and formally dressed. Someone had found her a new hooped petticoat. She even wore a fresh rose satin dress—an evening gown—though still five years out of date. Three white rosebuds nestled in her décolletage, a harmony to the purity of the skin beneath her gold locket. Under a fine dusting of powder, her face seemed carved alabaster.

She was perfect. A perfect court lady. Every lush curve, every female charm, offered with deliberate coquetry. Anything natural, human, vulnerable, was lost behind the flawless, artificial grooming. Alden felt almost as if he stared at her corpse.

Yet her eyes shimmered like violets, intensely blue and burning with rage.

With the grace of a queen, she flicked open a silver-and-ivory fan and arched both brows. "Lord Gracechurch? *Is it true?*"

"Madam," he said, bowing. "It is true."

Her skirts lifted as she stepped even closer. His pain intensified. Would she strike him?

"Then you might like to know this: earlier today Lord Edward Vane asked for my hand in marriage."

Constriction racked his gut as if he were about to be sick, or as if he might kill someone. His blade still hung sweetly enough at his hip. Yet he didn't seem to be able to move. His face felt rigid, as if it belonged to someone else.

"Struck dumb, sir?" Lord Edward asked. "How very entertaining! The wit of London caught at a loss for words! Perhaps you didn't know that Lady Elizabeth Juliet Amberleigh and myself were once engaged to be married?"

"Were you?" Alden heard himself ask as the words spun in his brain—*Lady Elizabeth Juliet Amberleigh?* "How odd, since the lady obviously married someone else—"

"My father's secretary." She turned away, her dress swaying in graceful folds. "Mr. George Hardcastle and I ran away together— much to my father's displeasure." Her spine like a ramrod, she moved into the center of the room. The men scrambled aside to make room for her skirts. "It created a great scandal. I'm sure everyone here has heard the story of Lord Felton's infamous daughter, except you, sir, since you were out of the country."

Alden realized then that he had snapped the stem of his wineglass. The bowl lay at his feet, slowly bleeding over the floorboards. He set the broken foot carefully onto the windowsill and tried to put together the shreds of the story.

Lady Elizabeth Juliet Amberleigh, daughter of the Earl of Felton. She had been engaged once to Lord Edward Vane. She had instead married this other man, her father's secretary, George Hardcastle, but been widowed . . .

She would marry Lord Edward now—?

Then why the devil the wager in London?

His entire world seemed to have become unglued, to be spiraling away into chaos.

Why the devil the wager?

The palm of his hand smarted. He glanced down at it. Not just wine. Blood. He had cut himself. Carefully controlling each movement, he wrapped his handkerchief about the small wound. Rage boiled just below the surface, a white-hot blaze of anger at Lord Edward Vane, at himself, at the world. If he were not careful, he might explode.

He raised his head and gazed at Juliet.

She fluttered the fan in her right hand, then moved it in front of her face.

Alden stared at her, reading the language of the ivory sticks: *Follow me!*

Follow me? Where? He looked again at her face. This time he saw it: the high courage and the hard beat of the pulse in her throat. Juliet was angry, but she was also terrified. Whatever she said, she was terrified, with a bone-deep terror. She glanced at the duke's son and her nostrils flared, just a little, while the tendons in her throat stood out like cords. He had once seen a man with that very same expression on the scaffold, before the hood was dragged over his head.

The engagement must have been announced. A great society wedding planned. Dowries and settlements agreed to—and she had repudiated a duke's son to elope with a secretary. The resulting scandal would have consumed society and the broadsheets. Had anyone ever imposed such a public humiliation on Lord Edward Vane and not paid in blood for it?

How the devil had she come here? What was Lord Edward to her? What was he to anyone who crossed him? A damned dangerous enemy!

Alden had no idea what she was doing, but she had clearly taken charge. Lord Edward stood in silence by the desk, his painted lips curved in a small smile. The other men were each caught, as if frozen, where they had been standing. Alden very deliberately relaxed his fingers. If any of these men did or said anything to increase her fear, he would have their blood, too, on his hands.

"Delightful," Alden said, shattering the silence. "An earl's daughter preferred a commoner over a duke's son! I wonder why?"

She raised both brows. "The secretary was a better figure of a man."

Lud! Alden leaned back against the wall and folded his arms across his chest. *It's your play, Juliet. Whether you hate me or not, let me know where you would lead me.*

"My dear." Lord Edward's patch flattened. "After this, there will never be another offer. Pray, think!"

Juliet curtsied. "But why should I *think*? I am here only to be decorative, am I not? In the gown you kept for me since our engagement five years ago and with my hair dressed by a woman you brought with you from town for that very purpose. Alas, I'm just an empty-headed female, whose words tumble without meaning from her mouth."

"You are naturally distressed to learn of your husband's recent death," Lord Edward said.

Recent death! Alden had thought her widowed years ago.

"So silly!" Juliet paced, fluttering the fan. "Until tonight I had thought that George lived, that I was still a married woman, until you were kind enough to tell me otherwise."

Shock compounded on shock. She had believed that her husband lived? While Alden had played out his wicked game of seduction, she had believed George Hardcastle to be alive—and only discovered otherwise tonight?

The implications spun and twisted, like mad flurries of leaves in a gale, all structure lost in turbulence. All along she had believed her husband to be alive. . . . Dear God!

To Alden's surprise, Lord Edward laughed. "A lady may follow any whim she chooses. I offer you my hand and with it, social redemption. Yet perhaps you prefer the reckless Lord Gracechurch to an honorable offer from a duke's son?"

She snapped her fan shut. "There is nothing between Lord Gracechurch and myself, Lord Edward, except a much simpler wager than yours. Alas, it remains unfulfilled—"

"And what, pray, was that wager, ma'am?" Dovenby asked. He had been standing quietly, watching their exchange.

She tipped her head. "You do agree, sir, that a lady's wager takes precedence over a gentleman's?"

Dovenby smiled. "Of course, ma'am. A lady's desires must always come first."

Skirts belling, she paced down the center of the room, like a queen with her court, until she faced the duke's son. "Lord Gracechurch and I must discover who wins our contest before you see which of you wins yours. You agree?"

Lord Edward was trapped. He nodded. "By all means, ma'am."

"What the deuce is this wager?" Denby blurted. "Damme!"

Her smile seemed almost sweet. "A chess match for each day this week, Sir Reginald, where the winner may ask for a boon. Lord Gracechurch still owes me our last game."

"I am content to concede the wager, ma'am," Alden said immediately. "Assume you have won and done as you wished from the beginning—sent me away."

"I do not wish for any such thing," she replied. "A wager is a wager. I would play our final chess match now."

Alden closed his eyes for a moment. He had no idea where this was going, yet he owed it to her to use him however she wished. To make up for what he had intended, he would owe her the world if she asked for it.

Fenborough threw back his head and guffawed. "Then you must agree, Gracechurch!" He slapped one hand on the arm of his chair. "Must he not, gentlemen?"

Dovenby took a pinch of snuff. "Definitely. You have a set, Denby?"

"A *chess* match?" Sir Reginald almost shouted. "Why the deuce should they play chess? We expected better sport than that tonight!"

Dovenby had the grace to look slightly uncomfortable. He closed his snuffbox with a snap. "One infamous wager at a time, don't you think?" He turned his head and glanced at Alden. "You demur, sir? Your last chess match with the lady?"

Juliet seemed calm, even amused, but her eyes were desperate. "It was promised, Lord Gracechurch."

Lord Edward lowered his lids and turned away. So the duke's son would not step in to prevent this. Alden glanced at the clock. Ninety-nine minutes to midnight.

It was promised.

Alden swept her a bow. "Your servant, ma'am, as always."

He did not want to play chess. Especially like this, with an audience.

When he won, what the deuce should he demand? *Take me to bed, Juliet, and save me?* He saw it then, the look on a couple of the men's faces—Bracefort and Denby. It was what they expected, anticipated with foul eagerness. A sick shiver ran up his spine. Had he ever been so damned that he had thought he could bed her here, at Marion Hall?

Fenborough walked over to a gaming table at the side of the room and flipped open the top. An inside leaf was inlaid with black and white squares. He picked up a box and shook out the chessmen, glanced at the clock, then grinned at Alden.

"If you plan to best the lady before midnight, Gracechurch, you had better start playing."

The furniture was instantly rearranged so the table stood in the center of the room with two small upright chairs on opposite sides for the players. Juliet's skirts billowed in waves of pink, brushing under the table against Alden's silk-covered shins. He felt the electric contact, silk-on-silk, like a small shock.

The audience refilled their wineglasses and gathered around. Lord Edward remained standing alone at the fireplace, a small smile fixed—like his patches—to his face.

A studied silence fell over the room.

She played a classic opening without surprises. Alden tried to plan his strategy—a fast, ruthless strike straight to victory. He knew her style of play, her weaknesses and strengths. It shouldn't be too difficult.

But what should he ask for when he won?

He could not read what she was thinking. Candlelight made a halo of her powdered hair, charmingly set with white bows. As she moved, flames glimmered around the edges of her ribbons like a miniature sunrise. Her low neckline offered shadowed curves, lush, tempting, beneath the erotic folds of the three rosebuds.

Tendrils of desire for her unfurled, blurring his judgment. He wanted her. He wanted her with an intensity that dazed him. Yet whatever the outcome of this, he would never, never be able to touch her again.

He glanced up at her shadowed face.

Her lashes formed a sweep of dusk on her cheeks. Her features were still, as if carved. It was as if all of her energies had coalesced into a bright, hard shaft of white light, focused on the board, on the grouping of pawns and bishops, knights and queens.

Where had she found the courage that enabled her to take her rage and terror to forge this intense determination? Why had she insisted on this one last game?

She made her move without looking up. He began to long for her glance, for her to meet his gaze. She did not.

Yet as black and white patterns formed and broke apart, a small frown chased the hint of a smile, then gathered again like storm clouds. Still Juliet did not look at him. Was she afraid of what her glance might reveal? That her emotions were worn too openly on her face? It seemed suddenly dishonest even to try to read them.

He looked down at her hands. A sparkle caught his eye as she moved her rook. She wore a ring. A diamond set in gold. With a sickening certainty he knew that Lord Edward had given it to her—along with the dress and the fan and the rosebuds. A ring! Would she truly marry the duke's son?

Cold sweat drenched his spine.

What should he ask for when he won?

Only that, Juliet! That you not marry this monster! You were wise enough to refuse him once and run away with your father's steward. Faith, don't marry him now!

Was he so noble? Unbidden, a small voice whispered of horrendous alternatives, temptations . . . to let her become a society wife like all those other discontented, sumptuous wives. To set her in a place where he could finally pursue his desire for her without scruple . . . where he could make her his paramour under her husband's nose. . . . And to ask—as his boon, if she became Lord Edward's wife—for a return of his fortune and his freedom?

Yet the thought of her marrying the duke's son, only to become mistress to an unprincipled rake like himself, only added more fuel to his mysterious, deep-seated fury.

He had already lost his fortune and his freedom. The outcome of this chess match could not change that now. There was only one gift he could in honor ask for when he won: that she leave Marion Hall and the company of all these dissolute rogues and never return.

She moved a knight. He glanced at the board in vague surprise. She had taken his king's bishop. It created a new balance on the board.

Well done, Juliet! I didn't see that coming—

He sat back to reassess the game. It was time for his final, fast thrust, an unassailable gambit for victory. Then, when he won, he must attempt to guess what she wanted him to claim. Idly she played with the captured bishop. In marked contrast to her ring and the lace cuffs that foamed over her round forearms, her hands were visibly worn by work. Hands that had cradled a baby chick; made wine from pale, whimsical cowslips; held hot compresses to his arm when he'd been stung by a bee.

Hands that had taken his face in a sweet caress as he had kissed her and put his soul into that kiss.

Emotions seemed to ferment and boil. He moved one heeled shoe clumsily, shaking the table. Her skirts enveloped his legs. Heat flooded his blood. Hot and cold, as if winter sprites and summer elves took turns to torment him. Devil take it! She could not marry Lord Edward, even if Alden Granville-Strachan, Viscount Gracechurch, had to commit cold-blooded murder and hang on a scaffold for his crime.

What should he ask for when he won?

A farewell kiss? Lord Edward's ring to give to Peter Primrose for Sherry? The ring and a promise that she would go back to Manston Mingate to live out her lovely, ordered country life forever? He thrust his remaining bishop along its diagonal. Lace trembled on the back of his hand. She could not go back to her secretive life in the redbrick house. Lord Edward Vane had found her. If she did not marry him, the duke's son would destroy her as surely as he had decided to destroy Alden—who was no longer in a position to help her.

Cold shivers seemed to emanate from some deep-seated reserve of ice buried in his heart. He couldn't think clearly. He knew only this: whether Juliet married the duke's son or not, if Lord Edward continued to persecute her, his new servant would undoubtedly kill him.

Juliet finished her next move and glanced up under her lashes. Distress seemed to have blinded him. Alden could no longer read her expression at all. She stood up suddenly and moved away from the table. The swish of pink satin and hooped petticoats broke the tense silence. The watching men let out a collective breath. Energy flowed suddenly, as if ice cracked to release streams of floodwater.

Bracefort pummeled one hand on the back of his chair, shaking the gilded wood. Fenborough turned and threw his glass with a crash to shatter in the fireplace. Trenton-Smith laughed aloud.

"Well done, ma'am!" Dovenby said quietly.

Lord Edward stepped forward to stare down at the board. The other men waited, visibly expectant, but he only smiled and turned away.

"Faith!" the duke's son said over his shoulder. "Very pretty."

The others broke ranks and followed Lord Edward to the wine table.

Juliet walked around the table and put her palm on Alden's shoulder. She leaned close to whisper a single word in his ear.

"Checkmate!"

CHAPTER NINE

⁂

*J*ULIET HAD WON?

Shock left Alden stunned for a moment, then incredulity gave way to a mad spurt of hilarity. He suppressed his wildly inappropriate mirth behind his handkerchief and wondered why laughter felt so deuced close to pain.

The prize was hers to demand, yet what could she ask of him now, when he had already lost everything, when he was about to become Lord Edward's property?

The duke's son turned from the wine table, glass in hand. "I am glad I did not wager on the outcome of *this* game," he said dryly. "I would have lost."

Fenborough's titter was echoed by Bracefort.

Dovenby walked away from the others to lean against the mantel. His gaze washed slowly over the chessboard, then fixed on Lord Edward's face.

"Lord Gracechurch now owes you a boon, does he not, ma'am?" the Dove asked, though he continued to look at the duke's son. "What do you demand for winning your game?"

Skirts rustled. Juliet sat down again. She closed her eyes.

Tiny sounds seemed to amplify in the silence. The slide of silk over silk. The slight clink of a wineglass. Then the hush became absolute as each man held his breath. What public humiliation would she demand? Infinite unpleasant possibilities presented themselves. Whatever she suggested, Alden would have to fulfill it, at whatever cost in degradation or embarrassment to himself.

"Madam," he said softly. "Your wish is my command."

Her lids flew open, revealing that stunning blue gaze.

"Very well, sir." She spoke clearly, concisely, without coquetry or shame. "All your worldly goods were lost last Sunday night at cards, unless you win them back by securing my favors before midnight tonight. I wish you to do so."

Pain flooded his chest.

Hideously aware of the watching faces, Alden stood up. The scrape of his chair and the rap of his heels rolled like thunder in his ears as he walked to the door. His mind seemed to have stopped working. He wanted nothing except fresh air and escape. Even the latch felt odd under his fingers, as if he had never opened a door before. He paused for a moment and stared at it.

In a susurration of skirts, she walked up behind him. He glanced down at her powdered hair. Her breath was coming too fast. The locket rose and fell over the enchanting swell of her breasts. Lovely. Desirable. Juliet.

She was willing? Why?

"Since your person is all that you have left, your favors are the forfeit I claim." She fluttered her fan and glanced at the clock. "It is just thirty minutes till midnight. That half hour is what I want."

Alden felt choked. "You would allow me to win my wager with Lord Edward?"

"I not only allow it," she replied, "I demand it."

His pulse hammered painfully. She would give him his heart's desire. She would grant him possession of her delectable body. She would save him from ruin.

She did not know about the one further stipulation of his infernal wager with the duke's son: her locket.

He tried to speak so only she would hear, but his words sizzled about the hushed room. "Juliet, don't ask this!"

She raised her chin in a gesture of pure defiance. "I insist on it."

In a sudden white rage Alden hated her. He hated the entire situation—that they should have such a conversation, like this, in public. Didn't she know she would become the sensation of the year? For a man, such an escapade was only another feather in his cap. For a woman it meant devastation. She would be a pariah. Whether he agreed or refused, she would be destroyed.

Furiously he determined to save her from this blind desire for sacrifice, turn her demands into a joke, save her reputation—if he could.

Alden bowed his head. "Ma'am, you have succeeded in achieving the unattainable: making Lord Gracechurch plead. As that was our true last wager, you have now won everything—"

Dovenby jerked, stepped back and caught his elbow on a tall candelabrum shaped like a standing goddess. The brass figure fell into the fireplace with a crash, catching a side table on its way. Another set of candlesticks started to slide. Flaming wax rolled across the floor. Heeled shoes pounded out a cacophony as men leaped to catch the flying objects and stamp out the fire.

Alden and Juliet were caught in a sudden cocoon of privacy.

"I insist on it," she repeated quietly. "I wish to throw Lord Edward's schemes in his face."

He retreated into his chilliest court manners, offering her only a tiny nod of the head, almost an insult. "You don't know how very tempting that is, ma'am. I must still refuse."

"Then I ask it to save a child named Sherry, and a deaf driver named John, and Mr. Primrose, and all of your other dependents at Gracechurch. You cannot refuse me."

"I can and do, ma'am."

"You *cannot*." She sounded furious. "When I have asked aloud in front of all these witnesses?"

"It pains me to embarrass you, ma'am, but I do not wish—"

"You selfish blackguard! Do you think I give a damn about

your wishes? When you won our previous chess games, I allowed all of your forfeits, even the Italian evening."

Alden pressed his handkerchief to his mouth, dismissive. "My forfeits were designed to enhance my wicked reputation. Your absurd wish is guaranteed to destroy the purity of yours. You are a widow. You have no one to defend or protect you. If you're determined on self-destruction, I would rather not be a party to it. I am trying my damnedest to allow you to retreat with some shred of dignity."

Her lip curled in scorn as she snapped open her fan. "Lud, sir. You have been trying to seduce me all week. Are you incapable of fulfilling that intention?"

A strange frenzy roared in his ears.

As if his body acted without conscious volition, his left hand pressed down on the door latch; the fingers of his other hand locked around her wrist. With a small cry, she shut her fan. Alden pulled her with him into the corridor. The door slammed closed behind them. The ruckus of swearing, half-drunken men was cut off, as if by a knife.

Alden barely registered the tranquil hallway. His hands closed on her bare shoulders. His palms feasted on warm skin, then slipped down over ripe, female curves. He pushed her against the wall, letting his thumb brush over one sweet arch of breast. Rosebuds shredded in his fingers, so he tore them away.

Without compunction he seized her head in both hands and brought his mouth down over hers. *Ecstasy.* He held nothing back, used no subtlety. One need overwhelmed: to invade her, possess her, transport her to the heights of sensual pleasure. To thrust into this one woman, to plunder her tenderness, plumb her mysteries and her sweetness and her heat, until she writhed and gasped beneath him—to hell with the consequences!

Overwhelmed by the stridency of his desire and his rage, he ravaged, not caring if he scorched her. Yet her mouth met his with a white-hot rage and passion of her own. It was a kiss born of desperation, seared by anger, that almost forced them both into hatred.

Alden tore his mouth away. Juliet leaned back against the wall, cheeks flushed, lips bruised. Her eyes swallowed darkness.

"You think to frighten me?" she asked. "I am not afraid of you. You are nothing but bravado and show, an empty man with an insufferable conceit. This is for me."

He stared at her pulse, rapid and hot in her throat. Hot breath roared in and out of his lungs. "Is this truly your own wish, ma'am? I thought perhaps you were Lord Edward's puppet."

He didn't know why he said it. It wasn't what he believed. If she wished to, she could throw those words in his face and walk away.

Instead she turned her head and took a deep breath. "I did not come here to Marion Hall of my own free will. Apart from what you owe me, that is the third reason you cannot refuse me."

As if a snuffer were dropped over a candle, his rage died. She faced him with that high, bright courage, tinged with a desperate bravado. It seemed essential to offer her every possible escape, to make at least that recompense for his theft of her peace.

"I am—Juliet, I am sorry. That is not how I have dreamed of winning you. There must be some other way out of this. You're an earl's daughter. Your father, surely, will protect you from Lord Edward?"

Juliet glanced back at him. She looked every inch a lady. "My father will not receive me. We have not spoken, nor corresponded, in five years. Why do you suppose I was living alone in Manston Mingate?"

A world of unspoken questions hung between them, yet throughout the house, clocks were ticking . . . *to midnight . . . to midnight . . . to midnight.*

"How did you come here?"

"Lord Edward walked into my cottage and told me about your wager in London: my body for a stranger's fortune. What an exquisite moment! To know the true reason for your attentions. To know that everything you said and did was a lie since the moment we met. Perhaps you can imagine the humiliation of that?"

"Believe it or not, an almost equal humiliation is mine." He tried to speak gently. "Thus, whatever your motives, I'm not sure I can bear the generosity of what you offer now. Why would you reward me for my venality?"

"Because Lord Edward also told me, with exquisite finesse, of my husband's death. Recently, apparently, in London. It was a . . . shock, unlooked for. While I struggled to comprehend that, he suggested I marry him. I refused, but he had menservants with him. I was thrown into a closed carriage and brought here."

"You were *kidnapped*?" His voice sounded raw.

She shuddered. "I have been washed and painted by strangers, dressed in this silk gown that he purchased for me when we were engaged to be married. He wants us to begin again."

"Then why did he arrange the unholy wager with me?"

"Lord Edward thinks he has now taught me a lesson about his power, so he can forgive my rejection of him five years ago. Perhaps he can. However, I prefer his disdain. There is only one way for me to avoid his persecution. His pride will never forgive another public insult. Win your wager and he will wash his hands of me. Otherwise, he will never leave me be."

"If he wants you so badly, why the devil did he risk the wager to begin with? I might have won."

"Might you? Lord Edward was supremely confident you would lose. Thus he could help himself to your fortune, while offering me a nice punishment." She glanced back at him, her eyes the color of bruised violets. "He learned of my husband's death and knew I was at last a free agent. He will try to force me to marry him. Nothing else will confound him, but this: you must win the wager."

Pain spread into every muscle, as if he had fenced until exhausted. The pieces fit, each move part of one overall gambit, bringing them both to this intolerable conclusion.

"With hindsight, it would appear that I was peculiarly thick-witted—"

"None of that matters." She tugged off the diamond ring and let it drop to roll away on the floor. "This is all I care about: Lord Edward will be forced to abandon his interest, if I publicly spend the next half hour in another man's bed."

It was true. Lord Edward was undoubtedly repudiating her right now and cared nothing for how it was done. He listened as a swell of masculine laughter echoed through the closed door behind him.

"Indeed, I see I am trapped, ma'am. You have pinned me and toppled my king, robbing me of dominion. The price, it seems, is my body—"

"La! The price of your original wager was mine."

"So we are both in demand tonight. Firstly, by Lord Edward. Now, me by you. You, obviously, have won."

Her neck curved like a sculpture of Venus. Her mouth was set, rigid, her back like a column.

"You cannot bear not to be in command, can you, Lord Gracechurch? You cannot bear it that the consummation of our game is due to my ultimatum, not yours, even when it is what you worked for so very hard?"

"You do not accuse me of being Lord Edward's accessory?" he asked. "You don't think I was part of this from the beginning?"

She spun about and walked away a few paces, heels clicking on the floor.

"No, of course not. Even you are not such a good actor. All you know is this: to labor, toil, slave to win yet another conquest, another lady's name to add to your endless string of meaningless encounters. Why else would Lord Edward choose you?"

The back of her neck seemed very tender beneath the clasp of gold chain that held her locket. A sweep of powdered hair rose above her bent nape, an echo of the sweetness of the curve of her shoulder. Whatever accusations she flung at him now, he de-

served. It was all true. He had accepted this profane wager. He
had intended to win it.

They both knew that he had almost succeeded.

He stepped toward her—and saw a faraway version of himself
stepping back. A large mirror gleamed at each end of the corridor.
They reflected into each other, an infinity of hallways, receding
and receding in a sparkle of candlelit glass. In each replicating
image he saw himself. The smallsword. The wide skirts of his
waistcoat and the silk-clad shape of his calves. His gilt hair worn
without powder, unless that was required for an audience with
royalty. A vanity that seemed hideous to him now, dressed like a
doll in the clothes of the court—except his jacket, of course, which
he had stripped off. Wise, always, to be able to reach one's blade
easily when surrounded by enemies.

His gaze slid away from his reflection to lock onto that infinity
of ladies, multiple images of rose silk, powdered hair, deep décolletage. Smaller and smaller, disappearing into the never-ending
corridor, each one stood with hooped skirts billowing, spine rigid
with courage. Each pair of blue eyes looked back into his with
disdain.

Juliet. He had told her he loved her. He had casually said the
same to a myriad women. Why on earth did he think he perhaps
meant it now?

"I have been asking myself what Lord Edward's real game was
all week," he said. "I do not usually lose at cards—"

"Nor with women, why is why he used you. Now it is my turn.
What matter if there is one more notch on your bow?"

"It matters, if you are not truly willing, Juliet."

Her fan snapped, the frail ivory wands splintering in her hands.
"Willing? Oh, your conceit is surely greater than that? You are
such a splendid lover, every woman is willing."

He swept her a bow. Up and down endless glass corridors,
blond heads bowed, getting smaller and smaller. He retreated into
the familiar game, the game he had perfected with so many
women.

"Then you will not change your mind?"

"I will not!"

He smiled, deliberately. "Ma'am, I desire your body with a quite reckless ferocity. I have never denied or attempted to hide that. When in addition, I stand to win back my fortune and my ancestral home, I am by no means noble enough to turn that down. I only hope you are prepared for what's about to happen."

She wavered then. He saw it in the nervous little jerk of her hand. "Prepared?"

"To share passion for our mutual pleasure, for as long as it lasts, with nothing else implied. I am ruthless about affairs. Mine are only of the body, not of the heart. That's what it means to be a rake. I will not marry you."

Rose satin flowed in the infinite mirrored images as she turned away. "Alas, but there is another condition, sir: After tonight, you will never see me again."

It was a small shock. He took the broken fan from her hands. "I did not mean anything quite so drastic. I shall delight in changing your mind."

"You will not seek me out again."

"After tonight, you may wish me to."

"But if I do not ask you, you will not contact me. I must have control in this."

He bowed his head. "Your wish is my command, Juliet."

"You are also, no doubt, experienced enough to guarantee not to get me with child?"

"Yes, I can guarantee that."

"Then, if we are to consummate our unholy treaty, we had better begin. There's not much time left."

The door flew open. Like a cork thrust forward on the wave of inebriated laughter from the room behind, Sir Reginald Denby's flushed face bobbed into the corridor.

"Well, Gracechurch? Do you agree to the lady's demands? We have a new wager riding on the outcome."

Alden swept him a formal bow. "You may tell Lord Edward

that the lady gains her desire. I trust you wagered on the winning side, sir, and that your distinguished guest is not too disappointed by his failure to win Gracechurch Abbey?" He turned back to Juliet and held out a hand. "Madam?"

Her fight for courage was palpable as she placed her fingers in his. A tremor ran up his arm. He laid his other hand over hers to keep it still. Her wide eyes glanced up into his. Alden pulled Juliet to his hip, crushing her hoops, doing his best to imbue her with confidence. Now it was too late to turn back, she was shaking like a leaf.

Sir Reginald seemed ecstatic. "Hah! I wagered you'd do it this time, Gracechurch. Deuced pretty filly, what? Would've had her myself—just for the sake of her eyes, dammit all!" He bellowed until a footman came running. "The green bedchamber, man! Show this lady and gentleman to the green bedchamber."

"I despise green, Denby," Alden said. "Did you not hear me tell Fenborough so?"

"The green room's the best—" Sir Reginald began.

Alden ignored him and smiled at the footman, standing awkwardly to one side. "You may go. The lady and I will choose our own accommodation."

The footman seemed distinctly confused. "My lord?"

Denby swayed against the wall. "Take 'em to the green chamber and be damned to it!"

Alden tapped Denby lightly on his plump cheek, not enough to hurt, just enough to humiliate. "I regret I must spoil the rest of your evening's entertainment, Sir Reginald. We'll find our own way."

Taking a tight grip of Juliet's fingers, he led her away, leaving the footman to support his drunk master as he slumped to the floor.

A stair led them up to several suites of bedrooms. Alden strode down corridors, throwing open doors, until he found what looked like a disused dressing room with a valet's sleeping couch against one wall. The couch had been made up with clean sheets. The room had no windows or other entrances, and it met one other vital criterion: a key in the lock.

He spun Juliet inside and closed and locked the door. The room plunged into instant darkness.

"Why here?" Her voice was sharp with bravado. "I have no aversion to green."

He reached for her face with both hands and cupped her cheeks while he kissed her on the forehead.

"Do you still not know what kind of men these really are, Juliet? Denby's green bedroom is infamous in the clubs of London."

"Infamous?" she asked faintly.

"For its walls and ceilings, even the bed canopy. The room is filled with mirrors, hidden doors, peepholes—"

"Why?"

"So that an audience may watch."

For a moment, her shattered breathing was her only response. "Oh," she said at last.

He groped forward in the pitch dark, still leading her by the hand. His fingers brushed over hanging garments, a dresser, a patch of plastered wall. The darkness muffled and obscured, leaving him only sound, scent and touch. Every little rustle, every sigh, magnified. Every scent, poignant, pungent, intoxicating. Every touch, a focused concentration of sensation.

The room smelled of clove-pinned oranges, sharp and sweet. Her skirts brushed against his legs, releasing the tang of lavender. Beneath all of it ran the scent of Juliet: musky, winsome, bathed in wildflower water, powdered with aromatic starch.

His senses fired.

He was aroused, alive, vibrant with desire. He felt for the couch and sat, pulling her down beside him. Her breathing sounded harsh and frightened. Her hooped skirts enveloped his legs. He held her hands in both of his and waited. Her fingers shook with a fine tremor. Her nervous breath brushed his cheek. For a moment, he thought perhaps she was crying. Everything else fled his mind but that one thought: had he made Juliet weep?

Somewhere in the house, he heard a clock strike. The single chime of the quarter hour. Fifteen minutes till midnight.

With one fingertip he traced her cheek and brushed his thumb over the curve of bone below her long lashes. Her eyes were dry, yet—somewhere in his heart—he still thought she wept.

Alden slipped one hand behind her head, feeling the stiff powder in her hair. Her stays creaked as he pulled her into his arms and laid her head to fit into the curve of his shoulder. For a few moments they sat in silence, two human beings embraced by the dark. He felt alive with a tenderness so strong that even his scorching ardor must wait in the face of it. With the fingers of one hand he smoothed the hair back from her forehead, until he heard her breathing grow quiet and steady.

"It's not too late, Juliet," he said. "You have sufficiently humiliated Lord Edward. I can take care of myself without this sacrifice."

She pulled away. He could imagine the proud tilt to her chin, the way her hands smoothed her skirts to make that slight crackle.

The air beside him cooled as she stood up.

"It's no sacrifice," she said. "I *need* you to best Lord Edward, and that is more than just bravado. Honor forbids that we lie about this."

He reached out one hand. It did not feel like chance that he immediately caught her fingers. An invisible cord stretched between them now. He could do nothing wrong.

"And what else, Juliet?" His arousal filled his world, a sharp convergence of carnality. "What else?"

"There is nothing else."

"But there is still something else that I hope is true, Juliet."

"What?" Her voice shadowed the dense, quiet darkness.

Could she feel the quick pulse of his desire? Sense the pleasure and anticipation building in his body? He gently separated her fingers and caressed each one, from knuckle to tip, lingering over the sensitive pads, letting his thumb stroke small circles in the center of her palm.

"This truth: That you would like to discover what a rake knows about women that an ordinary man can't imagine. All those long lessons in Italy. What he learned from the keen passions of the many women since, too many to count. All of that wickedness and pleasure, more intense than honest people know. Perhaps you want that, too. Just once. To sin in the dark with a stranger."

Her hand trembled. "I want only that you win your wager against Lord Edward."

He traced over the swell at the base of her thumb, around and around. "What if that isn't enough reason for us to make love, Juliet?"

"It has to be!" She sounded desperate, the tears closer to the surface.

He lifted her hand. She allowed him to carry her knuckles to his lips. Her fingers gripped his convulsively as he kissed them, one by one, carefully, fleetingly, in a caress designed to tantalize.

"Then it will be enough, because you wish it." He knew absolutely that he meant it. "So let us make this the most memorable night of our lives."

E RELEASED HER. INSTANTLY JULIET PRESSED HER HAND TO her lips. Sweet fire burned over the backs of her knuckles and licked at the center of her palm. Clenching her fingers into a fist, she stood bereft, abandoned in the night. Her corset constricted, laced tightly around her ribs where it forced up her breasts. Was that why her heart ached?

Everything she had said about the duke's son was true. It was worth anything, even this further destruction of her reputation, to disrupt his plans and force his public repudiation. Lord Edward would never forgive her, but he would also never pursue her again after what she had done downstairs.

Yet she did not intend for one moment to truly allow this rake's misuse of her body.

Her pulse raced. It felt like panic. She swallowed.

There was something else the duke's son had said to her when he'd told her about that base wager in London: *I knew Gracechurch would never succeed with you. You could neuter such a popinjay with the lift of one eyebrow.*

She had almost done it in the open carriage, when she had pretended to be unmoved by his kisses and seen that fleeting vulnerability cross his face. Let Alden Granville think he had secured her favors. Let him think he had won his wager and saved his fortune. Then let him find himself impotent in the face of her scorn! She would humiliate him, destroy him, strip him of his pride and conceit, and leave him shattered.

Black night filled her vision. She could hear his steady breathing. His keen, masculine scent filled her nostrils. She had inhaled it like fresh air when she'd first come up behind him in Sir Reginald's drawing room. The other men were doused with strong perfume. In contrast, Alden Granville carried only the bouquet of fresh water, like a fast-flowing brook, mixed with some indefinable maleness that she wanted to draw deep into her lungs. Damn him that he had used all of that beauty to deceive her!

"There can't be much time left," she said into the breathing silence.

Something clunked as it hit the floor. The sound echoed in her heart in a small burst of panic.

"What are you doing?"

"Removing my shoes," he replied calmly.

Metal made a small clink.

"What was that?"

"My smallsword. I don't usually wear it when I make love." His voice teased, full of confidence. Damn him!

"You are getting undressed?" Her voice was too high, almost a squeal. Juliet swallowed again and took a deep breath.

"Does that alarm you?"

That slight shush of satin must be his waistcoat sliding from his arms. She could imagine it, the rose-and-silver embroidery folding, dancing as it was shrugged off his strong shoulders and back.

"I don't— No, of course I'm not alarmed!" Yet she stood frozen in the dark.

Something fine and soft rustled, tiny sounds as if the bells in the pattern on his lace rang in some almost inaudible, miniature world.

"Then you will be glad to know I have now shed my shirt. My breeches come next."

Her eyes must be closed against the pitch dark, squeezed tightly shut, for she could see a vision of him moving as he had moved through her hayfield, golden and powerful. Heat flooded her, as if her skin caught fire in that imagined bright sun.

A muffled snap. Opening buttons?

The *shush* of sliding fabric. His breeches slipping down over his strong, slim hips?

The fire was spreading, smoldering up over her belly and sending long tendrils of flame deep inside. Let him build an answering fire of his own! Let him be desperate, pleading when she finally mocked and repudiated him!

The tiny shivering sound of soft underclothes being drawn down over bare muscled thighs.

His breathing, fast and strong.

Then—except for that steady cadence—silence.

"You are naked?" she asked at last.

"Yes." His voice smiled.

Scarlet shame burned over her face, but she must know. She must know that he was ready and keen and vulnerable. "You are aroused?"

"Yes."

She had to gulp down panic, try to breathe normally, but the heat was consuming her and she couldn't catch a proper breath. "You have that much desire?"

"I vibrate with desire—"

"You're invisible. I can't tell!" Her voice was tight with trepidation and this underlying, all-consuming rage.

"Yes, you can. You don't need eyes to know that I am aflame with intensity. You know it in your bones, Juliet, because you feel the same way."

Not yet! Not yet! He must be brought to the point of desperation before she took her revenge. Yet her legs wanted to fold, collapse into a heap of satin skirts and hoops. She reached out to steady herself and found nothing. She couldn't see. She didn't know where he was. She couldn't interpret the small sounds any longer.

"What happens now?" Panic vibrated in her voice. She gulped convulsively.

"Now it is up to you."

Her fingers flailed in the darkness, only to brush over something silky and soft. For a moment she was arrested in a kind of blind madness. But it was only his hair.

He was kneeling at her feet.

Juliet gasped in a breath, then another.

"Hush," he said. "Relax. Your wish is my command."

She stood stock still, her fingertips resting on those waves of unpowdered gold. Silky. Soft. Spun sunshine robbed of color by the dark, cheated of its visual splendor, leaving nothing but silken sensuality. She stroked back over his head, feeling the part and slide of that gold on her palms, the ripple of curl, then the heavy mass entrapped by the ribbon.

"Untie it, if you like," he said.

She did not want the distraction of words, only this floating sensation. She tried to focus again on her burning desire for revenge. "What?"

"My hair ribbon. You may untie it, if you like." His voice was amused, warm. "Then I will truly be—like the first man—entirely naked."

Juliet froze. She had demanded that he ravish her. When he was helpless with desire, she intended to destroy him, verbally emasculate him. Let him find himself helpless and flaccid, while she poured scorn on his impotence! He knelt defenseless at her feet. Yet she shook deep in her bones when he asked her to untie his hair?

Her breath rushed out as somewhere in the soaring confusion of heat and emotion she found the courage to continue.

"Very well. I do not— I do not have much practice at this. You will forgive my being a little clumsy?"

"It's only a ribbon."

She slipped her palms over his bent head, groping past the shock of his firm shoulder, his strong neck, his skin aflame, until her fingers closed over the ribbon.

He knelt at her feet like a knight errant and let her fumble. Juliet groped for the loops, identified the free ends and disentangled them from his thick hank of hair. She tugged until the knot slipped undone. Tentatively she ran her hands through the strands, separating them, letting the flow of liquid silk slide over her palms and between her fingers, lifting the rippling mass away from his face, smoothing it over his broad shoulders.

Heat emanated, a fine vibration, from his skin. His muscles flexed hard as he dropped his head forward, offering his vulnerable nape. Her hands slipped from his hair to feel the wonder of his muscled neck, knit so smoothly into his naked shoulders. A vision of his hot, golden skin scorched her memory. She traced over his strong upper arms, smooth as polished wood, yet vibrant, dynamic, warm with life.

Her fingers touched his face as he lifted his head. A fleeting fingertip over one cheekbone. A palm momentarily cupping the slight roughness of his jaw, then slipping down the strong line of his throat. His bright scent flooded her nostrils, bringing a new, deeper undertone. His breath came hot and fast. Yet he still knelt, not touching her. How could she bring him to the point of desperation, if he left everything to her?

"You must help me." It was almost a sob, as if her words swam in tears.

Without a word, he took one of her hands and kissed the center of her palm. The touch of his mouth burned: soft, dry lips; the moist flick of a tongue. The erotic charge made her legs shake—a simple kiss to one hand, firing every nerve with the intense expectation of pleasure.

"I must sit down," she said.

"You won't fall. I will support you."

"I am faint."

"Hush, hush. It is only the dark."

"I had not imagined so much darkness," she whispered.

"I wanted to see you," he said softly. "When I dreamed of us together, I visualized how you would look without this—" He ran his palms down over her stays. "Without these—" Her skirt rustled. "Without these—" His hands smoothed up her stockinged legs, pushing her petticoats aside.

Sharp satisfaction flooded her bones. She took one quick breath. In spite of the dark she looked down. *I saw you,* her memory whispered, *peeling off your jacket and waistcoat and shirt, cutting hay like a nature god. When later you lay at my feet, I never saw anything so beautiful in my life. And then I found out how you had deceived me!*

Over her chemise his firm palms stroked up her thighs, then down again. Ripples of feeling followed them, making her gasp. She bit her lip as his clever, experienced fingers lingered for a moment at her waist. When his hands slid back down to her ankles, her hooped petticoat came with them, falling in a heap about her feet.

"Hold on to my shoulders," he said.

"Alden—"

"Hush, Juliet. Just feel it."

He caught her hands to place them one at a time on each shoulder. His skin burned, but he felt solid, unshakable. While she clung to that strength, he lifted each of her feet in turn and slipped off her shoes. The heels clinked as they hit the floor.

Her stockinged toes curled as each sole sank into the mound of discarded petticoat. Still kneeling, he took her right foot and set it on his bent leg. Powerful thigh muscles flexed beneath her instep. His heat scorched through her thin silk stocking, sending a conflagration over her skin.

His palms rubbed firmly up her calves, stroking first one leg, then the other. Strong fingers caressed her instep and rubbed heel and ankle, only to move higher, and higher again, until he stroked the back of her knee and the inside of her garter. Intense pleasure surged in waves. She moaned into the darkness, clinging to his shoulders in case the intense delight turned her legs into straw and made her forget her purpose.

Not yet! Not yet! Let him think he had won!

Yet she moaned again as his fingers touched her naked thighs.

"May I remove your stockings?" His voice was husky, choked.

Only her stockings—a reprieve! So not yet! "Yes. Yes. If you like!"

Not yet!

Deftly he untied the knotted ribbons and slipped them away. His palms caressed her naked calves as he slowly rolled down each stocking. One by one he slid them off over her toes and set each foot back down on her crumpled petticoat. Cool air kissed her bare skin, but beneath it a white-hot fire consumed her to the bone.

Soon! Soon! Before the body's passion swept her away—

His fingers stroked her bare instep, making her want to sob with pleasure. His mouth followed, kissing over her ankle and up, up, until his lips scorched that tender, intimate spot at the back of her knee.

She cried out, an inarticulate groan.

"Alden—!"

His palms slid up her legs. Her skirts were carried with them as he stood.

Chemise, petticoat, and gathers and gathers of satin bunched and crushed in his hands to fold against her belly. Tiny blue lights crackled suddenly, small leaps of electricity dancing over her skirts, flickering about her petticoats, as if sparks leaped from his naked flesh to hers. Answering flames roared in her blood as his fingers traveled firmly up the backs of her thighs to cup her bare bottom.

Blue sparks danced madly in the dark. Her heart thundered. The scent of lavender and cloves mixed headily with musk and that deeply satisfying, clean male scent that was his alone.

He held her upright, her skirts crushed between them, while his fingertips slipped down over her buttocks. Electric intensity sparked after them, igniting passion, concentrating everything into one bright, hot center of exquisite pleasure.

"Alden!"

He closed her mouth with a kiss.

Juliet kissed back, her mouth invaded, her nakedness open to his fingers' clever exploration. Her breasts ached. Her skin burned. She flamed in a conflagration of glittering, blue-sparking skirts, supported against him, held up only by his strength. Her hands closed on his shoulders, her fingertips sank into firm skin and muscles, while tiny blue crackles fired in her nerves, popping like little cannon.

His hand slid under one thigh, lifting it in a flashing rustle of petticoats. He hooked her knee over his naked hip, pushing aside skirts as his fingers stroked her belly, then dropped lower to where she was moist and willing. Faith! She was more than willing, carried away on a rush of sensation, longing for the heavy weight of him, for his invasion.

Now was the moment to deny her own passion and destroy all of his! To leave him impotent, begging, mortified. *Now!*

Juliet tore her mouth away and dropped her forehead to his shoulder, sinking her nails into his arms. He lifted her higher. A velvety hardness nudged her naked flesh, seeking the intimate yielding between her legs.

Now! She must say it now: *You buffoon! You think that I want you? You think I am eager for you? Is this the vaunted potency of a rake? You leave me cold, indifferent. Hah! No wonder you have used so many women. Obviously you cannot satisfy any of them—*

Yet her breath clamored in her lungs. Her gasping tongue wouldn't work. Dense, velvety darkness crackling with flickers of blue flame consumed everything. The roaring burn of her own blood deafened. Somewhere deep in her belly the need demanded—for more, more of those acute sensations, that rush of pleasure and moisture and swelling that demanded to be fulfilled. Essential need overwhelmed her, engulfed her in desperation.

He lifted her higher. Intimate heat flared. Her body yearned to welcome his.

"Your wish is my command," he said—a whisper, vulnerable, human, tender in the dark, asking permission. "Say yes, Juliet."

Now! Her lips moved. Her tongue brushed over his hot, bare shoulder. She lifted her head as frantic yearning culminated in her mouth to form one simple word. The rest fled—all of her revenge, all of the cruel things she had planned to say—gone like dry grass before a flame.

"Yes," Juliet said.

Her toes lifted from the floor as with one lunge he thrust inside, filling her.

Somewhere in the darkness a bell began to ring. The sound saturated the dark room, reverberating in her shattered mind. *One . . . two . . .*

He held her still while the clock chimed. The blue crackles disintegrated, leaving only pitch blackness. The burning stretch between her legs consumed her, creating ripples of unbearably sweet sensation. He held her impaled there, taking her weight while he filled her with ecstasy. She dropped her head against his shoulder and felt the fine fire of his skin on her face.

The chimes rang in her ears . . . *eight . . . nine . . . ten . . .*

Her heart thundered, matching the tolling of that distant alarm. Juliet clung to him, her thighs locked about his hips, her soul inundated with rapturous sensuality.

His lips moved over her cheek, delicately, then he kissed her once, quickly, on the mouth.

. . . eleven . . . twelve.

"Midnight," he whispered.

CHAPTER TEN

HE LOWERED HIMSELF BACK TO THE COUCH, CARRYING HER with him so she straddled his hips, her skirts spread over their thighs. Her fingers clung, absorbing the perfection of stark muscle and tendon, while his hands kept her upright, supporting her as he held her impaled. Her whole existence concentrated on that one pulsing fire where their bodies joined, a focus of spellbinding sensation. Then his hands slid away, freeing her to move.

She began to rock her hips, seeking more—more intensity, more exhilaration. Her skirts crunched in a new haze of blue crackles. The rush of their hot, mingled breath clamored in her ears. Forever, forever, so long that she thought she might dissolve.

The sweet tension built. Musk and cloves. Running water and lavender.

Liquid fire.

Her womb convulsed, over and over again. Until at last she felt the rush of such an intense pleasure, she thought she might die.

"Juliet!"

The single name, *her* name, mingled with her own inarticulate cry as at last his powerful contractions fused with hers.

Afterward he cradled her in his arms for a long time, saying nothing, her head on his shoulder. Slowly he released fastenings, untied laces. Every element of her clothing surrendered to his knowledgeable fingers. Her dress slipped away, her white petticoat, her stays—each garment gave up its hold on her limp body.

Sometimes he gently rolled her in order to pull away the masses of fabric. She let him do it, malleable as a kitten, until finally she curled against him clad only in her thin chemise, breasts crushed against his chest.

In her belly, in her languorous limbs, in her heart, all her distress had dissolved into deep satisfaction.

He pulled a soft cover from the couch and wrapped them in it together.

"That was not what you intended, was it?" he asked.

"No." She kissed his shoulder. His flesh tasted salt on her lips.

"I thought you would reject me. I tried to allow you every opportunity to do so."

"Yes."

"I even put you on top, in command."

"I know."

"I could not believe, after you discovered what I had done, that you would be so generous."

She trailed her fingers over his chest. "I did not intend to be."

"You are not unhappy?"

"I don't know." Her rational mind had to wake up, with reluctance, as if from some spellbinding dream. "I should be. I felt your—" She bit her lip. "Did you lie when you said there could be no chance of a child?"

"I took precautions." His voice rumbled beneath her ear. "Prettily tied on with blue ribbon, though you couldn't see that, of course."

"Oh." George had never used any such thing. He had wanted, without success, to give her a baby. "So you were not *quite* naked?"

"It's the kind of thing rakes know about." He kissed her gently on the forehead. "Yet you risked even that. Why?"

"I wanted you to win your wager."

"No, you didn't." His lips touched her hairline, then teased at the corner of her eyebrow. "Can't you admit you would make love just for yourself?"

She snuggled closer to his warmth, running one hand over his delectable male skin. "Why? I thought you would rather believe that I did it for you."

His laugh reverberated. "Lud! You certainly don't owe me anything. Yet we don't need a cause to make love, Juliet. Desire is reason enough."

She raised up on both elbows, whispering into the dark. "Desire cost me everything I was born to—wealth, security, a good marriage—and brought me nothing but poverty and hard work. Why do you think I am interested in desire?"

"Because that's human nature. It's nothing to be ashamed of."

"Desire made me run away with George."

"I thought you fled Lord Edward."

"There was that, of course. Something about him terrified me. But I also wanted George to put his hands on my naked body. I longed for it. Does that horrify you?"

His hands caught in her hair, pulling her head down until his lips caressed her ear, then slid down the side of her neck. "No, it delights me."

She digested that in silence for a moment. "You don't think such desire wrong in a female?"

"We are all pleasure-seeking creatures, Juliet, men and women. Shall we prove it again?"

She had no denials left. This time it was languid, slow. He explored every inch of her body. She surrendered all control to his clever hands and seeking mouth.

All those long lessons in Italy. What he learned from the keen passions of the many women since, too many to count. All of that wickedness and pleasure, more intense than honest people know. Perhaps you want that, too. Just once. To sin in the dark with a stranger.

Yet he no longer felt like a stranger. He felt like a lover, more intimate, more trusted than she had ever imagined. This time their mutual climax rolled in long, slow waves, like a moon-dragged pulse through an ocean of ecstasy.

Juliet lay sprawled, satiated, cocooned in warmth, his arms around her, while she drifted in and out of sleep. Whenever she woke, he kissed her until her ardor fired again, only to find him already erect every time. In some deep, liberated place in her soul, a bright spurt of laughter surprised her. Smiling into the velvet night, she slid her hand down his belly and closed her fingers about his hardness.

"I had wanted to prove you impotent." She rubbed her nose against his neck. "I did mean to spurn you. I thought I could rob you of this." She stroked her fingers down the shaft. It seemed such a mystery, the heavy weight, both hard and smooth, the tender skin over the tip. "Now I see how absurd a thought that was."

He laughed, pulsing in her hand. "Why absurd?"

"Because I don't think a rake can fail—"

Soft laughter shook him. "Even a rake is just a man, Juliet." He arched his back, like a purring cat. "Ah, don't stop!"

The vulnerability of it caught at her heart, that he abandoned any defenses, trusted her so intimately.

"But a rake must know more than an ordinary man. So what is the secret? I had a husband for six months. You and I haven't done anything different than what I did with him—"

"Yet it felt different?"

She blushed, burning in the darkness, and ducked her hot face against his chest. "Yes. All those lessons in Italy? Is there a secret?"

He pulled her face up to his and kissed her. "There's only one secret, Juliet, and that is to think about the other person's pleasure more than your own. I like to please women." He rolled her over and began to tease a nipple with his forefinger. "I like to discover my lover's sweetest spots—sweetest to her, not to me, though they become like honey to me when I find them."

She writhed beneath him, laughing. *A sweet spot!* This time when he dressed his penis in its protective sheath, she helped tie the ribbons, fumbling in the dark, laughing with him, ecstatic over his silly jokes about jackets for little men.

"A very *large* little man," she said, almost hysterical.

"You think . . . I am . . . large?" He was gasping with laughter. "Ah, Juliet, you know just how . . . to flatter a man!"

"You are much bigger than George. I didn't know men could be so different."

"Do you like it?" He was suddenly serious.

Heat fired from her cheeks to her toes. "Lud! I like it— You fill me—"

"Hush," he said. "I think we must make s. .. Let me check that it's really a good fit."

Juliet lay back and focused on that sweet stretch as he eased inside, then buried himself once again to the hilt.

She awoke again later, drifting in a warm sea of safety. He still held her tightly. One palm rubbed slow circles over her back, delicious, kind, comforting.

"It was," she said sleepily.

"Was what?"

"A good fit."

His hand stopped, then resumed its slow circling. "Will you admit to desire now? Or must you still have a noble cause?"

She tried to find a genuine answer, searching her heart. One truth surfaced that she had already looked at, even mentioned. There was far more at stake this night than desire. It was part of what had given her courage.

"I had a little brother. He died. At least by winning your wager we have just saved the world of a small boy who still lives."

"Sherry? He's a stranger's bastard baby. Why should you wish to save him?"

The captivating circles rubbed up to her nape. She wanted to purr.

"I know there's no connection between the children, nothing that links them, but it seems right to save a little boy when we can. So think, if you like, that I do this because Sherry reminds me of Kit." The darkness and warmth breathed security, a refuge from the harsh realities of daylight. "My little brother, Christopher, Viscount Kittering. We all called him Kit."

"Can you tell me what happened?" The question was gentle.

It was something she had never told anyone except Miss Parrett. The pain of it festered like an unhealed wound. Yet she felt safe with this man who lay naked in the dark, holding her languid body against his. "He was seven when he drowned. It was my fault."

The words dragged out, dropping one by one into the safe cocoon of darkness. "Six months after I ran away with George, we wrote to my father. We hoped for his forgiveness. I had sold most of my jewelry by then, and George thought Lord Felton would relent, give us my dowry, and set us up in the world. At the same time I wrote to my mother, asking her to meet me secretly at an inn. I missed her. I thought she could intercede with my father. She brought Kit with her. She wanted me to leave George and come back home."

"But you refused."

"I was *married*."

His fingers stroked her hair. "You believe so strongly in marriage?"

"I made vows and paid a very great price for them. I would never be unfaithful. If George lived, I would not be here now."

"Yet you and he separated?"

"He left me. The night I met Kit and my mother that last time, there was a terrible storm. Their road home went through a ford. In the dark and the rain, their carriage overturned. They were all drowned, even the coachman."

He lay silent, his warmth and strength encircling her, but his fingers spoke of tenderness, of sympathy.

"There was no action left after that," she said. "Only blame. I don't know if my father would ever have accepted my eloping with George. My mother thought that he might, but after she and Kit died, George knew that any chance of wealth with me was ruined. So he left. I never saw him again."

"He abandoned you *then*? When you had just lost Kit and your mother?"

"It hardly mattered. I only wanted to die. My desire had destroyed my whole family."

His lips kissed away the sudden burn of tears. "Hush, hush. You had a right to your desire, to your own existence. You did not destroy your family. Fate did that. Fate and bad fortune."

"But they still died. My father still lives alone with a broken heart. I have nothing left but my locket."

His hands stilled. "Your *locket?*"

The gold felt warm and smooth in her hand as she touched it. "My mother gave it to me when Kit was born. It's a Felton heirloom, said to contain the key to a treasure. It became a symbol, perhaps, of how much we all loved each other, especially of how much I loved my little brother. Kit and I played endless games based on some funny old writing engraved inside. I have nothing else left."

She heard his breathing, broken by distress, but he said nothing.

"Do you understand now?" she asked. "Whether we admit to desire or not, it was vital that we do this for Sherry—the tiniest recompense, perhaps, for what happened to Kit."

His chest heaved as he took a deep breath. "What we did, what is happening between us, has nothing to do with Sherry or with Kit—any more than it has to do with my brother. There is no recompense for our loss, for their deaths. But our life goes on, Juliet. *Life!* We are *alive!*"

His hands reached for her jaw and held her face captive for a moment. Then his lips burned down over hers, in passion, in heat, almost in anger. Was grief so close to rage? Was desire more intense than either?

Without hesitation, Juliet kissed back, reaching for him with both hands, for the splendor of his body, for that glorious submersion in passion.

Later she dreamed that they talked in the grape arbor, where he held her close on his lap and asked her again: *Do you like it?*

In her dream she answered with the truth she could not quite admit to awake: *I have spent five years knowing that my husband lived. As long as he was alive, the future had closed all its doors. Those five years were lived in celibacy. Do you think they were lived without desire?*

So you do admit to desire? his dream image asked.

I have just given you my soul for it. Now I know that George is dead, I am free, Alden Granville. Free to love again.

Do you love me?

I love you, her dream self said. *Though it breaks my heart.*

ALDEN WOKE UP TO DARKNESS, BUT HE KNEW IT WAS MORNing. Juliet's steady breath fluttered against his shoulder. He reached for the delectable curve of her flank. How many times had they made love? How many times had he poured all of his passion, his ardor, his very essence into her lush body? He'd lost count. But then, he never counted.

Her flesh felt cool under his burning palm. To his surprise, his desire remained banked, only a smoldering fire. Why did he feel so disoriented, giddy, as if his mind were not quite his own? He slipped his hand away from her soft skin and sat up. A headache slammed into his skull. He shivered. Lud! Was he unwell? Another shiver racked him. He staggered from the bed. The door opened onto a silent corridor, lit by the dull light of a rainy morning. His naked flesh flamed in the cold air.

Fever!

He closed his eyes for a moment and remembered himself soaked to the skin, getting Sherry into his bath, making sure that the child took no chill. All the while, like a fool, he had worn his own damp clothes, his wet hair plastered to his head, until his blood ran like ice in his veins.

He shuddered, naked and burning. Tremors ran across his shoulders.

It was vital that we do this for Sherry.

Bloody hell! The wager was not over yet. Somewhere in the house Lord Edward waited for his proof.

Alden stumbled back into the little room. In the beam of gray light from the open doorway, Juliet slept like a child, a tiny smile curving her lips. Something moved in him, something that carried with it a strange thud of panic. He touched her shoulder. His hand shook, clumsy. She didn't wake.

I have nothing left but my locket.

It would be a madness to lose the wager over this one last thing. The panic beat harder, fear writhing in his heart as if he were undergoing some odd transformation. He fought it desperately. He was a rake. It was his vocation to use women.

I wanted you to win your wager.

A sudden sweat broke over his skin. Alden gathered his clothes from the floor. He found his handkerchief and wiped his face, before he strode to the door and tossed his clothes onto a chair in the corridor. He felt light-headed. His skin burned. His muscles wept over throbbing, aching bones. He stood in the doorway for a long minute, watching the rain trickle down the windows, hearing its dull hiss echo about the quiet house, while the fever played merry hell with his body.

He must win the wager!

She made a small sound. He spun about, but she had only turned in her sleep. In long drifts of powdered tangles, her hair spread over the cover. Alden strode back into the little room.

Wake up, Juliet! Tell me to go to hell!

Naked, shaking, he stood over her, willing her to wake. In her sleep she made a small gesture with one hand, as if to push him away. So they had shared a night of passion! What the hell did it mean more than that?

Cursing silently, he unsnapped her gold chain. Her locket flamed in his palm as if it would burn to the bone.

Next door he found an empty bedroom. A half-full pitcher stood on the washstand. Cold water scorched over his face and limbs as he ducked his head in the basin, then shook himself like an otter. With clumsy fingers he dried himself and donned his clothing. His face looked flushed, eyes glittering, in the mirror

over the dresser. In an ice-cold rage he searched the dresser drawers. He found powder and rouge, even a selection of patches in a
small tin.

The powder looked stark, too white. He spread rouge along his
cheekbones and added a large patch to distract attention from his
fever-bright eyes. A little cold water smoothed his hair before he
tied it back. As a last gesture, he shook out his lace and strapped
on his smallsword, before thrusting stockinged feet into gilt-
heeled shoes.

He spun around and stared into the mirror.

Alden Granville-Strachan, Viscount Gracechurch, stared back.
The rake who made a habit of breaking hearts. The man who had
wagered his own ruin against a woman's virtue and won.

Very deliberately he picked up Juliet's locket from the dresser
where he'd lain it. It was obviously more than a hundred years
old, with an odd design on the back. He wondered briefly if there
was anything inside—a lock of hair, a miniature painting. It
would be a violation of both honor and her privacy to look. How
simple to resist life's smaller temptations!

Her gold jewelry slipped unopened into his pocket.

*A*LDEN FOUND LORD EDWARD SITTING IN THE PARLOR WHERE
he'd played chess with Juliet. The pungent odor of coffee
glazed the stale smell of drink and perfume from the previous
night. Fingers steepled together, the duke's son lounged in a chair
by the empty fireplace and stared into the grate. He did not appear
to have gone to bed at all. On a side table at his elbow, something
glittered, sparkling in the gray light.

His rings! Alden had given them to Sir Reginald in London,
then forgotten all about them. His heels clicked on the floor as
he strode into the room.

"Good morning, Gracechurch." Lord Edward spoke over his
shoulder. "Coffee? Help yourself."

"No servants this morning, sir?"

"Surely you would not wish Sir Reginald's staff to witness our upcoming exchange?"

The mad temptation was to draw his sword, to silence that smooth drawl forever. Instead Alden poured coffee from the silver pot on the sideboard. "Why not? We had enough witnesses last night."

"When they had a purpose. Lud, sir! You make me nervous. You will be kind enough to lay aside your blade?" The duke's son watched Alden unbuckle his sword and set it down. He tapped at the rings. "Thank you. Here are your trinkets, sir."

Carrying his coffee, Alden walked to the fireplace and picked up the rings. "You are confident I have now redeemed them?"

"Of course. You have the locket?" The duke's son smiled. "Obviously you have had the lady—" Dried powder was caked on his face. "It was sweet?"

His rings slipped one by one into their familiar places. Alden spread his fingers and looked down at them. Either that, or make a fist to wipe the sneer off Lord Edward's face. "Wealth is sweeter."

"Yet you do not in truth have much wealth, do you, Gracechurch? You are sadly in debt, even now."

"My affairs are my own."

"Only after we have settled our wager. The locket, sir."

Alden picked up his coffee. Its heady fragrance filled his nostrils as he took the locket out of his pocket and dropped it onto the table.

"You give it up so easily? Have you no care at all for the lady?"

"I am a rake." With a certain ferocious satisfaction, he reveled in the statement. Of course it was true! "Do you really believe I have a heart?"

Lord Edward laughed. "No, sir, I am sure you have not." He reached inside his jacket and withdrew a handful of paper slips. One by one he tore them to shreds, then pulled out his betting book. He wrote in it, then handed it to Alden. "Satisfied?"

Alden scrawled his signature across the page. The flutter of torn paper fell about his feet like snow. He took another sip of coffee, the burning liquid icy in his scorched throat.

"There is also the matter of the promised five thousand."

"A banker's draft will be delivered to you tomorrow." Lord Edward held out a note. "My vowel in the meantime."

Alden set down his cup. The fever burned along his bones. Infuriatingly, his hand shook. "You may keep it."

The duke's son raised both brows. "Why?"

"In trade for the lady's jewelry. I have a collection of such mementos. It would make a pretty, if trifling, addition." It was a lie, of course, though not one that mattered.

Lord Edward slapped one palm down hard over the locket. "Not for sale, Gracechurch!"

Alden walked away to stare out of the window. His head thundered. The blood scalded in his veins. Beneath his fine jacket, the rose-and-silver waistcoat and all of his lace, he was sweating like a racehorse. God prevent him from passing out now!

He tried to concentrate.

"Everything is for sale, sir. It is just a matter of agreeing on a price."

"Lud! She has cozened you. You do give the lady your heart. How about your pretty hand in marriage?"

It was still raining outside, a dull drizzle, soaking the gardens. Water glistened over statues and topiary. "The lady is not interested in marriage. You hadn't noticed?"

"Faith! You refer to my offer yesterday?"

"You asked her to marry you. I am touched."

Lord Edward threw back his head and roared. "*Marry* her? I never had any intention of marrying her. I wanted her once—if you think she is delectable now, you should have seen her at sixteen—but now? Do you think I would stoop to sully myself with George Hardcastle's leavings? The man's grandfather was a butcher."

It was almost impossible to think through the pounding headache. His joints ached as if they were being attacked by a woods-man's saw. *Concentrate!*

"Then may I inquire why you asked her?"

"To frighten her."

"So your renewed pursuit was a bluff? I confess, sir, you leave me nonplused."

"My dear Gracechurch! Pray do not play the innocent with me. You may have no soul, but I expect you to understand revenge."

Alden pulled out his handkerchief to blot his dry, burning mouth. "Sadly, sir, your argument loses me. I have never pursued anything as tawdry as revenge."

"No, you would rather pursue women, which made you perfect for my purposes."

"The card game I was careless enough to lose in London?" He leaned back against the wall and crossed his arms over his chest to hide the shaking in his limbs. "Delighted to oblige, of course, but you will assuage my curiosity. *Was* the wine drugged that night?"

"Alas, sir, hardly a question one gentleman asks another."

"Yet you will agree that I was oddly light-headed, as you will concede that you allowed me to win in our little encounter with rapiers that morning?"

"I will even admit that you were a most worthy opponent, my dear Gracechurch. I have rarely been pressed so deuced hard. But certainly you would not have prevailed unless I had allowed it."

"How foolish of me not to question that at the time—nor to question my odd lack of judgment that night."

"You were foolhardy," Lord Edward said.

"Indeed. But you had to make certain of getting me in debt, and surely not even you would descend to marking the cards? Can you tell me your real purpose?"

Lord Edward had flushed beneath his paint. "By all means. I wanted the locket."

"If you had wanted only the locket, you could have taken it. After all, you compelled her to come here last night."

"Deplorably crude, but necessary. Will you call me out over it?"

Alden tipped back his head and studied the ceiling. Painful spasms attacked his spine. The patterns in the plaster seemed to move by themselves. *Concentrate!*

"I am tempted. In spite of your admittedly superior skill with a blade, I am tempted."

"But you will not?"

"A duel and its cause can hardly be kept secret. Sadly, I never make public my dealings with women: a caprice, but one I believe I am known for. Meanwhile no one else will speak of the events of last night. To do so would be to spread a tale in which Lord Edward Vane looks the fool, something which—after the scandal you survived five years ago—you will never tolerate again. You have thus already sworn all your cronies to secrecy, even though it leaves the lady's reputation untarnished."

"I care nothing for her reputation. She may keep it with my blessing."

"I thought so. Therefore, no duel—as you planned."

"Tell me, Gracechurch, how did you ever lose a chess game—especially to a woman? I would like to match you some time myself."

The longing to simply lie down was overwhelming. What a time to contract an ague! "We are playing right now, Lord Edward."

"But this time checkmate is mine. I have the locket. A worthless trinket, of course, but what do you offer me for it?"

He was running out of time. There was no choice but to move straight to the end gambit. "My person."

"Hah!" Lord Edward's coffee spilled to the floor as he flung both hands wide and stood up. "Not Gracechurch Abbey? Not your scattered investments? Only your person?"

The stain spread like blood over the floorboards. The cup had been full. Alden had no collection of ladies' trinkets. He wasn't even sure any longer why he'd said it. "There are others in need of the Abbey."

"But no one needs you? I am charmed."

The truth of it burned into his heart. No one needed him. Not his mother, not Sherry, not even Juliet.

"My person is my own to give or take as I wish. I am offering it."

"You are perceptive, sir." Lord Edward walked closer and stared into Alden's face. "You have hit upon the one thing that does indeed tempt me."

Alden set one hand on the shutter to steady himself. "Then we have a bargain?"

The duke's son stepped close enough to touch. "No, sir. You entirely misunderstand my revenge. You were never the target, only the tool. She ran away with a butcher's grandson and publicly rejected me. Now it is her turn to taste betrayal."

The bitter taste of the coffee filled his mouth. "Betrayal?"

"Of course. Why else did she sacrifice herself last night? She loves you. Isn't that what all your women do? Give body, heart and soul to the heartless, soulless Lord Gracechurch?"

"Except this lady. She had other motives."

"Don't underestimate your power, sir! You guess quite correctly what I would like from you—it is what everyone wants, man or woman, and my own eclectic tastes are well known, I believe. Yet, alas, I will forgo even that to know her pain when she finds out what you have done." Lord Edward held up the locket. It glimmered in the dull light as he tossed the gold disk, caught it, and thrust it into an inside pocket. "You took the only things she cares for in this world: her honor and her locket. She loves you and you betrayed her. What's more, you betrayed her to me."

Alden managed to walk to the couch. He clutched the carved back with one hand as he slid onto the brocade seat. The floor spun. Chair legs seemed to dance together in mad patterns of gilt and wood. The blood-dark stain had run into the edge of the fender.

"About the wine that night in London—" He swallowed, pressing his lace handkerchief to his lips. Shivers consumed him. "This coffee, also?"

Lord Edward's voice seemed to boom and echo as if from a great distance. "Perhaps. Yet I am surprised to see you so incapacitated—"

Alden laughed then. "You are in luck today, Lord Edward. Nature conspires to help you. I believe I have influenza."

Heels clicked on the floor. A strong hand set icy fingers on his forehead.

"Lud, sir! You are burning! Allow me to call your carriage."

It had been madness to risk the coffee, even so little, on top of his illness. Alden leaned back, allowing the couch to support him. "I prefer to stay."

Bony fingers ran down the side of his face, outlining his cheek. Lord Edward leaned closer. "I am ecstatic that you so enjoy my company." Vicious fingers locked in his hair, pulling his head back.

"If you kiss me," Alden said, "you will have to kill me, for I will certainly murder you later."

"Oh, Gracechurch! So passionate! I like that in a man." A sharp-edged ring briefly scraped his lips. Alden tasted blood. "Your carriage awaits. Your carriage, your deaf man John, and the rest of your useless dependents: the bastard tutor, the bastard child you keep so carefully at the Abbey, your mad mother. Your entire life awaits you—except Juliet, who will never speak to you again. By the way, I lied about the locket."

Alden stared up at the powdered face and cruel, rouged mouth. "You do *not* want it?"

"Oh, I want it, but I lied when I said it was worthless."

Someone knocked. Four footmen entered. At a nod from the duke's son, they hoisted Alden between them. It was useless to struggle. Yet he struggled. A chair splintered. A man reeled back, cursing. But after a sadly deficient amount of damage to the room, one of the footmen bent Alden's right arm behind his back and they carried him to the door.

Untouched, Lord Edward followed. A cold drizzle burned on Alden's face, wetting his hair and clothes, before they thrust him into the waiting carriage with two footmen to restrain him. Someone tossed his smallsword onto the seat opposite.

The duke's son rested one hand on the open carriage door. "I lied about some other things, too."

The fever rang in waves. Each raindrop bit like acid into his skin. Yet Alden called on what was left of his strength, measuring distances, weighing the deadly grip of the footmen.

"What else is there?"

"I' faith, Gracechurch! I thought you a better player than that. You didn't guess my two little falsehoods? The first: the locket contains the key to a fortune beyond anyone's wildest dreams."

"And the other?"

The carriage lurched as the horses started to move. Alden wrenched one arm free and reached for his sword, just as Lord Edward slammed the door.

"I lied about her husband's death. I just came from London where I spoke with the man. George Hardcastle is alive and well, though sadly short of funds. Furthermore, the butcher's grandson is most anxious to be reconciled with his faithless wife. Checkmate again, sir!"

Alden dropped his suddenly irrelevant blade.

Chapter Eleven

A SMALL NOISE WOKE HER. SOMETHING MOVED, CASTING A shadow.

"Alden?" she asked.

"Alas, ma'am," a man's voice said, not unkindly. "Lord Gracechurch has left."

She felt dazed, bruised with lovemaking and sleep. *"Left?"*

"I understand he has returned to the Abbey." Robert Dovenby stood in the open doorway, silhouetted against the dull light from the corridor.

Juliet clutched the cover to her breasts and sat up. "Gracechurch Abbey?"

"You will, no doubt, also wish to leave—before the rest of the household is awake?"

A defiant swell of laughter welled up in her chest. What else had she expected? That he would be there as she awoke to greet her with kisses? That he would swear undying love? He was a rake. This was what rakes did. Yet she felt ill, as if she'd been hit.

"I thought," she said acerbically, "that he would at least have had the courage to make his excuses in person. No matter. I should indeed like to go home. I have three cats to take care of."

Dovenby bowed. "My carriage is at your disposal, ma'am. As soon as you are dressed, take the second to last door on the right

in the hallway outside. It leads to a servants' stair. I shall wait at
the bottom."

"I am to creep out as if I am ashamed?"

He glanced away, the dull light catching his profile. He was a
handsome man, with something secretive and powerful about the
nose and jaw. "As you prefer, ma'am. Lord Edward Vane has already left. The others still sleep. However, Sir Reginald is downstairs. I fear he may attempt to offer you some insult."

"Because I have now publicly branded myself a harlot?"

"Because he is a boor, ma'am, with a sore head from too much
drink."

Juliet pressed her forehead to her upraised knees. What had
she thought? That Alden Granville would somehow rescue her
from this? That—in spite of what he'd said—he would offer marriage?

"You do not think, Mr. Dovenby, that discretion is irrelevant
now? When the other gentlemen reach London—"

"They will say nothing. Lord Edward has sworn all of us to
secrecy."

She looked up, surprised. "Then why—?"

"I have no idea. However, I advise discretion with Sir Reginald.
I would really rather not feel obliged to call him out."

"So I am to creep away to save *you*?"

Dovenby smiled. It was a surprisingly nice smile. "If you like."

He bowed again and left.

Juliet looked about. Her clothes lay piled beside the bed where
Alden had left them, after—

Tears burned, scalding. Those feelings! The languorous pleasure alternating with such sweet, rapturous intensity. She had
never dreamed, never imagined—

Damn him! Damn him and his lovely, lovely way with women!
She put one hand to her throat.

Her locket!

The tears stopped as if dried in a hot desert wind. Rage swept, scouring like a sandstorm. The force of it left her wanting to retch.

He had taken her locket?

Twenty minutes later she stepped into Dovenby's carriage.

*T*RAINED ALL THE REST OF THAT DAY. JULIET PACED ABOUT HER empty house.

He had taken her locket!

Dovenby had sent her home. He had not accompanied her himself. With no one to tend it, the fire in the kitchen had gone out. No hot water. No hot food. She didn't care. Perhaps she would never eat again. Meshach, Shadrach and Abednego stared at her with accusing eyes. Not even a meal of meat scraps compensated for their feline resentment at the lack of a fire. She fed the chickens, returning with wet feet to the cold, damp house.

Since I came back from Italy, ladies have berated me, cursed me, even tried to have me killed—or their husbands have.

She had no husband. She would have to kill him with her own two hands.

Juliet laughed. Then worried by her own bitterness, she set about building a fire.

It was over. The entire mad episode was over. Lord Edward would never approach her again. Neither would Alden Granville. She had his word on it.

It was over.

Even the sunshine. The rain came on harder that night, threatening to blow a gale. Water pelted the roof and windows, leaking onto the sills. For the sheer comfort of it, even though it was an outrageous extravagance, she lit a fire in her bedroom, hauling the fuel upstairs in a basket. Drops ran spitting down the chimney. Juliet huddled under her covers and shivered.

He had peeled away her defenses, laid open her soul, discovered what she cared for most in the world, then stolen it. She would hate him until she died. No, he didn't deserve the passion of hatred. She would regain perspective. She would be superbly indifferent.

Juliet turned over in bed. Oh, God. Oh, God. What did it matter what she felt or did? He would neither know, nor care. She would never see him again.

He had taken her locket!

Wind howled in the chimney and rattled the casement, as if in sympathy.

It was still raining when Tilly arrived in the morning. The maid was bedraggled, the hem of her cloak dragging mud. Time to pick up the reins of normal, everyday existence once again. Juliet made only one concession to what had happened. While Tilly fed the hens, Juliet walked into her kitchen and took down her chess set.

Without even opening the box, she threw both board and men into the fire.

The black and white squares crackled, peeling paint as the wood charred and smoked. The box cracked open, spilling pawns, queens and kings in a helpless melee into the devouring flames.

Her three cats rubbed around her ankles, purring.

*I*T WAS A BLIND, HELPLESS RAGE. ALDEN LAY IN HIS BED AND cursed. His blood scalded his veins. If he did not clench his jaw, his teeth rattled in his head like some macabre representation of death in the village pageant. He had tried to stand, only to fall back against the pillows. All he could do was curse. So he swore, sometimes aloud, sometimes silently, while servants padded about his room.

Soon the local doctor leaned over him, holding some foul-smelling potion under his nose. "Pray, drink this, my lord. Most efficacious to rid you of toxic humors."

The tremors felt too violent to trust speech, so Alden shook his head, clenching his teeth. The doctor gestured. Several men in livery gathered about the bed.

"Pray, do be pleased to drink it, my lord," one of them begged.

"I have a chill," Alden said as deliberately as he was able. "If you value your employment and your lives—"

Yet it seemed that his words were garbled, impossible to understand. He broke out in a cold sweat as the doctor closed in once again.

His brow furrowed, the doctor nodded to the servants. "Lord Gracechurch is delirious. As you love him, I pray you will assist me?"

Strong, devoted hands grabbed Alden's arms and legs and held him down. Someone grabbed his nose and forced his mouth open. His tongue gagged on the foul taste. He swallowed some as he fought for breath, then spat with his last remaining strength. The men leaped back, faces dabbled with drops of potion.

The doctor wiped his chin with a large handkerchief. "I fear for His Lordship's sanity. He must be bled."

With intense concentration Alden managed to grind out the words. "No bloody bleeding!"

Yet the footmen grabbed him again, nothing but concern in their faces. Alden caught a glimpse of a basin and razor. His own servants held him down as blood streamed from his arm.

"This is most inconsiderate," a new voice said. "Why was I not consulted right away? Oh, do go away, all of you! I wish to speak with my son."

"Mother!" Alden shouted. "How good of you to call."

The doctor bowed from the waist. "Your Ladyship! His Lordship is raving with fever. He must be bled."

"Well, of course," the viscountess said. "But not now. I need to consult him about something. Go away!"

The footmen had already retreated and were standing at attention, staring at the ceiling.

"Her Ladyship is not to be refused, sir." Alden managed to hold up his slashed arm. He thought perhaps he was making sense this time. "Your work is done. See? I bleed."

Lady Gracechurch promptly fainted. Alden lay neglected in the bed while the doctor and footmen gathered about his mother. She was lifted onto a chair and fanned. Her maidservant, who was hovering behind her, set fire to a feather. The acrid smell filled the room. . . .

*H*E WOKE TO THE STEADY DRONE OF A VOICE. HIS MOTHER'S voice. Alden wasn't quite sure what she was talking about. Her words blurred, humming along like meaningless music. Something about orchards and vegetable marrows. A complaint about the day he was born. A long diatribe on Mrs. Sherwood, so ungrateful, so wicked. He drifted in and out of sleep.

"And then Lord Felton—"

He snapped awake. "Who?"

"Lord Felton. Francis Amberleigh, the Earl of Felton. Really, Alden! Haven't you heard a word I've been saying?"

Alden sat up. He was soaked in sweat, but the fever had receded. He felt considerably stronger. The room lay quiet, lit by a few braces of candles. So it was night. Lady Gracechurch sat by the bed.

"Mother, how long have you been here?"

"It is so seldom I can have you to myself, Alden. I have been here since yesterday."

"Yesterday! Devil take it! Have I been that ill?"

"Nothing to be concerned about. As I told that doctor, this has been your habit since childhood. When others suffered long, stuffy colds, you always ran *such* a dramatic high fever, then were better within days. I sent the doctor about his business. I have never trusted doctors, not since the day you were born. You are quite well now?"

"Yes, thank you, Mama." The room stank, a mixture of potions and burned feathers. "Would you pray order me a bath and ask a footman to open the windows?"

His mother looked at him with eyebrows raised. Of course, she wouldn't dream of ringing a bell, if he were there to do it for her.

"It is raining," she said. "It is night."

Alden gathered his strength, reached from the bed and rang. A footman appeared, listened to his orders and disappeared, but the window remained closed.

"What were you saying about the Earl of Felton?"

She turned to him. "What, dear?"

"Lord Felton. You were speaking of him."

"Was I? I have quite forgot."

Alden leaned back and closed his eyes. His mother's visit was pure chance. Just as it was chance that she had chased the doctor away before the man killed his patient in an excess of medical zeal. Lady Gracechurch lived in a world of her own. She had seen nothing odd in sitting by her son's bedside, commanding his sole company and complaining about matters of business and gossip, while he shook and sweated with a fever.

"Lord Felton had a daughter, Lady Elizabeth Juliet Amberleigh," Alden said. "She ran away with her father's secretary, a man named George Hardcastle. Her mother and little brother were killed later in a carriage accident. Their deaths were commonly seen, so I understand, to be her fault. Or at least, her father never forgave her."

"Oh, lud! I wasn't talking about *that*. I was talking about the Felton treasure. The story is that a great fortune in gold is buried in the garden. Rumor has it that a new clue to its whereabouts has been discovered—"

"The key to a treasure."

"What, dear? Lord Felton says he will not countenance a lot of ruffians digging about in his grounds, looking for a treasure lost since the war."

"Which war?" Alden asked.

"That disgraceful business with Oliver Cromwell, of course. The family treasure was buried in the garden and lost. Such a romantic tale, though Felton claims there's not a shred of truth in it."

A buried treasure? A tale for children and idiots. If Juliet's locket carried the key to a fortune, why would she have lived in poverty in Manston Mingate? And yet there had been a truly rapacious gleam in Lord Edward's eyes.

The door opened. A stream of menservants entered, carrying a tub and pails of hot water. Lady Gracechurch retreated. Alden climbed from the bed and sank into the filled tub. After a night's sound sleep, he would be entirely fit again.

To do what?

To go to Juliet on bended knee and try to explain?

He had betrayed her.

The knowledge echoed in his mind like a pronouncement of doom, as if he had been sentenced to be dragged to a public place and hanged by the neck until dead.

He had betrayed her.

He felt numbed by the enormity of it, as if his heart had turned to stone.

Yet though the soul quaver, any jackanapes could find the courage to face the gallows with an outward show of bravado, wearing colored ribbons at the knee to flash defiance at fate. Alden Granville-Strachan, Lord Gracechurch, had plenty of colored silk and long years of laughing his defiance at the world.

Her husband is alive.

He must put Juliet behind him, as he had put so many other women behind him. London and its pleasures awaited.

So why this stinging tension, scalding behind his closed eyelids as if he might weep like a child?

He finished his bath in a burning rage. Plague take all doctors! The clumsy cuts in his arm—his sword arm, devil take it!—began bleeding again and had to be bound. Dressed in a long gown he walked to the window and pushed aside the drapes. Rainwater flooded down the glass. The frames rattled. A foul night.

Did Juliet lie in her narrow bed in Manston Mingate and rain curses on his name?

He hoped so. He hoped with a sudden desperate fierceness that her curses would prove effective and cast him into hell. Perhaps he had already condemned himself to Hades? That dreary round of gaming and drinking and affairs? The thought rang hideously empty and hollow, as if echoing an unnamed, unrecognized terror deep in his heart.

I would venture that both parties lost, sir, but that you have more pride, that is all. You are quicker to see the end coming and so you salvage yourself first . . . you have never had the nerve to risk anything else.

Risk? He shuddered at the thought of what he had been prepared to risk with Lord Edward for her sake. Yet in the end he had salvaged nothing, not even pride.

Her husband is alive.

Alden flung up the sash to breathe in the rain-soaked air.

Something moved, darting across the lawn. It was hard to see through the streaming downpour, but at last, even in the slashing night, he could make out the furious little figure, legs pumping wildly as he ran toward the house.

Alden spun about and rang the bell. A slightly sheepish footman appeared at the door: last seen helping to pinch closed his master's nostrils at the behest of the doctor.

"My lord?"

"A boy is approaching the house. I wish to speak to him immediately."

"A *boy*, my lord?"

"Faith! Must I repeat every order? Bring the lad up here. Immediately!"

"Very good, my lord."

The man bowed and retreated. Alden paced his bedroom.

A few minutes later the door opened.

"Lud! A drowned rat," Alden said. "Come in, lad, and sit down. You are thirsty, hungry?"

The boy nodded, panting hard. His hat was a soggy mass of wool. Water ran off his coat to pool about his feet.

Alden signaled to the footman. "Food and something hot to drink. Put brandy in it. And bring dry clothes."

The footman sniffed and left. The boy pulled off his sodden

cap and grimaced. He was gasping with each visible heave of thin shoulders. He was for the moment incapable of speech.

"Sit here." Alden indicated a chair beside the fire. "Relax and catch your breath. Whatever it is, it can wait a second or two. Then you may tell me why Master Jemmy Brambey of Manston Mingate has just run fifteen miles through a storm."

The freckled face contorted as the boy sucked in air and wiped away rainwater and tears with the back of one hand. Alden gave him a handkerchief and watched with a certain fascination as it came away not only wet, but dirty. The rainwater running off the boy's clothes would probably stain the carpet.

The footman returned with a tray. Alden forced himself to be patient while Jemmy sucked up hot liquids and bit into a large slab of pie.

"If you can eat, you can talk," Alden said at last. "Pray begin. You have a message?"

"My sister said I was to come to you, my lord," the boy said, spitting crumbs. "She's turned out."

"*Tilly* is turned out?"

Jemmy shook his head. "Mistress Juliet Seton! It's not her house. Men came this afternoon to oust her—lock, stock and barrel. Anything they didn't think they could sell, they smashed—"

Choking back dread, Alden went to his dresser and began flinging on clothes, practical riding clothes, the first he could find. "Go on!"

"They came in carriages. A whole gang of men. One of them claimed he was her husband, though we all know she's a widow. When she wouldn't go with him, he said he had already sold her house—seeing as it was really his, not hers, them being man and wife—and she could live under a tree for all he cared. She still wouldn't go with him. In the end, Tilly said, Mistress Seton held a pistol on him and threatened to shoot him, so he left."

Alden took his own weapons out of their case. He would like very much to take that damned doctor's blood in trade for his own, drop for drop, and force his foul potions down his own bloody incompetent throat.

"This man was named George Hardcastle?"

"I don't know what he called himself, my lord. Tilly said he was a big handsome fellow. He said if Mistress Seton came begging to him in London, he might take her in. Then in the face of her pistol and the way she was shaking as if it might go off any second, he upped and left, but the others stayed behind to turn her out. She couldn't stop them. Tilly says the gun wasn't even loaded, because there hadn't been time to load it, what with them coming so sudden and all."

Alden primed and loaded both pistols, then thrust them into his pockets.

"Where is she now?"

Jemmy took another bite of pie. "Don't know. Tilly was sent packing. Mistress Seton wouldn't go with her and told her not to come back. So Tilly ran home and told Ma what was going on. Ma sent me to you."

"You'll be rewarded. Now, get warm and dry. That footman will help you and show you to a bed."

The footman raised both brows.

"A *guest* bed," Alden said over his shoulder as he strode out of the door. "In a *guest* room."

T WAS PITCH DARK, RAIN PELTING DOWN. WIND ROARED through the elms, tossing the branches, tearing loose leaves to spiral away in the downpour. Alden swung from the carriage and stared at the redbrick house. His cloak was instantly soaked.

"Wait here," he told his coachman.

Deliberately not taking a light, he opened the gate. The path glimmered under the pounding rainwater, sparkling in a mad dance of splashing raindrops. Alden strode up through the garden and pounded on the front door. No answer. He tried the latch.

The door was locked. Rain streamed as he stepped back and looked up at the windows. They stared blankly at the night, inky black.

He had stopped for a moment at Tilly's house in the village.

"She wouldn't come back here, my lord," Tilly had said, weeping. "She said we'd only suffer for it, if Ma took her in." She'd indicated the rough little room, the ceiling so low that Alden had needed to bend down to enter. "And how could a lady live here with the likes of us? Oh, sir! What's to become of us all?"

He had left reassurances and coins, then come straight to Juliet's house.

Rain battered, running in waterfalls from the corners of his hat as he walked around the house. The garden seemed flattened, trampled, though he couldn't be sure in the driving darkness. In the yard with the work sheds, the pounding rain echoed and re-echoed around the small space. Alden cupped his hands about his mouth and yelled.

"Juliet!"

There was no answer. He went from shed to shed, trying doors. They were all locked. The flagstones were slippery, treacherous. The old wooden doors shone black with water.

He turned. Rain drove in sheets across the open expanse of hay meadow.

"Juliet!"

Only the roar of rain and the howling wind.

I lied about her husband's death. George Hardcastle. I just came from London where I spoke with the man. The butcher's grandson is alive and well, though sadly short of funds. Furthermore, he is most anxious to be reconciled with his faithless wife. Checkmate, sir!

Alden Granville-Strachan had fallen straight into the trap, played his pawn's role with zeal, while Lord Edward Vane laughed with his cronies over his exquisite revenge on his one-time fiancée. *Her husband is alive.*

"Juliet!"

The night answered with the mocking bellow of a rain-soaked gust.

Cloak flapping at his heels Alden strode down the path toward the chicken house. Something caught him hard in the shin. He fumbled in the wet darkness until his fingers identified the handle of the scythe, broken. The blade had been snapped and lay glimmering among the ruin of a pea patch. He stared until he could make out the heap of smashed implements, farm tools, shovels and rakes, piled up as if for a bonfire.

Rage consumed him. He shouted aloud into the uncaring night. "Bastards! Bastards! *Juliet!*"

Eggshells crushed under his boots. The chicken house lay silent, the door wrenched off its hinges. Obviously the hens were gone, scattered into the woods to become food for foxes. There was nothing he could do about it.

Once he stepped inside, the bellow of rain subsided to a dull roar. Somewhere, underneath that demented clamor, he heard something else. The sound was rhythmic, steady. A cat purring.

Alden reached into a pocket and pulled out his tinderbox. Crouching to shelter the spark from the wind, he formed a long twist of straw and lit it, setting it in the doorway where it wouldn't catch the henhouse on fire.

"How good of you to come," she said behind him. "It would be useless, I assume, to ask you to leave?"

"Juliet, thank God!" He spun to face her. "I thought if you saw a light coming through the garden, you might hide—"

"I *am* hiding," she replied. "Especially from you."

She sat huddled on the floor in the filth of straw and feathers. Meshach lay curled, purring, in her lap. One hand stroked rhythmically over the tabby coat, yet her eyes held a numb shock, like a puppy he had once seen that had almost drowned in a fish pond.

"Are you hurt?" he asked at last.

"*Hurt?*" She looked away, turning her head, the column of her throat stiff with reproach. "Of course, you mean physically. Perhaps a bruise or two, where I was seized by the arms and forcibly evicted. Otherwise I am quite well. George did not want his men to harm me *physically*."

Alden stared at her. Water trickled down his neck. He wanted to tear the world apart with his bare hands.

"Yes, George is alive. I am an adulteress. You knew, of course."

He took a deep breath. "No. Not until afterward. But I know what that means to you."

"It hardly matters now, does it? Lord Edward told George where to find me. My husband was apparently in need of instant funds, so he has sold this place and everything in it. He is quite within his rights. He is prepared to provide me with a home in London."

"Jemmy Brambey told me."

The wavering light danced over her face. "Did my maid's little brother also tell you that Lord Edward has been paying him to spy on me? Jemmy has been running to Marion Hall with regular reports. Lord Edward was kind enough to explain it all to George."

"Then your husband knows—"

"That I took an infamous rake for a lover? Publicly? Before witnesses? Yes, he knows."

Alden stared at his hands. His rings sparkled, reflecting the little flame behind him.

"Go away," she said. "You swore—"

"Then I am breaking my word."

"I do not wish to belabor the point, but you do see that I am left with no one I can trust? Not even my maid."

"In spite of everything, you will have to trust me."

She lifted Meshach to rub his head under her chin. "What use would I be to you? Everything I have, or had, belongs to George. Even my body. If you used it, you would be stealing from him."

Perhaps if he could only crack open the night like a walnut, there would be a different, less cruel world inside? "I can help, Juliet. You can't stay here."

Her eyes held no more expression than the tabby's—a terrifying, animal blankness. "George called me a harlot, but he would still take me back, even after I fornicated with you. Fancy that!"

"Whatever he called you, it is not true." The words bit, like mad dogs. "Nor is that description accurate for what passed between us."

"And what did pass between us? Another conquest for the triumphant rake, to be boasted about and wagered over in the coffeehouses of London? Well done, Lord Gracechurch!"

He knew she would flinch if he touched her. Damn it to hell! He wanted to touch her.

"Curse me, if you like. But you must get to shelter. I have a carriage waiting in the road."

"I can't leave." Her eyes glimmered suddenly. "Abednego and Shadrach are still lost. My cats were afraid of the nailed boots and loud voices and the crash of broken china. They fled into the garden. George's men hunted them through my flower beds with clubs and pistols. They thought it was great sport—"

His anger burned so clearly, he thought that if he looked down, he might see it squatting in his palms, like a fiend.

"If I can find these men, I will kill them for you."

She clutched Meshach till he yowled a little protest. "Faith! How very like a man! Somewhere out there in that roaring darkness two confused cats are cowering in terror, and all you can think of is killing some stupid, ignorant louts."

"I am thinking only of getting you to safety."

"I cannot leave my cats."

"Of course not," he said. "I brought a basket for them. I thought they might not let us carry them in the carriage otherwise."

Tears slipped suddenly down her cheeks. "You brought a *basket?*"

"Let me help you to the carriage. You can wait there while I find Abednego and Shadrach." He tried to meet her gaze with only the lightest, most noncommittal of glances. He didn't want to panic her with his black rage. "At least you found Meshach. A tabby would have been impossible to see outside in the dark."

She gave a small laugh, smoothing the striped coat. "They won't like the basket."

"They will love it. There's catnip inside. You will come, Juliet?"

Shadows traced over her face as she looked directly into his eyes. "Pray, do not call me by my given name."

Absurd to feel the impact of such a small thing as if it were a death knell. "As you wish, ma'am. But you will come with me?"

"I am not a fool, nor a martyr. I would rather be in hell than come with you. However, you have a basket for my cats and you owe me. But rest assured, my lord, that there will be very little satisfaction for you in my company."

The flame went out, plunging the henhouse into darkness. Alden rose and looked out. The rain had diminished to a steady drizzle. "I will make it up to you."

"I hope you try. I will find the greatest pleasure in creating whatever shreds of misery it's in my power to bring you."

"This was not what I wanted—"

"And what did you want? To forget me? Of course. You had already decided, no doubt, to move on. Don't try to tell me that's not true!"

He couldn't answer. It was true. He had thought he had no other choice.

Juliet stood, Meshach in her arms. "Faith! I wish I were a witch who could set demons to rip into your soul. Alas, I do not believe that you have one."

"No doubt you are right. It doesn't matter. We can hardly stand here in an empty henhouse and debate it."

The wind had died away. Damp darkness stretched, oddly quiet now, vibrating only with the steady pitter-patter of drizzle. Alden took off his cloak and held it out. She allowed him to set the heavy wool around her shoulders. It dragged the ground. He wanted to put an arm around her, but he stepped aside and let her lead the way through the ruined garden. The coach lamps glimmered like beacons beyond the gate.

As soon as Juliet was safely inside the carriage with Meshach curled on her lap, Alden strode back into the garden and began to search. This time he carried one of the coach lamps. Light streamed over bent stems and torn leaves. Moisture curled and steamed. Beyond the beam, it was pitch black.

A gleam of wet color caught his eye. He went closer to investigate. Clothes. Juliet's clothes, thrown in a sodden heap onto the carrots and marigolds. In a white fury he gathered the armful of dresses and petticoats and carried them back to the coach. He thrust them inside the boot and turned back to the garden.

How far might a frightened cat go? Away into the woods? Into the village to find a new hearth, less threatening than this one? Into some secret feline hideaway right here in the garden that Alden would never discover?

His boots scrunched through damp leaves and torn petals. He hunted through the thicket of shrubbery behind the limp hollyhocks, calling softly. He swung the lantern up, staring into the trees, looking for a cat among the great gnarled branches.

Nothing.

The drizzle began to thicken. Water dripped off his hat and wet the shoulders of his coat. He had left his cloak with Juliet in the carriage.

Alden hesitated for some time at the entrance to the grape arbor, letting the beam of light dance over the shredded vine, the black, broken posts. The table where he had teased Juliet with a chess game had been tipped over. Rage battered at him, flooded every pore, as he remembered snatches of their conversation, the way she had looked at him with desire smoldering in her cornflower eyes, the way he had looked back at her.

He turned away and leaned his head against a post. Anger and pain made bloody strange bedfellows! His pulse surged hot and fast. He felt almost light-headed, as if the fever might return. Yet he still didn't really want to care.

Rain began to patter audibly again. A small wind stirred the branches. Something moved, close to the ground. Alden bent down, shining the lamp into the space where the table top had fallen against one bench. Green demon eyes gleamed back. The light sparked gold off a marmalade coat. Shadrach!

He knelt on the wet stones and set down the lantern, calling softly. Shadrach retreated, balling himself into the farthest corner. Alden reached under the seat. The cat hissed. Entreaties, tapping fingers, a twirl of vine stem, nothing worked to tempt him out. The rain started to pound. At last Alden lay full length in the mire and reached with both hands. Carefully he pulled the cat from its hiding place. Moments later he carried Shadrach to the coach.

Juliet did not meet his eyes or speak to him. She sat in the corner of the seat and stared out of the opposite window, Meshach still purring on her lap. Alden set Shadrach in the basket and closed the lid.

He combed the garden and sheds for at least thirty minutes, calling softly, looking under bushes and in the hollow crotches of trees, above doorways and in the crannies of windowsills. Somewhere out there a white cat ghosted through the dark night. Perhaps Abednego had gone as far as Farmer Hames's distant barns? Or away through Mill Spinney? Perhaps a bullet or a blow from a club had found its mark?

He had no solution to this problem. Nothing in the way of wit, or strength, or skill—with a sword, a hand of cards, or a woman's soft body—could tell him the whereabouts of Juliet's white cat.

Alden strode one more time up the path to the henhouse, then back through the yard with the sheds. For a moment he stood calling under the porch of the back door. Silence. He looked up. Clouds were shredding, revealing an indigo sky. His coachman had moved the carriage away and brought it back several times, to keep the horses from standing. Yet he could not leave without Abednego.

I have taken your locket, Juliet. I have used your generosity and your lovely, lovely body. Now, because of me, your white cat is lost. And yet, after this night, there is little I can do to make amends, because you are another man's wife.

The strength of his desire to win her forgiveness took his breath away. The mix of emotions—rage and fear and guilt—clenched with cruel fingers in his gut. His mind burned with the knowledge that he had no power left, that he was impotent to help her, that it was all his fault.

He could seek out Lord Edward and create a pretext for a duel. He might even win. He might succeed in leaving the duke's son gasping his last breath in a pool of his own blood. Whatever momentary satisfaction that would bring, it would not make reparation. Nothing could restore Juliet's safety and equilibrium. Nothing could make up for what a careless rake had already done.

Deliberately he opened his hand and let the lantern smash on the path. The oil flamed and ran for a moment, then fizzled and went out, leaving him in darkness. He stepped out of the porch.

The white missile hit him like a cannonball. Tiny blades sank painfully through layers of clothes into his flesh and clung there. *Abednego!*

Alden gently disentangled the claws from his shoulder. The cat had hurtled onto his rescuer from the roof. Instantly Abednego began to purr.

He carried the cat to the carriage. Juliet lay back against the corner of the seat, her jaw shadowed above the long curve of her throat. Her face glimmered softly in the dark, her hair almost black in contrast. One hand rested in her lap. The other lay flung aside on the seat, the fingers curled up.

She was asleep.

Alden placed Abednego in the basket. The marmalade and tabby were already curled there together. The three cats immediately formed a single ball of contentment, purring.

Without waking Juliet, he settled on the seat opposite her. The horses started forward. Alden stared at her face and wondered what the devil was happening to him.

CHAPTER TWELVE

❦

*J*ULIET WOKE AS THE HORSES STOPPED. MEMORIES FLOODED BACK. The duke's son in her parlor. The mad night at Marion Hall. Waking to find Alden gone, her locket gone. How could she have been foolish enough to think it might end there? The arrival of George in Manston Mingate had crashed into her life like a tidal wave, bringing every implication of the previous week's events into shattering focus.

Her husband was alive. Now, as she'd feared for five years, George Hardcastle had exterminated her life as she'd known it and could control her happiness into the foreseeable future.

Alden, Lord Gracechurch, the lover she had unknowingly taken in adultery, had all along been in league—whether wittingly or not—with her one-time fiancé, Lord Edward Vane, who had lied about her husband's death to entrap her.

It hardly mattered that George's men had broken china and a handful of farm implements.

It hardly mattered that Lord Edward had conspired to destroy her.

Alden had shattered her soul.

"We have arrived," he said.

He sat with arms folded over his chest, head flung back, booted feet resting on the opposite seat. His clothes were soaked and splattered with mud. His hair was plastered to his head. Loose strands straggled over his cheeks. Yet even now—even after everything he had done—his sheer male beauty took her breath away.

Her agony crystallized into hatred.

He glanced directly at her.

Her hands clenched in her lap. She had allowed him to woo her and kiss her. She had let those carved lips caress hers. Those fine hands had explored her nakedness. She had opened her body and soul to his invasion—and been betrayed.

"You detest me," he said quietly. "Of course. I don't blame you."

"I hate you. More than I have ever hated anyone in my life."

He turned his head to look out of the window. Wet hair trailed over his shoulder. "Yes. I would feel the same."

"You have no idea of my depth of feeling. It would bring me great satisfaction to know for sure that you were going to burn in hell for all eternity."

A footman opened the door. Alden dropped his feet to the floor and stepped from the carriage. Turning, he held out a hand to assist her.

"Unfortunately I cannot make it to Hades quite so quickly, ma'am, so I will have a man fetch the basket and put the cats in your room."

The flambeaux around the house entrance cast a flickering light over his face. Two bright spots of color burned against his deadly white cheekbones. His eyes glittered.

Fear washed over her heart. "What is the matter?" she asked. "You are ill?"

"A small fever, ma'am." He smiled. "Perhaps it will consume me, as you wish."

It made her angry. Angry that for a moment she had cared. Juliet put her hand on his sleeve and stepped down.

"You have the pox?"

"Lud, no! A chill, that's all."

"A professional rake takes precautions against disease, of course. How fortunate I am that you did so with me!"

His smile disappeared. He took a deep breath, staring at her fingers on his cuff. "Don't try to make what we shared into something ugly. It was not."

"Not for you, perhaps," she said, removing her hand. "But it was very ugly for me."

She pushed past him and walked into the house. Years of training as an earl's daughter gave a rigid dignity to her spine. His boots rang on the floor behind her as he gave orders to servants. A room for her upstairs. Food, water and a soil box for the cats. To carry the basket carefully.

At the top of the main stairs, a maid appeared in front of her and curtsied.

"If you would please to follow me, ma'am?"

Juliet glanced back. Alden stood at the base of the stairs. Fever shone demon-bright in his eyes. Perhaps he really would be consumed by morning? Yet he lounged against the newel post with careless bravado, staring up at her.

She turned away. The tension in her body was fierce, painful, enough to make her want to fold over and gasp aloud. It hurt. This much hatred hurt like a burn. There was no compassion left in her heart. Only a black pit of rage and despair. This man had destroyed her future and robbed her past. She wanted him to hurt at least as much as she did.

"If I could, I would give you exactly what you wish," he said.

His words stopped her. She stood shaking in the hallway, but she refused to turn to meet his gaze. Only bitterness kept her upright.

"—with the rack and the wheel and the thumbscrews thrown in for good measure," he added.

She saw his reflection suddenly, in the tipped glass of an open round window, high on the wall. Wet, bedraggled, handsome as the devil. The tiny, distorted image was of a man she had thought for a moment she could love. He was burning with fever.

Her heart pounded. "Then to please me you would die tonight, for hell surely awaits you afterward."

From some deep reservoir of strength, he bowed with a flourish. "I shall do what I can, ma'am. Your wish is, as always, my command."

*J*ULIET WOKE IN THE MORNING SURPRISED TO FIND THAT FROM pure exhaustion she had slept deeply and well, without dreams. A steady purring echoed from the bed, where Shadrach, Meshach and Abednego lay curled in feline bliss on the cover.

Without disturbing the cats, she slipped from the bed and went to the window. Thin cotton brushed against her legs. The maid had produced a night rail the previous night, too long for Juliet, but serviceable. From the simple fabric and style, it was probably the girl's own. At least he had not sent her some prior mistress's night attire!

The storm had left the sky washed as blue as a forget-me-not. Yet pain still pressed, like an incubus, on her lungs. Somewhere far away across those fields and trees lay the home she had been given by Miss Parrett. The sanctuary a rake had invaded with his charm and deceit. The house her husband had seized and sold, when he had learned of her adultery.

Juliet turned away, sick at heart.

A gilt-and-plaster ceiling arched above her head. The furnishings were beautiful, costly. Other than the simple nightdress, every luxury a peer's home could provide was hers. The best wine and a selection of delicacies had been sent up on a tray the night before, the silver dishes gleaming in the extravagant light of dozens of wax candles. She had left the tray untouched, so the maid had taken it away.

Juliet walked restlessly across the thick carpet to look at the painting over the mantel. A sweep of trees and fields, dotted with black-and-white cows. Some stood hoof-deep in a stream near a picturesque folly, their reflections shimmering in the shallow water like a broken chessboard. A small brass plate read simply "Gracechurch."

All this, *all of it,* she had won back for him. Then he had taken her locket and abandoned her.

Her heart ached under her ribs. It was hard to breathe. But hatred alone would not be enough to sustain her. Fighting the temptation simply to retreat back to bed, Juliet rang the bell and ordered a bath and breakfast. Abednego stretched and dug his claws into the blue-and-rose cover. Shadrach thumped to the floor. The other two cats followed.

She led the way into the small dressing room and crouched to tap her finger on the dish that a footman had set there last night. Abednego took one look at the dried gravy remaining there, turned up his tail, and stalked away. Shadrach and Meshach rubbed at her ankles, complaining. She picked Meshach up in both hands and buried her face in his soft fur.

"I have fresh beef for them," Alden's voice said behind her.

Juliet froze, hideously aware of her loose hair and borrowed night attire. Immediately she was furious at such an absurd feeling. He had known her naked.

"Pray, do not ask me to leave," he said.

She set down the tabby and stood up, her back to him, glad of the voluminous folds of cheap cotton. "Because you won't go?"

"In London it is quite customary for a gentleman to visit a lady in her bedchamber. Since her toilette often takes till past noon, a married lady's bedroom becomes reception room, salon and breakfast parlor."

"But she has maids and footmen in attendance at the time. I do not."

"If you ask, I must leave, of course."

"Because my wish is your command?" She filled the question with sarcasm.

He crouched to scrape some scraps of meat from the plate in his hand into the cats' dish. Unlike her, he was fully, even formally, dressed, in a morning coat of pale cream brocade. His gleaming hair was bagged neatly in black silk.

The three felines began to gulp down their breakfast.

"Our mutual wish is to see the cats happy. Perhaps we can begin there."

"And my happiness?"

He stood up and set down the plate. "Is my only true concern."

She spun away. "Then why did you not die in the night as I wished?"

"Faith, ma'am!" He strode past her into the bedroom where he stood and stared from the window. "I thought you would prefer several weeks in which to torture me first. It should not be too difficult."

Juliet watched him from the doorway of the dressing room. Light pouring in the window outlined the graceful lines of his body, the powerful back and long legs. The sun sparkled in his hair like champagne. It still moved her, that masculine beauty. She despised the feeling.

"Do I have so much power over you?" she asked.

He turned to face her, his eyes dark against his pale skin. Even before he spoke, her answer was there: that naked desire, the unguarded male longing that left her floundering in confusion and resentment.

"All the power is yours," he said simply. He walked back to the fireplace and indicated a chair. His hands glittered with rings. "Pray, come and sit down, ma'am. I would be grateful to also take a seat."

She crossed her arms. The line of his profile might have been drawn in chalk. Yet he had not hesitated to become soaked to the skin hunting for her cats—

"You were very ill?"

He glanced up, with a flash of self-derision. "The barber liberated me of a wretched excess of blood—guaranteed to cool my evil humors. You should be glad."

Juliet stalked past him to the window. She knew he reached for lightness, and she usually hated to be petty. Though with this pain in her heart, how could she forgive him anything?

"I am surprised that a man so obsessed with appearances would admit to any infirmity, but it's no matter to me if you stand there until you fall."

"I make no complaint, ma'am, since it serves your purpose."

She spun around, surprised. "My purpose?"

He had crossed his arms and pressed his shoulders back against the paneling. "To torture me."

"How?"

"The sun shining through that nightgown torments me very well." His eyes glittered like starlight. "I have known their touch. I have visualized how long and lovely they must look. But I have never seen your legs. No doubt their shadow beneath that poor cotton is as close as I ever will. It is anguish enough."

Heat washed through her thighs and belly. Horrified, Juliet sensed the betraying desire invade her bones, as if they became limber and soft. "I think you are telling me the truth."

"Of course. Certainly I brought you back here to rescue you. I could hardly have left you to drown outside in a storm. But I was well aware what an acute punishment it would be—"

"What punishment?"

"To know that we'll never be lovers again will truly be a living hell for me." He leaned his head back and laughed.

She wanted to lie down. Just that. To lie down on the floor. Instead she took a deep breath and continued standing stiffly, staring at him. "I thought you preferred brief affairs?"

"Not quite so brief!"

"Of course. You always end them yourself. When *you* become tired—" She almost choked on the words.

"When it is naturally over. Alas, ma'am, I do not believe it is naturally over between us."

"It was hardly a natural beginning."

"I know that. Yet I hoped—"

"What?" The anger drove her to walk again. She paced from the window to the bed, then across to the dressing room door. The cats had finished eating. Shadrach was crouched over the water dish, drinking with typical feline concentration.

"Nothing. I did not know that your husband lived."

"I thought you liked to seduce married women?"

As if he felt as driven as she did, he pushed violently away from the wall. Sunshine glanced over his brocade and lace, edged the cream with gold as he strode past the window. "But you would not have acted as you did, had you known you were not free, would you?"

She hesitated. She and her family had paid far too high a price for her marriage vows for her to set them at no value, yet George had abandoned her so long ago! In what sense did they even have a marriage?

"*Would you?*" he insisted.

His face seemed almost translucent, the bones shadowed under the skin. He had obviously been desperately ill, not a slight chill, not a feigned convenience. Yet the hatred turned her heart into stone—it must!

"No," she said, moving back to the fireplace. "If I had known that George lived, I would not have done it. I wish to heaven I had never met you."

"Lud, Juliet! I did not willingly abandon you. Yet I have made you hate me."

"I do hate you. I can't help it!" She sat down, not sure she could stand any longer.

As if in defiance, he remained standing. "Thank you, ma'am."

Did he thank her for hating him? Or because he could no longer see her legs outlined beneath the thin cotton gown? Hysteria threatened. Juliet choked it down. She no longer knew how she felt, but it wasn't indifference.

She believed he hadn't known about George. He had, in fact, tried to give her every way out, before he had accepted her offer at Marion Hall with a passion that had scorched to her soul. He had even, last night, brought a basket for her cats. Yet as long as even a part of her emotion was this fervent anger, she must feed it.

"So you first became ill at Marion Hall?" she asked. "That next morning? *That* is your excuse for leaving without a word?"

"I realize it's a poor one. Yet it's the truth. Sir Reginald's menservants had to carry me out." He gazed at her steadily. "With any kind of influenza, I usually run a very high fever—fast, but severe. Then I recover more quickly than most. Do you think I *wanted* you to wake up alone? Lud, Juliet! Even if I'd been on my deathbed, I longed to make love to you again."

Pain twisted in her heart. "You still stole my locket! What did you do with it?"

He did not flinch or turn away. His eyes were very dark. "I gave it to Lord Edward."

Her knuckles shone as she clutched the chair arms in both hands. "Why?"

"It was the final condition of our wager—"

"Oh, God! Proof!" Hatred burned in her soul like a lamp, her only light in a sea of darkness.

"Yes, proof!" She thought he fought to remain calm, to keep his voice controlled and steady. "Without the locket your sacrifice would have gone for naught and Gracechurch Abbey would be his right now."

"You couldn't have told me that?"

He seemed pinned, standing with open palms beside the window. "I could have, but I didn't. Unfortunately, I misjudged his motives. The humiliation and revenge had been accomplished, so what did the locket matter? Yet he would not sell it back to me."

"How noble of you to try! What did you offer him for it?"

"Something I believed he would value far more. In fact, I was devilish certain of it." He turned to the window and leaned there, staring out. "I misjudged that, too. He wouldn't bite. Why did he want the locket so much, Juliet?"

"Don't use my name!"

His back became rigid. Suddenly he banged one fist on the shutter, making it rattle. "Faith, ma'am! We have been *lovers*!"

She leaped up. "Lovers? What the deuce do you know of love?"

"*Lovers!* You gave me your body. I gave you mine. Perhaps it was for all the wrong reasons. Perhaps it happened because an enemy's foul machinations threw us together. Yet for one night we were naked in each other's arms, innocent of anything but that one glorious fact."

"The animals in the barnyard do as much."

"Don't you dare tell me that!" He spun like a fencer, his body a weapon, his voice deadly. "Our hands gloried in the feel of each other's skin. Our lips and tongues and fingers ran free as the wind to seek and explore in pure delectation. Your legs wrapped eagerly about mine. My very soul emptied in worship of your body. We devoured each other as if it were the dawn of creation—"

"It meant nothing—a coupling!"

"I know you regret it. I *cannot*! And neither, devil take it, will I let you deny what really happened between us."

She pointed to the door, ablaze with anger. "Leave!"

"As you wish. But let us have this one thing clear: we were magnificent lovers—"

"What difference does it make?"

"This difference, Juliet." He stalked toward her until he stood close enough to touch. His clean male scent enveloped her. "The facts. You desire me as much as I desire you. I shall not act on it. I shall not—"

"I *hate* you," she insisted.

"Yes, you hate me." Sunlight dazzled behind his fair head. "That changes nothing. A desire like this flames with its own logic. If I were to kiss you now, you would kiss me back, with passion, with fervor, with an open, seeking mouth."

"I would not," she said, though her lips burned and heat ran in treacherous waves over her skin.

"Don't you dare deny it! If I were to touch you—even your shoulder or your hand—your legs would tremble, your body burst into flame, as mine would, as mine does just to stand this close. Your skin smolders now. I am scorched by the heat of it."

She closed her eyes and wrapped both arms over her breasts. "For pity's sake!"

"How the devil can I be merciful now?" His voice vibrated with passion. "I am in an agony of hunger for you. If I were to slide away that ugly gown and cup your naked breast—"

"Stop it!" she begged. "What are you trying to prove?"

His heels struck hard on the floorboards as he strode away and wrenched open the door. His answer came back as if he flung it.

"The sheer magnitude of what we give up, if we never make love again, and that even if you hate me, you can trust me to admit the bloody truth and still not act on it!"

The door slammed.

Juliet staggered to the bed and curled up. Her heart raced, thundering in her chest. He was right. Oh, God, he was right! Her whole being was consumed with longing. If he had kissed her or touched her, they would be together now, naked, in this bed. Her legs burned, her groin ached. Her body yearned to open and welcome him.

The shame of it scorched into her soul, burning a yet deeper trace of hatred. He never doubted his own allure. He was so certain of his potency, he no longer even tempered it with charm.

I fear my stay at the Three Tuns will require me to exchange pleasantries with rustics in the taproom, until I forget that I ever knew anything besides turnips and mangel-wurzels. You cannot be cruel enough to condemn me to such a fate—

He was right. She was not cruel enough. She must harden her heart, until she could become so.

Shadrach leaped onto the pillow—soft marmalade comfort. Meshach sat licking a paw in front of the fireplace. Abednego arched his back and hissed as the door opened and a string of servants entered with her breakfast and bath. Behind them came the maid who had shown Juliet to this room the night before. Her arms were full of clothes.

"Your things, ma'am." The maid curtsied.

The girl was carrying Juliet's own gowns and petticoats that

George's men had thrown out into the garden yesterday as valueless—all except the pink dress she had worn in the carriage with Alden, which they had carried off to sell. So in the dark, wet garden, he had even gathered up her dresses.

The maid blushed, reminding Juliet of Tilly—that nervous awareness such girls always showed around a man like Lord Gracechurch. "I have a message from His Lordship."

Juliet sat up, filled with a nervous awareness of her own. "A message?"

The girl looked at the ceiling, frowning with concentration, as if trying to retrieve each word exactly from memory.

"Lord Gracechurch said he hopes your clothes are adequately cleaned and pressed, ma'am, seeing as how he don't keep a ladies' wardrobe in the house. Even though, His Lordship said, he thought as how you might believe that he would."

The maid grinned triumphantly, bobbed another curtsy, and carried the clothes into the dressing room.

Juliet burst into laughter. It gave way, at last, to tears. The three cats jumped onto the bed and curled up beside her, as if to offer comfort.

*E*VEN IN HER BEST BLUE GOWN, JULIET KNEW SHE LOOKED NO better than any of the servants on their afternoon off. Nothing could be more irrelevant. As soon as she had eaten breakfast and dressed, she walked down into the gardens to find a quiet place where she could think.

How on earth to plan for the future? She had nothing, literally, but the clothes she stood up in. Her family had disowned her. Anything she possessed, or could earn or acquire, belonged, and would always belong, to her husband, who—in spite of everything—had offered her a home.

What other alternatives remained? Only prostitution of one kind or another. Disgraced wives had chosen before to live in scandal as another man's mistress. But not, of course, with this man. Lord Gracechurch might offer such a position, but only to use her, devour her soul, then cast her off. It was what such men did. Even with Alden Granville, even with him, it would only be harlotry in the end.

George knew that. He had known in Manston Mingate that her refusal to return with him was empty. Even if he starved her or beat her, even if he punished her for her adultery for the rest of her life, she had nowhere else to go.

If Lord Edward had been planning this revenge for five years, he had certainly planned it well!

A small rustle startled her. Juliet looked around and her breath stopped. A blond head was poking out from some bushes.

Air rushed from her lungs. "Sherry?"

The boy crawled on all fours onto the gravel walkway, then stood up and grinned at her. Leaves were caught in his hair.

"Have you seen Lord Gracechurch?" the child asked.

The stubborn little chin and something about the set of the nostrils reminded her so fiercely of Kit she felt ill. Juliet shook her head.

"I want to show him something." Sherry felt in a pocket with one grubby fist.

She was fifteen again, older sister to a little boy like this, the longed-for son who would inherit her father's lands and title, the baby who had been born after her mother had lost so many others—in the womb, in the cradle—with a solid grasp on his sister's heart. Viscount Kittering: with his death had come the end of the family's hopes. Now the earldom would die with her father.

Without thinking, she reached for her locket and found only naked skin.

Juliet took a deep breath, then another. At fifteen she had never been kissed, never had any thought for the future. Whenever George Hardcastle came across her in the house or garden, he had been respectful, deferential. She had thought of nothing in those endless summer days but playing games in the gardens with her brother, reading, sewing, riding in a decorous little party across her father's great estates, always with a groom, a maid. Yet George had still found ways to come upon her alone.

Kit was dead, drowned in a swollen ford.

This child lived.

"What do you have to show him?" she asked.

"We're collecting birds' eggs," Sherry said. "Mr. Primrose and me."

"I had a little brother once. He liked to find birds' eggs, too. How many do you have?"

Sherry pulled several little bundles of rags from his pockets and set them on the bench. He unwrapped them one at a time.

"A robin, a yellowhammer, a bullfinch, a hedge sparrow, a blackbird and a wren. That's six. Mr. Primrose said I'm to find ten different kinds, because we must never take more than one egg from a nest. Do you like birds?"

"Very much."

Yellow hair tumbled over the boy's forehead. Yet she folded her hands in her lap and watched him, holding in the pain and trying to bury it.

"This speckled blue-green one is a blackbird's. Bullfinch eggs are greenish, too, with these little brown marks." His forefinger pointed. "This one's the wren's."

The child's neck seemed so slender, such a slight thread supporting such a precious life.

"And who laid this one?"

He looked up, just as Kit would have looked up, with a tiny scorn. "That's a robin's. Everyone knows that! I found the nest in some broken bricks in the garden wall. This pink one with the purplish squiggles is a yellowhammer's, but sometimes they're more white, too."

"And the hedge sparrow's egg is as blue as a summer sky," a man's voice said. "Her nest is mossy and grassy, but not as neat as a chaffinch's. Did your sparrow line the inside of hers with wool, sir, or horsehair?"

Alden stood with arms folded, leaning against a tree a few feet away. He looked as if he had been standing there for a very long time. His gaze was shadowed, though the sun brightly burnished his hair and played lovingly over the rich cream brocade of his jacket. He met Juliet's startled gaze and smiled.

"Wool!" Sherry shouted. "*And* hair!"

Ignoring the man's costly clothes, the boy launched himself at his protector, shrieking as Alden swung him up in the air with both hands. Juliet felt instantly excluded. Man and child laughed together until breathless. It was a rough-and-tumble, masculine good humor—even in the little boy—banishing anything female and soft.

"The woodpile!" Sherry yelled. "I found it in the woodpile."

Still laughing, Alden set him down and allowed the child to lead him back to the seat. Juliet wanted to leap up and leave. For Sherry's sake, she did not. Instead she sat, her blue skirts spread next to the birds' eggs, and suppressed her rush of bodily awareness.

For several minutes man and boy studied the eggs. While Sherry chatted excitedly about birds, Alden added grave comments, taking the child's interest perfectly seriously. The wren's nest lined with feathers. The blackbird building her neat cup of grass and mud and dead leaves in the hedge. The handsome bullfinch with his rose-pink breast. His drab mate hiding her nest deep in a bramble patch, where only a determined child could wriggle his way in.

"Now, sir," Alden said at last. "Take the eggs to Mr. Primrose. He is waiting for you in the herb garden. He has some bugs to show you, and you can learn which ones the birds like to eat."

The boy obediently wrapped the eggs, thrust them back into his pockets and ran off.

Juliet stood up and watched him go, feeling as if part of her heart were running away on those stout little legs.

"I came here to apologize," Alden said. "I didn't expect to find Sherry."

"*Apologize?* For destroying my life, or for forgetting your manners?"

Alden closed his eyes, almost as if he were in pain. "The boy is safe here only thanks to you. I hope you may derive some comfort from that, at least."

Comfort? Sherry disturbed her, opened that aching, lost place in her heart where she had stored her memories of Kit: bittersweet memories that time had already blurred, however fiercely she tried to pay homage to them.

Now the child's guardian stood, tall and powerful, offering his empty repentance and refusing to meet her accusatory gaze.

She took a deep breath. "Yet it was your idea to risk his future and this entire place over a wager."

His lids flew open, revealing that passionate blue. "How very careless of me! When I have worked so deuced hard to save it."

"*Worked?*"

"Yes, ma'am. Worked. Unless you don't concede how much work it is to keep up appearances day after day, to manipulate, flatter, bluff a path through London society. I was not expected to inherit the title. I began without a penny. I am trying to build an empire of investments to keep this place afloat and pay off the mortgage until I can make the estate productive enough by itself. Unless I dress and behave as if money is nothing to me, I would not stand a chance."

Even though she was standing, he sat down on the bench, spreading both arms along the back, and glanced away. His hands lay quiet in their nest of lace. The fine hands that held the tiller of all this: house, estates, a child's happiness. The knowing hands that had explored every secret of her body.

"And your women? They are also vital to this laborious project, no doubt?"

"Those myriad ladies who have warmed my nights and cheered my days? I deny none of them. However, I do not use female companionship for any nefarious purpose. I take lovers because I glory in making love."

"So they have nothing to do with your brave efforts to save Gracechurch Abbey?"

"No." His lip curled as he looked up at her. "Though it doesn't hurt to maintain a bold reputation."

"Of course, you take no pleasure in gaming or carousing? That is all *work*."

"I take pleasure wherever I can find it." The warmth in his gaze brought hot color to her cheeks. "I like pleasure. But a great deal of what I am obliged to do in town is just grindingly hard work and the job isn't finished yet."

"Then I cannot conceive why you would risk everything on one hand of cards with Lord Edward Vane!"

Raked gravel crunched under her shoes as Juliet marched away. The sun dazzled off flowers and a succession of stone seats, placed at intervals in the shade of a yew hedge. Perhaps if only she could weep, this terrible pain would not press so hard on her heart?

Rapid footsteps strode up behind her. Alden caught her upper arm and forced her to stop. "I thought you had more courage than to flee," he said. "We must talk."

Juliet turned to face him. "Really? What about? Do you want to explain all those colorful male birds and their drab little mates to *me*? In spite of all that masculine flamboyance and brilliant plumage, they all pair up faithfully enough, don't they?"

"For that one season, when they both raise the young. Only the bullfinch mates for life."

"How odd, when he's the most decorative!"

"He's also the most destructive. He literally nips fruit blossoms in the bud."

"Does he?" she said. "How very stupid of him."

"Nevertheless, he provides well enough for his young and his mate." He released her arm. "Juliet, what do you intend to do? I know that you hate me. I don't blame you. But you have nowhere else to go. I want you to know that you may live here—"

"Playing what role?" She spat the words as if they were the dregs of bitter wine.

"As my lover, of course!" His voice incised, sarcastic. "Lud, Juliet, can't you credit me with any human decency?"

"Very little. You have caused too much pain in my heart."

He spun away, the skirts of his coat swirling behind him. "Because I took your locket and gave it to Lord Edward. Yes, I know. I cannot make that right."

"You can make *nothing* right. The realm is full of the results of careless actions that cannot be made right. I have a husband who is prepared to provide a home for me in London. If I continue to refuse that noble offer, I will get no sympathy from society or the law."

"You think I'm not aware of that?"

She wanted to push him beyond his control, as he pushed her. She could sense his discomfort and withdrawal. It made her want to dig at that golden surface and uncover whatever might lie there.

"What usually happens in your world when a husband is confronted with proof that you have publicly used his wife as a harlot?"

Glittering in the sun, he paced away a few strides. "I have never been careless enough to offer such obvious proof before, unless the husband was acquiescent."

"And the ones who are not? The men who are shamed, angry?"

"Demand a duel, of course."

"So you fight, unless the man is afraid to meet you?"

He turned back to face her, nostrils flared. *"Afraid?"*

"Because you always win, don't you? A duel with you is invariably an uneven match, dishonorable and cowardly by its very nature. How very brave you are, to fight duels where you face no risk at all!"

"No man *always* wins. Not me. Not even Lord Edward Vane."

"He is such a good swordsman?"

"The best. We have fenced. I would not want to face him again, if he had death on his mind."

Juliet walked away a few paces and sat down on the nearest

stone seat. She wanted him to lose his temper, rail and shout, so she would have the excuse to rage back.

"So if I want you dead, I should arrange for him to fight you? How generous you are to put such knowledge in my hands!"

"Use it, if you like! It doesn't matter a tinker's curse to me."

For a moment she thought he would leave, spin on his elegant heel and stalk away. Instead he walked up to her and stood blocking the sun. He held out both hands, palms up. They were steady, offering not rage, but control.

"Look at me, Juliet. Why the devil do you think I would prefer to use these hands to deal death? They will do so if forced to it, but your own flesh knows how well they prefer softer employment."

Her skin burned with awareness. Her face flooded with color, remembering, remembering.

"You think to confront me with my *desire*? Faith, sir, it is too late for that."

"I have already tried it. I know." Rue lay dry and sweet in his tone, in his curled palms. "It was for that I thought I should apologize. Just know I have never killed a man in a duel."

She looked away from the shadow at the base of his thumb, the tender, capable fingers. "So the poor husband is left alive, but humiliated. Yet what if he did prevail and prove his point?"

"Then there might be a private settlement, or he can bring a criminal conversation suit for damages—"

"For money?"

"Of course." He paced away. "Because I have alienated his rightful property and deprived him of its use."

"Splendid!" Suddenly she longed only for the peace and quiet of her little house in Manston Mingate, with the three cats sunning themselves on her brick path. "Another game played by men for dishonest stakes."

"Do you think the pain is all yours? None of this is what I expected or wanted. You must know that."

Juliet stood up. "Then what did you expect?"

"I expected a night's pleasure. I had that beyond measure."

"And what did you want?"

He took a deep breath. "I thought I wanted no entanglement. I thought I wanted to walk away. Now I'm not sure."

"Not sure of what? Why?"

"You think when I describe myself as a rake, it's just words? It is not. I adore women, but no one woman. I am captivated by pleasure, but I abhor responsibility."

"Then you deny Sherry?"

"A child? It's not the same thing." He spun about and caught her by both arms, strong fingers gripping her sleeves. "I know you will never consent to be my mistress. I don't want that!"

"Then what do you want, Lord Gracechurch?"

His eyes blazed. "I am breaking faith with everything I have ever lived by. I am asking you to be my wife!"

CHAPTER THIRTEEN

❧❦❧

SHE WAS STUNNED INTO SILENCE.

For a moment she thought he would kiss her, try to force her to accept him, but he dropped his hands and ran both palms back over his hair.

"Lud, Juliet!" He stepped back and bowed with a wry smile. "I didn't ever think to shout my first proposal of marriage."

"Does it still escape you, Lord Gracechurch," she said at last, "that I am already married?"

"I will ask your husband to divorce you. I will pay whatever it takes."

"So I am to be bought and sold? After first having my name dragged through the mud."

"That couldn't be avoided, of course." His voice was steady now, almost emotionless, as if he still needed to prove his control. "He would have no other grounds, so your adultery would have to be proved in court. I would shield you as well as I could."

She whirled away, her steps crunching on the gravel. "And how well would that be? Don't such cases require every intimacy to be revealed, described in the most degrading detail for the satisfaction of some slavering judge and the prurient public? George will have to call witnesses: Tilly, Kate, all the men who were there that night at Marion Hall. You and I would be forced to recount under oath every sinful act. Sir Reginald Denby and his friends would certainly enjoy every moment."

The gravel path ended in a short flight of steps. Juliet ran up them and found herself on a stone-flagged terrace. A formal garden spread below it. A wheel of radiating flower beds, cut in patterns like an intricate maze, divided a series of stone paths, each bordered by a miniature box hedge. The paths converged on a fountain, where carved dolphins spouted endless falls of water.

Alden took the steps two at a time and came up behind her. "We could survive it."

"Perhaps a reckless rake might think so. Perhaps in the white heat of desire, I might even be fool enough to believe it, too. But you were in Italy—" The water ran, wearing away the stone fins, the blunted snouts on the dolphins. "When I eloped with George, London erupted in broadsheets. Cartoons. George with me in every conceivable—" She had to fight for breath, suffocated by memories. "Cartoons about Lord Edward that were even worse. Vile. Things I had never even imagined." She turned to face him. "That's what scandal means."

"I do not dismiss it, Juliet."

"Yet you say we could survive it? And what of George? Why do you think my husband would consent to this outrageous plan?"

Alden propped himself against the stone rail of the terrace. The gardens quilted a backdrop for his graceful slouch. "He will—for enough money."

"You don't even know him."

"I know he doesn't love you."

It trapped her where she stood, as if the air were spun sugar, sparkling and thick in the sunshine. She felt brittle. Did the pain stretch her past her breaking point?

"And you do?"

He looked away across the flower beds, his profile startlingly attractive, his blond head glimmering. White light reflected off sugared stone, sparkling water, the falls of lace at his throat, as if all of this—the man, his home, the very sky—was unreal, all part of an intricate confection.

"No. I don't know. I don't think so. Love? I think that takes more time than we have had, Juliet."

"Well, that is honest, at least!" She narrowed her eyes against the brightness. When had an English summer day been so bright? "How flattering that you ask me to marry you, when you know I cannot! How very gallant! Such an easy way to salve your conscience!"

His fists clenched on the stone parapet. "Do you think *conscience* would drag me to the altar?"

"*Drag?*" Juliet sank onto the stone bench behind her. Was she going to faint? "So—after we have cavorted through the divorce courts, survived the cartoonists, and paid a fortune in compensation to George—you really intend marriage, though up to this point you have avoided it like the plague. Perhaps you think to do your duty by your name? Very well, I will divorce George and marry you, so you can leave me here, my belly filled with your child, while you go to London, the tables and your more willing women—"

"It would not be like that."

She raised her chin, forcing her back as upright as if she wore the tightest corset. "Then how would it be, my lord? A life in hiding and shame, with every footman and scullery maid in England giggling over every detail of our lechery? I could never appear in society. You would never be content to live without it."

"I could live very happily without it."

Juliet burst out laughing, a shivery, fragile mirth. "Why on earth should I believe you?"

He pushed away from the parapet and began to pace. "I don't know. How can I prove it? I have enjoyed scores of women. I seduced you cynically. I had to. I wanted to win the wager."

"You admit that?"

His coat fit lovingly, drum tight over his taut back and at the waist, before the flare of cream skirts framed his long legs. "I have never denied it. I am trying to tell you the truth. So know that this, too, is true about what happened in Manston Mingate:

though my body burned to know yours, I also, against my better judgment, found myself liking you, respecting you. A great deal, as it happens."

"Against your better judgment!" The water in the fountain soared and wept behind him.

"Do you *want* flattery and lies? Of course, it was against my better judgment! In the past I have chosen only equal relationships, with ladies who offer themselves as cynically as I do. I don't fall in love. I don't involve hearts. And never before have I offered marriage!"

She glanced back at the dark yews with their poisonous branches. "What on earth could you know of love? It would be impossible for you to imagine."

"I loved my brother," he said starkly.

"If we are talking of proof, prove that!"

His brow contracted. "How the devil can I? Lud, Juliet—do you want me to tell you that I love you as I loved Gregory, my brother? I won't. It's not true."

The pain burned beneath her ribs. Perhaps she was already hollow inside, just a blackened empty shell? "If I am to know that you would cherish and protect me as your wife, you must prove your capacity for devotion and caring." Juliet looked directly at the man she hated and desired, at all his treacherous glamour and strength. "Tell me about Gregory's death!"

Alden stopped pacing. Bright color burned again in each cheek, in startling contrast to his chalky skin. This time it wasn't fever. It was distress.

"I don't—" He turned back and stared out across the garden, where the fountain leaped and played, never-ending. "The news reached me in Florence."

She made herself push. Let him break, like a sugar fantasy smashed with a hammer! "What did you do when you received it?"

He gripped the parapet with both hands. "I paid the messenger."

"And then?"

"I went without hesitation to my new mistress of the moment."
Pain spiraled in ever-deeper waves. "You went to a *mistress?*"

He slammed one fist onto the unforgiving stone. "What will
it prove, if I don't tell you the truth? Maria was dead. I had a new
mistress. She lived out in the country. I rode fast to her house and
we burned away the night in a haze of lasciviousness. Only later,
riding home in the dying moonlight, did I realize I was numb."
His voice shivered with pain. "Numb as if I had been beaten with
sticks."

Memories flooded her heart, stopping it dead in her breast. *I
am sorry, ma'am. They are both drowned, the countess and Lord Kittering.*

"Go on," she said.

His face was rigid, as if he had to force each word, as if he were
being tortured.

"In that same unfeeling daze I rode along roads stark with
shadows, losing my way, riding along track after track until dawn
began to break. I remember it clearly: the new light flooded the
landscape with peach, green and silver, made smoke out of trees,
cast bottle-green fingers over the harsh Italian soil. The most
beautiful dawn I have ever seen. My tired horse stumbled and
almost fell."

*They should never have tried to cross the ford, ma'am, in such a
storm—what with the water being so high! The horses couldn't keep their
footing. Couldn't the little boy swim?*

His rings sparked in the sunshine, sending out piercing flashes
of white light, as his fingers burned into the parapet. "I remember
dismounting and tying the nag to a tree. I walked through a grove
until the trunks thinned and the blue sky blazed openly above
my head. It was hot, very different from England—"

He stopped.

"You must tell me," Juliet insisted.

"Tell you what?" He spun about to face her, his expression
ravaged, ferocious. "That that's when the pain began? I lay full
length on the unforgiving ground. I was racked with grief, torn

apart as if devoured by wolves. I heard noises—grotesque noises like a wounded animal—gouging my tongue, filling my mouth with bitterness."

Her nails bit into her palms. "Why?"

"*Why?*" He began to pace again. "I loved him and he was dead. What more will you bleed from me?"

"So you left Italy—"

"I had to. I was the new heir. I arrived at Gracechurch Abbey to find my father had dropped dead of an apoplexy after gaming away the estate. But Gregory died first. He had fought a duel over some matter of family honor—I don't know exactly what. My brother was not a very good swordsman. He bled to death."

*A*LDEN FELT NAKED AND BRUISED. *NUMB AS IF HE HAD BEEN beaten with sticks.*

Juliet must understand. She, too, had lost a brother. Perhaps that was why he had felt he could, indeed, tell her when she asked. He had never told anyone else. Who else could he trust with the truth?

Yet now he stood entirely unprotected, vulnerable, as if he had peeled away his skin to expose his soul. He raised his head as she stood up. Juliet walked away a few paces, her neck fragile, her shoulders lovely.

"And you call that love?" she asked. "To be in a foreign country when your brother died, doing something you could have done better? To let him die alone, without you, while you lived as a servile puppy to an Italian man's wife? God save me, Lord Gracechurch, from your idea of love!"

Something shattered, explosively, sending shards of pain into every limb. For a moment he thought he had been struck down by summer lightning, striking hard and fast from the blazing sky. Alden glanced down at his cuffs and at his elegant heeled shoes. All there. He still stood upright. His body was still knitted together.

Nothing in the garden had changed. Yet agony bored through his chest.

"It is true," he said at last. "Do you think I'm not aware of it?"

Juliet stood rigid and said nothing.

He took a deep breath. "If you wished to wound me, ma'am, you have indeed succeeded."

Alden spun on his heel and began to walk away.

"Yes," she cried suddenly. Her skirts swished as she spun about. "Yes, I want to hurt you!"

He stopped, keeping his back to her, fury and pain knotted together in his stomach.

"Did you really think you and I could make a future?" she shouted. "Suffer together through my divorce and win any kind of peace afterward? You are mad!"

"Perhaps. For, if indeed I harbored any such fantasy, you have successfully rid me of it. I knew you were wounded. I did not know you were so bloody cruel."

"Cruel? I hope so, Lord Gracechurch!"

Alden glanced back at her. Tears streamed down her face.

"Yes, I pretended to be someone I was not. I pretended not to want your bright games and your knowing body. I, too, was dishonest. But it will take more than my desire to make me stay with you, more than you can offer or could ever offer."

Helplessly he stepped toward her.

A searing, terrible self-knowledge saturated her gaze. "For where was I," she asked, "when my little brother and mother drowned in a ford? Living in lust with my father's secretary—"

He knew what he must do. It had moved past words into the simple human need to comfort, to hold. Perhaps he could never win her. Perhaps he would never make love to her again. But he could still offer her the warmth of human contact, a shoulder to cry on.

He took one more step.

"If you try to touch me now," she said. "I swear I will laugh out loud."

As if an icy wind blew into his soul, all feeling froze and died. He stopped and bowed, with an elegant flourish, the gesture as insultingly careless as he could make it.

"Nothing could persuade me ever to touch you again, ma'am," he said.

His heels clicked as he strode along the length of the terrace. Sun blinded. His coat skirts flew out behind him. The steps at the far end plunged into the shadow of the yew hedge. Just as he reached the top step, something moved. Senses instantly alert, Alden stopped. A waver of mist and darkness took form in the shade. For a moment he thought he was seeing ghosts.

But a stranger emerged from the darkness to block Alden's path.

The fellow was tall, well-built, with cleanly carved features. A young man, fit and strong, though his green coat fit loosely, like a merchant's or a gentleman's down on his luck. Black eyebrows and olive skin betrayed that his hair would be naturally dark beneath his wig—as dark as his frown.

"You are Lord Gracechurch?" the man asked.

"If you have estate business," Alden said with deliberate hauteur, "pray address yourself to my steward."

The stranger glanced down at the naked blade in his right hand.

"No, my lord," he said. "My business is with you."

Alden had automatically reached for the sword at his hip. His hand had come away empty. He did not usually wear a smallsword when strolling about on his own grounds.

He lifted both brows. "I assume I have the pleasure to make the acquaintance of Mr. George Hardcastle?"

George advanced steadily. Light glanced off the cold length of metal as he held his sword before him. He pressed the tip against Alden's chest.

"You may not think it such a pleasure, my lord, when we become better acquainted."

Alden backed up a step. There was nothing to hand he could use for a weapon.

"Faith, sir, since I always choose only those companions who please me, I foresee a sadly short acquaintance."

George Hardcastle laughed. "How short would you like it to be, my lord?"

The back of Alden's waist bumped into the parapet. He crossed one ankle over the other and rested his hands on the harsh stone behind him. He gazed at Juliet's husband quite steadily, the way he might study a dog he intended to buy.

"As short as possible, sir. You have something with which to reproach me? I trust it won't take long. I am a busy man."

A button fell away, sliced from his coat, to roll off among the moss between the flagstones.

"I came here to kill you," George said. "It will take hardly a moment to press home this blade."

The sharp metal cut easily through brocade, lace and linen. Alden shrugged, feeling a slight cut to the skin on his chest.

"Go ahead," he said. "It will make deuced little difference to the state of my heart."

George stared at him. "You have stolen my wife's affections—"

"Really? Why don't you ask her?"

From the corner of his eye, he saw Juliet. She had marched resolutely across the flagstones to stand within ten feet of the two men. As long as Alden did not know her husband's mood concerning her, he could not vault over the parapet to escape the blade. He resigned himself to another bloodletting.

"Yes, George," she said. "Pray, ask me."

The blade shook. "Lud, Julie, I'm deuced sorry! I never meant your little house to be destroyed like that. But Lord Edward told me such things—"

"They were all true," Juliet said. "I believed you were dead."

"I'll make it up to you," George said. "I've found the nicest little place in London. We can start all over again. I didn't mean any of those things I said in Manston Mingate. I'd been drinking. You know how a little drink goes to my head."

I'll make it up to you! Was that what every man promised her?

"It doesn't matter," she replied.

"I had some reverses in business," George went on. "But I've just been offered a new chance to rebuild."

"Good," Juliet said. "Then we may live together in a modicum of comfort."

The sword dropped, slicing open waistcoat and shirt to score a thin red path down Alden's chest, as George turned to face his wife.

"You mean you'll come back with me?"

"Of course," Juliet said, chin high. She looked like a queen: the red queen, sun shining copper and chestnut in her hair. "You're my husband."

"Yet honor demands—" George began.

"Lord Gracechurch would not be worth your time to meet in a duel, Mr. Hardcastle," Juliet said.

"Faith, ma'am!" Alden glanced down at his naked chest. The cut welled tiny beads of blood. "Let your husband offer any insult he likes, even this amateur bloodletting, I refuse to meet him."

George looked back at him. "But I came here—"

Juliet shrugged. "If you mean to dispatch him, it will have to be now, in cold blood. I should stand here and applaud, but the law may not look upon His Lordship's murder as kindly as I would."

"As you see, sir, I have hardly stolen her affections," Alden said. "Allow me to call for your carriage, Mr. Hardcastle. I'm sure you and your wife would prefer to leave right away?"

"Yes." George sheathed his sword. He looked stunned.

"Lud, sir!" Alden said. "Do not look quite so disappointed. To bring a lawsuit against me for my sins might have added a little to your wealth, but of course you cannot subject your wife to the scandal of such a thing, if you are to remain in business in London."

"As you say, my lord," George replied. "Yet, alas, business of late—"

"Whereas," Alden interrupted, "if we all keep quiet and I also invest in your ventures, I imagine you and Mrs. Hardcastle might achieve a small level of domestic respectability. It might not be tranquil, but I imagine it will prove interesting. Perhaps you would take these rings, sir? A small token, should I have caused your wife any unintended distress?"

Alden peeled his father's diamonds once again from his fingers and knew that this time they would be sold, disappear beyond recovery. He dropped them to clink, one by one, on the terrace.

George bent immediately to gather them.

Alden walked up to Juliet. "This is truly your choice, ma'am?"

"Yes," she said firmly.

"Then you know I will not interfere. I have never deliberately damaged a marriage."

She said nothing, though he saw a new anxiety flare in her eyes.

"The cats?" he asked quietly.

"I can't take them." Her voice burned. "George doesn't like cats."

Doesn't like—the man's minions had tried to have her pets killed!

Alden bowed over her hand. "Rest assured, ma'am. 'Blessed be the God of Shadrach, Meshach and Abednego, who hath sent his angel and delivered his servants that trusted in him.' They may reside here in feline felicity, and Sherry will love it."

HE DID NOT CALL FOR MENSERVANTS TO DETAIN THEM. HE DID not call for his sword to run George through on the spot. He did not wrest her from her husband's control, so he could flee with her to Paris, to Rome, to Timbuktu. He allowed them to leave: Mr. and Mrs. George Hardcastle.

He didn't care!

Silence descended over the terrace. Alden gripped the parapet in his ringless fingers until his joints went numb.

I have never cared! I do not care now! Women are all alike. One is as good as another in the dark!

He thought suddenly of Maria, the first time he had learned she was unfaithful to him, as well as to her husband. Her genuine amazement at his surprise. Her concern for his hurt. *Why, sir! Would you try to possess me? Be a man!*

The sound of voices made him glance up. Sherry raced down one of the paths to the fountain. Peter Primrose strolled after him. The child turned and waved, his blond head a golden coin in the sunshine. It had been worth it—every last moment! Alden would do it all again and with even more swagger the next time. What had he lost? A handful of rings. Meanwhile he had gained back an entire estate and beguiled yet another woman into his bed.

Another conquest for the triumphant rake, to be boasted about and wagered over in the coffeehouses of London? Well done, Lord Gracechurch!

Then why the devil did he feel as if he deserved to be whipped?

"My lord?"

Alden looked up to see one of the gardeners staring at him: Harry Appleby, his head gardener's son.

"Whence the deuce do you find the temerity to disturb me in my own damned garden?"

Harry flushed and touched his forehead. "Beg pardon, my lord, but Your Lordship is bleeding onto the parapet."

Alden glanced down. His slashed waistcoat and shirt framed the long cut George Hardcastle had given him. A tiny trail of red, like little petals, bloomed on the white stone.

He pulled out his lace-edged handkerchief and pressed it over the wound. It would hurt to laugh, but he still did it.

"Never mind, Harry, the next rain will make all as good as new."

*   *   *

HE CARRIAGE ROCKED. JULIET FOLDED HER HANDS IN HER LAP.
"Gold!" George exclaimed, fingering Alden's rings.
"Keep us alive for a month or two! Maybe you should spend a few
more nights in some aristocrat's bed?"

Her husband leaned back and laughed. He was still handsome.
It was easy to see how a naive girl had been impressed and flattered
by his attention. George was tall and limber, with lovely hands.
She remembered kissing him the first time. She remembered falling in love. A lifetime ago. Now she was incapable of ever falling
in love again.

"They told me you were dead," she said. "Other than intimacy,
I have every intention of being a dutiful wife."

He leaned forward and touched her hand. "But I can't afford
you, Julie, not unless you do something to earn your keep. Someone's been targeting my business, someone powerful. I couldn't
maintain trade. I got delayed indefinitely by customs and denied
permits for months at a time. Rivals brought in shiploads of timber, while mine rotted at sea or on the quay of some godforsaken
Russian port. It went on for months. I'm just about destroyed.
Your father—"

She moved her hand so he couldn't reach it. "Wanted to ruin
you immediately after we ran away, yes. But that was five years
ago. My father wouldn't interfere now. I doubt he knows, or cares,
whether we live or die."

"Then who the devil was it, Julie? Who wanted to ruin me?"

"I don't know," she said. "Recently, it seemed that I was the
target of ruinous plotting. Lord Edward Vane was behind it."

George looked uncomfortable. "He's a powerful man. It doesn't
do to cross him."

"But we did. Five years ago."

"Lud, he's forgiven us now. He's invited me to become a partner
in his new venture: the Isle of Dogs Muscovy Pelt and Sable Company. Make my fortune."

"*Lord Edward Vane* promises to rescue us from ruin?"

"Why not?"

A chill shivered down Juliet's spine. She almost welcomed it. Anything was better than this leaden numbness, the weight that was crushing her heart.

"Surely," she asked, "there are conditions for his generosity?"

George stared from the window, avoiding her gaze. "Well, of course—there are bound to be conditions."

She closed her eyes against sudden, mysterious tears. Fear? Grief? She didn't know, but she could afford neither. Five years ago she had married. Whatever happened now, nothing could change that. She must make the best of it.

"You were such a peach, Julie." George sounded almost plaintive. "I did love you."

"Not as much," she replied dryly, "as I thought I loved you."

S UMMER DAYS AT GRACECHURCH. THERE WERE FEW PLACES lovelier in the world and few places as suddenly empty. Within three days the cats claimed the run of the place. Fickle creatures, content wherever they found food and shelter with affection on demand. While the cats sunned themselves on the terraces, Alden gave his daylight hours to Sherry and to estate business. After all, he had five thousand pounds won from Lord Edward to invest. Every day when he left Sherry, he rode until he was exhausted, then came home to pore over the account books and farm registers until his eyes burned like flames in dry sockets.

It wasn't enough.

The agony became acute in the long summer evenings after Sherry had gone to bed, when her cats butted at his ankles or claimed his lap. In the cruel, restless nights, his pain became torture. However much he exhausted himself, he couldn't sleep. He thought he was haunted by women: every woman he had ever let down or disappointed; every woman who had ever deceived or wounded him.

Why had he never married, even though it was his clear duty to produce a legitimate heir? Did he think he wanted more from marriage than he had believed it possible to find there? Any woman he had ever thought he might marry had already been wed to someone else. Had he deliberately chosen married women as a way to minimize the risk of truly sharing trust? Even Juliet! *Even Juliet!*

He had never cared like this before, when a mistress had gone back to her husband. The thought of Juliet in George Hardcastle's bed made him physically ill. Desire for any other woman was ground into dust. What else could cause that, but rage and wounded pride? Yet there was *nothing* he could do about it, nothing he could ever hope to offer her in recompense, except, of course, to retrieve her locket.

Tell me, Gracechurch, how did you ever lose a chess game—especially to a woman? I would like to match you some time myself.

We are playing right now, Lord Edward.

He had forever lost Juliet, but the battle between Lord Edward Vane and Lord Gracechurch had hardly begun. There was nothing left to Alden now, except revenge.

He dismissed the first and most obvious answer. Now that enough time had passed, he could easily force Lord Edward to a duel over any triviality without involving Juliet's reputation, but if he died on that more proficient sword, her locket would never be recovered and Gracechurch Abbey would be abandoned, after all. One of his cousins would inherit and the fellow was an unworldly man of the cloth, sadly incompetent to continue what Alden had been working for so damned hard: to rescue the estates and all the people dependent upon them.

A challenge would also reveal to Lord Edward how much Alden cared about what had happened at Marion Hall. Thus, no duel.

However, another gambit had been played out in Sir Reginald's country home, the taunt the duke's son had not been able to resist: *The locket contains the key to a fortune—*

It demonstrated a weakness shared by most men: greed. Yet unreasonable greed often revealed desperation. Perhaps Lord Edward was more financially vulnerable than anyone had realized. And the next move in the game was Alden's.

*H*E RODE UP TO LONDON IN HIS CARRIAGE. THE NEXT DAY, dressed in fawn-and-gold brocade, he took a sedan chair to his favorite coffeehouse. The room overflowed with talk. Gentlemen and lords, flamboyant as peacocks, were debating, laughing, even occasionally drinking coffee. Lord Gracechurch fit in among them as if he had never been away.

Only one man there had also been present at Marion Hall, the man Alden had come to seek: Robert Dovenby. Alden leaned one hand—fingers empty of rings—on the back of a chair at the Dove's table, as if only stopping for a moment.

"I believe, sir," he said, "that we might have an interest in common."

The Dove raised a dark brow. "Really?" A serving man brought coffee, fragrant and hot. Robert Dovenby sipped at his cup. Alden said nothing, only waited. The other man sat back as if to assess him. "Not, I trust, about our last unfortunate meeting? I assure you I have forgotten every detail."

Alden laughed. He didn't know Robert Dovenby, but his instinct was to rather like the man. "It did not escape me, sir, that you created a diversion that evening in a most timely fashion. I do not imagine you are usually that clumsy."

"The brass goddess? The side table? The ensuing conflagration?"

"It gave the lady a most welcome moment of privacy. Was that merely chivalry, or was it your intention to obstruct a certain person's plans?"

"Chivalry, of course. I would never wish to annoy our mutual friend."

Alden studied the man's face. The bland expression gave little away, but he decided to take the next step. He had to know, if he was going to see Lord Edward ruined.

"Yet what if it were a question of something a little stronger than annoyance?"

Dovenby set his empty cup on the table. "Then I should suggest we discuss it."

"Shall we meet later, sir?" Alden indicated the room. "Without this busy audience?"

"By all means, Lord Gracechurch. I always prefer to conduct such business with discretion."

Alden bent close enough to murmur in the Dove's ear as he slipped a paper with an address and time into his pocket. "I thought so."

T HERE WERE SEVERAL PLACES IN LONDON WHERE TWO GENTLE-men might meet at night in absolute secrecy. Alden's suggestion had been a spare room in Lord Bracefort's townhouse, while that lord was conducting a party. It was a party without ladies, or rather, without his wife, who was visiting family in the country. The women who attended such select gatherings did not claim to be ladies. Alden wasn't invited, of course. It didn't matter. By the time he arrived, everyone was drunk, including the footman at the door.

Alden walked through several rooms interestingly decorated with half-naked women. Lord Bracefort displayed a lace-trimmed garter tied around his bald pate. His wig and jacket were missing, as were the fastenings on his breeches. Like pennies, the brass buttons lay scattered on a table. His companion sported His Lordship's wig and little else. She held a small fruit knife in one hand and was carefully slicing more thread. Buttons plinked while His Lordship giggled, oblivious to his surroundings.

Robert Dovenby was waiting in a disused box room at the top of the house. He sat carelessly on the draped arm of a chair. The skirts of his gray coat flowed over the dust cloth. Both men could be observed arriving and leaving separately without arousing suspicion. With a house filled by such luscious guests, it was highly unlikely anyone would believe they had come to meet each other.

"You stayed out of London longer than I expected," Dovenby began.

"I was busy with some new cats." Alden did not want to admit how he had raged and brooded at Gracechurch Abbey.

"The lady's pets? She mentioned them."

Alden propped his shoulders against the wall and crossed his arms. "I didn't know you were acquainted."

"Since you were otherwise occupied, I saw that she returned safely home that next morning," the Dove said frankly.

"Thank you. I should have done it. Unfortunately, I was sadly incapacitated. One more bone to pick with our mutual friend."

"How did you ever fall into his clutches to begin with?"

Alden shrugged. "Carelessness. He was the spider. I was the fly. You are aware of the original scandal—"

"I was in London at the time. Not only were she and the butcher's grandson held up to vicious ridicule, but the broadsheets were full of very vigorous cartoons about our mutual friend that were extremely close to the bone."

"His tastes are indiscriminate," Alden said, "like a cat's."

The Dove stretched out long legs. His shoes boasted discreet silver buckles. "I doubt if he ever felt anything as honest as simple lust. He hungers only for the further inflation of his pride, rather publicly damaged, of course, by the lady. Marion Hall was his idea of revenge?"

"It goes further than that. He also wanted her locket. He chose a particularly diabolical way to secure it, but the locket itself was one of his aims."

"Because the lady valued it?"

It was pure instinct to think he could rely on this man, yet Alden trusted him.

"That was his first incentive. For sentimental reasons, she valued it more than anything she possessed. No one could have told our friend that, except her husband. Yet one would think these two men would never be on speaking terms: a duke's son and the commoner who stole away his intended bride. So I assume they had business dealings?"

"They did," the Dove said.

"I thought so. Did Lord Edward deliberately ruin Hardcastle's timber business to gain control over him?"

"Ah," the Dove said. "I believed you to be a perceptive man. George Hardcastle does not know that, of course."

"Or he would hardly have told Lord Edward about his wife's locket. Yet Hardcastle must think it valueless—"

"Why do you think any of this would be of interest to me?" Dovenby asked.

"I made a few inquiries," Alden said. "Discreetly, through an agent. You also have business dealings with our mutual friend."

"To my benefit. Not, unfortunately—though he doesn't know it yet—to his."

"Yet he trusts you. He invited you to Marion Hall. I would like to know whether he is just driven by greed, or if he is in truth in need of funds?"

Dovenby studied his shoe buckles, a small grin bending the corners of his long mouth. "One might say that his affairs are in considerable disarray. Yet he knows only that he needs vast amounts more capital to continue to invest in his dearest business ventures. His intention is to become the wealthiest man in England."

"It's not easy being a younger son," Alden commented dryly.

The grin became wider. "Greed is an unfortunate attribute. It can blind one to reality. I have wondered why he seemed so incredibly overconfident lately, though I have found his hubris most useful. You imply the lady's locket has some critical role to play?"

"He wouldn't sell it back to me—not for blood, nor even for money. I believe he thinks it will lead him to the Felton treasure: a legendary hoard buried about a hundred years ago and never recovered, a fortune in gold and jewelry."

"Which explains a great deal," Dovenby said. "Thank you for

this information. May I advise you not to invest in the Isle of Dogs Muscovy Pelt and Sable Company, where our mutual friend is now so heavily committed?"

"Yet perhaps I have my own plans for his downfall," Alden replied quietly.

Dovenby closed his eyes as if he were making up his mind to something. "You don't have time. There is another task for you, if you're interested. The details of this new Muscovy venture do not auger well for the lady."

Alden's small shred of satisfaction vanished. "What the devil do you mean?"

The other man glanced up, his face calm, but a small pulse beat visibly at the side of his jaw. "What use is his wife to George Hardcastle? He abandoned her five years ago. She is only in the way now. To get him to bring her to London, Lord Edward ruined Hardcastle's business, trapped her into adultery, then told her husband where to find her in Manston Mingate. One would think his revenge on her complete. Yet now, for no apparent reason, the duke's son has given her husband a partnership in his new Muscovy Company. Lord Edward believes—if mistakenly—that it is going to make him very rich. Now he voluntarily shares that wealth with a man he despises?"

Dread seized Alden by the throat. He paced away across the room. "The devil! On what conditions? What the hell has he demanded from George Hardcastle in return?"

"Sir Reginald Denby—no doubt in his role as lackey for Lord Edward—has been collecting affidavits: from a woman in the village who worked for the lady, even a lady's maid from your mother's house—"

"*Tilly? Kate?*" Alden spun about to stare at Dovenby. "What about?"

"Her servants swear she ate flowers. Just to turn down a duke's son and run away with the steward is enough proof of lunacy in the right quarters—"

Alden's hands closed on a length of linen. Without conscious thought, he grasped fabric in both fists and ripped. The dust sheet tore to reveal the marble statue of a woman.

"He *cannot* make such accusations stick!"

"Of course he can." Dovenby was white about the nostrils. "With the husband complicit and Lord Edward paying the doctors?"

"And she behaved with exquisite insanity at Marion Hall?" Rage formed a sick knot in his throat. It was his fault! *His fault!* To be declared mad was worse than death. "She has already been locked away? Where?"

"Perhaps you can find out." The Dove held out a folded slip of paper. "I had planned to go after her myself, but perhaps the task is rightfully yours. Leave our financial revenge on Lord Edward to me, and I shall—with a certain personal reluctance, I admit— leave the lady's rescue to you. Here is Hardcastle's address."

"She's not in Bedlam?" The question almost choked him.

"No," Dovenby said, standing. "A private asylum, I understand—I don't know where."

Alden strode blindly back across the room. Appalling images flooded his mind. The Bethlam Royal Hospital lay north of the old London Wall at Moorgate, where bored ladies and gentlemen paid a fee to laugh at the lunatics—an afternoon's entertainment, to watch the filthy, witless creatures shout and swear and rattle their chains.

Was Juliet now locked in such a place?

With his fingers on the door latch, Alden forced himself to stop and look back. "Thank you, sir. We'll stay in touch? I will find the lady, but I'm not done with Lord Edward."

Dovenby walked to the window and looked out, palms clasped behind his back.

"I'll keep you informed, Lord Gracechurch."

The statue appeared to be staring past him. With one hand the marble woman clutched her Greek robes to her breast. In the other she held out a ball of fine thread.

"Ariadne," Alden said.

Dovenby looked around and cocked a brow.

Alden nodded at the statue. "The king's daughter who led Theseus out of the labyrinth after he killed the Minotaur, only to be abandoned on the isle of Naxos by the hero she had rescued. Is it ever possible to rewrite myth and find a happy ending?"

"I don't know," the other man replied. "But good luck."

CHAPTER FOURTEEN

𝒜 LDEN'S FIRST IMPULSE WAS TO OPENLY CONFRONT GEORGE
Hardcastle or the duke's son. To find out where Juliet had
been sent, he could easily justify the infliction of pain. Yet he
knew a physical confrontation would be useless. His enemies
could lie, prevaricate, delay. Lord Edward would relish being
given such power. Meanwhile a simple message would see Juliet
moved, farther and farther from Alden's reach, until she had disappeared so deeply that no one could ever find her.

He walked blindly through Bracefort's house, ignoring the naked women, the couples copulating in the hallways. The thought
flitted vaguely through his mind that this was the longest he'd
gone without sex for ten years. He dismissed it, concentrating
only on Juliet. He did not love her, but he was damned if he'd
see her incarcerated for life as a lunatic!

"You are to be congratulated, sir, on your narrow escape," a
man's voice said.

For a moment, Alden's rage was so intense that he could have
murdered with his bare hands. Instead he raised both brows and
stared back at Lord Edward Vane.

"From what, sir?"

The duke's son burst out laughing, two patches dancing on his
cheeks. "From any deeper entanglement with sweet Juliet, of
course. She has gone mad. Did you know?"

It took every ounce of self-control, but Alden shrugged. "Really? I fail to see, sir, how that doleful fact concerns me."

Was Lord Edward disconcerted, even for a moment? "Faith, sir! You truly are a coldhearted dog."

Alden gave the duke's son a careless bow. "Hearts, sir, were never at issue. I trust Mr. Hardcastle and his mad wife may dance along merrily enough together?"

He managed to walk away. He even stopped casually in the hallway to exchange a lewd joke with Trenton-Smith, who appeared to have forgotten their small misunderstanding over the man's unholy sister.

At last Alden walked out into the stench of London streets and called for a sedan chair. If he was to best Lord Edward in this, he must overcome his murderous rage—the impulse to drive too fast across the board. Winning had never before been this important, and this time the checkmate must be absolute. The chair jolted along the cobbles. Alden leaned back and forced himself to think, to concentrate on a gambit for victory. He had no legal or social justification whatsoever to interfere in what they had done to Juliet. She was another man's property. Doctors had declared her insane.

Ariadne, the king's daughter who led Theseus out of the labyrinth after he killed the Minotaur, only to be abandoned on the isle of Naxos by the hero she had rescued.

If he was to save her this time, it meant disappearing into the labyrinth himself.

*J*ULIET SAT IN STONY SILENCE AND STARED AT THE SOUP. TINY black specks floated among the brown chunks of mutton. She did not think they were edible. In fact, she very much feared the specks had once enjoyed individual lives of their own. Nevertheless she dipped her spoon into the liquid and swallowed. The woman in the next room had been refusing food. They had tied her hands and legs to force a physic down her throat. The woman had retched and screamed for an entire night.

Juliet ate the soup.

The room was tiny, little more than a cell, somewhere near the top of a large house. Light filtered in through a barred window high up on the wall. She had no idea what kind of house, because they had arrived in the dark and she had been bound and gagged.

A madwoman! Since then this little space was all she had known. It held a bed, a wooden chair by a shelf against the wall, and a chamber pot. The bed was equipped with large leather straps. There were, she was sure, worse places to house a lunatic. At least she had her own room and the public did not pay a fee to look at her.

A woman in a white apron came and took away the bowl. She was sandy-haired, no longer young, with a fearful look about the nostrils, as if she had never received quite enough air.

"Excellent soup, Mistress Welland," Juliet said. "An imaginative recipe. I am glad to know that Lord Edward is getting his money's worth."

"Any more talk like that and it'll be the gag," the sandy-haired woman replied. "Or the dark cell. I have my orders."

The dark cell was, Juliet had learned, a place in the cellar with no windows at all, where lunatics could be left for days at a time in pitch blackness. Confinement was considered therapeutic. At least as long as she stayed in this room, she had daylight.

"My apologies, ma'am. Your chef would grace the king's own kitchens, of course."

Mistress Welland shouted. Footsteps pounded in the corridor. Two men burst into the room and grasped Juliet by both arms, dragging her from her chair. The woman thrust a rag into Juliet's mouth and tied it behind her head, while the men strapped her down to the bed.

"You're not to be allowed to pretend to be a lady! That's the conditions!"

Helplessly Juliet shook her head as straps and padlocks snapped into place. She must try to think about something else. A hay meadow, sweet and bright in the sunshine. Her arbor, draped in white muslin and moonlight. The cluck of chickens as they scratched and dusted in the shade. Her cats: Shadrach, Meshach and Abednego, named for the men of faith who had been rescued from a fiery furnace by an angel. Not a man. Not a man with hair like a summer day and a dastardly way with women.

Yet she had the rest of her life to do nothing but think. Alden had tried, in his own way, to behave with honor. He had touched her to the soul. Why had she let them part with harsh words? Why hadn't she tried harder to understand? Now it was too late.

THE STUDY IN LORD EDWARD'S TOWNHOUSE SLEPT QUIETLY enough. The house sighed occasionally, as if the furnishings relaxed in their own secret slumber. His face blackened with soot, his hair covered, Alden sat for a moment on the windowsill and contemplated the dark room. This was where he had lost Grace-church Abbey in a game of cards, where he had wondered how he could be so foxed on so little wine, where Lord Edward had no doubt slipped him some concoction to blur his judgment: all to make Juliet suffer.

The card table drowsed, its treacherous surface dumb. The side table stood empty and voiceless. But something in this house must be forced to talk: to give up its secrets and tell him where Juliet had been taken.

Alden slipped silently into the room. He believed that the duke's son was out, but the house was full of servants. If he was discovered, he might be slain before he could prove his identity and attempt to laugh it all off as a joke between gentlemen. Smiling a little at the splendor of the risk, he opened the shutter on his lantern and began to search.

He was methodical and thorough. When he found locked drawers, he took keys out of his pocket and unlocked them. How fortunate that the duke's son had chosen to visit a particular courtesan who had also in the past favored Alden! Lovely Clarinda Kennedy had agreed, with a little persuasion, to steal the keys from Lord Edward's pocket. While the duke's son spent the rest of the night enjoying her delectable services, Alden was getting copies made.

Now desk drawers willingly surrendered to his skilled hands. In absolute silence, lit by the steady beam from the lantern, Alden studied papers and receipts. He learned what Dovenby had meant about Lord Edward's empire of investments. He skimmed letters from abandoned women. He found a copy of the agreement that the duke's son had drawn up to include George Hardcastle in his business schemes. He did not discover where they had taken Juliet.

Closing the shutter on the lantern, Alden stepped into the hallway. A few moments later a stair sagged under his weight, shouting its complaint. He froze for a moment, but no doors opened. No servants came racing with cudgels and pistols. He walked into Lord Edward's bedroom and took out the replica keys once again.

Drawers slid open. Dressers revealed neat stacks of shirts. Nothing! Why would Lord Edward write down where he had sent her? He had no doubt washed his hands of her, content in the knowledge that Juliet was locked away forever. Alden almost wished that the door would open and the duke's son walk unsuspecting into the room. He could very easily justify murder.

Sick at heart, Alden went to the window and looked out on the moonlit chimneys of London. The quiet scene was a lie. Beneath those roofs men and women schemed and cursed and caroused, battling fate or their own damnable nature, fighting to survive in a world that seldom cared whether they lived or died. It had been his life since he had come back from Italy—a meaningless pattern of coldhearted risks. Now he didn't give a damn if he never saw London's hells and coffeehouses again.

Closing his lantern, he turned and strode back through Lord Edward's chamber. A shaft of moonlight streamed across brocade hangings and the small table beside the bed. The white wax of a half-burned candle gleamed in a gilt candlestick, a leather-bound book beside it. Alden stopped and looked at it. Within three strides he had opened the book. Several sheets of paper lay folded inside.

His pulse beat hard as he opened the lantern shutter and read the crabbed writing. Not directions to where Juliet had been taken. She was mentioned nowhere on the tattered sheets. But if he could only find her, this information might free her yet.

"*Y*OU MUST NOT ASK FOR BOOKS OR WRITING MATERIALS," Mistress Welland said. "You can't read or write. Such mad questions will only overheat your brain. You are to be gagged whenever you say such things. If you persist, you'll be put in the dark cell."

Juliet stared up at the high window and said nothing. She didn't even dislike Mistress Welland. At least as long as she was there, the men wouldn't touch her. Juliet listened to the click of her shoes as the woman crossed the room. Keys rattled on the ring at her waist.

A man's voice sounded from the corridor: Bill, one of the attendants.

For a moment, Juliet lay absolutely still, barely daring to breathe. *Don't leave, ma'am, I pray!* From the bed she couldn't see the door, because her head was trapped in a kind of wooden cradle. She had been strapped down once again, because she had been pacing the room. They said it was the repetitive, senseless motion of a lunatic.

The keys clinked. The woman's footsteps receded down the hallway. But the man's heavy tread turned back into her room. Juliet closed her eyes and swallowed hard as his breath wafted over her face.

"You're a pretty trollop, Polly," Bill said.

She lay rigid, trying not to flinch, but she knew what was

coming. A fumbling at her clothes. Hands on the neck of her dress. Coarse fingers thrust down the front of her bodice, curdling her blood, corrupting every bright memory.

"Do you like that?" A rough fingertip felt for her nipple. "They say you can't get enough of a man. Shall I come back tonight?"

A woman's scream pierced the air. Bill cursed. Juliet heard the grate of his nailed boots, before the door slammed shut and the key turned in the lock. A hideous stain seemed to have soaked to her bones. He had not visited her at night yet. But of course it was only a matter of time. Then, perhaps, she truly would go insane.

ALDEN LINGERED FOR A MOMENT ACROSS THE STREET FROM Hardcastle's house—a small row house in a respectable merchant neighborhood, the address Robert Dovenby had given him—to watch Juliet's husband leave for the day. This was where George had brought Juliet after they left Gracechurch Abbey. This is where doctors had examined her and declared her a lunatic.

They had used the affidavits from Kate and Tilly, of course, and twisted her behavior into more condemnatory evidence. Perhaps she had been drugged, to appear almost senseless when examined. Alden hoped so. He hoped the hell she had not been conscious when they put her through that. Yet she must have woken up and found herself imprisoned, with nothing but the shrieks and wails of madwomen for company.

He clenched both fists. Pray God she was incarcerated only with women!

"Here, you! Move about your business!"

A man in a white wig and blue coat waved his stick in Alden's face. In that first split second, Alden almost gave away the whole game, then he remembered. He was dressed like a tradesman's servant, a man who put his back into his work. To be certain his true identity could not be detected, he had found himself a genuine job, where he ate, slept and drank with the other men. He could not remember ever being this dirty in his life.

Alden slouched, tugged at the lock of hair over his forehead, stepped into the gutter, and adopted a scurrilous accent. "Beg pardon, sir. No harm meant."

The gentleman pushed past him without a backward glance.

Alden adjusted the heavy load on his shoulder and dodged through the carriages and horsemen thronging the roadway. It had taken two weeks to get to this point: to be welcomed and trusted in the kitchen of Hardcastle's house, while his network of agents scoured the lunatic asylums and madhouses of Britain. To no avail. No Juliet Seton or Lady Elizabeth Amberleigh or Mrs. George Hardcastle was recorded as a patient in any of them. Nothing was left but this—how well he had charmed George's servants.

Ignoring the front entrance, Alden thumped down the stairs to the servants' portal below the street. The door opened to reveal the face of a kitchen maid.

"Delivery." Alden gave the girl a wink.

"Well, don't just stand there," the maid answered. "Bring it in. But mind you don't mark up our clean floor, else Cook'll have my hide."

Alden grinned and gave her another wink. "Then I'd better take my boots off."

"And that's not all you'd like to have off, I reckon!" The girl blushed scarlet.

He laughed, bent his head and stepped through the doorway. Setting down his burden, Alden caught the maid around the waist, tipping up her face with one finger under her chin.

She gazed into his eyes in open adoration. "You villain! I'll lose my place!"

"No, you won't, Emmy! Not like I've lost my heart."

The girl closed her eyes for his kiss. He made it slow and thorough. Her limber little hands stroked his back. He thought with dismay that she must be a virgin. The latch rattled. The maid leaped away and smoothed down her apron. Her eyes shone.

Cook bustled into the kitchen. "Brought my beef, you rogue?"

"And your five chickens and the goose. But you can only have 'em in trade for a kiss and some of your apple pie, Cook."

The older woman took a good-natured swipe at his head, but Alden kissed her, too, before they all sat down at the kitchen table. A few moments later he wiped the crumbs from his mouth with his shirt cuff, while the two women devoured him with their eyes.

"So what's the latest gossip?" he asked.

"I told you the mistress was taken off for a lunatic?" Cook's voice dropped to a conspiratorial whisper. "Well, now! I've found out where!"

His heart missed a beat. It was everything Alden could do not to grasp Cook by both plump shoulders and shake her, but they mustn't know that he cared.

"Have you now?" he asked. "To the backside of the moon, most like!"

Emmy screeched with laughter. "I told you she was mad, didn't I? The master brings home his wife that ran away from him five years ago and she won't let him touch her."

He winked again. "You wouldn't bar the bedroom door against *me*, now, would you, Emmy?"

The girl blushed and giggled. Alden knew she would give him her virginity and her heart as eagerly as she swallowed her pie. He felt almost ashamed as he squeezed her fingers under the table.

Cook stood up to poke the kitchen fire. "Who ever heard the like? To refuse his marital rights to a handsome young gentleman like Mr. Hardcastle!"

"Only goes to show she was crazy," Alden said, though he could have bedded Cook herself when he'd first heard it: Juliet had locked her door against her husband at night. It was one bright candle burning in his storm of black rage.

"Well, that's neither here nor there now, is it?" Cook rattled the poker. "Harry Oldacre down the road knows Tim Roland, like I told you, as works on occasion for Mr. Grimble. Mr. Grimble's ostler is friends with a fellow named Dave Peck, who has a sister called Meg. Well, guess, now!" She turned and waved both hands, the pots on the wall in imminent danger from the poker. "That same Meg is kin to the coachman that came to take the mistress away. Harry told me the whole story."

"It'd better be a good one!" Alden curbed his impatience and grinned at Emmy.

Cook sat back at the table. "The mistress asked the coachman to let her off in the middle of nowhere. She said she had to stop for a call of nature and instead took off into the woods like a March hare, throwing out shreds of cloth as if she were trying to leave a trail. Poor mad thing. They tied her hands after that."

He didn't know if he could bear it. *They had tied her hands!* Yet, clever Juliet, she had first done something to make the coachman remember her.

"So where did they take her?" Emmy asked.

"To a place in Wiltshire—Blackthorn Manor, it's called. Of course, it's not Mr. Hardcastle as is paying for it—it's that lord as came here and oversaw her being taken away."

"Never heard of it, nor your fancy lords," Alden said, choking down his rage. "And what's more, I don't care." He let go of the maid's hand and stood up. "Here's what I care about: I'm going away, Emmy. Remember my brother's little farm in Devon, the one I told you about? He's asked me to go there and help out, like I said he might. I'm off tomorrow. No more town deliveries for me."

"Off tomorrow?" The maid's eyes swam with tears.

He leaned down and kissed the top of her little linen cap. "Don't fret for me, now, will you?"

Emmy pushed him away and stood up. "Fret for the likes of you, a butcher's fellow! I'll have you know that Harry Oldacre asked me only yesterday to walk out with him on my afternoon off."

Alden picked up his basket and swaggered to the door. "Then it's good-bye, isn't it? Thanks for the pie, Cook. Don't work for any more lunatics, will you?"

He dodged out of the doorway as Cook tossed a cabbage at his head. Emmy's sad little sobs followed him all the way up the stairs. He would make sure that the girl received a surprise message in a couple of weeks: a distant relative, perhaps, someone she'd never heard of, who had left her a small legacy. Emmy wanted to leave domestic service and have a little shop of her own. Perhaps Harry Oldacre would like to be a part of that bright new future.

"*Y*ES, MY LORD," A MAN'S VOICE SAID. "WE COULD INDEED, most certainly. Blackthorn Manor would be honored to help in the case of Your Lordship's sister."

Juliet snapped awake. Every bone and muscle ached. Sunlight poured in through the high window. She had been left strapped to her bed the previous evening and no one had come to release her this morning. She was desperate to use the chamber pot.

Footsteps sounded in the hallway. One set echoed with the rap of a gentleman's heeled shoes. She recognized the heavier tread: Mr. Upbridge, the man who ran the place. They had not exactly been introduced. Mr. Upbridge had inspected her when she had first been carried in, gagged and bound. He had listened to her captors' account of her behavior and studied some documents handed him by the men Lord Edward had hired. Without asking for the gag to be removed, Upbridge had gravely shaken his head and told the men to take her to this room, where she was to be encouraged to become sane. Now she heard him propounding his theories to someone else.

"Indeed a most interesting case, my lord. Delusions are common among lunatics. You say your sister believes she is Queen of Scots? We've had women claiming to be Joan of Arc or Cleopatra.

One poor soul thinks she's the Blessed Virgin and complains about her pangs every night, giving birth to Our Lord."

Another male voice replied, too softly for her to hear. The footsteps stopped. She heard the little sliding hatch in the door being opened. She couldn't lift her head to look at the faces peering in at her. Neither would they see much of her beyond a body lying strapped beneath blankets.

"This one claims she's an earl's daughter," Upbridge said. "Though in God's truth, she's an actress, quite out of her wits. A disorder caused by poisonous humors from the womb, brought about by insatiable wantonness. Fortunately, a gentleman took pity on her and had her brought here for treatment—an act of great charity. We do not allow her to mix with our other patients, of course, the ladies of real breeding."

The other man murmured something.

"Very simple, my lord. If she insists on her delusions, she is corrected. Nothing cruel or pernicious, even for females who are lewdly given. We gag our patients for wrong speech. Tie them down with leather straps for wrong actions. It's very effective in most cases. In addition we use purgatives and cold baths. She is to be started on a course of physic on Monday."

The other man asked a soft question.

"Such cases are seldom tractable, sadly, but our attendants are well trained in dealing with such difficulties as the lunatics may present."

The sliding hatch snapped shut. Juliet closed her eyes.

To her surprise the door opened. The men's footsteps crossed the room. Juliet automatically flinched, though she tried not to show her fear. She even forced herself to look up into the face that leaned over the bed, then she relaxed. Mr. Upbridge, of course, who wouldn't dream of touching her. She tried to smile at him.

"Doing better this morning, are we?" he asked. "Now, tell this gentleman who you are."

Juliet knew perfectly well what she was supposed to say: *I am an actress. I have lived like a harlot, driven by unbridled lust.*

"I am Lady Elizabeth Juliet Amberleigh, the daughter of the Earl of Felton," she said. "I would like my father to be told I am here."

"Lud!" the other man said with a trace of Scots accent. "What's her true name?"

"Polly Brown," Upbridge replied.

Juliet barely heard him. Desperately she tried to turn her head to look at the visitor. Shadows and sun moved over the plaster. The newcomer leaned his palm on the wall above her head. His cuff was embroidered, beautiful, the cut extravagant. Cascades of snowy lace with a pattern of tiny bells and angels fell away from an elegant white hand.

"Polly Brown?" A kind of bored hauteur colored his voice. "Why, I believe you are right, sir! I have seen her myself playing some Italian role."

"One of those lewd operas, no doubt?" Mr. Upbridge asked. "A looseness in morals often leads to lunacy."

The guest leaned over the bed and smiled down at her. Sunlight glowed in a halo around his white wig. Juliet smiled back through a wash of tears as he brushed one finger over his lips to indicate silence.

Alden gazed down at her with no other change in expression. "Perhaps your attendant—Mistress Welland?—should bring breakfast."

"No breakfast, my lord. Food given too early in the day—"

"Lud, sir! I should not like to think that my sister would go hungry so late in the morning."

". . . of course, my lord, in our better wing, where your sister would live . . ."

Alden leaned close enough to whisper in her ear. "Tonight. Do or say nothing out of the ordinary. Trust me, Juliet. You are rescued."

Upbridge was still burbling.

"I am sorry," Alden said as he walked away. "When I see this poor creature here, neither washed nor fed, I am not sure that Blackthorn Manor is appropriate for my sister, after all."

The door opened and closed again, but almost immediately Mistress Welland came in to undo Juliet's straps. She looked flushed and excited.

"A most distinguished visitor that was, from Scotland," she said. "Perhaps you know him?" Her breathless voice implied that Lady Elizabeth or Polly Brown might be equally intimate with a member of the Scots aristocracy. "Lord Maze, his name is, handsome as daylight." She grinned to herself, as if at a secret. "He's an earl."

"An earl?" Juliet sat up and laughed. She hoped it wasn't the mad cackle of a lunatic. "I thought he was an angel."

THE IMPOSING CHIMNEYS OF BLACKTHORN MANOR BULKED against shifting clouds, edged with moonlight. Alden had stalked down through the asylum that morning in such a white-hot rage he hadn't been sure he could trust himself. His ire was not for Mr. Upbridge, who obviously did his best to care for the inmates, but for Lord Edward Vane, who had conceived and paid for the whole scheme.

Yet he had controlled the anger. Even knowing that Juliet was imprisoned upstairs, he had spent three more hours that morning at Blackthorn, laying the groundwork for tonight. He had no authority to demand Juliet's release, no valid excuse to interfere. Mr. Upbridge was being well-paid to keep her, so he had no motivation whatsoever to let her go. It would have to be done with stealth.

At last Alden saw the signal he had been waiting for: a candle in a downstairs window. Carrying a selection of bottles in one hand, he walked rapidly across the short stretch of grass. A door opened. Alden stepped through into blackness. A female hand, wiry and strong, clasped his.

"Oh, lud! I wasn't sure Your Lordship would really come—"

She opened another door into a small bedroom lit by a single candle. The flame glimmered over hair softened to honey in the dim light. In her nightdress and with her tight bun combed out, she looked almost pretty. Alden smiled down into the nervous face of Mistress Nell Welland. Without compunction he slid one arm about her thin waist to pull her into his embrace.

"Faith, my lord!" she said, close to breathless. "You waste no time at all!"

He kissed the corner of her dry mouth. "Because there's no time to waste, Nell. I have to leave for Aberdeen tomorrow. You won't come?"

She shook her head, as he had known she would. He had learned that morning that she was an orphan, too afraid of the world outside Blackthorn to venture into it. Yet Lord Maze, the imaginary Scottish earl, had flattered and beguiled Nell Welland that morning, until she had agreed to this assignation tonight—to taste wine, he had suggested, to taste a little touch of wickedness.

Her small breasts thrust against his chest as he kissed her again. He could not afford to hurry and lose her trust, so he lingered, making the kiss as skilled as he knew how, calling on all those years of experience to soften her, weaken her, until she would agree to anything. Her lips trembled under his, firing his body. Thank God!

Alden was also determined that poor lonely Nell, imprisoned here among her lunatic charges, would never know that he didn't really want to do this. She would only remember that a Scottish earl had found her lovely and asked to spend a few hours in her company. She might also remember that he had brought her a present of exquisite and very strong wine—better than she had ever tasted in her life—and insisted that, between caresses, they share glass after glass.

For Alden didn't want her slender little body or surprisingly comely hair, he only wanted her keys.

*　　*　　*

*J*ULIET'S EARS STRAINED FOR ANY NOISE: A MOUSE SCRATCHING behind the plaster; beetles in the walls. Was this how a lunatic listened? Darkness spread over the room, as if pressing black kisses into the corners. There was no sound at all. Not even the muffled mumbling of the woman next door. Perhaps, while no one noticed, she had died and now lay stiff and cold in the night.

When the key turned in the lock, Juliet jerked—awake perhaps? She didn't know any longer whether she slept and dreamed, or whether she lay awake in the dark, waiting for footsteps—

The door slid open and a man's boots trod steadily across the floor.

"Juliet?" Alden said softly.

"It's dark," she replied, choking back panic. "I can't see you."

"Hush, don't move."

His quick, strong fingers snapped the padlocks open and worked at the straps. One by one they fell away, freeing her numb limbs. He slipped an arm about her shoulders and helped her sit up.

"I am afraid I am dreaming," she said with a small laugh. "It's hard to know sometimes."

"Don't talk. Put your arms about my neck. I'm going to carry you out of here."

"I can walk," she whispered back.

Warm breath tickled her cheek. She turned to it as a kitten turns to its mother: blindly, rooting for comfort. He pressed his lips to her ear.

"No, you can't. You are barefoot. Besides, you've been kept trussed like a package and your muscles won't work."

Without further ado, he swung her into his arms and carried her down the stairs. Juliet could no longer help herself. Though she did it in complete silence, she wept onto his shoulder the entire way.

*   *   *

T HE COACH MOVED THROUGH DARK LANES, THE SOUND OF THE horses' hooves loud in the quiet night. Or was it her own heart beating in her chest like a drum? Alden sat opposite her. His hands lay quietly in his lap. He had not touched her again after setting her inside his carriage. Juliet couldn't clearly see his face, beyond the glimmer of white skin and hair. He still wore the powdered wig. Now that her second chance was here, she was terrified.

"I stink," she said. She looked down at the shoes he had brought for her, her own shoes, a pair left behind at Gracechurch Abbey.

"Indeed, ma'am. A warm bath, I think, is a priority."

"How did you get the keys?"

"From Nell Welland, your keeper."

She stared out at the black hedges. "Surely she did not just hand them to you?"

"Alas, no. I stole them while she was soundly asleep and contented, I hope."

Her head snapped around. "You mean—?"

"Yes, all those skills from Italy." His voice was even and steady. "Useful in so many ways."

Juliet leaned her head back. "Of course, no woman can ever refuse you—which in this case was fortunate for me. But even Mistress Welland? I'm amazed!"

"She was quite attractive once she let her hair down," he said dryly. "We also drank wine together, a little stronger and in greater quantities than Nell was quite used to." Juliet thought he smiled, but perhaps it was a grimace that made his teeth glimmer whitely in the darkness. "I didn't have to go quite as far as I feared, but further, alas, than I'd hoped."

"I don't care," Juliet said, amazed that it was true. "Should I care? I am just so glad to be out of that place! How did you discover Blackthorn Manor?"

"Not from Lord Edward."

She closed her eyes against the night, trying to find a safer darkness within her own mind. "I didn't imagine he would tell you!"

"I searched his whole damn house for a clue. He hadn't cared enough to write it down. Your husband's servants found out for me in the end. Thanks to your little trick in the woods, the coachman remembered you. I had to practice my wiles on Emmy, with additional small attentions to Cook. I have paid court to a great many women looking for you, but I did them no harm."

"How can you be sure? Your very presence is dangerous to women."

"Dangerous? I made Emmy's heart beat faster. I tempted her a little. I taught her how to kiss. The beneficiary of those lessons is likely to be a stalwart young fellow named Harry Oldacre. Emmy is no worse for the experience."

Was it arrogance or just a simple statement of truth? Should a man like this pretend he didn't know what he could give women?

"Lud!" she said. "If your business is temptation, you know how to offer every woman her heart's desire, don't you?"

"I hope so. It is all I have practiced for years. But it was done only for you, to bring you your heart's desire."

"I'd have left with Lucifer—" Her voice caught. She had to take a deep breath and start again, hating herself for being such a coward. "But in the morning they will find out. They will come looking for me. Lord Edward is controlling George, and my husband has legal charge of my destiny. Next time they will hide me better—"

"No, they won't. Mr. Upbridge will be looking for an actress named Polly Brown, not for Lady Elizabeth Juliet Amberleigh."

How could his voice sound so confident, so certain? "Yes, I know they said I was called Polly. They also said I was a harlot. Why does it matter?"

"All the lunacy orders are in Polly Brown's name. Lord Edward claimed she was an actress, his mistress. He did it that way so that no one could find you, so that you could be buried in the madhouse forever, but you do see what it means?"

Her little glimmer of hope was almost painful. "That no one knows what really happened to me?"

"Exactly. Your husband has no proof that his wife was ever found insane. If Lady Elizabeth Juliet Amberleigh, daughter of the Earl of Felton, emerges triumphantly in public and is obviously not lunatic, Lord Edward and your husband cannot do this to you again."

His solid shape was warmly reassuring in the dark carriage. Perhaps she could even make out the shadow of a wry smile tilting the corners of his mouth?

"So the butterfly must emerge from its bondage in the chrysalis? How can I spread new wings in society?" It was hardly necessary to speak the obvious answer aloud, but she did so anyway, even though—after Bill—there was no question of their living together. "As your acknowledged mistress?"

"It's one solution, certainly. Any lady who did so would be seen as wicked, but *never* as lunatic. I am very tempted to tell you that there's no other choice, but there is, of course."

The lightness in his voice was absurdly welcome. She tried hard to match it. "I await with bated breath! You need a housekeeper, a chambermaid? Your best friend's brother is looking for a mistress? Your favorite brothel—?"

"Faith, Juliet! You would prefer *that* to my company? No, the answer is treasure."

"*Treasure?*"

"The Felton Hoard."

"The ancestral treasure of the Feltons has been lost since the Black Death. It's a myth, a story for children."

"No, Juliet. It is real. Lord Edward came across letters attesting to its rediscovery in the reign of Richard the Third and its final reburial during the Civil War. He has been assiduously collecting relevant documents ever since. I have read them."

"*Lord Edward?*"

"Did you think he wanted only your destruction? He also wants the fabled wealth of the Felton Hoard, which is why he wanted your locket. He believes that the key to the treasure's location is hidden inside."

She stared at his shadowy face for a moment, then she laughed. "Surely you see what an absurdity this is! If I had been carrying about the key to a fortune, why would I have lived as I did in Manston Mingate?"

He leaned back and crossed his arms. "I have wondered the same thing."

Juliet waved both hands. "The hoard was supposed to consist of jewelry, necklaces, gold bracelets, adornments for a woman. The story is they were a gift to an ancestor of mine from Harald Fairhair, when she married one of his Viking lords. She was an only child who brought extensive lands as a dowry, so her father demanded the treasure be settled exclusively upon her and her daughters to be passed down in the female line. How lovely if it existed! Sadly, it does not. Kit and I looked for it."

"But if it does, all that ancient gold would be yours, not your father's, not your husband's. I have read the documents. I believe your claim would hold up in court. Lord Edward intends to steal it."

"And finding this treasure is your sole answer for my future security?"

"Not at all. I was about to propose that while we wait for the duke's son to show his hand, you move in as my mother's companion."

"At the Dower House?" She hoped it didn't sound as squeaky to him as it did to her.

"Why not? For an earl's daughter to leave her merchant husband to live respectably with a dowager viscountess will be seen as eminently sane in all the right quarters."

"Your mother would agree?"

"She would barely notice you. You would have a great deal of freedom."

Juliet remembered her one brief encounter with his mother with a small trickle of trepidation. "This is my best option for the future?"

"My mother's brother is a marquess, which makes her almost untouchable in society." He stretched one arm along his seat back—a lazy movement, full of male confidence. "Besides, she is very touchy on the subject of lunacy."

"Why?"

Alden laughed. "Because she is quite mad herself, of course."

Juliet lapsed into silence. Anything was better than Blackthorn Manor. Yet it meant that her life as an independent woman was over. Even though Manston Mingate had brought its daily round of hard work, she had been free there. *Though never free from fear,* added a small voice—afraid, always, that George would find her.

Yet Alden had broken into Lord Edward's townhouse and seduced women who obviously hadn't interested him, in order to rescue her. He was offering her a future with his mother, where her husband couldn't harm her, even though he knew she would never consent to be his mistress. Why?

"I am not sure why you are doing this for me," she said after a few moments. "After what was said at our last meeting."

Moonlight glimmered on his cheek as he ducked his head to look out of the window. "You said nothing to me that I didn't deserve."

"I truly hated you."

"It doesn't matter if you still do. I am not about to proposition you."

"Then why did you rescue me?"

He was silent for a moment. "Shall we just say that we have a mutual enemy?"

"Lord Edward gives us a shared interest?"

"I intend to destroy him." It was said simply, the way a man might say he needed to see the weeds in his driveway destroyed.

So he had rescued her just for that: to foil the duke's son. Not because he cared, or because he felt he owed it to her. Perhaps it was better this way, safer. She still felt numb. What feelings might surface, if she ever allowed herself to truly feel again?

"By the way," Alden said with a new touch of mischief in his voice. "Did you really eat flowers?"

It caught her off guard. "Yes," she said. "When you sent me the pineapple, I ate part of the rose—petals fell into the butter . . ."

His laughter shook the carriage, shouts of pure glee. "Lud!" he said at last. "I am glad!"

"*Glad?* Why?"

He did not lean forward. He did not reach for her hand. Yet she felt as if his spirit reached out and touched her. "Because it means you were feeling foolish and merry—that I did something at least that brought you a moment of happiness."

A moment! If she was honest with herself, he had given her almost a week of happiness: impossibly golden, brilliant days, and that one night—

The coach rocked, then stopped. Light flooded in through the windows from several flambeaux outside, glittering on his wig and dancing over the smooth lines of his face. The face that was ruin to women.

"We are here," he said. "The Black Horse, a modest but decent hostelry. It's too far to go to Gracechurch tonight, so I hired us rooms earlier. Wrap yourself in this." He picked up a hooded cloak from the seat and held it out. His smile was blazing, almost defiant. "A hot bath awaits."

CHAPTER FIFTEEN

❦

*A*LDEN WANTED ONLY TO SMOOTH THE FILTHY, MATTED HAIR away from her forehead, press kisses on her sad lips and brave eyelids. . . . He had no right to any of it. He could only buy her a bath and a meal and a safe bed for the night—and new clothing, of course. The rags she was wearing must be burned.

But which rooms to reserve? The thought had burned, but wouldn't she want to be as far away from him as possible? Though how could he leave her alone, entirely surrounded by strangers? In the end he had chosen two chambers with a connecting door. She could always lock it against him.

After a solitary meal and a bath of his own, Alden paced his chamber, dressed in his nightshirt and dressing gown, thinking about women. He liked women. He liked their company and their minds. He loved their bodies. Why did a future inhabited only by a succession of ever-changing female faces now seem so bleak?

What the devil had Juliet done to him?

He had thought Lord Edward had concocted a fiendish enough revenge that night at Marion Hall. Nothing had prepared him for what he had found at Blackthorn Manor. Rage still flared, but a new, terrifying emotion he couldn't name burned even deeper. She was so damned courageous, his Juliet. No, not *his,* alas!

Could he resist trying to seduce her again—trying to cajole, beguile, to possess that lush body? The thought of making love to her seared through his blood. Could he make it through the rest of his life and never know that sweetness again?

He strode to the door connecting their rooms and stood there, his forehead pressed into the wood, his fingers clenched on the latch. She slept, warm, bathed and fed, on the other side. Without making a sound, he released the latch and turned, leaning his head back against the wooden panels.

Devil take it! *Juliet!* He wanted to shout her name at the moon.

A kitten mewed.

Alden stood stock still. He heard the sound again, a plaintive little wail, filled with terror. The cry formed itself into words, barely intelligible at first, then jelling into recognizable syllables: *please, please, please, please . . .*

Juliet was imploring—

Alden spun about, wrenched at the latch and stepped into her room.

Candlelight streamed through the open doorway behind him. Yellow beams traced across the bed to spark amber and mahogany in the long braid of hair moving on her shoulder. She lay rigid on her back, her arms immobile at her sides, while her head thrashed from side to side.

"Please, please, please, please . . ."

He strode immediately to the crumpled bed with its tossed covers. She was wearing the night rail he had purchased for her, modest and simple. He had thought it was right, though he wasn't sure why—only that it would definitely be wrong to buy her something provocative, something to reflect his own base desires.

"Juliet?"

"I will not say anything, anything, anything. . . . I won't beg, I won't beg. . . . I won't let myself say anything . . . please, please, please—"

He touched her shoulder. Immediately she jerked awake. Her pupils like pits, she stared up at him from a chalk-white face.

"It's only me," he said. "You were having a nightmare."

She turned her face away. "I'm sorry. I didn't mean to wake you."

He felt helpless. "Faith, Juliet, what did they do to you?"

"What do you think?" Her voice was muffled.

Perhaps the floor opened. Perhaps his heart broke into shards like dropped glass. Perhaps he was run through with an unseen blade to fell him where he stood. She had been *raped?* As if his legs turned to straw, Alden sank to his knees beside the bed and buried his face in both hands against the cover.

"Can you tell me?" he said at last. "Can I help?"

Her hand grasped the sleeve of his dressing gown, her fingers pressed into the fabric. "It was at night. The nights when they tied me down."

Her nails must be marking his arm. He barely noticed.

"I wasn't ravished," she said. "Not—" She shivered. "It was little enough at first: just a fumbling—furtive, fast, incomplete— as if he still didn't quite have enough courage."

Alden wanted to be sick. *Lord Edward will die for this!* "Who?"

The shaft of light cast her face into shadow, her skin ghostly against the bed hangings. "One of the male attendants—the one they called Bill. He had been told I was a harlot."

The Minotaur roared somewhere deep in his skull. "What difference does that make?"

"It wasn't really that much," she said, as if her nerve failed her. "I should forget it."

Alden stared at her white knuckles, stark where she still clutched his sleeve. He wanted to hold her solidly against his broken heart. "It's bloody foul. Damnable. That any man should touch a woman against her will! God, Juliet, if our bodies aren't ours, then what is?"

She released his sleeve and curled back against the pillows. "A married woman's body is her husband's. He has a right to it."

"Yet you refused George in London, because rights come with duties. A man's duty is to entice, attract, ensure that his lover welcomes him. If she does not, he has no rights at all!"

"You can say that because you know how to please women. How was George to know that a rake had spoiled me for ordinary men?"

He stood up and turned away, stunned by her bravado. "You think that justifies his sending you to Blackthorn Manor where some lout could terrorize you?" Alden thrust out a hand and caught the hangings at the foot of the bed. He stared blindly at his fist: the heavy velvet under his fingers, the silk cuff of his dressing gown and nightshirt. "I can't even begin to imagine your rage and despair!"

"No." Her voice rang with a kind of desperate courage. "You probably can't, but you might rip the bed to shreds trying. If I were to ask you for some other kind of help, could you give it?"

He released the hangings and turned to face her. "Name it."

She sat up, wrapping her arms about her knees. "I do not like you or love you, but I trust your control."

Amazed, he stared at her profile, the turn of her cheek and neck—lush, lovely, Juliet. As she glanced back at him again he saw her need written plainly in her eyes. Alden took one stride and held out his hands, palm up. "Tell me, Juliet."

"I thought about it." She closed her eyes as the words tumbled out. "I had plenty of time to think. It wasn't just to be touched like that, but to be strapped down in the dark, while a stranger's hand felt up my leg or down my bodice . . . I had to bite my tongue to keep from shouting or begging. Any complaint would only have meant more hours in the straps, or confinement in a dark cell under the house. I hoped if I lay absolutely still, with no reaction at all, he would get bored and go away."

Alden sat down on the edge of the bed. He felt as if ice had settled in his soul. She had been forced to endure it. Surely he could endure hearing it?

"But it got worse?"

"Each time he came back, he was a little bolder, went a little further. I began to think I really would go mad. Not from what he did, because it never actually went that far—" Her voice broke on a little half-laugh. "It's hard to rape a woman whose legs are strapped together."

Alden made himself say it, face what she had been forced to face. "Yet you knew that one night he might get bold enough to undo those straps."

"I wondered if anyone would care or object, if I were found one day to be mysteriously with child. Yet most nights, he didn't come at all. Sometimes I thought crazily that those might almost be the worst—to lie there and imagine what he might do the next time . . . and the time after that . . . or if he was visiting another woman and doing worse things to her."

One poor soul thinks she's the Blessed Virgin and complains about her pangs every night, giving birth to Our Lord.

Bill was as good as dead, as were Lord Edward Vane and George Hardcastle—the bastard who had once tricked her into thinking she loved him.

She shivered. "I thought it would go on for the rest of my life—"

Fury crushed like a glacier in his chest, but compassion pressed more strongly, allowing him to sit quietly on the bed, not touching her.

"It's over now," he said. "You are safe."

"No," she said. "It is not over. With my eyes closed, I can still feel his fingers."

He felt helpless, lost for a way to help her. He knew only his deep anger.

She turned her back and swung her feet to the floor on the opposite side of the bed. Her plait followed the curve of her spine. The shaft of candlelight outlined her jaw and the small flash of skin above the collar of her nightdress.

"I don't want that to be my last memory of what happens between men and women."

Alden stared at that naked flesh, painfully tender. "What do you mean?"

"Do you think I want to stay celibate the rest of my life, having nightmares? I won't hide again. I spent five years hiding in Manston Mingate. I tried to deny my feelings and yearnings. I tried to tell myself I could be happy alone. I was not happy alone."

He looked down at his empty fingers. She was presenting him with an almost painful honesty. What could a man like him do with such a gift?

"This is what you thought about?"

"I lay in the dark in Blackthorn and thought if I ever had the chance to start again, I would grasp it with both hands." She stood up and spun about. "You have just given me that chance. As your mother's companion, I can go into society. I can travel to London. What reputation do I have to care about? None. As a married woman living apart from her husband, I shall be expected to take lovers. I intend to take lovers. I want to find pleasure in it. Like Maria!"

He leaped to his feet and backed away from the bed. "I don't want you to be like Maria!"

Her lip curled in scorn. "You think that I care what *you* want me to be?"

"What the devil do you want from me, Juliet?" His hands closed into fists. "I cannot undo what's been done."

"Yes, you can. There is no one else I can ask. I want you to take away the dark and replace it with brilliance. And it can't wait! I am very sure it can't wait!"

He felt almost as if he were a disembodied spirit watching someone else standing helplessly on the carpet. "What do you want me to do?"

"I want you to light candles—crates of them. I want you to make this room hot and bright. I want to see red-hot flame in your hair and on your arms and legs and stomach. I want to see you. I want you naked in front of me, here in this room."

"You want me *stripped*? Why?"

"Faith, Alden!" Her voice raged. Her eyes looked ravaged, ugly.

"I want you to bed me! You used my body. Now it's my turn to use yours!"

He spun about and strode into his own room. He had never felt less aroused. The image of that attendant touching her legs and breasts while she lay strapped and defenseless ate like a canker at his desire. He didn't want sex. He wanted to kill. Lovemaking was a pleasure, a pastime, an answer to boredom, not this!

Yet she had asked and he must answer.

He gathered candlesticks. He raided drawers and cupboards and pulled every candle from its holder. He carried them all into Juliet's room. He thrust half-burned candles into empty sconces and glued them with melted wax to her supper plates. He filled the cold fireplace and set candlesticks on every horizontal surface. Then he spread flame from wick to wick.

When the walls burned with light, Alden turned to face her. A terrible finality shone in her eyes.

"Naked," she said.

He wrenched away his dressing gown and let it fall to the floor. Using both hands, he pulled his nightshirt over his head and tossed it to a chair. With one bent finger he tugged away the ribbon, so his hair fell freely over his shoulders. The glare of flames licked over his naked body like a thousand lovers.

He strode to the bed and stood at the foot of it.

Color rose in her face as she met his gaze, a flush like a fever, the antithesis of desire.

"I would never deny you, Juliet," he said quietly. "Nor will I give you hypocrisy."

HER HEART POUNDED IN A CACOPHONY OF MAD RHYTHMS, AS if it leaped and bounded within a cage of chains. He was beautiful. Soul-shatteringly beautiful. The corded legs and arms; the flat, tight stomach and narrow hips; the hard flare of muscle over chest and ribs. Beautiful. Beautiful.

Blond strands curled, caressing, over his shoulders. His skin gleamed gilt in the blaze of candlelight, his sex darker, bronze against his thigh: the man's body she had worshipped with mouth and womb and fingers at Marion Hall, but never seen—and then he had betrayed her.

The wild pulse of her angry heart ran deeper and deeper, aching between her cramped, ugly legs. She had felt ugly ever since Blackthorn: ugly, hideous, as if her very soul had become twisted and deformed.

"I am determined to become free," she said. "I will be free of you, too."

"Yes," he replied. "If you like."

"I want to touch you." The madness careened, making her dizzy.

He walked around the bed, his arms relaxed at his sides, a tiny smile at the corners of his mouth. His naked skin gleamed, defenseless in the candlelight. She could hurt him, if she wished. Why wasn't he afraid?

Yet he stood confident and unashamed by her bed.

Juliet rose up on her knees and set both palms flat on his chest, against the soft crinkle of hair and the compact muscle beneath. His sex stirred and hardened.

"You feel desire for me?" she asked. "Even now?"

"I am a fool of desire, Juliet. I desire you to the depths of my soul."

She slid both hands down to rest on his hips, then leaned forward to lay her forehead in the firm hollow of his shoulder. His arousal lay heavy against her nightdress. The thin fabric was all that held her together, stopped her from shattering into tiny, brittle pieces. She lifted her face.

"Kiss me," she said. He began to lift his arms. Juliet pulled back. "Don't touch me with your hands!"

He dropped his hands and tipped his chin for a moment to stare at the ceiling. He was stripped, this lovely man, this fool of desire, totally vulnerable to her furious whim and her ugliness. A pulse beat hard and fast in his strong white throat.

"Mouth only?" he asked.

"Mouth only. Kiss me, Alden."

He lowered his head and smiled. *Smiled.* The shiver of anger raced up from her heart to explode on her empty tongue. Gripping both of his shoulders she leaned forward and pressed her mouth to his. His lips softened under her assault, allowing it, allowing her angry pillaging of his masculine beauty, while his sex reared, hard and firm, against her belly.

Juliet thrust her tongue between his teeth, plundering the wine-dark secrets inside. Her fingernails sank into the muscles of his shoulders. Her breasts pressed against his chest, separated only by the fine fabric of her nightdress. She was monstrous, as if all her limbs had become distorted and grotesque.

Why wouldn't he lead her from this clumsy, wild assault into those skilled, lovely embraces they had shared before? In spite of his rampant arousal, he stood passive in her arms, letting her lead him. His tongue matched hers, his lips responded, touch for touch. He kissed, but he did not take charge.

She pulled away at last, filled with fury.

"What is this?" she asked. "Kiss me!"

He stepped back, staring into her eyes. "If we would replace all your horrific memories with tender ones, then we mustn't couple in anger, Juliet."

"In anger! What the deuce do you care what my emotions are? Concentrate only on your own needs, as you usually do. Your flesh is ready enough. This need be nothing to you but another episode, like all the others. What use is a rake to me, otherwise?"

"I promised not to give you hypocrisy," he said, frowning.

"Why? Why think you must do anything more than pretend? I don't want you to! Don't pretend tenderness. Don't pretend that you care. Just do it. Burn into me, burn into my body!"

Pain flared deep in his eyes. "If you wish it, you shall have that. You want skill? You can have it. You want potency?" He glanced down at his erection, then back into her eyes. "I am on fire for you, in spite of your hatred. But ask yourself first, Juliet, if that's really what you want. Because once we have gone down that road, we can never go back."

"Good. I want it to be too late. I want to be free of you forever."

"You have been hurt," he said, opening his hands. "This won't free you."

She took the hem of her nightgown in both hands and wrenched it off over her head, before she threw herself back on the bed. She felt repulsive, her limbs twisted like tree roots, her breasts horrible. Perhaps he would spin on his heel and leave, or perhaps he would obey that imperious sexual demand between his legs, push himself over her and thrust her thighs apart.

Either way, she would win.

Alden did neither.

"This is not an episode," he said. "It never was. If only you will let me, I will prove it."

He bent to retrieve her nightgown. Before she could move, he tossed the fabric over her and wrapped her securely in its capacious folds, pinning her arms to her sides. Panic burst like a thundercloud as he slipped onto the bed next to her and pulled her against his chest. Juliet fought, trying to knee him. He trapped her legs with one of his and held her pinioned.

"Now, hush," he said. "We aren't enemies, Juliet. I'm on your side. Look at me."

She stared up into his lean face, framed in gold. Candlelight blazed, adding to the warmth of the summer night. With sure, gentle fingers, he stroked the hair back from her forehead.

"There," he said. "That's better. Now fit your head against my shoulder and let me hold you."

"Hold me?"

He grinned, but something else burned intently in his eyes. "Women like to be held. Every rake knows that."

Alden lay back, fitting her head against his shoulder, holding it there with one hand, while he rubbed the other over and over down her back. Juliet drew up her knees like a child, while he pulled her closer into his embrace. She didn't have the energy to fight. If he wanted to, he could seal forever into her soul the stain of Bill's assault.

"I have liked being a rake." His voice feathered away into the bright room. "I have reveled in the way women soften when I glance at them, the way they blush and melt if I give them a certain smile. To bring that look to a woman's eyes whenever I wished—it made me feel I could conquer the world. Power is very addictive, Juliet. But it's the power to win willing surrender, not the power to coerce that is headier than wine. You don't need to coerce me. I am willing. I surrendered to you a long time ago."

He kissed her earlobes and temples, before again finding her mouth.

The frantic anger still beat at her heart, yet Juliet heard a moan. Her moan, shivering up from her lungs. His lips touched tenderly, to the corners of her mouth, to her tongue, to her upper lip only, then to the lower one. Tears sprang, stinging her eyelids. His lips brushed over each eyelid in turn, as if he would kiss away her pain.

"You want brightness, Juliet, the body's brightness—but that's based on pleasure, on the mutual delight of skin to skin. You are beautiful, rare. I am confounded by the depth of my desire, but your body belongs to you. The power is all yours."

"I am defeated," she said. "I cannot take charge any longer. Help me, Alden."

His lips pressed gently on her forehead. "Relax. You are safe with me."

He picked up her plait. Deftly, he untied ribbons and unraveled her braid. One by one, long strands slipped through his fingers, drifting over her breasts in a warm, familiar skein of mahogany.

She felt protected, wrapped in a cocoon of her own hair.

Saying nothing, Alden took her right hand in both of his. His palms rubbed firmly, from elbow to wrist, his fingers seeking each knotted muscle, each concentration of ugliness. He massaged steadily, rubbing away tension and pain with calm certainty.

Juliet lay helpless and let it happen.

Almost as if her bones sighed and relaxed, her arm seemed to grow longer, like a bud unfurling from a dry, wrinkled seed buried too long underground. The dicot unfolded, the true leaves sprang strongly from the stem. She was a spring plant, running green with new sap.

As if reaching for the sun, her forearm grew straight and strong.

Her left arm, in contrast, still felt like a monkey's, shriveled against her side.

At last he kissed her palm and laid down her hand, before he took her left forearm in both hands and began to work the same magic.

His face was almost stern, concentrated and intent. Light scattered in her eyelashes. He burned in bright threads of golden flame, a sheer, breathtaking splendor—even his hardened sex, magnificent and tender in the candlelight.

As if the dawn sang to a sunflower, her arm shed its warped distortion and turned evenly, fearlessly to his life-giving heat.

He laid her hand down, almost reverently, and rotated her onto her stomach. Her nightdress slid away. Juliet flopped like a fish, trailing her tight legs behind her, yet her long, blissful arms seemed to float.

His hands brushed her shoulders as he gathered her hair and stroked it aside. A shivering sensation thrilled over her skull, as if her hair sang.

She pressed her face into the pillow, robbed of the sight of him, as he began to work down each side of her spine, pressing with both thumbs, forcing away the demons of disfigurement. Her skin softened beneath his palms. Her back became limber. Her bottom sprang supple beneath his fingers. She was becoming expansive and lovely, her back strong, her legs stretching away to infinity, her feet sighing in bliss.

Each limb stroked, then gently shaken, scattering all the misshapen ugliness and replacing it with serenity. Every surface caressed, every muscle cajoled into luminous surrender. When it was complete, when there was nothing left to unravel, as if every limb had burst into radiant bloom, he lifted her in his arms to smile down into her dazed eyes.

"You are as lovely as daylight," he said. "I am honored to touch you."

Juliet put her arms about his waist and burst into tears.

He held her, stroking her back. His kisses pressed on the top of her head, on her ears, on her temple. As her tears dried, she tipped her head and smiled at him. He smiled back.

"Let us make love, Juliet. Not fight. Not fornicate. Make love. Now, kiss me again."

His mouth found hers as flames of brilliance burned cleanly through her blood.

His ready body discovered hers a few moments later, in a plunge of slippery, throbbing sensation. With wild jubilation, she cried out, a gasp of delight, as if her lungs and throat emptied any last shreds of corruption. An image of his ecstatic face flooded her mind: his hair rimmed in gilt, his skin golden. Perhaps Jupiter ravished her in a torrent of luminous coins. Lord of the gods— witty and clever, sinful and noble—making love to her with the powerful demon wisdom of a rake, until she felt beautiful, glorious, and emptied of hatred.

S HE SLEPT, EXHAUSTED, AGAINST HIS CHEST, WHILE ALDEN LAY and stared at the ceiling.

This need be nothing to you but another episode, like all the others. What use is a rake to me, otherwise?

He had spent his adult life pursuing nothing but episodes. The stimulation of the chase. The intensity of its inevitable culmination. He had never failed to seduce a woman he wanted. Never. One after another, those safely available women had fallen into his arms and his bed. He had of course chosen only women who were experienced and dependable: married women, secure in their miserable but necessary marriages; cynical widows with no desire to marry again; even professional courtesans, as long as they were exclusive, sought-after and hard-to-get.

He had thought Juliet a widow, safely attainable. She had turned out to be trapped in a miserable marriage, which ought to make her all the more perfect for a brief—or preferably lengthy— affair. He had never achieved quite this level of physical ecstasy before and he was loath to give that up. Why the devil was it so impossible to foresee a future where she would live as his mistress?

The candles began to die, one by one. The last few cast small, dancing shadows over the uneven plaster. The building creaked as it settled down for the long, cool hours until dawn. Alden pulled the covers over Juliet and himself, still holding her.

The light flickered. Growing steadily darker, the room smelled of smoke and wax, overlain with the musk of their lovemaking. The last candle went out. His arm had gone numb, cradling her, but he did not move a muscle.

*A*LDEN WOKE TO A GLIMMER OF LIGHT. A FEW BIRDS TWIT- tered outside.

Barely dawn.

As he turned his head his blood surged. Juliet slept soundly. Her hair gleamed in the pink-tinged half light. Her arm was cushioned by his; her breasts pressed against his chest. He wanted to kiss her awake, bring that contented, soft look once again to her eyes. As he reached to move a strand of chestnut from her cheek, her eyelashes lifted.

"Good morning," he said.

She looked shy, as if she were surprised to find herself naked, her legs entwined with his. "I wondered if I dreamed it," she said.

"So did I." He ran a strand of her tangled hair between thumb and forefinger. "Did it work?"

A small frown pulled her brows together for an instant. "Work?"

"Did we chase away the dark memories? Can you go freely now

into the arms of any man you choose?" He tried to make it light, an easy banter, the way he would talk to any lover.

"Yes," she said. "Yes. You made me feel beautiful."

"You are beautiful."

She sat up, allowing his hand to settle on the curve of her waist, where the slim back flared into her woman's hips. Had she noticed his erection?

"Perhaps it worked too well," she said. "I don't want us to do it again."

Astonishment robbed him of breath, until he remembered how easily he could make her change her mind.

"Why not?"

She sat in silence for a moment, as if debating with herself. He traced up her spine with his palm.

"Very well," she said, twisting to face him, covering her naked breasts with her arms. "I have nothing to lose from the truth. If we do it again, you will make me fall in love with you."

"And that would be a mistake?"

Juliet bent to retrieve her nightgown from the floor. His hand slipped away from her waist.

"You're not a man with whom it's wise to fall in love. You break hearts. You always move on." Her back was lovely, fluid and slender. Female. She pulled the nightdress over her head, hiding her glorious breasts, her lovely woman's belly. "Why have you never married?"

His retreat from the question was automatic—from this sudden invasion into his privacy, into something that was none of her business—

"Nature calls," he said. He didn't mean it to sound so sharp, but his disappointment that they wouldn't immediately make love again was bitter. "May I answer her queries first?"

He slipped from the bed and grabbed his dressing gown, before he went into his own room to use the chamber pot. He had to allow his arousal to die away first. Alden watched himself, slightly bemused. Did women understand such simple, primal facts about men: that the average male usually woke from sleep instantly aroused, ready to tumble the nearest wench foolish enough to be that close?

The physical impulse to make love to her again dominated his thinking. He desired her with an almost painful ferocity. Why must she demand more of him than he wanted to give? He had seduced scores of women. He had never lied to them, but neither had any of them truly become friends, privy to his secrets, aware of his inner life.

What made him so afraid to take that next step?

Afraid? The thought shivered through him like a waterfall. He had been *afraid*?

He forced himself to face it. *Fear?* Fear of what? Abandonment? Intimacy? He stood in stark confusion for a moment.

Alden splashed cold water over his skin and cleaned his teeth, allowing her time to do the same, then he walked back into her room. Juliet gazed up at him from a chair beside the fireplace. She was wrapped in the dressing gown he had bought for her.

"I have decided to answer you honestly," he said.

"Why? Were you tempted to lie about it?"

"No, I was tempted simply not to answer. But first I'd like a truth from you. I would very much like us both to get back into that bed. I refuse to believe you do not want that, too."

Her eyes blazed. "Of course I desire it! Lud! I am trying to save myself from making such a mistake."

"A mistake?"

She was every inch the lady, proud and upright, as if armored by that training. "You *want* me to fall in love with you, when we can't have a future? I am still married. You are Lord Gracechurch and you must marry an heiress. I won't become your mistress so you can break my heart when you wed someone else."

It seemed a minor objection. "What if I promise never to marry?"

"How can you? I am only wondering why you haven't wed already."

Alden walked to the cold fireplace and leaned there among the wreckage of burned wicks and candle wax. How odd that this took more courage than facing a naked blade on a dueling ground!

"Gregory was the heir. It was up to him to produce a string of little Granville-Strachans to inherit the title."

"Yet it's your duty now. Why did you delay?"

It would be easy to avoid this painful probing. If he touched her, she would melt. They could make glorious, memorable love and drown all these awkward questions in the body's far simpler ecstasy. Yet he groped for the truth, whatever the risk.

"Perhaps because I didn't want someone like me to seduce my wife."

"Ah," she said. "Is no marriage safe from the charms of someone like you?"

"Some, of course. Rare ones. Yet the relationships I have indulged in have been far more honest and less hurtful than I thought wedlock could ever be. I didn't believe it was in my nature to love exclusively, or create one of those exceptional marriages. I do know I could never have loved any of those virgin girls I might be expected to marry."

"So you wanted to be in love with your wife?"

"I suppose I did. How extravagant of me! This isn't something I have really thought very hard about, Juliet. But men and women only truly get to know each other in bed. Why marry a stranger, only to find we hated each other and were stuck for life?"

She stood up and paced across the room. "You've never made love to a virgin?"

Alden watched her with devouring need. He had nothing to offer but his own flawed self, but he plunged on blindly, searching out the naked truth, deliberately abandoning charm and wit.

"I never thought it was fair. Virgins have false expectations, illusions that are impossible to fulfill."

"As I did, when I ran away with George?"

Her silk wrapper flowed like a river from her shoulders, her hair rioting over it. Carriages were stirring outside. The sound of men, horses and wheeled vehicles echoed up into the room.

"Faith, Juliet! Deflowering dewy-eyed misses is not a responsibility that has ever appealed to me. It's at heart dishonest and exploitative, unless the man is genuinely in love."

She stood with her back to him. "That doesn't stop most men."

"Juliet, what the deuce do you know about men? There are only three reasons why an experienced man seeks a virgin. Either he must, because he needs her for a bride. Or he's addicted to that kind of ugly discrepancy in power. Or he believes some nonsense about a virgin curing his pox or his impotence."

"And which of those made George marry me?" She turned to stare across at the window. Light chased over her profile. "Perhaps all three of them? Or perhaps it was just money. You're right, of course. My silly little head was filled with all kinds of fantasies. George soon divested me of them. Yet I liked what we did in bed together. I thought it was wonderful."

He glanced back at the bed where they had made love. "What do you think now?"

"At the risk of further inflating your exaggerated pride, I see now that I was too ignorant to know any better. I wanted the attention." Her words clashed with the roll of iron-shod wheels bouncing over the cobbles in the inn yard, but he heard the wry note in her voice. "I didn't know, of course, that there could be so much more to it."

He crossed his empty arms over his chest. "And now you do?"

"Now I can go out there into the world and find out. I can compare men as you have compared women. This one is better, that one is worse—"

"I have *not* compared women!"

She spun about to face him. "I thought you said I was the best?"

"The best?" He flung his hands apart. "What the devil would that mean? You are unique to me, Juliet, but not only because of what your body does to mine."

"Am I?" Her tone almost teased, but desperation was there, too.

He knew he was about to take the greatest risk of his life. The words would tear his heart open, because he thought this time they really might be true. He said them anyway. "I'm in love with you."

"The rakes' most practiced lie!"

"Lud, ma'am!" He didn't mean to shout, but his voice roared as he strode across the room to stand over her. He grasped her shoulders in both hands. "Those are not words I've ever truly meant before. *I am in love with you!*"

Her eyes dilated as she stared up at him. "What fools we both are, Lord Gracechurch! My heart aches with what I want to call love for you. My soul wants to believe you, to believe your offer of marriage. But I can't! Don't you understand? I can't!"

"Why not?"

He wanted to press his mouth over hers, force her to give in to what her body so obviously wanted.

"If I become your mistress, you can no doubt force George to seek a divorce, but he will not make it easy, not even to salvage his pride. You can pay whatever price he demands—with money or a sword, it doesn't matter—you may even prevail. But however much we might think now that we want it, we could never make a marriage afterward."

"*Why the devil not?*"

She turned her head. "Because there would be too much ugliness first. Because I have made this mistake once before: thought my body's reaction to a man meant that I was in love and that our love could survive any scandal, any adversity. I was wrong. Now I am doing it again. You think that you want me. Easy to say while I am safely unattainable. What will happen after all the bitterness and public shame of a divorce? We are not in love, Lord Gracechurch. We only think that we are."

"This is real," he said. "Don't deny it."

"Even if it is, it cannot survive," she replied. "There are too many obstacles in our way. If I agree to become your mistress now, you would live to regret it. I could not bear that."

The door still stood open into his room, waiting for him to close it behind him. Alden released her.

"Then what the hell do we have left?"

"We have Lord Edward to bring to justice." A note of ridicule crept into her voice. "And perhaps even the treasure of Harald Fairhair to find."

CHAPTER SIXTEEN

LONE IN HER ROOM AT THE BLACK HORSE, JULIET OPENED
the trunks and cases Alden had brought for her: under-
skirts, overskirts, petticoats, bodices, sleeves. Lace and ribbons.
Hats, veils. Matching shoes and stockings. He must have had her
clothes measured at Gracechurch Abbey. He must have ordered
all this then. Her heart beat hard as her fingers strayed over the
luxurious silks and brocades.

*He must have planned then for her to stay with him! Even then he
had wanted her this much!*

Someone knocked at the door. In her nightdress, staring at the
soft colors and rich fabrics—and the brushes, combs, toiletries,
cosmetics—Juliet called permission to enter.

"Oh, ma'am," Tilly Brambey said, a quavering wail in her
voice. "Lord Gracechurch said as how you needed a lady's maid.
But I don't really know how, do I? And I didn't know . . . when
those men came questioning—" The maid's voice broke on a sob.

Juliet looked up, crossed the room and took Tilly's hands.

"Nonsense. I am delighted to see you, Tilly. I can show you
what to do."

Two hours later, with Tilly stepping proudly at her heels, Juliet
walked down the inn stairs, spine straight, the curve of her breasts
deliberately exhibited by her tight lacing. Layers of ivory and
cream floated above her high-heeled shoes. A rich sweep of feather

curled from her hat. Juliet had entered this place as a madwoman.
She was leaving as a lady.

Alden was waiting by the carriage. Her heart skipped a beat
as she saw him, the lover she could never truly win.

Silver-thread flowers rioted along the facings of his waistcoat.
He held out one hand, lace foaming from his cuff. "I am outshone
in magnificence at last, ma'am," he said, bowing over her fingers,
while amusement warred with appreciation in his eyes. "We are
two birds of paradise. Let us take the world by storm."

JULIET STUDIED HIM—THE BLOND HAIR, THE STONE-CUT FEA-
tures—as they jounced along the high road. After helping
her into the carriage, Alden had bent his head over some letters
that had just been delivered to him at the inn. Using a walnut
writing case, he penned a series of quick replies, which he sanded
and sealed, then tucked into his pocket. A second carriage trailed
behind, carrying Tilly, some other servants, and their luggage.
Alden had, apparently, determined to travel in style.

What did she think she understood about him? His gorgeous
appearance was only the first layer, yet it was one that she savored
now as if she had been hungry for it all of her life. A wealth of
lace and silk on a man was something she had always taken for
granted. It spoke of power and social status, vital to the structure
of society.

Yet Alden had turned it into something else.

His appearance was both beautiful and witty, almost as if he
celebrated the irony of hiding masculine muscle beneath such
essentially feminine frippery. For a woman to put her hand on a
man's sleeve and feel the hard tension of his arm beneath the silk
was intensely erotic. Perhaps no age had ever been as blatantly
sensual as this one. No wonder men like Alden reveled in it,
reaping woman after woman like a scythe harvesting flowers.

Was she to be one of them? One of those casually mown blossoms?

Juliet touched the lace over her own forearm. She tried to look at her wrist as it must appear to him. A woman's bones were so slender compared to a man's. Was that what fascinated men? For whatever reason, he had made her feel beautiful when she had thought ugliness had contaminated her to the bone. It had not been only her body he had healed.

I have already given him my soul, she thought. *Why lie to myself? If I cannot trust him now with the truth, then truth does not exist in the universe. Yet the truth is that I am not free. Even if George divorces me, will I ever be free enough?*

He glanced up and smiled at her.

"Where did you learn such very odd ideals about marriage when you were so young, Juliet?"

She was taken aback for a moment, then she laughed. "From romances."

He raised both brows. "Romances?"

"All those tales of King Arthur and his knights. I'm sure it sounds foolish, but they convey such an ideal of love."

"Faith! Guinevere was one of the most notoriously unfaithful wives in history."

"Yet it was a grand passion."

He listened perfectly seriously. "So you wanted a knight in shining armor?"

"If I did," she said with a wry smile, "I made a bad choice. In the end it was as if I had married Mordred instead. Yet George truly attracted me. Perhaps we could have made a good marriage, if my father had not . . . if Kit and my mother—"

"No. George Hardcastle didn't deserve you for a moment. But we all make mistakes when we're young."

"Did you?"

"Of course. Maria was a mistake. Haven't you guessed?"

He leaned one shoulder against the side of the carriage, arms folded over his chest. Lace from his wrists foamed across his powerful thighs. The gilt heels and silk stockings only accentuated the hard muscles of his calves, as if even his shoes were a wonderful joke, an arrogant wink from a jester, laughing at the world. Yet he seemed stripped of both arrogance and mockery now.

"I was probably as romantic as you were," he went on. "I also wanted that single grand passion, the one woman who would meld into my soul as Adam's rib fit beneath his heart. Thus I ignored what I saw in my own home, even ignored Gregory's example—"

She felt breathless with surprise—that he should talk so openly. "What do you mean?"

His eyes shone as innocently as cornflowers beneath his thick lashes. "Lud! My mother and father had a typical society marriage—seen as a great success. He barely tolerated her. She retreated into fragile eccentricity, becoming ever more demanding. The more she demanded, the more he ignored her."

"They didn't love each other at all?"

"My father didn't love my mother at all. And she—? I don't know. I don't think she loved him either, yet she was bitterly wounded whenever he was unfaithful."

It seemed infinitely precious, these simple revelations, simply told. Her own parents' marriage had fallen somewhere between that cold-blooded social contract and a true melding of souls. There had been tension sometimes, difficulties, but they had loved each other.

"I think any woman feels that way, once she has committed herself. He was the father of her children." She took a deep breath, gathering courage. "What did you mean about Gregory?"

His gaze was almost amused, as if acknowledging her hesitation and his own, as if—like two castaways in a leaky boat—they shared one risk and were forced to embrace it together: this tentative attempt at trust.

"I adored him." Alden seemed to search for words, as if they were disused, rusty with time. "He was my only brother and several years older. In the eyes of a young boy he embodied gallantry and courage. Women couldn't get enough of him. I still love him. I always will. Yet, when I was sixteen and fell in love for the first time, he deliberately—"

He turned his head, his expression suddenly shuttered as if he lost his nerve, after all.

"Tell me." She spoke the words just as he had spoken them to her the night before, not sure if he would trust her enough, not sure if she could trust herself to listen.

Alden glanced back and smiled. The smile was a gift, a gift of faith. Juliet met it with one of her own, but tentative, breathless, whereas his was filled with sudden confidence.

"Her name was Emily. The daughter of the local schoolmaster. She was lovely. One of those fragile, ethereal girls who don't seem quite strong enough to cope with the life they're born into."

"How did you meet?"

"I first saw her at church and found a moment to speak to her while my father dispensed condescension among the parishioners. She and I soon met secretly, little clandestine meetings in the grounds at Gracechurch Abbey, at prearranged spots in the village. We talked about poetry and debated philosophy."

"She was well read?"

"Well enough, and she had a good mind. We fell passionately in love. There is nothing more intense and absolute, of course, than a boy's first love—caught on the threshold of manhood, untested and uncontaminated by the world. I worshipped her. We even exchanged a few uncertain kisses. It was so deuced exciting to touch her. . . ." He leaned his head back and closed his eyes, a tiny hint of self-mockery in his voice. "My mouth sang with the pure lyricism of it, that delicate, butterfly touch from those virgin lips. Yet I was determined to honor her purity, though her pretty restraint was like tinder to the flame in my loins. I wanted to marry her."

Juliet knew what was coming. She knew it in her bones. It was what she would have done, if she'd had an older sister.

"So you went to Gregory and poured out your heart?"

Alden laughed, not bitterly, but with a kind of sad wisdom.

"Gregory was very gentle. He pointed out that she would never make an acceptable wife for the son of a viscount, that such girls were destined for quite another use by men of our class. When I demurred, he offered to prove it. Emily was only fifteen. Within two months she was carrying his child."

The carriage rocked, dust beginning to coat the half-open windows. The sound of hoofbeats melded with her heavily beating heart. "What became of them?"

"Her father tried to challenge Gregory to a duel, but my father saw that the man was dismissed and the family sent away. The child died in the womb—fortuitously, you might say. Emily married a year later. Quite respectably, I believe." Alden gave her a wry smile. "An affecting tale. One you would think I could have used to seduce innumerable women over the years. Oddly, I've never told anyone before how the very first love of my life betrayed me."

"Emily?"

"Oh, no." His voice was still light. "The poor child couldn't help herself. The restraint she'd shown me was absolutely genuine, but my brother was irresistible. No, it was Gregory's betrayal that sent me to Italy and kept me there. And yet, I never stopped loving him."

"Of course," Juliet said. "He was your brother."

Sunlight sparkled through his spotless lace as he laid his hand against the glass for a moment. He pushed the window closed.

"He did it from love. He wanted to save me from making the mistake of my life. Yet however I look at it, however much I credit those motives, he was wrong. His treatment of Emily was barbarous. He prevented my finding or helping her. It was deuced hard to forgive that, though with hindsight it seems only foolish and self-pitying—the behavior of a child—to fling myself into the arms of Maria to let her teach me to be as cold and calculating as Gregory had been."

"But how could you stay in the same house with your brother after he had seduced your first love?"

"Not easily. But I could also have recognized the extent to which he was right. To have eloped with Emily would have destroyed both of us. There was no real depth to that calf love. Our marriage would have been a disaster. Gregory just might have picked a kinder way to demonstrate it."

"Perhaps first love is always doomed. We are such babies at sixteen. I wouldn't want to be that young again."

He laughed suddenly. "Lud, no! Nor I!"

They sat in a surprisingly companionable silence, as if this exchange of confidences had moved their relationship to a new level, one that did not need to be explained aloud. She did not even need to express her sympathy and horror over what Gregory had done. Alden already understood it.

What else is this sense of safety, of trust, if not love?

"Intensity," she said. "You spoke about it once before."

"Did I?" His beautiful hands lay casually on his writing case, with its burden of letters, paper and quills.

"When we shared our Italian supper, you were explaining why you did not want constancy, why you had sought out so many women. You were searching for an intensity, you said, that never lasts."

"Brave words! That is how I trained myself, what I used to believe."

"You don't now?"

"Now I find myself loving with a far greater and more genuinely passionate intensity than anything I have ever experienced before. Can you believe that?"

She looked down, almost afraid to meet his gaze, while her heart thumped. "Perhaps."

"This intensity assails my heart even when I am not with the lady. I have an absolute certainty that any other woman would only bore me to tears. You have ruined me, Juliet."

In spite of her emotion, she laughed. "Ruined? How?"

"It's deuced terrifying to know that, whatever happens now, my days as a rake are over."

"Just a sign that you're sliding into your dotage."

"No." His tone was indignant. "Just a sign that I have finally come to my senses."

"Faith, sir!" she replied. "Ever since I first laid eyes on you, you have been robbing me of mine."

She turned her head away, yet she knew he studied her, his gaze straying over her extravagant bonnet, the low neckline of the fashionable gown, the fitted bodice with its sets of tiny bows and seed pearl embroidery. His lazy inspection sent tiny waves of breathless delight over her skin, as if she bloomed for him, unfolded petals to offer her vulnerable heart.

"You love me," he said.

Juliet nodded.

"Then here we both sit, in all our finery, two fools of love."

"Yet how can we be certain it is real?" Juliet insisted. "We both thought ourselves in love before."

He folded his arms again, as if resisting an impulse to touch her. "Because this is nothing like that first childish infatuation, at once so exciting and naughty. This love frees and transforms. If, for whatever reason, we must now lose each other, it would be nothing like our cynical response to the loss of that first love—"

She was genuinely surprised. "Your reaction may have been cynical. But mine?"

"To retreat to Manston Mingate to play chess with an old woman was deeply cynical, Juliet. It was as much a denial of the needs of the heart as what I did by becoming a rake. By the way, who *was* Miss Parrett?"

Of course, he must change the subject. What use to talk about their feelings for each other? *If, for whatever reason, we must now lose each other*— Nothing could change the fact that she was still married to someone else. Juliet took the lead he had offered.

"Miss Parrett had been my grandmother's companion. Whenever we visited, she was there: this valiant woman who knew just how to offer real warmth to children. Kit and I adored her. We missed her terribly after my grandmother died. Only I knew that she had eventually retired to Manston Mingate. After I eloped with George, she was the only person I wrote to, except for that one letter to my mother, when it was too late."

"So Miss Parrett knew the name of the inn where you were staying?"

Juliet nodded. "And when my letters stopped, she wrote to inquire after me, but when my mother's carriage turned over, I'd run out into the storm and almost drowned, too. I caught a lung fever and was too sick to be moved. The inn sent back a message demanding payment for the room and the removal of my useless self, which is how Miss Parrett found out about the accident at the ford. That was when she discovered I had been abandoned by George and that my father had shut himself away, receiving no messages."

"Almost dead with grief—pale as a ghost and sick with a fever."

It had been such a soft murmur she hadn't quite been sure of his words. "What?"

"Nothing. Just something the innkeeper at the Three Tuns said once. Go on."

"Miss Parrett dipped into her slender resources to hire a private carriage and she came to fetch me. It's no exaggeration to say she saved my life."

"She is buried in Manston Mingate?"

"In the churchyard. I used to visit her grave every Sunday."

"I'd have liked to have known her," Alden said. "To say thank you."

The carriage lurched as it turned into another inn yard. Hooves boomed and rang as fresh teams were rushed out of the stables and the tired horses led away.

Alden swung down as soon as their coach stopped. Juliet leaned from the door and watched him exchange letters with a man on horseback: a groom from Gracechurch Abbey. As their new team was being hitched, the groom turned his horse and galloped away.

The coach dipped as Alden stepped back inside. He opened another short letter and perused it.

"You conduct urgent business?" Juliet asked.

"*Our* business," he said, smiling. "Lord Edward spun a spider's web to entrap us. For the last several weeks, I have been spinning one of my own. With any luck, we'll turn the duke's son from spider to fly."

"Can you tell me about it?"

"Of course. I have sent out a network of messages. The first was a note to inform Blackthorn Manor that a certain assistant named Bill was responsible for your escape and was motivated by secret information he had gleaned from you concerning a treasure. That message will immediately get back to Lord Edward. Bill may expect a knife in the back."

"Lord Edward will murder him?"

"I doubt very seriously that he will do it himself," Alden replied dryly. "Though we live in a world where children are executed for stealing a spoon. If Bill is lucky, Mr. Upbridge will ask him about the message. If he is wise, Bill will flee before retribution arrives. As it happens, I believe the man is stupid. Let us leave him to providence and the duke's son, Juliet, but either way he'll be removed from Blackthorn Manor."

Alden had faced death himself several times at the end of a blade. It was another reason why gentlemen wore all that lace and silk, to disguise the lethal capability beneath, yet she shuddered.

"I *should* want mercy for the man, but I can't quite—"

"In another few days, he would have raped you. He has been abusing other women for years—night after night, helpless lunatics, tied to their beds. He deserves to hang. Starvation in an alley or a knife in the dark is almost too good for him."

"I am glad," she said, "that no other women will suffer. And the other letters?"

Alden opened his writing case. "Are from a network of spies I have set to watch Lord Edward. We aren't the only ones with reason to wish ill to the duke's son. For several months he has been encouraged to invest ever more wildly, in ever more extravagant schemes. I have done what I can to exacerbate that. He will have to go after the treasure very soon or face ruin, but he can't move until your father leaves Felton Hall. Even a duke's son can't chance being discovered digging pits in a peer's grounds at night."

"Then send him a message telling him my father has left for London."

Alden grinned with wicked confidence. "I already have."

"Though you know there is no treasure," she said.

"I know no such thing."

"Alden, I grew up with the legend. Kit and I analyzed patterns wherever we found them, looked for imaginary clues in every ragtag collection of books and documents at Felton Hall, then dug holes all over my father's estate."

"And the locket?" The feather danced as his quill scratched over the paper.

"Kit and I studied it, too—the numbers and symbols inscribed inside were meant to be a code telling where the treasure was hidden. Five or six new holes were dug as a result. Why would Lord Edward risk so much over the implausible existence of this lost hoard?"

Alden folded another note, pressing his seal into the wax. "It's the nature of our age, Juliet. We are all gaming mad."

"Does the game ever stop?"

"How can it?" He closed the writing case and set it aside. "Yet you and I have already thrown our cards onto the table."

"What do you mean?"

"I mean that we began with a rather wicked game. I initiated it, but you didn't shrink from the gamble. Faith! To invite a perfect stranger into your kitchen at Manston Mingate? To agree to play chess with him? Now we have stopped playing and passed the turning point."

"What turning point?"

His eyes were dark, lovely, as he smiled. "The one when you must risk showing another person the truth about yourself, including your pettiness, your mistakes. At that moment you are vulnerable to a terrible hurt, but if you don't take that risk, intimacy is never possible. Not that I ever thought before that true intimacy was what I wanted."

"But you have risked it with me?"

"I have risked it with you. It's a matter of discovering whether you can trust. I trust you. I love you. I am fighting now to see if we can truly have a future."

"I am almost afraid to think of it," she said. "I am still another man's wife."

He turned to stare through the dirty glass. "That is the subject of my third set of letters. I am trying to find out everything there is to know about George."

"How can that help?"

"I don't know. But it can't hurt."

*T*HEY STOPPED IN SEVEN MILES TO CHANGE HORSES AGAIN. ALDEN received another batch of letters. While he read them, Juliet drew a plan for him of her father's estate, marking the places she had dug up with Kit. He studied it. The carriage rocked on. She watched him with thinly concealed craving, the ardent hands, the quick intelligence, and waited.

"So where is the Felton Hoard?" he asked at last. "Your best guess based entirely on the locket?"

She pointed out the spot where she had sketched a spring near the corner of a pasture. "Here, without question. I can describe every blade of grass, if you like, though it has changed since Kit and I were children. My father drained the little pond, here, ditched below it, and put in a new trough for the cattle. . . ."

He listened intently until she had finished, then grinned. "A perfect spot for some revelry. Invitations of one kind or another will now be issued to all the interested parties."

"Including George?"

He snapped open the silver lid of the inkpot in his writing case. "Is that all right?"

"I am not afraid of George," Juliet said, "as long as I'm with you."

"Yet the result may not be pretty." He touched a letter he had received at their last stop. "Lord Edward has just been informed he needs a titanic infusion of cash now. He has already made his move to go after the treasure."

"So we must go straight to Felton Hall?"

He was writing rapidly, folding and sealing note after note. "Things are moving even faster than I'd dared hope. You don't have to come, Juliet."

"No." She tried to make her voice as courageous, as carelessly certain, as his. "No, I am sure that I must be there—now I am learning to be quite good at risking things—"

His smile opened like a sunrise. "Then we are about to get involved in some midnight capers."

*J*ULIET HAD THOUGHT FOR A MOMENT THAT THEY MIGHT HAVE to hide their presence in Feltonbridge, the nearest town to the ancestral seat of the earls of Felton. But how could they, with two carriages and a train of servants? They pulled up in front of the largest inn in town. Alden had already sent a message ahead to reserve the grandest suite of rooms. An extremely expensive light supper was immediately delivered. After washing the dust of the road from her hands and face, Juliet sat down at a table laden with champagne and delicacies.

Alden exchanged a few words with one of his menservants, then closed the door. He leaned against the wall to read yet another new letter. Candlelight danced over his hair, as if the sun kissed a field of buttercups. Juliet watched his fine hands as he crushed the paper into a ball and tossed it into the fireplace.

He looked up, met her gaze and smiled, then walked to his chair. He stood for a few moments, both hands resting lightly on the carved crest rail, and stared down at her.

"There will never be anyone else," he said evenly. "For the rest of my life. Whatever it takes, whatever we must go through, once you are free—and you *will* be free—will you marry me, Juliet?"

She laid both hands flat on the fine tablecloth, while her pulse thundered in her ears. The trust he had shown, his revelations about Gregory and Emily and Maria, her own truths offered in exchange—this one day had changed her yet again, made her ready to take any leap of faith, whatever the risk.

"If I am ever free—*when* I am free—whatever it takes, I will, Alden, gladly."

"Then I am saved. But in the meantime—" He looked down at his fingers resting on the chair back. The crumpled letter lay like a doom in the fireplace. Juliet stared at it, as if she could read its dark message through the destroyed paper. Alden followed her gaze and nodded to the crushed writing. "My man of law sends his advice, almost a decree, that we don't live together now, if we ever wish to marry."

Startled, she looked back at him.

"I am confident that George will come to an agreement—for enough money." He gave a wry smile. "Perhaps for the Felton Hoard he will let you go. But your adultery is his only grounds, so the divorce might be conditional on your *not* marrying me afterward."

"Why?"

He turned and paced away. Juliet stared at the fitted waist of his coat and the elegant flare of the skirts.

"I am your seducer. Divorce isn't allowed to reward sin. It seems that I must give you up, even if freeing you from your marriage takes years."

She closed her eyes and dropped her head into both palms. "Can you?"

"I can do even that, if I must. I don't say it will be easy, but I will wait for you, Juliet. There will be no one else, ever."

"Is that a promise?"

His heels clicked on the floor as he walked up to her. "Let us plight our troth here, Juliet." She looked up to see him smiling down at her, holding out one hand. "Let us make our promises before these witnesses." He waved the other hand to indicate the room. "These candles and hangings. These chairs and this table. The oyster patties and the champagne. The bread and the butter. My only regret is that I gave all my bloody rings to your husband."

Juliet pushed back her chair and stood up. She put her right hand in his. "If we don't have a ring," she said. "Let us seal our promise with a kiss."

He smiled, charming, the lovely smile that had seduced countless women, now only for her. "Dare you risk it?"

"I do. And I will risk whatever comes afterward. If we are to be parted, Alden, then let us take one last memory with us to sustain us in these damnable celibate months to come."

He spun her so she was pressed against the table. With a grin of pure wickedness he bent her backward over one arm. Deliberately, with infinite patience, he trailed fingertips down her throat, over her collarbone and the swell of her breasts.

"Kiss you where?" he said, trailing a shivering path of fire over her naked skin. "Here?"

He touched her nipple through the fabric with his thumb. "Here?"

He moved back to brush over the sensitive spot below her ear. "Here?"

"Here," she said, breathless, blood pounding. "On the mouth."

He pressed his lips to hers.

Was it different when you had admitted that you loved a man with all your heart? Did everything change, because he had said he loved you and you believed it at last? Juliet knew only that her very soul craved his touch, that her heart opened and surrendered long before his clever mouth and ecstatic tongue began to ravish her mouth.

As if he had traveled over parched deserts to find her—

As if he had slashed for a year and a day at a thorn hedge to find a lost castle, asleep for one hundred years—

As if he had climbed a labyrinth of stairs, combating magic

mirrors, brushing through a century of spiderwebs, to lift the sleeping princess to his mouth, Juliet felt bright life flood through her bones.

They had played games of temptation in the dark. They had shared painful tenderness in a blaze of candlelight. Now he showed her at last what it felt like to love without restraint.

Her clothes fell away, one silken element at a time. His clever fingers released ribbons and hooks. Her skirts fell with a whisper to the floor. Her stiff bodice peeled back like a crab shell. Overdress, underdress, corset, chemise: all slid away, one soft murmur after another.

Meanwhile her palms caressed the sleeves of his brocade coat, feasting ravenously on the erotic contrast of his hard flesh beneath. He shrugged his shoulders. His coat slid through her fingers to drop to the floor. Beneath it his silk waistcoat was buttoned from chest to knee. She followed the line of buttons, releasing each one. The stiff embroidery opened to rub against her nipple.

A jolt of sensation ricocheted into her heart and plummeted to her groin, firing an ache so intense she groaned aloud. He caught her ragged exhalation on his lips and breathed it in, mingling her moan with one of his own. His waistcoat followed his coat to the floor. To peel his shirt over his head they would have to break the kiss. She couldn't bear it. She couldn't bear to stop kissing. His mouth was a well from which she could drink forever.

Even as her chemise fell away, leaving her naked in his arms, she kept drinking from his mouth. His lips smiled into hers as he thrust both hands between their bodies for a moment. His knuckles brushed her breasts as he ripped the fine lawn of his shirt from top to bottom to shrug it from his shoulders. His breeches followed. His erection sprang strongly between them as he slid away his underdrawers, although he stepped back into his beribboned shoes.

His palms rubbed up her spine to her head, his fingers pulling away hairpins until her hair tumbled down her back. As he did it, she reached to tug away his ribbon and run her hands through his hair. He pulled his mouth away suddenly, breathless and laughing, before catching her face in both palms.

"We are reborn," he said. "Rising from the sea foam like Aphrodite on her shell."

Juliet pressed into him, rubbing her belly against his arousal. "Is that what you call it?"

His penis shook against her as he laughed. "All this at our feet. We stand naked in a sea of silk. Apart from our shoes and stockings, we are as innocent as the day we were born."

"We can take them off, too."

"No, I don't think so," he replied, briefly kissing her again. "It's too damned erotic to leave them on."

He swung her into his arms. Juliet clutched both hands about his neck as he carried her to the bed, his heeled shoes rapping on the floor, hers swinging freely, both of them naked from the knees up.

Without ceremony he dumped her onto the bed and stood looking down at her for a moment. He was glorious, triumphant, his eyes black with desire.

She wriggled back against the pillows and watched as he, after all, stepped out of his shoes and onto the bed, then tied on the sheath that protected her from bearing his child. He rolled slowly over her, supporting his weight easily on his hands, but entwining his silk-clad calves with hers. His erection reared between them, proud and imperious. Juliet ached to receive it, to feel the slide of it reaching deeply inside her, but with devilish skill he forced her to wait. Every other inch of her skin must first receive his homage, even her ribs and the inside of her knees.

When he entered her at last, she burned like a furnace, only to cry instant ecstasy into his shoulder. He waited for a moment, smiling down at her, before beginning to thrust, driving an intensity of sensation deeper and deeper.

Mad thoughts careened beneath the exquisite sensations. She was his forever. She loved him. She might never be able to marry him. He had said he would wait, but could she believe it? He thought he could now, but when celibacy turned into weeks or months—? Yet for this one night, she wouldn't care. She wouldn't care. She had given a rake her heart, and devil take the consequences. She opened her eyes to fix his face forever in her memory.

The shudder of his climax rippled over his body, taking her to delirious depths of release. His head was thrown back, his expression sublime. Juliet closed her eyes and wept her rapture openly, until she found the sleep of pure exhaustion in his encircling arms.

She woke to a mouth on hers and a hand tenderly brushing hair from her forehead. In her sleep she kissed back, as if she kissed the night demon come to take her to paradise.

"Midnight capers," Alden whispered against her lips. "It is time to go after Harald Fairhair's pretty treasure."

CHAPTER SEVENTEEN

❧

*J*ULIET STRUGGLED AWAKE. ALDEN WAS ALREADY DRESSED—BUT simply, in a dark coat and breeches with riding boots—and standing beside the bed. He held a candle in one hand and shielded her eyes from its direct flame with the other.

"What did you do to me?" she asked. "I feel as if the blood has been drained from my body and replaced with silly happiness."

He grinned like Abednego given cream. "Why silly?"

She stared up at his features, caressed by candlelight. "Oh, I am a very fool for love, Alden Granville-Strachan. How am I to bear celibacy now, after that?"

He leaned down and kissed her mouth once more. "As I will, one day at a time."

Juliet sat up, still weak in every limb. "Is it morning?"

"Almost dawn. We left midnight behind several hours ago. Lord Edward is on his way. I must be after him. Are you still sure you want to come?"

Was hesitation foolish? After all, she had not seen Felton Hall since she had run away with George all those years ago. And perhaps her father had not gone to London at all. Swallowing her trickle of trepidation, Juliet nodded.

She slipped from the bed and found hot water already waiting in a basin. She washed rapidly, not caring that Alden's eyes devoured her as she did so, nor that he was obviously aroused by the sight. She almost hoped he would not be able to resist and would—instead of riding out to confront their enemy—stride across the chamber to make love with her again.

"I would," he said as if reading her mind. "God knows I want to. But if I am to be celibate for some impossible length of time into the future, perhaps I'd better start now. Besides we mustn't lose Lord Edward."

*D*AWN SPREAD WATERY FINGERS ACROSS A SKY LIKE AN OPAL-escent eggshell. Juliet stood with Alden under a small stand of trees and shivered—not from cold, though the early morning air was chilly and damp with dew. The great house before them, still sleeping darkly beneath the wash of pink and green-yellow sky, was Felton Hall. This was where she had grown up, played with Kit, walked sedately beneath these trees with her mother—whence she had run away with George Hardcastle, handsome and charming, but a man without depth and with no essential core of kindness. Little shivers ran through her blood like a hoard of tiny imps.

Without a word, Alden reached back and took her hand. They stood in absolute silence for several more minutes. At last a group of shadows materialized from the woods opposite them: a troop of misshapen creatures, like a small herd of strange beasts with bizarrely long necks and stiff heads bobbing at each step.

"Our enemy," Alden whispered then. "He brings minions."

The shapes moved closer, jigging their strange heads. Juliet stared at them: four men carrying picks and shovels over their shoulders. Ahead of the group, one figure devoured the turf with ferocious strides, the tails of his coat flying behind him: Lord Edward Vane.

The duke's son stopped in the corner of the pasture and directed his men to start digging. Alden turned to Juliet and put one finger to his lips. His smile ghosted in the half-light and her heart turned over.

Two picks swung up, then thudded into the ground: a sheltered, somewhat boggy patch at the base of a small rise. It was the spot she had shown Alden on her map. When she and Kit were children, a spring had bubbled up there, but a new drainage ditch had been dug below it since then. Now it was a place that became just occasionally damp, enough to support a few wild irises and a little coarse marsh grass, but no longer a place where cattle could drink.

To one side, the ruins of a brick building had crumbled into a few ragged walls, invaded by brambles. On the other, a group of low bushes straggled into the base of the hillside above. The slope itself was thickly clustered with trees, offering their protection now to Juliet and Alden.

Clods of dirt flew. *Suck. Thud. Thud.* Lord Edward stood and watched.

Alden sank to the ground, pulling Juliet down beside him. He took off his coat and wrapped it over her shoulders. She had no idea what he planned to do next and she hadn't asked him. They sat side by side in absolute silence, while the irises were trampled and the marsh grass cut away. There seemed to be no good outcome to any of this—whether Lord Edward found Harald Fairhair's treasure or not, she was still married to George Hardcastle.

A cock crowed somewhere, then another, a raucous echo from the home farms. Ducks startled into sudden flight from the lake near the house, rattling the air with their wings as they passed. The eggshell colors bleached from the sky, mutating into the clear blue of an early summer morning.

Juliet let her hand lie in Alden's palm and listened to the throb of her own heart as the picks rose and fell, and the duke's son paced beside an ever-growing pile of dirt. It was an hour, maybe two, before the sun broke over the treetops to flood the diggers with color. Lord Edward's gray coat flushed to rose pink, his face leaped into focus, stark with powder and rouge and the patches that covered his scars. He pulled off his tricorn and scratched under his wig.

The soil in the pit was becoming damper. The picks had given way to shovels now. At each stroke they sucked and popped as bricks of earth were removed. Juliet watched with her heart in her mouth. She knew there was another kind of treasure here. She just didn't know what she'd do if Lord Edward found it.

*A*LDEN WATCHED THE MEN LABOR. HE HAD THROWN HIS NET wide, weaving this trap. A dozen things could go wrong. Devil take it, a hundred things could go wrong, yet none of it truly mattered, not even revenge on Lord Edward, as long as Juliet loved him. She sat beside him in the damp, shadowy morning, her hand in his. He knew that this invasion of her childhood home distressed her, and he had taken a further risk she didn't know about: he had sent a letter explaining everything to her father, for he knew that Lord Felton was home. If the earl didn't come, she would never know that her father still turned his back on her. Yet if he did—?

The desire to protect her, save her from harm or distress, seared Alden's heart.

I would slay dragons for you, Juliet. I would storm the walls of Troy. I would fight the hoards of Genghis Khan. Anything to protect you and save you from harm. My heart trembles and swells, Juliet. Is this love?

Yet he could not save her from this: this witnessing at her childhood home or the results of that, if what he had planned didn't happen as he hoped.

Lord Edward's boots wore a dark track in the dew-soaked grass. Across a distant field a small herd of cows began to stream toward their barn, ready for morning milking. The sun grew warmer.

The laborers were working in shifts now. The hole was growing deeper. A pick clanged against something hard.

Lord Edward spun about.

"You have something?"

The laborer bent and began to scrape with his shovel. "Looks like a box, my lord."

"*A box!*" Ignoring the damage to his breeches, the duke's son dropped to both knees in the dirt at the edge of the pit. "Lud, man! Hand it here!" He reached down with both hands.

The laborer handed him a mud-covered cube.

And all hell broke loose.

Juliet tore her hand from Alden's and raced down the slope, shouting.

Alden sprang up and ran after her.

Several men jumped out from behind the ruined brick wall and began to run toward them.

Across a far field, a man on horseback came galloping ever closer.

Lord Edward's laborers flung aside their tools and took to their heels.

"How dare you!" Juliet yelled. "That's mine!"

Clutching the box to his chest, the duke's son scrambled to his feet, stepped back and slipped into the pit.

In a flurry of skirts, Juliet skidded to a halt at the edge of the dirt pile. Alden caught her, just as the other men came up behind them, led by an older man, obviously a peer, in a white wig and expensive green frock coat.

Juliet lifted her head and met the man's raw gaze. For a moment they stared at each other in silence.

"Lud!" she said at last with a half-laugh. "Father?"

"Well, madam." As if paper blew in a storm, Lord Felton's face crumpled. "It has been a long time, but you find me well enough, daughter."

He held out his arms. Alden watched as Juliet walked directly into her father's embrace. Thank God!

"Perhaps," Alden said to the gaping servants, "someone should help Lord Edward out of the mire?"

Immediately several of the earl's servants reached down. Smeared with mud, Lord Edward was pulled onto the grass. As he stood, his wig fell, revealing the stubble of his shaved head beneath. The powdered headpiece lay ignored on the ground, where one of the menservants inadvertently ground it into the mud.

"Damme, Lord Edward!" the earl said. "What the devil do you think you're about, digging a great pit on my land, what?"

The duke's son bowed, still hugging the box. "Lord Felton, your servant, sir. Your indulgence, I pray." Bareheaded in the early dawn light, Lord Edward shimmered like a shard of ice, hard, brilliant, with no loss of dignity. "Your daughter and I were once engaged to be married—"

"I am aware of that, sir," the earl said.

Lord Edward bowed again. "I have been forbearing, you must agree, sir, even in the face of ridicule and scandal. I have been constant, even in the face of faithlessness." He glanced pointedly at Alden. "Even now, when I discover your daughter once more in such unfortunate company—"

The earl looked uncomfortable. His hands dropped, then he waved his servants away, out of earshot. "I have no quarrel with you on that score, sir. My daughter has much to answer for, I don't deny it."

The powdered face smiled. "Yet I have only wished to regain her affections. To find her treasure seemed but a small step—"

"Then you admit the box is mine," Juliet interrupted, stepping forward.

"Ma'am, my heart is yours." Lord Edward spun to face her, eyes glittering, a muscle leaping in his jaw, though his tone was bland. "But this box? Perhaps you forget what happened at Marion Hall?"

Juliet stopped dead.

The moment stretched, ripe with chaotic possibilities.

Pink coat skirts belled as the duke's son turned back to the earl. "Sir Reginald Denby's country seat—"

Juliet stood like a birch tree, white-faced, on the grass.

"Perhaps you have heard of it, sir?" Alden interjected helpfully. "A place known for its interesting architecture."

With a puzzled frown, the earl stared at the duke's son, then broke the silence as if he broke glass. "To what the devil do you refer, sir? My *daughter* was at Marion Hall?"

"Alas, and in the company of Gracechurch, whose reputation is well known."

"In spite of which sad fact," Alden said, "Lord Edward once again offered for your daughter's hand, which he would hardly have done if she had been in any way compromised by my unsteady self—"

"She refused me." Lord Edward's voice rang. *"But she gave me her locket and the rights to this box, if I could find it."*

Juliet looked stunned.

"This is true?" the earl asked.

"Gracechurch will no doubt corroborate what I say," the duke's son said, triumphant. "Unless he remembers the evening differently? Do you, Gracechurch? Must I bore her father with more details of what Lady Elizabeth Juliet Amberleigh said and did that night?"

"Quite unnecessary, I am sure," Alden said faintly. A mad urge to laugh was almost his undoing.

"Then who would dispute that this box is indeed mine?"

"No one here, Lord Edward," Juliet said. "Since I apparently gave it to you so freely, by all means, keep the box. Yet I will give you the value in cash of its contents."

"Are you mad, ma'am? Harald Fairhair's treasure?"

Alden swept the duke's son a bow worthy of any drawing room, using his handkerchief to add a particularly insulting flourish. The lace caught a clear ray of light breaking over the trees, flashing for a moment like a white bird.

"Alas, sir," he said. "If Harald Fairhair put his gold in that box, I'm afraid he must have traveled forward in time to do so. That is a tea chest, I believe, made about twenty years ago?"

"Which I once buried here," Juliet said gaily, "with Kit. The soil must have subsided, to make our box sink so deeply into the ground."

Lord Edward glanced down at the mud-caked wood. Without

a word he pulled open the lid. Beneath the rouge and patches, his face turned white.

The box fell to the ground as he reached into a pocket and brought out the locket. He stared at it for a moment, his mouth frozen in an odd grimace.

Alden plucked Juliet's gold from his enemy's suddenly nerveless fingers. "Disappointed, sir?"

With arctic bravado, his face a wax mask, the duke's son raised both brows. "Lud, sir, a mere trifle—"

"Compared to the Isle of Dogs Company? The fur trade? That nice network of investments recommended by Robert Dovenby?"

Like a marionette, Lord Edward jerked. "What the *devil* do you know about that?"

Alden smiled as he ran his thumb over Juliet's locket, then handed it to her. "Only that you are betrayed in your turn, sir. Did you really think the Dove was your friend? You are ruined, I'm afraid. Would you like all the details?"

One by one, he began to name them: the nonexistent ships, the cargoes never purchased, the empire of fraud and greed so willingly entered into . . .

A catalogue of ruin.

The duke's son ground ringed knuckles against his discolored teeth, his jaw working. Sliding down into a crouch, rose skirts crushed over the scabbard at his hip, he clutched his prickly head in both shaking hands. The silence was deafening.

Alden leaned down and picked up the box. "It's a charming feeling, isn't it?" he asked quietly. "Good for the bowels."

Leaving the duke's son huddled on the dirt pile, Alden gave the box to Juliet. "So what *is* inside? I must admit to a natural curiosity."

Juliet took Alden's handkerchief and spread it on the ground. She lifted the lid of the box and poured out the contents. A tumble of tiny men fell onto the square of linen.

"Ah," Alden said, dropping to one knee to look at them. "Toy soldiers."

Juliet met his gaze and smiled, before she turned to her father. "Yes, toy soldiers. Kit's favorites. We buried them here in fun, then couldn't find them again, however much we dug for them. It was just a child's game, based on the cryptic numbers in the locket."

"Child's game, what?" Lord Felton said, bending over the toys. "Then my daughter played a trick on you, Lord Edward, when she sent you here to dig a hole to Hades on my property. And from what Lord Gracechurch has written me about your affairs, sir, your trickery, your fraud, *and your treatment of my daughter*— with proof, I might add, sir, with proof—I'd say the jig is up for you, sir. My daughter deserves a better man than you, Lord Edward Vane!"

Face wet, as if slick with melting ice, eyes fixed on Juliet, the duke's son sprang to his feet. Too quickly for Alden to protect her from what Lord Edward did next.

I would slay dragons for you. I would storm the walls of Troy. I would fight the hoards of Genghis Khan to protect you and save you from harm.

But he was too far away, sword hanging useless at his side, and kneeling.

As if he watched from some great distance, Alden saw Lord Edward smile at her. As slowly as honey dripping from a spoon, the duke's son reached inside his coat and drew something out. The object caught a flash of sunlight as it turned, sparking in the cold morning, piercing, brilliant, striking like a knife into Alden's heart—although the lethal intent wasn't for him.

It was for Juliet.

Too late, she flung up a hand as Lord Edward raised a dagger and made ready to throw.

Alden had only that slow, nightmare split second to leap ten feet, to draw a pistol, to shout, to stop time. As he threw himself toward Juliet, hell seemed to close around him, roaring demonic screams in his ears, stopping his heart cold in his chest. All he could achieve was the shout: the last word she would hear on this earth, filled with the entire contents of his soul.

"Juliet!"

An echoing retort rang in his ears. Eyes wide with shock, Lord Edward dropped the dagger and crumpled to the ground. Alden crushed Juliet unharmed in his arms as he stared up into the smoking barrel of a pistol and another face, contorted with fury: the horseman.

The horseman who had been thundering toward them all across the pasture, brought from London by one of Alden's messages.

"Lud," Alden said. "It's Hamlet. Will anyone be left standing at the end of the play besides Horatio?"

"Bastard!" shouted the horseman. "The bloody bastard!"

Lord Edward writhed on the ground, clutching his shoulder where blood oozed between his fingers. "Hardcastle? Lud, sir! You shot me?"

His face murderous, George swung from his horse and stalked toward the duke's son. Before he reached him, at a signal from the earl, several of Lord Felton's men caught his arms and held him pinioned. The earl moved to stand beside his daughter. Juliet glanced at her father and grasped his arm, allowing Alden to move away, freed for action.

"We are ruined, sir!" George hissed, staring at Lord Edward. *"Ruined!"* Tugging against the restraining arms, he thrust his head forward and spat. "Your investment schemes have proved to be a bloody bubble, sir. Our creditors already know it. Everyone knows it. Everything has imploded. *Everything!"*

"Alas, Mr. Hardcastle," Alden said. "Lord Edward has already discovered the depth of his own deceptions. Your news is only confirming it."

"He ruined my business to start with! Set himself up in competition with my timber trade, ruined me, then offered to help me out, so he could ruin me more completely." George swung his head back toward the duke's son. "They're after us for fraud, sir, and embezzlement. I could hang."

"Then hang, sir!" Lord Edward retched once into the dirt. "And curse your father's ignoble blood, which won't protect you from the gallows."

"Damme, sir! If we hang, we hang together!" shouted George.

"Alas, whatever he has done, they will not hang a peer's son, Mr. Hardcastle, but they might hang you," Alden said. "However, if you leave now for France, you may yet escape the noose. Though not before you and I settle a few differences, of course."

Blood seeped steadily between the long fingers clenched on the pink coat, yet with mad defiance, Lord Edward laughed and sat up. "You would duel with scum like that, Gracechurch?"

"Lud, sir," Alden said with the lift of one brow. "Sooner than I would duel with scum like you."

The duke's son sprang back to his feet, sunlight blazing from his now drawn sword. For a moment he stood poised, that lethal, practiced fencing partner, one of the best swordsmen in England. Yet he was losing blood, his cuff stained red, his sword hilt slick in his palm.

Purely in self-defense, Alden's own blade hissed into his hand. Yet with a short bow, he gestured as if to throw the rapier aside. "I *never* duel with a bleeding man, Lord Edward. It makes him mean—and it removes all the art from the game."

Face glassy, ignoring Alden's undefended stance, Lord Edward thrust hard for the heart.

Alden parried and sidestepped. At his enemy's next lunge, he disarmed him. Scooping up both the dropped rapier and dagger, Alden threw the weapons aside, where one of the menservants gathered them, then began to toss his own sword to Lord Felton.

Yet as he turned, Juliet screamed. Lord Edward had grabbed the handle of an abandoned pick. He swung it with mad strength, the heavy steel dull, spattering mud. Alden's rapier shattered, blade severed from the guard, the shock of it numbing his arm to the shoulder as he barely deflected the blow. He ducked, snatched, and averted the next strike with a shovel.

"Faith, sir, a most original choice of weapons." Alden dodged again as the pick crashed past his head. "What about a duel with scythes?"

"Fight me, damn you!" Lord Edward shouted, though his sleeve bloomed with red poppies, streaming to the wrist.

"Get well, sir," Alden said kindly, "and I will meet you in a hay meadow. I guarantee to best you by the third windrow."

Metal rang again as Alden snared the head of the pick with his shovel. He twisted hard. The pick fell to the ground.

Lord Edward sank to his knees as if his puppetmaster had severed his strings. "I should have poisoned you like vermin——" he began, but he looked over his shoulder and grinned like a death mask.

George had wrenched away from his gaping captors. Before anyone could stop him, he launched himself at Lord Edward and flung him to the ground. As George's fist crashed into his injured shoulder, the duke's son shrieked once and fainted.

"Scum?" George shouted. "Scum!" Without compunction, he reared up on both knees, grabbed a rock from the dirt pile and brought it down with a sickening crash on Lord Edward's naked head.

Alden leaped, pinning George down with one knee and trapping the man's arms behind his back. He wrenched off his cravat and used the strip of linen to bind George's hands, before handing him back into the custody of Lord Felton's men.

"Lud, Mr. Hardcastle," he said. "You have just murdered the son of a peer of the realm. I am damned sorry for it, because—— once he was fit—I had every intention of murdering him myself." He dusted off his palms with a fresh handkerchief and bit back real anger. "Though I'm damned if I would have slaughtered an injured man in front of my wife."

Her back rigid, her hair rich in the now bright morning sun, Juliet had pressed one hand to her mouth and spun about to walk away, followed by Alden's silent, agonized apologies: that he had relied on those heedless menservants, had not seen this coming—and prevented it.

George glanced after her. "The damned whore! She's no bloody wife to me!" He swung his head. "When we first married, she tupped me like a sailor's doxy, but now she won't even f—"

Lord Felton brought his stick down across George's mouth.

Alden caught the earl by the arm. "Enough death, perhaps, for one morning? I didn't mean that business about Hamlet literally. Mr. Hardcastle is distraught over his financial losses. He did not intend to become a murderer."

Lord Felton turned to Alden, his face set in lines of command, a peer of the realm witnessing mayhem in his own domain. "Yet murder is what happened. You planned all this, what? When you sent me that letter asking me to come out here this morning— intercept Lord Edward and his men, meet my daughter again— you had all this planned?"

Alden glanced at George. Blood welled from a cut on the man's handsome face. *Planned?* Not quite. It was an odd feeling, as if dice rattled in his brain.

"I wanted to see Mr. Hardcastle face the wrath of the law over his fraudulent investment schemes. I hoped that, brought to extremity, he would agree to a more reasonable divorce. I meant to pay him enough to live in comfort in France."

Lord Felton pointed to the duke's son. "And Lord Edward, sir, who now lies there a corpse?"

"I hoped to see Lord Edward prove himself capable of the outright theft of a treasure with yourself as eyewitness, to show what kind of man he really was, to ruin him in society, with his family and with his creditors. I wanted to shame him, embarrass him, then I hoped to dispatch him myself in a duel."

"So you did intend his death," Lord Felton said baldly.

"I intended his death," Alden replied. "But not like this."

"Then it was at the risk of his own," Juliet said. "Lord Edward Vane was known to be a demon with a blade." She shuddered suddenly, walked off to a low part of the crumbling brick wall and sat down.

Lord Felton glanced back at Alden and studied his face. "I have not forgotten the suit you pressed for in your letter, sir, but as of this moment she is still a married woman." He indicated the scene, the crumpled form of Lord Edward, George in the hands of his servants. "I do not entirely lay the blame for all this at your door, Gracechurch, but I think my daughter and I need some time, sir. Five years to make up for, what? Her home, while her husband still lives, is here at Felton Hall with me."

"Of course," Alden said. "In the circumstances. If that is her choice—"

Juliet sat with both hands over her eyes. "I will stay here with you, Father."

The earl shook his head and stared off toward Felton Hall. "I wanted a duke's son for her, my only daughter. Perhaps a viscount will do, but I'm damned if she'll marry a commoner a second time."

"A great disadvantage to be born without a title," Alden said dryly. He closed Lord Edward's eyes, before draping his own waistcoat over his enemy's face.

George licked his split lip and laughed. "Then look to your own title, *Lord* Gracechurch! Lord Edward told me. He thought it was the greatest joke of all. He was saving it to throw in your face when the time was right: my marriage may have been a sham, but your precious brother's was real enough and so is his son's existence. What about *that*?"

"What son?" Alden stared at him. "What marriage?"

George spat.

"What marriage?"

"You'll not find out from me, *my lord*," George replied. "But you might ask your mother."

Lord Felton signaled to the servants. "What the devil is he talking about? Take the damned fellow away."

George was dragged off across the pasture.

His son's existence. His son's existence. Alden bent to gather the handkerchief with the toy soldiers. He walked up to Juliet and set them in her hands. A wealth of words were needed, too many to speak.

"I understand. You must give this time to your father. I shall go back to Gracechurch to uncover whatever truth I may."

She looked up and met his gaze. He thought her soul lay in her eyes.

"The truth between us will not change," she said. "Whatever the world offers."

Lord Felton walked up to his daughter and held out his arm. Alden bowed and stepped back. With her back straight and her chin high, Juliet placed her hand on her father's sleeve and allowed him to lead her away toward Felton Hall.

Alden stood by the gaping hole in the ground, the oddly decorative body of the duke's son at his feet, and watched them leave.

*J*ULIET FELT A DEVASTATING NAUSEA: *NUMB AS IF I HAD BEEN beaten with sticks.* George had murdered Lord Edward. She ought to have been glad. The fear she had lived with for five years had been lifted. Yet to see one's enemy slain before one's eyes by one's husband was not something she ever wanted to see again— and now George would be hanged. Dragged before a court, found guilty of murder and forced to walk to the scaffold to kick away his last breath before a jeering crowd.

Yet he had saved her life.

She had never really loved him, but George had won her first girlish infatuation. They had shared a bed, in pleasure, in real passion. Though he had proved to be weak and spiteful, she had never thought he was evil. What was she to believe now? That she had been seduced by a murderer, or that all men were capable of murder, given enough provocation?

Meanwhile, she had left Alden standing by the spring, to return to her childhood home with her father. She had valued these days, awkward conversations with the earl, weeping once in his presence, only to look up to see his eyes filled also with tears. They had lost a wife and son, a mother and brother, and then lost five years in bitter separation. Her father, too, had been taken ill after the accident. He had not known she lay near death at an inn. By the time he discovered that George had abandoned her, she had already disappeared into Miss Parrett's care.

They had to make up all that time and rediscover each other.

It was as if she had slept away those days in Manston Mingate, until Alden had forced her to wake up and live again. Unfortunately, living was painful as well as exciting. Difficult as well as fulfilling.

Juliet must take this time for her father, but what was she to do about the man that she loved and the harsh fact that she was still married, though her husband now rotted in the town jail awaiting the assizes? And what of George's odd threat, that Alden was not truly Lord Gracechurch? That his brother Gregory had left a legitimate son?

She sent decent food and clean clothes to George, and wondered if money and title were, in the end, all that mattered to Lord Felton.

H E HAD BEEN ALLOWED TO KEEP THE CLOTHES. HE HAD A ROOM to himself, decently furnished, looking through a barred window out over the yard of the town hall. They had even allowed him paper and quills. Yet George sat on the walnut chair, leaned his head in his hands at the fine desk and felt sorry for himself. She sent food and clean cravats, the bitch, but she didn't come to see him.

When a visitor was finally shown in, George refused to stand, even though Alden Granville made an elegant leg and respectful bow, almost as if the butcher's grandson were also the son of a peer.

"You have come to gloat?" George said. "Or to beg for more information? You won't get it from me."

"My mother, sir—though reluctantly—has already told me

everything Lord Edward Vane found out from Gregory." He smiled, entirely without rancor. "I'm afraid it does not distress me as much as you probably hope. That is not why I came."

"Then why?" George asked. "You couldn't wait to watch me hang?"

Heels rapped as the blond man walked to the barred window and looked out. George knew the view intimately. It was where he would die.

"Why assume the rope?" Alden asked. "Lord Edward would have killed Juliet. By shooting him, you saved her life. Although you then had the misfortune to crush his skull with a rock, a good defense might yet save you from the gallows."

"I can't afford a lawyer."

"If you want one, I will pay."

Astonishment stupefied him for a moment. "Why, in the devil's name?"

"For the same reason I would spare you the public scaffold: for her sake." The blond man turned to face him. "Lord Edward's father is a duke. His influence is immense. He may have been ready to strike off his son without a penny, but he will never forgive his murder. There is no way around that unfortunate fact. Thus you could not escape transportation or life in the hulks, but you might live—if you want to fight for the chance."

"I'd rather be dead," George said.

"Do you mean that? Then why not behave with honor for the first time in your life?"

George stared up, feeling hot shame stain his face. His visitor was immaculate, from curled buttercup hair to heeled shoes. It made him feel shabby, menial.

"What the hell do you mean—for the first time?"

"I mean that I have just read your marriage papers, sir," the blond man said.

His heart thumped uncomfortably. "It was all legal, done before witnesses."

Alden Granville shook out his lace and folded his arms, reminding George of the man's power, carefully restrained.

"Not quite. In spite of the witnesses, it was not done exactly according to all the terms of the recent Marriage Act, Mr. Hardcastle. It could easily be argued that the marriage was unlawful and that you perpetrated a fraud. You knew this, of course. You have always known it, as I believe Lord Edward knew it. He was a busy man, the duke's son, gathering information on everybody."

"You're trying to bargain with me? You'll pay my lawyer's fees, but only if I agree that our marriage was fraudulent? What do you want? A signed affidavit that we were never legally wed? Should it say that our marriage was never consummated? *That* would be a lie!"

If he hoped to upset his visitor, he failed.

"Her father is an earl," Alden said. "He also has considerable influence in this. Perhaps, by doing right by his daughter—"

George leaped up. "Yet *you* offer me my life in trade for Juliet's freedom to wed you?"

"I don't really give a damn about your life, Mr. Hardcastle." The hard face was calm, with no exultation at all in the blue eyes—only the faintest glimmer of a thinly veiled exasperation. "I am simply trying to remind you of the facts. I will pay for a barrister either way. As for your marriage, whatever you do, the flaws in the ceremony will give her father a simple way to free her. If you die out there in that square, of course, the point is moot. She is no longer your wife, either way."

"But you don't like the idea that in the meantime she is married to a murderer. That there'll be a hell of a scandal at the trial. You want her free *now*, don't you?"

"You don't think you owe her that much? You seduced her from her home when she was little more than a child. You abandoned her when she faced the greatest tragedy of her life. Five years later you destroyed without compunction the new life she had made. She loved you once. You could make this a great deal easier for her, if you wished."

"What are you going to do?" George asked. His hands felt clammy.

"I don't know," Alden replied. "I rather wish you would ask yourself what you should do, sir, if you wish to be remembered as a gentleman."

The blond man spun on his heel and stalked out.

George sat for a long time at the desk, staring at the walls as dark fell in loving fingers through the barred windows. Transportation, the hulks, or death on the scaffold. If he let Alden Granville lord it over him by providing a barrister, he'd owe his wretched life to those ringed white hands that had never done a day's honest work. Yet he was damned if he'd let that facile voice laugh at him as he was led to be hanged.

A butcher's grandson he might be, but he'd show all those damned aristocrats that they were no better gentlemen than George Hardcastle!

He stood up and washed his face and hands. Stripping off his clothes, he pulled on a pair of green stockings and tugged a clean white shirt over his head, carefully arranging the neck and cuffs. His best dark green suit followed, the one with the embroidered waistcoat. With a quick rub, he shined his black shoes before he thrust them back onto his gaily colored feet, then freshly powdered his wig and placed it carefully over his dark head.

For a moment George stared at himself in the mirror, then he turned back to the open dresser drawer and took out a long white cravat.

SHERRY CLUNG LIKE A SQUIRREL, ABOUT FIFTEEN FEET FROM THE ground, in the branches of a large oak tree. Alden lay back in the grass and watched him. If the child slipped and fell, he might be killed. But all small boys climbed trees. A boy couldn't grow into a man without taking risks, and Alden would catch him long before he plummeted onto the grass.

Footsteps crunched on the gravel path behind him. A footman bowed and gave Alden two packages.

Alden waited until Sherry was safely back on the ground and in the charge of Peter Primrose, before he walked back to Gracechurch Abbey.

He unfolded the paper around the smaller package. Juliet had written three sentences.

I love you. I believe in you. Whether in this life or the next, I will marry you.

Nestled in the creased paper lay her locket. Alden opened it and looked at the writing inside: the key to a treasure. Perhaps, now he had time on his hands, he would try to decipher the message for himself.

With a smile, he untied the larger package. Toy soldiers spilled onto his desk, her little brother's toys, once buried at the spring by the ruined brick walls. Unable to take treasure from the earth, Juliet and little Kit had given it. This time she had written three words: *For Sherry—Juliet.*

For Sherry. Alden glanced up at the walls of the study, the sprawl of another well-loved wing of Gracechurch Abbey visible from the window. Juliet's cats were sunning in the courtyard.

For Sherry.

He could not put it off any longer. Alden sharpened a quill and smoothed out a sheet of paper.

Gracechurch Abbey
   The Right Honorable the Earl of Felton.
   My lord: As I previously wrote, it was my intention, with Your Lordship's permission, to seek your daughter's hand in marriage as soon as she was free to wed again. I do not withdraw my suit, but I am obliged to inform Your Lordship of a change in my circumstances.

Alden stopped and looked up for a moment, with a wry grin at his reluctance to put it on paper: the facts he had gleaned from his mother. It had taken cajoling and orange biscuits, the drying of copious tears on lace-edged handkerchiefs, before she produced the papers she had hidden and admitted the truth she had known all along.

"Mrs. Sherwood's child!" Lady Gracechurch had wailed. "I don't think it right!"

But it was right, of course. Alden dipped the quill in the inkwell and kept writing.

My brother did indeed legally marry. I now have proof of it. Lord Edward Vane fell into Gregory's confidence quite by accident, during a drinking bout in London. The duke's son kept the secret—

—presumably waiting until he could find a way to use it for his personal gain! If Lord Edward had not been killed, no doubt he would have spilled the facts far more cruelly than Hardcastle had done. The secret must have brought the duke's son so many gloating moments over the years. Yet he had died before he could make use of his knowledge.

Alden began writing again.

My mother also knew, but she found the circumstances—

He stopped and considered for a moment before he chose an adjective. How to express his mother's ability to thrust unpleasant facts from consciousness? Impossible for someone like Lord Felton to comprehend.

—distressing and therefore acted as if the marriage had never taken place.

—the circumstances that had torn Gracechurch Abbey apart while he was in Italy. Alden could imagine the pain the situation must have caused. An unscrupulous young man had seduced his father's lover. For whatever reason, perhaps even a real love, he had married her, but no wonder they had kept the marriage secret! Alden attempted to write the facts dispassionately.

My brother's wife was a widow named Mrs. Sherwood, who was my father's mistress. My father discovered their liaison, but did not know of their wedding. The marriage was legal, but Gregory was killed before he could make it public. Mrs. Sherwood died in child-bed. . . .

Giving birth to Sherry. She must have relied on Alden's mother to secure her baby's rights, thinking that Lady Gracechurch would want to see her grandchild claim his proper place and title. Instead, his mother had betrayed Gregory's trust and retreated to the Dower House, denying the baby's existence.

Thus the child living at Gracechurch Abbey under the name James Sherwood is, in fact, James Granville-Strachan, my brother's legitimate son, now revealed to be the true Viscount Gracechurch. Although Gracechurch Abbey is not entailed, when James reaches his majority, I shall gift the house and estates to him as the rightful heir. Until that time, I shall remain in residence as his guardian.

Alden stopped. The crux of it: he was not Lord Gracechurch and never had been. He was merely a younger son once again, an adventurer, with no long-term prospects other than what he could create through his own brains and wit. Yet, because it was Sherry, he honestly did not resent it.

I can no longer offer your daughter a title, and I cannot offer our children the inheritance of Gracechurch Abbey. Yet I have come to believe, my lord, that love can conquer all obstacles. Therefore, once she is free to entertain it, I do not withdraw my suit, unless that is your daughter's own wish.
I am, your obedient, humble servant, Alden Granville-Strachan.

He sanded the letter and reread it, before he folded the paper. He could no longer impress the Gracechurch crest into the red wax. It was a damned shadowy future to offer an earl's daughter. Yet with Juliet at his side—if she would have him—he was prepared to face anything.

ULIET WALKED INTO HER FATHER'S STUDY AT FELTON HALL AND stopped dead. The earl stood at the window, hands clasped behind his back, staring out. His stout figure, his white wig, were dearly familiar now. Why had she not attempted a reconciliation years ago?

"Well, m' dear," Lord Felton said over his shoulder. "Letter arrived from your swain, fellow who's been calling himself Lord Gracechurch. Better read it."

—been calling himself?

Her mother's portrait hung on the wall. The eyes seemed to watch in sympathy as Juliet crossed the room to the desk and picked up the letter. His writing. She sat down and read it through twice.

"Rum business, what?" the earl said.

She closed her eyes, imagining the pain Alden must have felt to discover all this, knowing what it must have cost him to decide to give up all claim to Gracechurch Abbey, the home he passionately loved. Yet it was Sherry who benefited!

Her father turned. "Now what do we do?"

"As soon as I am free, we have a wedding," Juliet said firmly.

Lord Felton stared at her. "You'd take this fellow with nothing but the clothes on his back?"

Juliet smiled. "Excellent clothes, my lord, on an excellent fellow. Of course, I would."

"Damme!" The earl collapsed onto the window seat.

She crossed the room to kneel beside him. "If that letter doesn't prove his worth, what could? Alden will give up his estates to his brother's child! He doesn't have to. He cannot keep the title, but he could keep the property. Instead he will continue to build wealth for Sherry—"

"Sherry?"

"Little James, Viscount Gracechurch."

The earl shook his head as if bewildered. "This child lived at Gracechurch Abbey, even though Alden Granville-Strachan thought him the son of his father's mistress by a stranger—a nameless bastard?"

"Sherry was born there," Juliet said. "Where else should he live?"

Lord Felton patted her sleeve in silence for a moment, before he spoke again.

"But your suitor is left with nothing! He's a well-known rake and gambler. He's broken hearts all across Europe and England. How can I let him have my only daughter?"

"Easily," Juliet said. "You do as I have done and say yes."

The earl pushed himself to his feet. "There is other news, too, m' dear. Better sit down."

She felt the blood drain from her face at his sudden change in tone and sat down in the nearest chair.

"George Hardcastle," the earl said. "No way to put this, but to just come out and say it. The man hanged himself yesterday. In all his best clothes. Left a note."

He thrust out a second slip of paper.

Don't judge me too harshly. This is the only way out. Hardcastle.

"You are free now," the earl said. "There won't have to be a trial. Somehow the chap found the courage to do the honorable thing. So, now, do you still want this Alden Granville for a husband? Even if he's no claim to Gracechurch?"

She closed her eyes to hide her sudden rush of tears. "Yes. With my whole heart."

"Then, after a decent interval, you may take your new swain, if you wish. But he'd better prove himself first, what?"

"Prove himself? How much more can he prove?"

"He's a fine man, I won't deny it, but he is still a notorious rake. Let him wait for you. Let him show he wants no other woman. Let him wait a year and a day. If he still wants you then, if he stays faithful all that time, then he can have you."

"A year and a day? That's unfair!"

"Hah! So you think he can't wait? That if he's not in your bed, he'll find solace in another's?"

"I think it would prove nothing whether he did or not. A year and a day, Father! After Mama and Kit died, I thought I deserved any chastisement. I don't believe that any longer. I know Alden loves me. I know we'll be happy together. Don't you think we've been punished enough?"

The earl gazed up at his wife's portrait. "Your mother only ever wanted you to be happy. Very well, m' dear. We'll compromise. Let George Hardcastle rest decently in his grave for three months. Pay his memory, however unworthy, that much respect. Let Alden Granville prove himself faithful in the meantime. If he can do it, I won't stand in the way of your wedding. But if he can't, then you marry this man over my dead body."

CHAPTER EIGHTEEN

❧❧

$\mathcal{S}$UMMER SLID INTO AUTUMN. FLYING BANDS OF GEESE DREW strange runes across the sky. Juliet walked to the corner of the pasture by the ruins of the brick wall, to the spot where she and Kit had once dug for treasure and buried the lead soldiers. Workmen had filled in Lord Edward's pit and spread hay over the bare dirt, so it would seed new grass in the spring, but there was still a scar there, marring the pasture.

It was three months to the day that she had heard of George's death, read Alden's letter about his brother's secret marriage, and accepted her father's demand that they wait.

Had that been a risk? A man so used to sensual indulgence—

Yet beneath her fretful attempts to find doubt, burned the bright flame of a far deeper knowledge: how completely Alden must love her and just what an extraordinary man he really was. She had, for the first time in her life, discovered what love truly meant.

And so they had waited, while every last corner of her soul knew how severely she missed him.

In accordance with her father's wishes, Alden had not visited, but he had written every day: sending news of Sherry, of her cats, of the improvements he continued to make at Gracechurch Abbey for the benefit now of his brother's child—along with more personal, private messages for her alone.

And then, that last witty, incisive touch, so typical of him: at the end of every letter he wrote out a chess move, to which each day she responded with a move of her own. So that as the weeks had passed, at Gracechurch and at Felton Hall, two sets of chessmen reflected one pattern, one game, one heart.

Yet one of Alden's letters had made her sit down, heart pounding.

I received a visitor yesterday. Mr. Dovenby arrived on horseback. We have become friends of a kind, though the mysterious Dove does not seem to make friends very readily. Did I ever tell you that he had already contrived plans to destroy the duke's son, that he had his own reasons for vengeance, when I first asked for his help? We owe him a great debt, Juliet, but his reasons for hating Lord Edward are his own and he keeps his own counsel. When I pressed him, he would say only this: that if he ever thought he could fall in love with a lady, it would have been you. How can I blame him?

Why did that strange admission affect her at all? Robert Dovenby was one of the few men she had ever met who had *not* looked at her as if she were something he had the right to devour. She knew now how vital a part he had played in allowing her and Alden to find each other, that he had almost been her guardian angel, yet she knew nothing else about him.

She knew only this: all her woman's intuition had told her that she would not see much of Mr. Dovenby in the future. Now she knew why.

Juliet sat down on a section of the broken wall and closed her eyes.

The thud of a horse's hooves pounded across the pasture. With awareness tingling at the back of her neck, she waited. The hoofbeats came closer. A small metallic jingle from the bit, a little snort. The horse had stopped.

Warmth spread through her blood as if the sun shone directly into her heart.

"I am sorry there's no treasure," she said, letting her joy run freely.

"Indeed, ma'am. Devil take it! Why else ask you to meet me here, where the Felton Hoard was supposed to be buried? After all, I have longed only to see you draped in Harald Fairhair's gold," his voice replied, rich with laughter and love. "A massive torque around your neck. Barbaric arm rings and necklaces. A Viking hoard of solid gold draped over your body."

She grinned as the balm of his presence spread its soothing, brilliant light. "What gown could I possibly wear with such jewelry?"

"No gown at all, of course: only the treasure and nothing else. I have had to find a great deal of solace in memory and imagination these last three months."

Mirth bubbled in her, as if the spring found its way once more to the surface. "You imagined me *naked,* sir?"

"Every day!"

Juliet opened her eyes and stood up. Alden swept off his tricorn. He was dressed entirely in white: coat, waistcoat, a froth of snowy lace, even the ivory tricorn pulled from his golden head. Only his boots shone black, while his mount's coat gleamed like a pearl, the mane and tail a sweep of liquid frost.

The horse moved restively and pawed the ground.

"A white stallion," Alden said. "It seemed appropriate."

"It doesn't matter. Only that you are here!"

"You no longer wish for a knight on a white horse, ma'am?" He grinned. "Alas, I am shattered."

"No, the treasure. The treasure doesn't matter."

"It never did," Alden replied.

"You still wish to marry me, even without my mythic ancestral fortune?"

"If you'll take a penniless younger son. We can live at Grace-church while Sherry is little. By the time he is old enough to pick up the reins for himself, I trust I'll have created enough wealth of my own to keep us in comfort—at least enough to buy us a cottage with some chickens and pigs."

"I never kept pigs."

"As you wish, wife. Will you be content to be plain Mrs. Granville-Strachan?"

"I should be content to be plain Polly Brown, if it means we can be together. But I have something for you."

From her pocket, she pulled out a letter her father had written and sealed, addressed to Alden. Controlling the horse with one hand, he read for a moment in silence, then spun his mount back to face her.

"Alas, ma'am. It would seem that we shall not have the option to remain plain Mr. and Mrs. Granville-Strachan forever, after all."

Juliet stared up at him, her heart suddenly plummeting. "What do you mean?"

He dropped the letter into her hand and laughed. "Only this, Juliet: the earldom of Felton will die with your father—"

"I know that. It made Kit's death even worse."

"So your father has petitioned the king to re-create the title on his death and bestow it on whichever man is fool enough to marry you. The king has agreed. If you marry me, we shan't be Lord and Lady Gracechurch, but one day we'll be Lord and Lady Felton instead."

Juliet stared up at him in open amazement for a moment, then she began to laugh also. She waved both hands, indicating the huge estate around her.

"All of this will come with the earldom: mansion, grounds, farms, land—"

"Faith, ma'am," Alden said between shouts of mirth. "I am deuced disappointed! I was determined on a cottage and you will saddle me with all this." He held out one hand, eyes sparkling with mischief. "Yet I believe I must agree to your father's terms. As you are no doubt aware, I am only interested in your wealth, ma'am—been the case from the beginning."

"I am certainly relieved, sir, that you are not interested at all in my body."

"Faith, then you may not marry me, after all. I am on fire for your body."

"While I, sir, am only on fire for your bright mind. We have our last chess match to finish."

"Not the last," he said. "The first of many more. But the truth is I am desolate, lonely and pining for your presence: in my life, in my heart, in my bed."

She stepped closer to the horse and laid one hand on its glossy neck.

"Me, too," she said, holding up her hand.

Alden reached down and took it. Juliet picked up her skirts and set her foot on top of his boot in the stirrup. In the next instant he had swung her onto the horse with him and his mouth hungrily found hers.

The stallion began to dance, uncomfortable with its double burden.

"Damnation!" Alden broke the kiss, forced to give at least part of his attention to their fractious mount. "This carrying away the maiden on the white stallion is more complex than I thought."

Juliet settled into his embrace. Alden turned the horse's head and began to canter it in spirals around the meadow.

"We're going nowhere!"

"You are correct," he said, kissing her ear. "I thought you might like to know what I think about your treasure."

She leaned back into his strength. "What do you mean?"

"That you do indeed have gold here, sweetheart, if you want it for your daughter's dowry."

"The heavy, metallic, materially valuable kind? Kit and I followed the instructions in my mother's locket to the letter, so did Lord Edward Vane. Nothing was ever found."

"Look at the mud patch," Alden said as the horse cantered past the disturbed ground. "Burying boxes in the ground is a deuced bad way of hiding things. If the Felton Hoard had been buried like that, Oliver Cromwell's men would have found it in an instant."

"So we had it all wrong?"

"No, just a tiny bit of it. That wall," he nodded to the old brickwork, "has been here a very long time. Perhaps originally it was a mill, but the bricks are Roman. It was definitely here at the time of the Civil War. What better place to hide treasure than in its crumbling walls?"

She clutched his sleeve as the horse began to prance. "But the locket says the treasure is five feet from the surface of the spring."

"Indeed it does, but five feet *above* the surface, not below it. What do you wager, ma'am, that if our sons and daughters break out bricks the right distance above the ground, they'll find Harald Fairhair's gold?"

"*Our sons and daughters*—something about that sounds very, very good. What would you like me to wager?" Juliet asked. "My shabby virtue?"

His lips brushed the back of her neck, sending a keen rush of yearning down her spine. "I've already had that. How about giving me your promise to love me forever? You have mine. Forever, Juliet."

"In that case, husband, I don't really care about any other treasure."

"Good," he said. "Harald Fairhair's gold has lain here for a hundred years. If it exists, it can wait another century. Meanwhile, this damnable stallion is desperate to stretch his legs. Shall we gallop away into the misty distance and live happily ever after?"

"With you," Juliet said, breathing in his scent, reveling in his bright presence, secure in the embrace of his powerful arm, "I shall live happily ever after anywhere you want to take me."

Alden spun the stallion about and gave the horse its head.